Native Author
Web: www.thisisacircle.com
Email: whawk@sympatico.ca
416-710-9319

SHILOH

SHILOH
A NATIVE AMERICAN JESUS

A Novel about the Rebirth of Love

STEVEN WINTERHAWK

This is a Circle Part 2

iUniverse, Inc.
Bloomington

SHILOH
A Native American Jesus

Copyright © 2012 by Steven WinterHawk.

All rights reserved. No part of this book may be used or reproduced by any means, graphic, electronic, or mechanical, including photocopying, recording, taping or by any information storage retrieval system without the written permission of the publisher except in the case of brief quotations embodied in critical articles and reviews.

iUniverse books may be ordered through booksellers or by contacting:

iUniverse
1663 Liberty Drive
Bloomington, IN 47403
www.iuniverse.com
1-800-Authors (1-800-288-4677)

Because of the dynamic nature of the Internet, any web addresses or links contained in this book may have changed since publication and may no longer be valid. The views expressed in this work are solely those of the author and do not necessarily reflect the views of the publisher, and the publisher hereby disclaims any responsibility for them.

Any people depicted in stock imagery provided by Thinkstock are models, and such images are being used for illustrative purposes only.
Certain stock imagery © Thinkstock.

ISBN: 978-1-4759-6166-9 (sc)
ISBN: 978-1-4759-6167-6 (ebk)

Library of Congress Control Number: 2012921348

Printed in the United States of America

iUniverse rev. date: 11/13/2012

CONTENTS

Acknowledgments ix
Prelude: The Three Sisters xxi
Chapter 1:   Childhood in Kansa 1
Chapter 2:   A Young Man in New Rome 18
Chapter 3:   A Second Chance? 37
Chapter 4:   My Destiny? 48
Chapter 5:   The Path of Beauty 66
Chapter 6:   The Pipe 80
Chapter 7:   Another Arrow 95
Chapter 8:   A Dream Within a Dream 111
Chapter 9:   Returning Home With a Purpose 131
Chapter 10: Amanda A Rose by any other Name 139
Chapter 11: Sundance: The First Day 150
Chapter 12: The Gift of Truth 154
Chapter 13: Another Gift of Truth Amanda's 170
Chapter 14: Is This MY Destiny? Sundance (The Second Day) ... 183
Chapter 15: Sharing on the Mountain 192
Chapter 16: Another Mountain—The Wheel of Life 204
Chapter 17: The Winds of Change The Wheel turns 219
Chapter 18: Aurora The World Changes—and Why It Does ... 229
Chapter 19: Grace—And Betrayal? 247
Chapter 20: Once On a Blue Moon 261
Chapter 21: The Last Sundance 278
Chapter 22: After The Sun Dance 296
Chapter 23: Where the Vision Quest Leads 315
Chapter 24: To Search for the White Buffalo 327
Chapter 25: The Hunting 338
Chapter 26: Death—and new Beginnings 353
Chapter 27: Some of us return to Eden: In our own Way ... 362
Epilogue: Eden? 365

These Words (are a Give-away)

These Words belong to the White Buffalo
Can you speak her language?
These words cannot be translated
They are the language of the Heart.
These words are about Sacrifice
This can only be given freely
These words are about Compassion
When your Heart has been opened.
These words are about the Arrow
The Arrow is not the Truth
These words point to the Truth.
The Truth that is in your Heart
These words are a Give-away.

Acknowledgments

I would like to say Miiguetch (Ojibway for 'thank you') first and foremost to my Mother and Father for providing the perfect way to learn to walk the Traditional Native American Spiritual path—just by being themselves. I was born of a White Christian Mother and an Ojibway Father. Both my Mother and Father encouraged me to follow my Dreams. I will also say Miiguetch to my Soulmate who called me into the Dreams and Visions, and then appeared in my waking Dream as my partner Cidalia to share her Heart with me.

I also thank my good friend and Editor, Heather Embree for helping to transform my dreams into a readable book. And I thank my close friend Tony (Youngfox) Kitchen, an intuitive photographer, for the cover art in the form of a picture of a hand-drum with a Solar Cross illuminated appropriately by the sun.

Chee Miiguetch

Disclaimer:
And All that went Before

This is a Native American story, similar to the stories that my ancestors have shared around a campfire and is therefore true—in the telling and in the hearts and minds of the storyteller. In the Traditional Way, every dream is connected and part of a Greater Story. This story is based on my dreams, on stories that were passed down orally through generations and my personal view of the Bible (and the prophesies therein). All of the characters in this story are symbolic but are not named by co-incidence. Quantum Physics includes the theory of Alternate Universes and some stretch that theory to include untold numbers of worlds, that we create or change though our focus (by being the observer of the event). Aboriginal People, like me, have simply called this 'Dreaming', and we travel to these different realities in Dreamtime.

I have never intended that this story be a 'how-to' for someone who is interested in Spirit matters or Dream travel. It is a personal story about my experiences in learning to be Spiritually responsible for my actions and to walk the Path of Beauty as my ancestors did before me. I believe that our connection with God—the Great Spirit—is a personal journey. Most of this story originated in a Vision Quest that took place over the span of about a year and a half. I am including here a brief re-visiting of my first book '*This is a Circle: Mary and Joseph*" All of what was relevant in the first book is true in this second part of the ongoing story of '*What if Jesus was born as a Native American*,' with the focus of this story being on Shiloh, the child of Mary and Joseph. This is the second part of the story that came together in my Vision

Quest and therefore you will find parts of numerous dreams and dream worlds that I have visited. Believe what you may, I am neither asking nor expecting confirmation of the reality of dream travel to other worlds. This is real in a way I cannot explain—except in a story similar to that which my ancestors told. For anyone else, this may be a seen as a complete work of fiction.

Before my previous book came into being, I had written 5 novels about Soul Mates and Native Beliefs, which are yet to be published. These stories became part of a "living" dream journal until, on a whim that I cannot describe; I followed a burning curiosity to inquire deeper into the "Truth" about what was written in the Bible, and how it fit with my own personal, sometimes conflicting, beliefs. So I began a story that I tentatively entitled "*The Eastern Door*," This novel began with a young boy (me) living in a world that has ended in destruction. There are only a few people left alive, including this boy and his mother, who gives up her life so that he can go on. Eventually, this boy, having grown to the age of about 10, arrives naked at the entrance of a valley (similar to the fabled Shangri-La) where time stands still. In this Valley there are people, like the boy, who are Red-skinned and who have aged to the point of maturity and remain suspended in time. There is one Elder that he calls 'Grandmother', who cares for and teaches the boy about the blissful life in this Valley until he nears the age of maturity. His curiosity tells his Grandmother that he should go to the mountain and take part in a Vision Quest.

On the Vision Quest I was guided to change the title to "*This is a Circle*," birthing a series of stories—the previous one and the one you are about to read. Mary and Joseph marry and complete their destiny by bringing a boy into the world that will be like Jesus—except he will be a Native American Jesus. This boy's name is Shiloh.

This is a Circle
The West is a Spirit Circle
The End is also the Beginning
This Spirit Dance
Is the Mystery Dance.
Spirit is the part of the Mystery
that Remembers.
This Circle Is a Journey of Remembering.
…Steven WinterHawk (1992)

The End ...

The warrior who was given the arrow that ended the life of "the man with the yellow hair" at the battle of the Little Big Horn is sleeping peacefully now. It was a good Dream. Mary and Joseph and their baby are safe. Although he is content with his memories, this man who is also called Shane is aware that this Circle is not complete.

When the baby is of age to fulfill his destiny, there will be those that recall the story in a different way. Some will be prepared to forget that this man of peace ever lived and deny his message that is the Arrow of Truth. Others will continue the mistreatment of their brothers and sisters, including the animals and all creatures, and the Mother Earth. The trees will be cut down and the waters (the life blood of the Mother) and the air will be polluted. In the world that Shane calls home, many of these people, those that claim to remember, will be prepared to accept the death of the man who was born of Joseph and Mary. They will say that the blood of this man will save them and they will no longer be responsible for the so-called mistakes that they continue until the end of this world. But as the ancestors of the red skinned People were aware, this is a Circle.

Even as he sleeps, Shane is wondering if there is a better way.

In his mind and heart are memories of Sarah. In his obsession with his dreams, their relationship changed to the support of friendship, which is also good, but the fire of passion has become a smouldering ember. The gift of the Buffalo Calf maiden is one of his treasured memories—that will not be denied.

And so, he turns over in his sleep, the Vision Quest continues and the Dreams begin again.

...The Beginning

I looked up—in the new dream, it was morning again—early morning. A large bird passed overhead, accompanied by a loud roaring sound. It was like no bird I had ever seen before. I am sure that it was not the bird that cried out to me a moment ago—the bird that called me into this dream. The sun flared from this huge bird's wings and, at first, I imagined it to be on fire, but then, as it came down into the trees to my far right, I saw that the sun was reflecting off its feathers. I decided that this bird, however fearful it seemed, must be a messenger from the Great Spirit. So I stood up and set off along a rocky beach.

The beach seemed to stretch on forever. I had never seen this beach before, even in a dream. Even more astounding, was the body of water that sent endless waves crashing upon this rocky shore. Peering out to my left, I could only see endless rolling water—to a far horizon. There was a clear but distinct smell in the air. The smell filled my nostrils and my lungs, refreshing me, however, when I stopped and brought a handful of the water to my lips...it was bitter—I had to spit it out—it was undrinkable.

I continued walking toward the trees where I had seen the great bird come to earth. My curiosity had gotten the better of my fear. I also hoped to find water that was clean—my mouth was parched and although I now knew that this was another dream, the thirst and the curiosity would not go away.

Finally, I entered the forest that was on a piece of land reaching out into the water and I came to a wide pathway that was cut into the trees and beyond that was a small standing of trees, and...

....and there it was....the large shiny bird. It was on the strange pathway, further inland. I was considering going closer until I heard voices—many voices. The voices came from beyond the next stretch of trees. The combination of finding the large bird and the water that was undrinkable, along with voices speaking in a strange language, convinced me that I had to be dreaming again. I followed the voices and came out of the forest onto another beach where a large group of people were gathered, all talking at once, staring out at the water. Out in the water was a canoe (I recognized it from a story that my Grandmother had told me). This large canoe had a tree in the middle of it, draped with cloth!

Almost immediately a man left the group, and walked to meet me. As he walked toward me his back was to the sun, rising out of the distant horizon. There was a light surrounding his body and I thought it must be the water or the sun at the back of this man. There was a peaceful power about him—even more powerful than the leader of the tribe in my last dream. He extended his hand.

"Miighan," he said (which I heard with my mind-sense).

I thought this might be some kind greeting in his language.

"Mighan?" I answered and clasped his arm in the manner of my people.

"Mayingun," he said, as though to clarify with a broad smile crossing his face. "That is the name I will call you this time around. We have met." Then he sighed and, still smiling broadly, "Perhaps it would be better to say that we will meet in another place and time."

"I came here to find answers. I came to find out who I am. My Grandmother said that I might see an animal in my dreams and that four-legged would be my Totem. I did not think I would meet a Shaman." I was overcome with wonder at my good fortune.

"A Shaman?" he mused. "Yes, you could call me that. But then I would need an appropriate name as well—since this is your dream." His smile touched my heart. "You can call me....but wait, you have questions. I am getting ahead of myself," he laughed right out loud. "And considering that we will meet in a future place, I guess we are...? But there are no coincidences. My Father would have us meet for a reason. Perhaps I can help you on your Quest? Share your dream with me and we will both learn about your name."

This man was a friend that I had not yet met! I could feel this. I would trust this man…with my deepest secrets. I would trust this Shaman, this Sacred man, with my life. So I sat down on a rock near him and began to tell him about my previous dream and how I came to be on the Vision Quest.

He listened quietly and then said: "the Eagle whose cry began this dream and opened the door is not your personal Totem. Although Eagle will never send you somewhere you are not meant to go. Your Totem will be a four-legged that you have met—your ancestors were wise to look at their animal brothers and sisters to find their way on this Earth Walk." His eyes shone and he gazed toward the sky, "What did you see just before this Dream?"

"I saw a cloud person, in an animal shape!" I exclaimed.

"Now think back to your first dream," he instructed. "Did you see this four-legged in that dream?"

My mind retraced—one dream to another, and then, at the point of the first dream, after I had bid my companions farewell, I stepped into the entrance of the valley and turned back to see…the tail of an animal disappearing into the trees. My heart thumped in my chest. I was about to awaken again. I had seen my Totem—my Spirit-naming animal but my mind could not grasp the truth. This Shaman, who had helped me, was fading—only the sound of his voice remained.

"Wait—who are you? How will I know you again?" I called out.

"You can call me Two-Fishes. That is my Shaman name."

Then he was gone from my dream.

* * *

As this Dream Vision ended, I was aware that the meeting with this Shaman had altered me. Even as the morning sun's rays touched my face, I felt that my heart had been opened and I was still connected to that dream. Throughout the next day, I sat in meditative silence, unable to let go, with an acute anticipation of the next Dream that was to come.

Prelude
The Three Sisters

This begins with a re-telling of the Native story about the Three Sisters. In the Traditional Way, every dream is connected and part of a Greater Story.

A familiar version of this story is about the three main staple foods (squash, corn and beans) of the Native life that were planted together. In the Aboriginal ways of living that depended on vegetables for sustenance—instead of hunting—this story was an important teaching. But in the true way of Traditional teaching, a story can be re-told and adapted to the needs of the People or the individual.

In this re-telling, the Three Sisters are three human girls, daughters born to the couple James and Petra. It is important to note that in the Native tradition, one child would not be considered more important or more loved than another. We are all part of the Creator's plan. No one is less than another. Part of our Vision Quest, however, is about finding how we fit in the overall scheme of things that we call the Mystery. In the Native Way, a child is encouraged to find their "calling" by following their Heart. The Sisters' father, James, was a great Shaman in his own way. Their Mother, Petra, was originally born in a faraway tribe but Petra became a keeper of the tribal laws and an herbal healer. Because of this, Petra was reluctant to leave their tribal land even though their home was close to the City of Vega which was singled out as the target for the first nuclear bomb by the President of New Rome. This President now had the power that belonged to the Emperor, who died a mysterious death. Some say that his death was from the disease that he helped to create—the disease that steals one's natural immunity. But this could not be proven due to his solitary life.

When the eclipse and the darkness came, James convinced his wife that they should flee with their children into the hills to escape the destruction that he knew would come. One promise that the President of Rome did keep was the timing of the bombing of Vega.

The family headed towards the hills in their van. They had only two days, including the day that was filled with the seven hours of darkness, to get as far away as possible. At the foot of the hills, James parked the van and urged his family to travel the rest of the way on foot. "Hurry," he urged. "And don't look back. I can keep a spell alive which will protect us from the effects of the blast—but it will not last long and can only protect us if we keep together as a family."

This was part of a vision that James had been given by the Creator. He was promised that his family would survive so that they could carry on the Traditional Ways. The vision also showed James a cave that would protect them. They reached the plateau that was the source of a stream which fed the valley below. This was a wide stretch of land that reached out into a valley that once had been home to great Buffalo herds. At one time, the People, who were hunters, had used the cliff close to the cave, which James sought, to drive the Buffalo to the sacrifice of death. James could see the mouth of the cave. "That way," he pointed. "We will be safe in that cave."

But Petra remembered this plateau. She was a keeper of the Tribal Knowledge. She remembered that this plateau was where the Buffalo gave their gift of life. She remembered her family's home back in the land where her children had been born, and her husband's warnings and promptings fell on deaf ears. James and the three sisters went safely into the cave. But she turned around and walked to the edge of the plateau—the edge of the Sacred Black Hills—and she gazed longingly at the valley with the City of Vega in the far distance.

And then the first bomb hit. The sky was alit and on fire. Petra held her arms to the Creator and accepted her fate. She absorbed all of the wonders that had been the teaching of her People and, in a moment of Grace, the Creator turned her into a pillar of salt. Her sacrifice was to be a source of food for the Buffalo when they returned—when the cycle of life began anew.

* * *

"Take this potion at your own risk," the Elder Shaman told James. Its properties are hallucinogenic and it will open doors that the untrained mind might not be able to handle. At the very worst, a person can get trapped in a dream and not be able to awaken. And if he does wake up accidentally or otherwise, he may not be able to understand the sense of Oneness that is the result of the dream."

"This does not seem like a dangerous thing," James enquired. "To know that you are one with Creation is something to strive for."

"That is true," the Elder agreed. "But it is also something that one must earn over time. To wake to that knowing without remembering the journey can be a dangerous thing for the mind to comprehend. It will need the guidance of a father or mother who has walked this path before. One will need to be awakened gently by using his birth name."

"And then…?" James was curious… "what would happen next?"

"After he awakens to this Oneness, he will naturally be inclined to connect and share with his own kind. Then he will be shape-shifted into the form of his personal and tribal totem animal. As I stated before, this will also need the guidance and sharing by teachers. Otherwise they may never regain the form that they knew before ingesting the potion."

"This still does not seem like a bad thing," James was puzzled. "I sense that you believe that I'll have a need for this potion, and that I'll share it with others?"

"You are right," the older man smiled. "The future is not written in stone—although the Grandfathers—the Stone People will remember it for us. I am giving you this potion because a vision tells me that you and your family will experience a disaster that is beyond your mind's remembrance. You will need to hibernate as your animal cousins do—until the worst is over. I cannot say how long this sleep will be, but when the time comes, only one who has journeyed into the worlds of Dreams—a Shaman—will instinctively know that the first winter is over."

James awoke first. He fumbled around in the darkness to find his flashlight. The light would not come on.

"Either the bulb was broken in the shaking of the earth, or…?"

His other guess would be that the batteries had decayed with time.

When he had given his daughters and then himself a sleeping potion made from an old recipe, he was not sure how long they would remain asleep. This sleeping potion had been given to him by his teacher and the Elder had simply included the instructions that it was only to be taken in times of great danger.

"You might need to hide from danger," the aged man had said. "This will put you in a deep sleep—like the White man's story about a man called Rip Van Winkle." This was to be a good example of the situation that James and his family found themselves.

Perhaps the Shaman had a vision like the one that told James where to go so that his family would be safe. Either way, James had no idea how much time had passed. He removed candles and the matches that were kept in a small metal case from his pack. All that was required to wake his daughters was to speak their name—their true names that they had been given at birth. The two older sisters sat up, rubbing their eyes…and they began to change—even as he started to speak their younger sister's name. Then he remembered the other part of the sleeping potion's effect. The words of the Elder shaman echoed in his mind: "You will have just enough time to awaken your daughters before you begin to shape shift. You will begin to change into the totem of your tribe."

The Elder's warning was fading in a mind that no longer understood the spoken word. And the sound that was to be his younger daughter's name became a series of yips that changed into a mournful howl. It was a father's fur covered snout that nuzzled the sleeping child before he and his two daughters turned tail and slipped out into the night—to join in a serenade to the moon.

* * *

Prophesy

It may begin so simply
having just an Open Heart?
the Courage to accept
our part
in what has gone before
and what may come
to pass?

It may begin so simply
listening now, at the start
a quiet Voice
a burning bush?
Heard not with the ears,
but with the Heart
but alas…

We write it down
carve it in Stone
and our part becomes
obscure and hidden,
the words alone
become the Law
now given.

And then we cringe
in fear and hate
a Demon we have named
that takes our place
our responsibility…
controls our Fate
Forgotten…

Forgotten now
our part of this creation

forgotten the Creator
else, how could we hate
how could we fear
knowing the true All Powerful
ONE?

And now we kill the Messenger
the One that we pretend to Hear
the One whose words
we twist within our minds
to match the words in Stone
And now—are we Lost
and so alone?

And in our Desperation
we open once again
our Hearts
to find we are not alone
this prophesy has many parts
shared throughout the Earth
and many Hearts.

But…we are too late!
The End is near!
we cry in resignation
for in this Mayan calendar
we find certain
similar and foreboding Fate
Too Late!

This prophesy is not a gift
we proclaim—a curse!
it speaks of Judgment
for our actions
the fires of Hell—or worse

…but wait? How can this be?
Just wait?

Look closer now and still
your mind
for carved upon the Mayan stone
these are not words of Fate we find
but symbols to interpret
not with our fearful minds
but Hearts!

And now step back
and if attained
the Creator's view
of all we've seen?
this is a Circle—after all,
is there a second chance?
…it Starts…Again!

                …WinterHawk

Chapter 1

CHILDHOOD IN KANSA

The country called Kansa was quite a different place than Joseph had imagined—all he had to go on was the stories as related by Mary's father. On the internet and during his initial visit where he met Mary at the Pow-wow, he was made aware that things had not remained the way Soma had found it when he returned from his Vision Quest in the Black Hills. The City of Vega was still there, and it was like nothing else that Joseph had heard about anywhere in the world.

"A Star in the Desert" was on the sign that greeted a traveler at the outskirts of the large sprawling city. These words were also on the web site and various TV ads that played throughout New Rome. In Joseph's mind (or perhaps it was his judgment) the city might be a slightly tarnished Star—if that was what it represented. The reason for the comparison escaped him, until he learned that Vega was also the name of an actual Star—like Sirius. Vega, he learned, was a place that advertised "a lifestyle of freedom—complete freedom to be yourself." Anyone who vacationed in Vega was immediately aware of the truth that the words conveyed. In Vega, anything goes—literally. There were no laws—except the involvement of someone else in your fantasy. It is none of their business what you do—to yourself. But if you do harm to anyone else—you will be deported back to the country that you came from. And everyone knew how drastic the courts of Rome could be in dealing with those they described as Sinners. One other strictly enforced rule of Vega forbade children under the age of seventeen within the city limits. This was related to the first rule: Enjoy yourself—but be willing to be responsible for the consequences.

Outside the city limits of Vega, the country had undergone changes since the departure of Soma and his followers into the desert. For about 75 years since the exodus by the People to their homeland south of the Red River, Kansa had become a near "carbon copy" of the land that they had escaped. The land had been systematically divided into States that had their individual governments and borders. There were 10 large States that were answerable first to the Federal Government in Ottawa (a city named after the Algonquian tribe) and secondly to a group of Chiefs that met once a month in the city of Dallas—on the other side of the country.

One day, the Chiefs in Dallas received a message from the elected President of Kansa, requesting their presence. The request came actually from the President's Minister of Finance, informing the Chiefs that a bill was being drafted that needed their approval. When all 10 Chiefs traveled to Ottawa to meet with the President, he was somewhere else.

"Our President is meeting with the President of New Rome at this time," the Minister of Finance informed the Chiefs after the house was called to order. "We have negotiated an agreement that will mean free trade between our countries." Following this pronouncement there was an uproar that involved shouting and banging of desks between the ruling party and the official opposition. One of the Chiefs, an Elder of more than 80 years, waited for everything to calm down before he addressed the government.

"We were not informed of such a bill," the Elder said. "How can it be possible to have free trade between two countries that are not of similar or equal beliefs?"

"As you are aware," the Finance Minister stated in a manner that seemed to indicate that he felt himself superior, "the government of Kansa has been patterned after the successful example of our neighbours to the North. Our tax systems and financial budgets are a good reason that we are now in a surplus and that free trade would work so both countries benefit." He was quite near smug as he turned to another round of approval and boos.

The Chief sighed, "I am old enough to recall a different life. One that included Residential schools and concentration camps that our neighbours to the North called reservations. There were many agreements—many treaties before that—all of which were broken. And now they want free access to our resources again. If this agreement passes, they will want our trees and our water—not to mention the oil that has recently been discovered on our lands. And what do they promise in return?"

"In return, the government of New Rome will make us rich—and every Native person in Kansa and New Rome will be granted a status that will declare us tax free," the Finance Minister beamed. He and most of the elected representatives were much younger Native men and had not lived through the experience that the older man spoke about.

The Elder Chief remained standing. "And what of the taxes that we pay now? We pay a property tax and an income tax, and just this year we have been given a State tax to be added to the Federal tax that we pay on all things that we buy. Will this end these taxes?"

At this point, the younger Finance Minister made a grave mistake—the least of which was the underestimating of the 10 Chiefs. "Old man," he said with a smirk, "you have lost contact with this world. Things have changed. The taxes that you pay are needed to keep our country running in the manner that you and your grandchildren have become accustomed." The house reverberated to another bout of desk thumping and name calling.

Another of the Chiefs rose to his feet. "It is you who have lost contact with what is important—including the respect of your Elder," he stated in a firm voice. "What I have witnessed here is a disrespectful group of children. My sons and daughters would not act in this manner at our family table. I would hardly expect this at a school play ground." His glance silenced the offending members of government. "You talk about a surplus of money? And for what is this money being used? I do not see our roads being repaired as was the promise that brought the last tax upon us. You act as though this money belonged to you. Is this not the reason that you granted yourselves a great raise in pay? Yet, on the reservation that I live our People go hungry. When I return to my reservation—yes I still call it that—I will ask my People for a vote. I will ask all Chiefs to call a vote and the People will decide who is to be in charge of our country and the true meaning of free trade. I will ask for free trade—a sharing between all the States that are part of Kansa… and as for the offer of tax free status," the second chief continued, "when I look at the Grandfather that you spoke to in this manner, I can see that he is one of our People—I do not need someone to tell me this. I can see that he is free—and will be free of your taxes, as it should be for all our People. That is all I have to say at this time. We will see what the People decide."

The country called Kansa that Joseph chose as a good place to raise a family was originally tax-free. It was a country that had other problems, but for the most part, those problems were shared. Following the incident involving the free-trade tax dispute, the government in Ottawa was disbanded—as a result of a countrywide vote where all new taxes were abolished. Soma, the man who led his People over the Red River to this Promised Land, would have been proud. The borders between the individual States of Kansa were also erased—to be replaced with a tribal system. There were then 100 tribal allocations of land—looked after by the remaining 100 tribes and their elected Chiefs—sadly, still called reservations. One Elder noted, with equal sadness, that before the White man arrived, there had been over 500 known tribes living on the lands that were now called Kansa and The United States of New Rome.

"The Elder who spoke up about the disrespect that led to the unemployment of the politicians in Ottawa was Chief Seattle," Mary's father told Joseph and his daughter, while bouncing his grandson on his knee "Seattle was elected Grand Chief and negotiated new treaties with New Rome. At first, our People blockaded the Golden Gate Bridge, the only way to cross the Red River, and our Chiefs declared that there would be a high tax on everything coming and going from our Country. "We do not need what you have to sell us," they told the government and the industries across the river. We can grow our own food and we have the resources to sustain us. You, however, need us. The Red People like to buy the cars and televisions that your factories produce—this is a well-known fact. But if you want to be able to sell those things to us, you will need to build more factories in Kansa and employ Native workers. We will not accept factories and we will not allow businesses to operate in Kansa that do not employ 80% Native workers. This is true to this day—although the treaties have been broken more times than a politician can open his mouth. Our secret—the only thing that has worked so far—is that we do not have politicians. Chief Seattle would joke about how dealing with a politician was like trying to do business with a man or woman who has an incurable disease—one that clouds his brain. This disease is one part greed and the other part addiction to power. It causes a man to make promises that any sane person will know that he will not (or cannot) keep."

"But what about the armies of Rome and the USNR?" Joseph asked. "Weren't the people of Kansa in fear of being invaded again?"

"At first we were on guard," Wind-in-His-Ears held the baby high above his head and chuckled. "But then we realized that they would need to justify such an action in the eyes of their own people. Your people have become wiser since the times of the Indian wars (as well as the Red-Skinned). They really want to live the Christian way that they talk about—and many feel guilty about what happened in the past—except for the politicians, of course." He laughed aloud. "Their brains are too infected with the disease. But this disease recognizes what they call *sin*—so many of your people are caught in a dilemma—stuck between their minds and hearts. There has been an uneasy Peace—one that is fuelled by but kept in place with a memory of how the Creator helped our People escape the reservations North of the Red River—only to create new ones in this land we have named Kansa."

"We do not have an army," Mary chipped in, as she accepted her baby back into her arms. "We cannot afford it from a financial way and from a Spiritual way. Without an army, we are not a threat to our neighbours to the North."

"And we do not need an army because our Great Brother will protect us," her Father added. "Our Great Brother wants what we have, so he will protect us. Besides that—we could not match the technology that they have. This is a spiritually-wise way to live."

"But there is something missing—for both of our Peoples," Mary proceeded to feed the baby. "It will never cease to amaze me how Spirit could say that this small child could be the answer. He seems so helpless—so needful of our protection."

"What about the Spirits that you saw?" Joseph asked. Mary had heard the baby making sounds, like he was trying to talk to someone, after she had put him to sleep one evening. She went back to the bedroom and saw two Spirits bending over the crib. Shiloh was shaking his rattle at the Spirits and laughing like only babies can. "They were laughing, too," Mary told Joseph, "and I recognized that one of the Spirits was my Mother." Later, when she described the other Spirit to Joseph, he produced an old faded picture from his wallet and she agreed that the other Spirit was Joseph's Father. "Our son is being watched over by his Grandparents from the Spirit world," she announced.

"But if you have no army," Joseph had asked, "who is there to enforce the laws—if there are laws—and to keep peace?"

"An army is not needed to keep Peace," Mary's father informed him. "An army is needed to go to war—and to defend your country. We have no need to make war and our country is defended by the best air force and army that Rome can put together. Kansa does, however have strong and faithful police forces. Like that TV program you told me about that you watch late at night—called *West or East of something?*" Joseph had told Mary's Father about a TV program that he was able to pick up using his antenna at the cottage in Bethany. "I can only get it on nights when the wind blows and the stars seem out of focus," he said. "It is an Aboriginal station—I thought that it must come from Kansa." Mary's Father assured him that the only TV station that originated from Kansa came from within Vega—and it was not a channel that aired programs that included Native crafts and homespun drama. The Channel from Vega was always being blocked by the NRTVC—the New Roman TV Censorship board.

"Our police force does quite well in upholding the few laws that we require to keep our children safe," Mary's father insisted. "If you will notice—like your TV program—we do not have jails that are meant to keep people more than one night. We just give them time to sleep it off."

"But what about the serious offenders—what if someone does serious harm to another?"

"Depending on how serious the offence is—we give them up to four chances to do the right thing. After that—and if they have committed murder or harmed a child—they will be banished into the desert. A person of such anger will most likely join the Sons of Soma—the group that still roams the desert seeking vengeance or they will be killed by them."

"Sounds pretty drastic," Joseph commented. "Does it work?"

"We have a low crime rate. But we are aware that there are those that fall through the cracks. It is hard to do anything about the man who gets drunk and beats his wife—if the wife will not tell. Or the young people who are addicted to sniffing gasoline or drugs. This was the reason that Mary journeyed to your country. A Shaman told us that many of our people had lost their souls—and we believed that we knew where the damage was done."

"And what do you think now?" Joseph watched as his son was being fed in the natural way.

"I think that it is something that is common in both of our countries," Mary answered. "There are many who have lost their way—and just as many who say that their way is the only one. At this moment, I am holding this child—our son—and I am with the man who loves me. I do not feel lost. If I could give this moment to our People to know—there would be fewer problems in this world."

* * *

Shiloh spent most of the first five or six years on a farm that Joseph and Mary shared with Mary's family. The family and friends had helped Joseph build a house on one part of the land, and they put in a garden. They also had some livestock—a few chickens for eggs to eat and a couple of cows—just for milk. Both Mary and Joseph had given up eating red meat. On any given day during the weekend that Joseph was not working his trade, he would be found with his family sharing time walking in the woods nearby. On this particular day, however, Mary and Joseph were at the kitchen table watching their five-year-old son feeding the chickens at the far end of their fenced in yard.

"He spends a lot of time with the animals," Joseph remarked.

"Yes," Mary agreed. "He talks to them, you know."

"You mean that he talks in chicken talk?"

"No, silly, but he is able to communicate with animals—all animals. Our son is gifted you know."

"I know," Joseph agreed. "I just had a thought? Does he know that we will eat some of the chickens?"

"Yes—he says that they know. All animals know this."

"Hmmmm?" This was beyond Joseph's comprehension. How a five-year-old could understand this was…unthinkable. "I wonder what else he knows—or can see—that is beyond our seeing."

"I think that until it is trained out of them, most children are aware of things we adults only dimly recall," Mary smiled and sipped her tea.

On the other side of the yard, the parents of this gifted child might be frightened for the safety of their son—if they could see what he saw. A shape—undetectable to the eye had stepped boldly over the small wire mesh fence and stood watching the boy feed the chickens. The boy's head turned and stared intently.

"You can see me?" the black hooded man muttered under his breath. "This stealth cloak is not detectable even by radar at ground level. Maybe there is something special about you? I think you must be the One that I was told about. It took me a long time to find you—but, at any rate, I will end this now, just in case." The invisible man raised a cane that was actually a laser weapon with the intention…, but he was not able to point it at the boy. "What…is this?" he tried again, but to no avail.

"Damn!" the man in black muttered in frustration. "Is there something wrong with this?" He aimed the weapon at the nearest chicken and it flopped over—dead.

The boy calmly reached out his hand, touched the chicken, and it sprang to life.

"What?" the man exclaimed almost aloud. "You can…?" He tried again. Zapped the chicken and the boy re-animated it. This time, the boy held his hand above the bird, as though indicating what he would do.

"You can heal," the man exclaimed. "No—you can bring back the dead! This is impossible—I am only now getting close to this with a room full of computers and DNA equipment and this boy can do it on a whim."

The man looked about the yard. He saw the parents at the kitchen window. "Well since I know that you are the One that I was warned about, if I can't get to you in one way...maybe there is another." He raised his weapon in the direction of the child's parents and..., it refused to fire! "Damn! Damn! There will be another time." At that the man in black left—walked off into the forest nearby where a secluded helicopter—protected by the same stealth technology that had hidden the man—stood waiting to take him back to Rome.

Later, when Shiloh came in from the yard, Mary asked him if he had a good time playing.

"Yes," the boy smiled as though satisfied with himself. "But there was a bad man."

"A bad man?" Mary looked at Joseph. "I didn't let him out of my sight for a minute. Are you sure—I didn't see anyone."

"He was not there. But I could see him. Can I go play now?"

"Yes," Mary answered. "After dinner you can play in the house. Please go with your father and wash your hands."

"What do you make of that?" she asked Joseph.

He shrugged. "You would know more about Spirits than I. This is one thing that scares me—maybe we need to talk to the Shaman about this?"

"How do you get an appointment with a Shaman anyways?" Joseph recalled his experience when he needed a doctor's signature for the form to apply for his passport. He was put on a waiting list and given an appointment three weeks later for a physical that he didn't need.

"You just call her—and she will know if you need help right now or if you can wait, or even if you need to see her at all," Mary explained the next day on the way to see Sarah White-Eagle. Sarah was the Shaman who suggested that Mary go to Rome—to seek out a healing for her People. She was also the one who performed the marriage ceremony for Joseph and Mary. When Joseph looked back, his mind was so focused on his wife-to-be that he scarcely recalled the Shaman called Sarah White Eagle. She got her name when her hair turned completely white

9

at the age of thirteen. She started to talk for the Spirits that same day. "Some say she is about 60 years old (Mary told her husband) but, except for the white hair, she does not look a day over 30." When Sarah greeted them at the door to her dilapidated shack, Joseph was amazed once more. She was quite young for her so-called age. Her long, white hair hung down to her waist and her skin looked supple and full of life for a woman who appeared to be extremely anorexic.

"Come in—do come in," she urged. "Can I make you a tea?" when Mary agreed, she held out her hands for the baby. "My—how he has grown. Yes—yes. I can see and I can feel it."

"What do you see?" Joseph asked.

"The protection of the Angels," She sat in a nearby rocker and cradled Shiloh on her boney knees. "I saw it around both of you when I joined you in marriage. It is still there. And now it is there for your son—I think it will remain until he is old enough to accept his Path—until he knows his destiny."

"Whoa!" Joseph shuddered. "I have heard that too many times. And it gives me a chill. What is this about my son's destiny? Mary was told that he would be like—dare I say—Jesus? Please don't tell me that Shiloh will need to face a similar fate?"

"Not at all—not at all," she rocked contentedly. "Our destiny is not written in stone. And think twice if you believe that the Creator of All Things would send his son to be put to death—the first or second time."

"But the story about the sacrifice...?" Joseph wondered.

"A sacrifice is not genuine unless the creature—be it two-legged or animal gives of themselves willingly," she told them. Joseph remembered this from Wind-in-His-Ears' story. "The Father of All Things has sent his son—again, to be an example of the true meaning of Love. This is the simple truth for now, for the past, and for all futures. Back then some of the people made a choice—to reject his teaching and to continue their belief in the sacrifice of blood. It was his choice to be the sacrifice—or it would not have happened. Your son will face a similar choice—but do not be alarmed. His actions and those of the One, who came before, are concerning the same choices that any of us might be called to make. HE will lead the Way—it is that simple."

At the beginning of her mentioning the word *sacrifice*, Sarah White-Eagle's voice had changed. It was softer, and sweeter; younger than a woman of her reputed age. "I am called Ariel," she said. "I am what you would call the Angel of. Nature. It was my sister Gabrielle that came to Mary and told her of this baby's birth. We are from a place not far away—but beyond the veil of your understanding. We have watched over you since the beginning of time. The Creator of All Things gave us this purpose—one that we perform with Love."

"You said sister?" Joseph's voice was hoarse. Some part of him was in disbelief of what he had heard. "Are you all female? What about male Angels?"

"Well—you know of Michael? We are a balance of both and when the need arises, the Angel that is right will be there. We are another true step on what you might call *evolution*. Forget the silly story about Monkeys and Mankind. There are some animals that are more evolved than some humans. You each have your purpose in the eyes of the All Father and Mother. Gaze with love upon your wife Mary—does she not seem like an Angel to you? One day she will be—and so will you. There is no hurry—you have both been selected for this task of Love, like so many Mothers and Fathers before you. Be the Loving parents—that is in your Heart to be and worry not about the challenges of tomorrow. Know that you and your son are protected. This is so—and I am content in this."

Sarah's eyes lost just a bit of their sparkle and her voice returned. "Thank the Spirits for you and your son," she said, and set Shiloh down on the floor. Later, after the tea, Sarah joined Shiloh on the hearth to play with small figurines that she had carved and painted. "This little boy is you," she explained. "See how happy he is playing with the chickens." Shiloh engrossed himself in the game and after a while, Sarah asked: "Is there anyone else playing with you?"

"No—no one playing," as he picked up another figurine that resembled a wizard. "This man is watching," he said.

"Are you frightened?" Sarah asked.

"I am playing," he simply replied.

"He has no fear," the Shaman told Joseph and Mary, who watched this all from the kitchen table. "He knows that he has no reason to be afraid."

"Why is this man here?" she asked.

"Don't know. He is bad."

Sarah looked quizzically at the parents before asking. "How is he bad? He does not look bad to me."

"He is not bad—he does bad things—to the chickens—but I make them better. Then he is angry and he goes away," he continued playing happily with Sarah.

Sarah played along and then joined Mary and Joseph at the table for another tea. "He is not in any danger. And he is quite sane—as sane as any well-adjusted child that has the ability to see the invisible and to heal—maybe…if I am interpreting this right, he seems to believe that he brought the chickens back from the Spirit world."

"You mean that he could heal…the dead?" Joseph was aghast.

"No—, Yes," Sarah smiled. "I do not believe this is possible, unless it wasn't a person's time to go. Maybe this chicken, for example, was harmed by someone we cannot see. Well—it may be possible that your son could protect this animal—even after the fact. He is still so young and does not believe—I mean he doesn't disbelieve that there is anything he can't do."

"We have tried to help him be open—and to not lose that childhood imagination and wonder," Mary said. "Soon he will go to school, but we will make sure that the logical learning does not extinguish his natural knowing and his curiosity."

"This is a good thing," Sarah agreed. "And I do not think there is anything to worry about—although someone is watching. I can sense him here tonight. Do not be alarmed. It might be a good thing for him to know that, if he doesn't already from the incident with the chickens, that Shiloh cannot be harmed. He is protected by Angels—whether anyone believes that or not."

Later, when the family was gathered at the door, Sarah said: "We do not have a word for Good-bye," hugging Joseph. "As you must know by now. So I will say "I will see you again—'*meenawa*,' and in this door step—this safe place between worlds—I will tell you that Shiloh will soon have a playmate. You will have another baby."

"What do you think of that?" she kneeled to hug the boy.

"A baby sister," he said confidently.

* * *

Martha Anne-Marie was born to Joseph and Mary about eight months after that visit to the Shaman Sarah White-Eagles' home. She became a happy companion to Shiloh for five years and then contracted a childhood disease called meningitis.

Sarah held the small girl that Shiloh loved to call Anna (despite that her given name had been Martha) in her arms. All of the hospitals had been consulted, to no avail. "I can't do anything," Sarah proclaimed with tears in her eyes. "She is protected just like the rest of your family but she only came to share this time with you. She was Shiloh's sister in another dream, another life, and that night she saw him through my eyes, so she decided to join him here for a brief time."

Shiloh stood near. He was 10 years old now and full of memories shared with his sister Anna. Those memories streamed from his eyes. He raised his hand over his beloved sister. "I will…" he began.

"No, Shiloh," the small girl's voice was gentle and sweet. She spoke beyond her years. "This is my time. I must go now. But I will not be lost. You can find me again when you are ready. I will always be with you."

Thinking back through tear-filled eyes Mary had to believe that when Shiloh began his schooling—his logical schooling—that his true teaching had been accomplished through the sharing of an earthly Angel.

For a time following his sister's passing, Shiloh became quiet and withdrawn. Mary could only recall one other instance in her son's childhood that had impacted him nearly this much. This happened while she was in the early pregnancy with Martha. Thinking to please her husband, Mary suggested that the family attend a local church during the Easter holiday. Joseph showed a bit of hesitancy which Mary did not understand, but he agreed. Mary and Joseph sat in the church pews where he seemed to be relaxing into memories of his own childhood (as he was whispering them to his wife). Then the church resounded with a loud scream—from the back room where the children were. Shiloh came running out with tears running down his face, completely disrupting the service. He buried his face in his mother's arms, sobbing. "They want to hurt me," he cried. Mary looked to Joseph for an answer that he could not supply. She picked up her five-year-old son and together they made their way to the room where the rest of the children were gathered. A kind elderly Nun greeted the family at the door. "I do not understand," were her first words. Once inside, Mary asked what the lady had been talking to the children about. "It's Easter Sunday—we were talking about the crucifixion. And well...your son's eyes got bigger and bigger, and when I pointed to that small wooden statue of Jesus on the cross—he screamed in fear. It was as if he believed...I don't understand."

"I think I do," Mary said gently. "My son has this belief that whatever happened to the man you know as Jesus could happen to anyone—including him. I cannot explain it. We had best be going now."

"That was fast thinking," Joseph said when they were outside the church. "That was more my fault than anything. I should have told you why I left the church. I guess I just assumed that our son, being really who we have been told he is, would feel at home there—even if I didn't. Please forgive me for not speaking up. In the future, we should leave it up to our son—if he ever decides to be involved in religion. As they say—the Mystery deepens." Shiloh was quiet and appeared shaken for a few days, and then the promise of a baby sister seemed to restore his trust in life.

"Take a bit of time off school," Mary suggested to her son. "Take as long as you need. Hang around and help your dad if you want. Just remember—I am here when you need me."

A week went by and Shiloh spent most of his time reading out under the large maple tree in their back yard. He did not say much and his parents did not push. Then one afternoon into the second week, Mary heard a sound from his bedroom. Joseph and Mary had given him the rattle when he was a baby. The rest of the gifts from the four Spirits they held onto until they decided the time was right. After the incident in the church, Joseph hung up the Medicine Wheel and the drum on Shiloh's bedroom wall for him to ask about or use as he saw fit. The boy had played with the drum occasionally and just as infrequently asked his Mother to explain the meaning of the wheel.

This afternoon she heard him, as quietly as possible, playing the Drum.

Mary gently opened the door to the bedroom. She had her own hand-drum with her. "Can I join you?" she asked. He nodded and they drummed together—and time stood still. He finally stopped drumming and said: "We can't own another person—can we?" And when she was silent, he said: "And we can't hold onto them when it is time for them to go."

Mary answered: "There was a Poet called Kahlil Gibran who wrote that 'our children do not belong to us—they are the sons and daughters of Life's longing for itself.' Can you tell me—what does this mean to you?"

"It means that we are all children of the Creator—including you and dad and me…and Anna. I know that you do not own me—and that does not stop you from loving me. And I know that Anna is really an Angel that wanted to share love with us but that does not make it any easier. All of our sisters and brothers and mothers and fathers are really Spirits—they are Angels that have chosen to share time with us. But Anna is my sister (besides being an Angel) and I don't want to forget her. Do I need to let her go?"

Mary was quiet until she could address her own feelings. "Letting go of someone you love does not mean you need to forget them," she said. "This is the kind of Love that the Creator has for all people, and all mothers and fathers need to learn it. I love you with all my heart, but I must give you the freedom to spread your wings and be the kind of man—or Angel, or Spirit that you can be. There is an old saying that if we have a bird in a cage we should let it be free…and if it comes back…and well, you know the rest."

"This saying is only partly right—because when it comes back it still doesn't mean that I own that bird. It means that I still have to be ready to give it freedom—'cause maybe the bird just came back to thank me, and tell me that it loves me."

"Yes. Love is about freedom," she fought back a tear. "And one day we will see your sister again. I hope you believe that?"

He nodded and they began to drum again. Shiloh returned to school the next week but he had become a more serious young man. Mary and Joseph were glad that they had chosen to keep the arrow which the Spirits had called the *Arrow of Truth*, until he first knew his Heart.

* * *

Seven years passed in the blink of an eye—almost. The first two (after Anna's death) saw life in Kansa for the Renauldi family settle into a kind of normal state. During those two years, to paraphrase an old saying: *some things changed, and some found a balance.* One of Mary's relatives that had moved to New Rome shipped their unruly son back to live with his Grandmother on the reserve. The Grandmother did her best for about six months then had to let go.

James, at the age of thirteen, came to live with Joseph and Mary. He found a place to hang out in the renovated bedroom that Joseph had added on for his daughter. With Joseph's firm, caring hand and Mary's unconditional love, James became one of the family. He soon became the doting older brother to a quiet Shiloh. Meanwhile, Shiloh found books. He read everything that was in the small library in the local school and started on the library in the nearby town of Natchez—and his retention was remarkable. The two brothers were like night and day—James found his niche in Lacrosse, and Shiloh came home one day with a scholarship and an offer to be part of a student exchange program.

After much pleading Shiloh left for a six-month tenure in China. Joseph gave in; believing that this might be what was needed to open his heart and mind. James was sad to see his newly acquired brother leave. "Hey little brother," he kidded, "wish me happy hunting, but don't stay away too long. I am gonna work hard to keep the local girls happy until you come back," he winked. It was a private joke—since Shiloh was overly shy and James was forever encouraging him to participate in the weekend "hunt for buffalo". In six months, Shiloh came home only to leave again—this time for a year in Japan.

"What are you learning?" Mary asked when Shiloh had been home from Japan about a week and was planning his next adventure abroad.

"Are you kidding?" James overheard. "You should ask—what is he not learning. Tell our mother about that Aikido thing. That is totally rude!"

"Don't you mean *Rad*?" Joseph asked, thinking to be hip.

"*Rad* is out—*Rude* is…Rude!" James explained.

"You should have seen him—my little brother the shy boy," James could not keep silent. "This beefy kid was bothering my bro'—what a nerve—I offered to lean on him a bit but Shiloh says—no, let me show you something I learned in Japan. Well the next thing you know the beef was making like a beach ball—totally rude!" he slapped Shiloh on the back.

"Shiloh? I am surprised," his mother hid a smile. "You were always such a peaceful young man."

"It was a little bit different than James tells it," Shiloh explained. "But I have to admit that the results were the about the same. When I was in Japan, I met an Elder in the gym one day practicing some moves that looked like Kung-Fu. I asked him what he was doing and he explained a bit—he called it Aikido. 'Everything happens in a circle,' he said, and that had me hooked. I came back every noon hour until the man offered to show me a bit. It turns out that I am a natural at this. I trained every day for the rest of the semester, and the Elder told me 'You have learned all that I can teach you. I think you must have done this in a different life.'

"What do you think?" Shiloh asked his Mother and Father. Do you believe in past lives?" When Joseph just shrugged, the young man said: "I am not sure that I would call it that—but there are some things I am learning that seem to be more remembering than anything."

Chapter 2

A YOUNG MAN IN NEW ROME

Seven years had passed since his sister Anna's death and Shiloh arrived back home to the family cottage in Bethany, finished with traveling the world. His mother suggested to Joseph that they should spend time in his home country. She believed it was part of their union to help promote a healing between four colours—the races of the world. This was the reason, as the Angel had told Mary, that her son was born. (So, they had moved to the United States of New Rome less than a year ago.)

James, who had been learning the guitar with the help of Joseph for almost six years, now enlisted his "uncle" Jake to get a degree of professionalism by forming a band. The band was called *The James Gang*. "They are loud and nasty," Jake said. ("But they do have a bit of originality. If their music wasn't so angry, I would believe that they might do a bit better. But *c'est la vie...*") James was over 18, and able to act as an adult, so when Shiloh arrived in Bethany—*The James Gang* was (so-called) touring the country.

"Your father and I agreed that this was the time to give you the last gift of the four riders," Mary presented Shiloh with the Arrow of Truth.

"Whose version of the truth do you think the name signifies? Is it our People's Truth or the ultimate Truth?" He was already aware of the answer, but decided that he wanted his parents' take on it.

"Your question is more about—is there only one Truth?" Mary answered. "You have had time to learn that in your Heart—you know the difference between Right and Wrong. The war that Custer was part of was wrong. This arrow speaks to this—but it also recognized that the time had come for a change. Custer was not to be honoured for his acts of cruelty upon our People—he was honoured for being the bringer of change. There is a right thing and a wrong thing, but there is the most compassionate thing to do at any given time. This is why our People do not have a comparable word that means sin."

"I agree with your Mother," Joseph said. "There are parts of the White man's religion that I like—because it still resonates as true, but sin does not work—except for those who feel a need to judge. The concept of sin is for those that believe they have the only answer."

"I have had the privilege to learn what the world's people think about the Creator and his creations—all our Relations," Shiloh weighted the arrow in his hands before placing it in the quiver on his back which was also his carrying case for his flute, just how his father does it. "But that discussion is for a different time—if at all. Right now—I think I heard mom saying that she was taking a ride into town—I'd like to tag along."

"I am going to pursue my new hobby," Mary chuckled. "I am going shopping—for a new pair of shoes. But while I am getting ready, your Father has something else to speak about. Take as long as you need—both of you. I will be driving the new Jeep and your father's old mustang is still available for a dependable young man who has his new drivers licence. What do you think, dad?"

Joseph smiled, "For sure."

When Mary left the room, Joseph began his man-to-man talk with: "In the story about the Buffalo maiden, she gifted the young man with similar things that the four riders gave to you. There is one thing that she gave the man who was to be her husband—the only thing a female can share, besides the drum. As a way for him to know his Heart, the White Buffalo Maiden gave the man a Pipe."

"I know what the Pipe stands for," Shiloh blushed. "It is about the Sacred union between man and woman. And dad—I do know about sex, if this is where this conversation is headed."

"I know that," Joseph affirmed. "But I well your mother and I have been wondering because we have not seen any young women around—except for the ones that your brother brings home. Do you have a healthy—I mean are you…"

"Am I gay?" Shiloh sighed. "No, I am not. I have a very healthy urge when I see a young woman but I also have a fear."

"Please explain," Joseph requested when his son was silent.

"I guess you know that I can see where my life is headed. I am the one that will bring HIS message again. My message is about Peace and Respect and Freedom. This has not always been easy for many people to accept—especially those who would be in charge of people's minds. I have a fear—not for myself, but for what this will mean for you and my mother, and any young woman who might get attached to me."

"You are young and it is important to share Love," Joseph said. "My relationship with your mother has meant more to me than anything I can think about—in fact it's not about thinking. Your mother completes me—even though I am complete within myself. This is the Mystery that she has been teaching me since the first day I saw her. This is the Mystery that is the Love between a man and a woman—more than with a friend—any friend, of any gender. Your Spirit Father and I would not expect you to be on this Earth without this. And as for your mother and I—we accepted that you might not have an easy life when we brought you into this world. It must be the same for any caring parents. And I think that when some young woman finds it in her Heart to love you—she will be like you—I believe in this. You would not choose to share with someone who has a 'victim' attitude. Am I right?"

"Right, dad. I'll keep your advice in my mind. I hear mom calling. Maybe I will catch a ride to town and do a little buffalo hunting—like James says," he winked (and blushed), and quickly went his way.

On the drive into town, Mary asked: "How did the talk go?"

"Mom!" he admonished her. "That is between dad and me. It's a man thing."

"Oh gosh!" she exclaimed. "I know that. But the Pipe is about more. So much more. And don't be put off—I am your mother. If you can't talk openly to your mother—who can you discuss Spirit with?"

"In many cultures around the world—there is an uneasy connection between...sex...and Spirituality," he pointed out.

"But not with aboriginal races," she offered. "We are not ashamed of our primitive connections—as you so aptly put it. And the Pipe symbolizes this. The Sacred Pipe will hold a pinch of Tobacco to represent the entire Universe, and this is also part of the Sacred Marriage—the union of the Male and Female energy of Creation."

"Like the yin-yang that the Asian people believe in."

"Yes—that's right. Our Pipe is to be smoked in a Sacred way. Like the honouring of a relationship of a man and his wife. When we smoke the Pipe, we are praying—and our prayers are made visible in the smoke that goes up to the Creator. Our view of the universe is that everything is Sacred—a relationship that may or may not create a baby is sacred and every baby that is born is a son or daughter of the Great Spirit."

"Point taken—this is the way I see Life, too." He was sure that his mother needed to hear that—although she must already be aware…his thoughts drifted off—back to another time when they had a similar conversation.

Mary parked the Jeep and Shiloh followed her to a shoe store. "I will be about my business," he announced. "I am going to wander. I think I just came along to spend some time with you, but I am not a shopper—so you do your thing and I think I will find a place to get an ice cream. See you later."

Leaning back on a park bench and enjoying the ice cream, Shiloh's eyes scanned the opposite side of the street. Directly across from the ice cream parlour was a huge Catholic Church. The ornate copper spire that topped the roof and the brass cross (*sans* Jesus) caught his attention. The large stained-glass windows, however, portrayed the Stations of the Cross and the story of the crucifixion. His travels to different countries had been mainly a learning venture. It was not about judging one way better or worse than another—that was not his nature at any rate. He had come to see that many people have their unique ways of finding God. Around the world, he had also found an interest in the ancient and modern architecture involved in building a church. He finished his ice cream; he got up and sauntered across the quiet street to check out the church.

The front door to the church was locked. "Strange?" he mused, bending backwards to admire the spire. He knocked. "Isn't a place of worship supposed to be open at all times—for those in need?" He knocked louder—amazed at his own impertinence. He knocked until he heard the latch being unlocked.

"What can I do for you?" A man resembling Father O'Malley of Bing Crosby TV and movie fame answered the door. Except the man was abrupt—not like the Father that Bing had portrayed. "C'mon young man—state your business—I don't have all day."

"I am sorry father—but I was under the impression that you did have all day and this was the house of God that is open to anyone. I apologize if I misunderstood why you are here."

The man blinked as though trying to decide if this young upstart was just being sarcastic. "Who are you? And why are you knocking at this door. It is not Sunday, you know."

"I know Father. But I was across the street there and felt a need to talk to someone." This was not a lie (Shiloh could not recall ever telling a lie—unless you were to count silence as a form of lying). Something had drawn him here—some urge that he couldn't define.

"Oh alright—come in. There is a confessional booth over to the east side. Wait there and I will join you shortly."

Shiloh stepped inside. "I have no need for confession," he stated, while breathing in the atmosphere, and surveying the high arching ceiling. "I just want to talk. I have just returned from traveling the world and I wanted to talk about Religion and Spirituality."

"Then you should come back another time," the priest motioned toward the door. "We are in the midst of a discussion with our head Father—from the Diocese in New Rome and...I don't know why I am telling you this—please leave."

"Perhaps I should leave," the young man straightened his shoulders. "This is not my house. This is your house. My house is where any two or more people gather in my Father's Name. This could be in the quietude of a forest or a valley by a mountain stream. My house would be open to help a homeless person or to feed the poor," he turned to go.

"Wait—an aged man stepped through a nearby, partly opened door. "Who is your Father? Why are you here?"

"My Father who sent me here is the One Father of all Creatures. I have been here before and now I have come again—although I have never left."

The Elder man appeared thoughtful. "That is a big statement for one so young," he said, tilting his head to one side. "The light is odd in here right now, don't you think?" He directed the question at the man who had opened the door to let Shiloh in.

"Yes, Father—if you say…" The other man gasped. "Mother Mary! Who is this man? He…Glows!"

"Is it possible—that he is who he says he is? Or would that be blasphemy?" The older man took a step backward. "Should we bow down—or call for security?"

"I am not here to be bowed down to—and the last time—no, the second last time I was physically present in such a house—I was under arrest." Shiloh found these memories to be his—but not his at the same time. He brought up his hands to show the other men. There were scars—rope burns around the wrists, and the unmistakable scars in the palms of each hand. "I was tied and then nailed," he explained. "My hands could not have supported my weight otherwise."

"Oh my! I have often wondered about this." The Elder priest took the young man's hands in his to examine them more closely. "These wounds are real. Yes this was how I believe it was done," he agreed. "Come into the vestibule. We will talk with you—even if you are an impostor—it would be interesting to find out more about someone who would go to this length."

When he entered the vestibule, there was an atmosphere of expectation that hit him like a wall. He was momentarily engulfed. "I need to sit down," Shiloh gasped as the pain in his side was like a knife. "If I don't get control of this…" he looked at his hands. The men standing round him watched in fascination as the blood pooled in the palm of each hand and dripped onto the floor. He took a deep breath and centered himself in the chair. He visualized and then felt the familiar circle that came with his Aikido training. "Good!" A gentle voice sounded in his ears. "Seek the protection of your identity—reaffirm who you are—let go of the expectations." The wounds in his hands shrank and healed, and then the pain in his side was no more. "Whew! That's better," he breathed easier.

"Stigmatism," the Elder priest proclaimed to the other men—including two other priests that Shiloh had not yet met. "I have heard of cases like this, where the person actually relives the crucifixion of Christ." They drew up chairs in a semi-circle with Shiloh in the North. Strangely enough he realized that he was in the place of Dreams on the Medicine wheel.

"You could call it that. If that makes you feel better," he managed a smile.

"What else could it be?" one of the other men asked.

"It could be a Dream. It may be a Dream that will show you the Truth."

"And what is the Truth? Is it something that you think we are not capable of understanding," the Father that had opened the door for him was almost being smug.

"Not at all," Shiloh answered with not so much as a blink to show that he was aware of the other man's obvious disbelief—or was it one-sided belief. "Your Truth is perfectly capable of explaining things from your perspective. And your version of the Truth is correct for you—and many others that follow your Religion. Another way of seeing this is called a Dream."

"Is this Dream that you speak of real?" The Elder of the priests queried.

"It is so real. The difference between what you would call reality and this Dream cannot be defined. There is a Mystery story that goes like this: a man is put to death in a horrible way—he is whipped and hung from a tree and stabbed. This man dies. This is real. This does not seem like a Dream, although what happens next will confuse the senses of anyone who watches. There is a 'lie' that is told that if a man dies in a Dream—he will die in his "waking life." This is only a Truth for those who cannot see beyond the lie. For One who is truly awake, this lie does not apply. When he dies, he awakens in another Dream. One that is as real as the first Dream and when he is ready, after three days, he steps back into the Dream where he died."

"Is he a Ghost?" one of the men asked.

"No—he is so real—see—you can touch him, and even feel the wounds in his hands."

"I have heard this theory. Your Native ancestors believed this—and a number of aboriginal races—especially the Australian Bushmen believe in something called Dreamtime. You would have to show me something tangible to get me to believe." A third man who had been silent until now spoke up.

"But isn't this the basis of your Religion?" Shiloh asked. "This man was said to have provided this proof."

"Yes—but...?"

"I am here today—born into this Dream to tell you that the lie is not a lie—it is a misconception. If a person—more so a race—or over 50 % of the world believes in something, can it be said to be a lie? When enough people believe in something it becomes what your scientists will call conceptual reality—simply put a shared version of the Truth. It is, at best, a half truth but true for many of the believers that "buy into" the theory. At some point in time, the theory becomes a law and it is then that the followers of Religion or Science have lost touch with reality."

"So what is this lie that you say we have bought into?"

"That is my point—to anyone who believes, it is not a lie. In your words, it can be lumped into a collective one-size-fits-all word called *sin*."

"I don't see your point," the third man said again.

"If we do not accept our Divinity—our Spiritual Purity—we believe that we will always be missing the mark. And the reverse is also true—. when we accept the lie that says we are not worthy, we will not be worthy to follow the way of the man who can be alive in another Dream."

"And if this is a Dream, then who is Dreaming?" the Elder priest asked.

"You would not ask this if you did not already know that we all Dream of the One Great Dreamer. But imagine this Beautiful thought: we have been granted the Gift to be like the One who created us. We have been made in "His" image and thus we can be free to create and live our own Dreams."

"Spiritual mumbo jumbo," the first man declared. "We have the written word that is the One Truth. That is all we need."

"Yes, I agree. And it is written therein that the Word became flesh and lived among us. The messenger was here, he was put to death for daring to question the Truth. But he was beyond the lie. It may surprise you to know that many of our world's Religions and Spiritual beliefs are based on the story of a messenger—in one form or the other. It comes down to my knocking at your door today. The message is: *If you open your door and see a homeless person or a person who is in need of a meal, I am that man or woman who knocks at your door. When you feed this person you are feeding me. If you turn one person away—you deny that I am alive. This is your home—it is not my house unless you invite me in.*"

There was a mutually agreed moment of silence. "We are gathered here today to consider the fate of this church," the head Father explained. "Is that why you are here? The attendance has dropped off to the extent that this church is no longer financially sustainable. Is that why you are here?"

"I cannot say," Shiloh admitted. "I was drawn to come here. As far as I am concerned, I admire the architecture but any simple dwelling would do. It is not the structure that contains Spirit. Spirit cannot be contained. Do what you must. My Father does not require worshiping—my Father only asks for Love."

"There is so much new age talk like this," the first man said again. "There is even a man who claims to speak to God. This is blasphemy."

"How so?" Shiloh sighed. "If we all have a spark of the Holy Spirit within us, as the messenger said, then is it such a stretch of the imagination to think that we could have conversations with that Divine Source?"

"It is for me. That voice may be the tempter—the Dark one."

"Then so be it. Believe what you may but be open to Love. If you are open to Love then you will attract the same. That is all that I have to say. That is my message."

"We will give your message some consideration," the Elder Father said. "In the meantime, I will pray for a sign."

"What kind of sign?" Shiloh asked.

"If you are who you say you are and your message is sincere, then it is not too much to ask God to send us a sign." He had scarcely finished crossing himself when a commotion was heard in the foyer beyond the half-open door.

"That is just father Carmel returning with the new altar boys," the priest who had opened the door for Shiloh explained.

"Father Carmel is quite liberal in his choice of words," Shiloh noted to himself as he listened to the man beyond the door who obviously believed himself to be alone with the group of boys. The boys were roughly ordered to go to the main hall of the church where he would be joining them as soon as he dealt with the impudent one. The other boys could be heard leaving and then in the quiet that ensued, a resounding "wack" was heard, and the priest exclaimed: "John—Johnny, what am I to do with you? You just will not behave. Let me tell you what I will do." The following was a whisper that Shiloh could not make out but he had heard enough. He stood and quickly opened the door wide. He found the man who had spoken, bent over a cowering boy of about 10 years with his hand raised to deliver another blow.

"That will be enough!" Shiloh's voice was not loud but it had an unmistakably commanding tone.

"And who are you to tell me how I should discipline my boys?" the man shot back.

"In the first place," Shiloh's tone was now clear and even. "These are not your boys. They have been entrusted into your care and it seems that the trust was misplaced. In the second place…" his voice resounded within the lobby of the cathedral. "In the second place—I AM the protector of children and those who cannot protect themselves. I AM the One who has come again to right the wrongs that have been done in MY Name!"

The boy regained his feet, and ran to stand behind Shiloh. The man rose fully, stretched his shoulders, and his face changed.

"I know you—you are the Son of Mary and Joseph! You are the one who falsely claimed himself to be the Saviour. Suffer the little children to come unto me. Is that not your pitiful cry?" The man's voice had an extremely mocking ring.

"That was also a misinterpretation," Shiloh replied. "I will say again: Bless the children who come to me—for I will give them shelter."

The man laughed—a diabolical laugh. "And how will you give them shelter—how will you, a Peace-Loving, non-violent man be able to protect these children?"

Shiloh stepped forward. "I have the Arrow of Truth!" he proclaimed. "You do not know me in the way you think you do but I know you!" he pointed his finger at the man and the man drew back, clutching his chest."

"You will not harm me. I do not fear you," he rasped.

"I am not seeking to harm anyone," Shiloh replied. "And there is no reason for you to fear—if you have nothing to hide. But I see that is not true. I can see the darkness that is hidden in your heart, I COMMAND that darkness to BE GONE. Dark Spirit—leave this man—and let him be healed. HO—this will be so!"

The man who had been menacing the boy shuddered and fell to his knees. He clasped his hands and begged, "please forgive me. I did not believe—I have been led astray."

"Get up—you are healed and you are forgiven. Now go your way—and do not darken these doors again." Shiloh pointed to the front door of the church and added: "It is my Father's wish that you do not find yourself in a position that will allow you to be near children again." When the man had gone, Shiloh turned to the boy noting that all of this had been witnessed by the group within the vestibule. "You will be safe now," he said placing his hand on the boy's head. "And I need you to know that none of this was your fault." The boy stared wide eyed. "I need you to know that you are innocent of all that happened and that My Spirit Father and the Angels will protect you." The boy nodded.

"Please call this boy's parents to come and pick him up." Shiloh demanded. I will remain until they arrive."

While waiting, Shiloh brought the child into the vestibule and seated the boy in a chair beside him. "If I had even a question about this man's previous behaviour—I would have called the police," he informed the other men, now silent, in the circle. "I could see however that until now, he had been pushy and verbally abusive. I cannot tell you how I could see this—perhaps the Arrow that I spoke of was the symbol to enable this Gift? This man was about to take this abuse to the next level—as you could see and hear." The other men simply nodded. "This man comes from a family where he was the victim. But this does not give him the right to pass on this curse. I healed him by casting out the dark spirit that had taken possession of his heart but with an adult like him there is 'free will' that now comes into play. He must not be entrusted with children—the pain and anger are still there and it could attract the darkness once again. You are all elders and I grant you the due respect, but you should see that the Dark is not the cause. It is the result. We must become responsible for our own healing by learning to give and receive forgiveness—otherwise the One who is sacrificed will be forever on the cross and this circle will exist for eternity."

When the boy's mother had come to collect her son, Shiloh crossed the road and proceeded silently on his way. He glanced back before rounding a corner and saw a slightly different building in the place where the church had been. There was a sign on the building that read *Bethany Hostel for the Poor and Homeless.* He did not question the truth of this far-seeing—but wondered if he were to look again… No—it's better to let this part of the Mystery be."

When Shiloh returned to where the Jeep was parked, he found his Mother talking to a couple of young men in a beat-up pickup. She introduced the boys as a couple of James' friends that sometimes rehearsed with the band.

"Your brother, James, is a cool dude," one of the young men told Shiloh. "He really has a heart of gold but I can't find it in myself to join the band on the road. They are just too rude—to the ninth degree," the other boy agreed.

Shiloh talked with James' friends until his mother suggested she was ready to return home and then one of them named Mark asked if Shiloh wanted to come join them the next day on a drive to New Rome.

"There is a Peace rally that we are attending. Non-violent for sure—or John and I would not go. The event is a TV broadcast. The Vice President is scheduled be there—to give a speech about homeland security."

Late afternoon the next day, Shiloh and the other two young men were in a line up to enter the campus of a large university in the city of

New Rome. This site was obviously picked because it was a controlled and secure environment. All vehicles and pedestrians had to pass a guard shack where they were required to produce a photo ID. Shiloh had been aware of this, and brought along his well-used passport. After passing the inspection at the entrance, they joined a slow moving line of vehicles on a two-laned driveway that ended at the main entrance to a large courtyard. Within the courtyard, Shiloh was told there was a university campus that resembled a modern day castle. There would be plenty of parking available for their truck with its back loaded with peace signs that they would share with other friends.

"What is the hold up?" John asked. He sat in the middle and Mark and Shiloh leaned out of the windows on either side to have a look. "There is a group of marines directing the cars," Mark sighed. "We could be here awhile."

Shiloh leaned out of the passenger window. He saw a small refreshment van about three cars ahead. It was still a bit back from the main entrance. "I'll be right back," he told the other boys. Before they could voice their questions about where he was going, he was out on the pavement and walked up to where the coffee truck was waiting in the line up.

He noted that there was a Native man—a few years older than himself, at the wheel of the vehicle. Shiloh tapped on the window to get the man's attention. The other man gave him a quick look and motioned for him to go away. Shiloh tried the door handle but it was locked. He motioned again to catch the driver's attention and made a motion with his hand asking the man to roll down the window. The driver must have realised that Shiloh was not going to give up, so he put the van in park and rolled the window down just enough to utter a curse, and to tell Shiloh to go away—in no uncertain terms.

"Open the door or I will tell someone what you are doing here," Shiloh insisted.

"What the hell are you talking about?" the other man spat out.

Shiloh leaned close enough to be able to say in a low voice: "I am talking about the explosives in the compartment under your seat."

The driver gave Shiloh another nasty look and reluctantly unlocked the passenger door. "If you believe what you are saying, then you must know that I can press a hidden button at any time and blow us all to hell and back."

"I know." Shiloh got in and closed the door. "I am here to ask you to turn around and go back the way you came."

"Well you can just blow smoke if you think I am going to pass up the chance to takeout that war-monger of a Vice President. I am here to get revenge for the way these Whites have treated our People. I am prepared to die in the process. I have been waiting for this chance for two years. Today is a good day to die! Are you ready to die with me? You had better be—or get out of this truck now. And if you so much as make a step towards one of those marines, it will be all over, Charlie."

"My name is not Charlie. I am called Shiloh," he said quietly. "And I am prepared to die, too, if need be—but not for the reason that you think. Revenge is wrong and this kind of blind revenge will end up harming a lot of innocent people. It is one thing to go into battle against a foe that is prepared to fight you and it is another thing altogether to forget about honour and respect."

"Honour and Respect! What a laugh! These people do not know about either. They are guilty of the worst crimes against our People. They are guilty of torturing and slaughtering our women and children. I will spit in their faces when I kill the man who orders this to be done."

Shiloh drew a deep breath. "You are talking about the past. It was a terrible thing what this man's people did—and there have been equally terrible acts by our People—all in the name of protecting our land and our children. We can say that we were like the wolf that will fight ferociously when he is cornered and that may seem to justify what has gone before. But…like I said, that was the past. It's time to put this behind us and regain our path of Honour and Respect and Peace."

"I will not forget and I will not forgive the harm that was done to the children in the name of the White man's God. This is too much," the young man's eyes were glazed with hatred.

"Then what about the harm you are about to do? Isn't your revenge just as wrong when it involves the murder of innocent people—especially children?"

"I am here to kill the one who is in charge of the senseless wars that the White people are still waging all over the Earth. I am not here to kill his children—that would be a coward's way."

"And if you do succeed in killing him—another will take his place with revenge as his battle cry. Revenge only breeds revenge. Especially when there are innocents involved. What you do not know is, in the killing of this man, you will also be ending the life of a bus-full of school children that is parked just beyond this wall. Your need for revenge has blinded you. You will do this without seeing or thinking."

"You are lying!" The driver clutched the wheel with one hand, in white-knuckled anger. The other hand was hidden, making Shiloh think that perhaps it was near the trigger of the explosives. "How could you know about what is beyond these walls?"

"I have seen beyond these walls and I have seen the result of your actions," Shiloh explained. "This will be difficult to understand but think about the ways of our People and our belief in the Dream. You and I have already driven beyond the gate ahead and into the courtyard. When we were parked, you still refused to listen to me. The moment you caught sight of the man that is the target of your hate, you pressed the button that killed everyone within eyesight—including a bus loaded with school children who had come to meet the Vice President."

"Do you think I am stupid?" the angry young Native man put the vehicle into gear and edged forward another foot. "If I believe that you could know this then why would you be in this truck with me? You must know that you are about to die. Why are you here?"

"I am here for the children," Shiloh explained in a quiet voice. "And I am here for you, too. But you have a choice and they do not." The truck inched forward another foot or so. The marines were clearing the traffic ahead and then a uniformed man stepped forward and motioned them through the gate. Something clicked into place that Shiloh could not explain. One moment they were about to drive into the glaring blood-red setting sun and the next moment they were in darkness. The young man at the wheel let his foot off the brake and the small truck lurched forward into a courtyard that was illuminated by a single spotlight mounted on the side of the main building.

"What is this?" the driver exclaimed. "Are you some kind of black magician? What did you do?"

"I didn't do anything—that I know of" Shiloh answered. "This is the work of Spirit. This is the doing of the Great Spirit. We have a few moments to decide what to do next. The way I see it, there will be men at the main guard shack where we came in. When they discover us, they will come running. Shut off the engine and we will talk."

"Talk? What is there to talk about—do you know what happened?"

"The explosives were set off. Look at the wall—it is black with the results. And there is still a smell in the air—but strangely not much for such an explosion."

"Are you trying to tell me that we are dead? Are we ghosts?"

"No—we are not ghosts. But we were killed in the blast, at least the Dreaming part of us. We crossed over into this dream. You and I and the truck are from another dream."

"So—is this like the stories that the White man tells about the Christmas past and all that rubbish? Are you about to tell me that if I change my mind and do what you think is the right thing, we can go back in time and everything will be OK?"

"There is no going back in time," Shiloh said evenly. "What is done—is done."

The young Native man slumped over the wheel. "This is crazy. What the hell happened? I don't buy your story for a minute. I think you hypnotized me and we drove to another place or something. I want you to take me back now."

"Maybe you should ask the men that are coming," Shiloh said. "I suggest that you ask them before doing something real crazy and setting off the bomb again. How many times do you think you need to die to satisfy your revenge?"

Two men carrying flashlights and brandishing hand guns arrived at the doors to the truck. "OK, you—inside the vehicle. Step out with your hands where I can see them," one of the guards ordered.

The driver hesitated for a moment, and then relaxed, and complied with the request, as did Shiloh, on the opposite side of the van.

"What are you doing here?" one of the men asked in amazement. "I didn't see you drive by."

"You must have dozed off for a moment?" Shiloh offered. "We were driving by and came in to check out what happened here. There were rumours at the catering company but we wanted to see for ourselves."

"Yeah? Well you should not be here. Don't you listen to the news? There was a big explosion here four days ago and a lot of people were killed—including the Vice President, some TV reporters, and a school bus full of children."

Shiloh noted that his companion's face lit up at the mention of the Vice President but fell when the guard confirmed the death of the children. "I am sorry to hear about this," Shiloh said. "Sorry about the intrusion. Is it OK if we leave now? We will be overdue back at the shop."

"What do you think, Fred?" The one guard asked his partner. "What's been done is done. There is nothing here that they could harm if they wanted."

"Yeah, sure," the other man agreed. "This is pretty weird, though. I heard that they found the remains of a coffee truck like this in the explosion. I think we need to call in the plate number and write up a report."

Shiloh and the driver of the van were allowed to get back in and drive the truck back out to the main road where a police car waited. "The truck was not reported stolen," the police officer confirmed. "Still, you should not be nosing around a sensitive site like this. Go on home—I will be checking in with the company you work for when it opens in the morning."

Once they had driven far enough, the young Native man who had been so angry earlier was now subdued and thoughtful. He pulled over and parked at an all-night doughnut shop. "What happens now?" he asked. "Can you take us back? I am half-way believing your story."

"I don't know," Shiloh replied. "There must be some reason that we are still here. We don't really belong here but Spirit has given me the duty to protect children. The way I see it they did die but for the children in that bus, this will be a bad Dream. We will know different. I think that it is up to you. The fate of the children in the world we come from is still up in the air. Do you still feel a need to set off the bomb? I will not go back. Part of me is already committed to the sacrifice—I will give up my life to protect those children."

"You already died. Don't you think once is enough?" The other man was pensive. "Who are you, anyways? How could you know the things you do?"

"I have memories of who I am…" Shiloh began to explain and then another memory surfaced. "This may sound crazy but maybe not—considering what already happened today—I mean tonight, but I need to ask you. What did you have to gain—other than revenge for killing this man?"

"Anything else is unimportant to me. I told the people who got me the job at the catering company two years ago that I would do this and be ready when time arrived to do my part. They offered me money and promised me that I would go to a heaven in the sky where I would have seven virgin wives."

"A lot of good the money would do when you're dead," Shiloh remarked. "And did you really believe the seven virgin story?"

"The money would have been given to my mother but if you knew my mother, well she would not have accepted blood money—no matter how desperate she was, especially if she knew how it came to be. And the seven virgins—I would not want any girl or woman to be given to me like a piece of property to be used. That would be completely dishonourable. Before my life fell apart, I had dreams of finding a woman who loved me for myself. When my mother left my father he had become an alcoholic and threatened to kill us all—my mother, my sister and me. I was angry at him and at the White man's ways that had taken away his dignity. I wanted revenge for all the crap that my life had become—so bad that it burned inside me and the only thing that could put out that fire was the killing of that man."

"So the SOS used your need for revenge to get you to do what they wanted—never mind who else got hurt in the process?"

"The…yeah, the Sons of Soma. I guess that I fit right into their plans. I guess that I am just like them. They want to turn back the clock to the way it was before the White man came. They have one agenda—revenge."

"You are not like them," Shiloh said. "Yes you were angry—maybe you still are. Maybe you feel you have a right to be angry and that you and your family were victims. Well, here is a thought. A man can only be a victim once. After that, it is his choice to continue or to move on. In the Spiritual ways of our People, a warrior takes responsibility for his life and makes a choice to live with respect and dignity and honour. That man is no longer a victim. When we say "today is a good day to die" this is really about living the good way, no matter what or who thinks differently. My Earth Father is White and he has a saying: 'what anyone thinks about me is none of my business.' I have come to see that it is not the colour of a man's skin nor where he is born that makes him wise."

Chapter 3

A SECOND CHANCE?

"I remember hearing a sound, just before we crossed over," Shiloh told the other man named Mat. "It was like…?" He removed his small knapsack and searched for…"It was like this," he exclaimed, holding up a Spirit Rattle and shaking it gently. The room began to blur.

"Whoa! Hold it for a minute," Mat cautioned. "How do you know where we will end up if you keep shaking that?"

"You said that you want to go back?" Shiloh reminded him. "Besides, I still feel that we are not done here. You haven't changed your mind and your heart is still full of anger. We will go back when you have resolved this—or not at all."

"So you are saying that we are stuck in never-never land? We do not belong here because we are dead and we can't return to the place where we are live. I don't think it is about me now. I have resolved my need for revenge. I succeeded in ending the life of the man who was the source of that desire but I am remorseful for having harmed those children. I would not do it again—if I had a second chance. The lives of those children are too precious when balanced by my revenge. I am empty—I no longer have a purpose but I am willing to go back and find it. I think it is now about you."

"I would like to believe that you are ready for a second chance but that is not my choice or my right to judge," Shiloh shrugged and ordered another coffee in the all-night doughnut shop. "Judgement is not part of the equation of Life—it is about Balance. There is no judgment required," he pondered, while sipping the coffee. "Do you have a family here? You mentioned a sister and your Mother."

"If this Dream is anything like the one I am familiar with, my mother looks after a home for homeless and abused women. Mostly young women that have been forced into prostitution. It is a long story but she and my sister rescue them off the street. And now, as if it weren't enough, she has lost her son. Maybe I am meant to stay here?"

"I think that if you went to sleep here, you would wake up from this Dream in the world we came from and nothing would have changed. You would probably believe it was all a bad dream and you might even go ahead with your plan to kill the Vice President. A Dream is of little use if we do not believe in it. It would be like receiving a vision and believing it was meant to be. Can we drive somewhere?"

"OK—but you better figure this out because we will need to sleep sooner or later." When they were back on the road, Mathew asked: "Maybe it is something like that movie *Back to the Future* and we need to be in the same spot that we left for it to work out, right?" Shiloh noticed that the other man's mood had truly changed from the first time they met.

"Let's drive to the part of town where your mother lives," Shiloh suggested. "There was a memory or something that came up when you told me about helping the young women get off the street." They drove in silence. The streets became seedier and the two young men began to see women hanging around the street corners. Shiloh asked Mat to slow down. "The government of Rome pretty well denies that these women exist. And these are the young women that the SOS would say you will be given as a reward for a job well done. Or at least this is where they end up. I have seen this in almost every city of the world. By the way, what time is it?" he enquired.

"It's about 1:30 in the morning," Mathew answered. "No respectable young woman like that should be out on the street now." He pointed to a particular girl that looked about 14 or less and pulled over to the curb. "Young lady—shouldn't you be at home?" He did not expect a civil answer.

She stepped out of the shadow towards the truck and said in a quivering voice: "This is my first night and I need money. Would you two like to hire me?"

"Your first night? Great Spirit! Are you even 16? What are you doing out here?" Mathew was shocked even after hearing the stories about the girls that his mother and sister brought home.

"Yes," she insisted. "I need the money…and I have no home to go to. I have no family in this city," she began to sob. "I just learned that my brother committed suicide…and there is nothing left for me to care about." She stepped closer to the truck.

Shiloh tried to think of something comforting to say and as he leaned over to the driver's window her voice sounded vaguely familiar—from another time and another place. "What was your brother's name?" he asked.

"My brother's name was Shiloh," she answered. "I ran away from home and came to the city to look for him but he died four days ago," she leaned against the truck for support. Her dark, black hair was dishevelled and her shirt and jeans were torn and looked like she had slept in them. But her face was familiar—about seven years older than Shiloh remembered.

"Anna?" he gasped. "Is that you?"

"Shiloh?" she blinked. "How could that be you? I met some boys who were friends of our cousin, James, and they told me that they saw you get into a truck that was blown up. The police told me that you must have committed suicide. I didn't believe it at first and I ran away when they tried to take me back home." She bolted around the truck and sobbed in his arms.

"This is…your Sister?" Mathew was astounded. He drove away with Shiloh comforting the young girl in his arms. They returned to the doughnut shop and parked. "She looks like she could use something to eat?" he suggested.

While the girl, who was actually a teenaged Anna, wolfed down a sandwich, she brought Shiloh up-to-date on what had happened since he had left home to live in New Rome. Shiloh just kept mum and listened. It began with: "After you healed me and became well-known and after you moved to New Rome to live your 'destiny' as a shaman, you did not have much time for your family. I am sorry brother but that is the truth." And she ended with: "Then everything fell apart. Mom and Dad tried to patch it up and make things OK for me, but nothing seemed to work. Shiloh—I don't blame you for doing what you were born to do but we needed you, too. I guess what I am really saying is that I missed my big brother being there while I was growing up. Most of the rest you already know. I failed to graduate from high school, and I ran away from home because I was too ashamed to tell our parents. I hitched rides and hid in the back of a truck crossing the Bridge to the States. If the customs had checked further, they would probably have sent me back home. But I didn't care—I was so determined to find you that I was prepared to run away again."

"But Anna," he sighed. "You are an Angel—a real Angel. Don't you remember?" She stopped eating, and stared wide-eyed. Then she shrugged and shook her head.

"I don't feel very much like an Angel," she replied. "I felt so worthless, that I was ready to sell my body just to be able to eat." Her eyes welled up with tears. "What is an Angel anyway. Seems to me it is someone's idea of the kind of person or Spirit being that no one would be capable of living up to…"

"Perhaps you might reconsider that if you knew that it was an Angel that inspired me to learn to be the best I can be. You are that Angel, Anna. An Angel is just…no, not just—what I mean to say is: an Angel can be someone who leads a simple life. An Angel is someone who knows who they are and lives from that place of balance—from the Heart. For me—you were the Angel that taught me to live that way. And Anna, I have to tell you something: without you, I might not have had the courage to give up my life for a school-bus load of children that I did not even know."

"What are you talking about, Shiloh? Are you daft? You were able to escape that explosion—maybe you even rescued the children. I believe that there isn't anything that you can't do. Either that or you are a ghost?" She reached over the table and pinched him. "Nope—you are not a ghost."

He caught her hand. And looked her straight in the eye. "Anna—I want you to remember the day you nearly died. Just relax and go there in your mind."

She sighed and did as he requested. "Now just for a moment, think of what you said to me when I was about to bring you back from death's door."

"I...I asked you not to heal me. Oh, Shiloh!" she clutched his hand. "Did we make a mistake—do you think that the last seven years were wasted?" She hung on for dear life.

"Think about what happened since then," he suggested: "Life is never a mistake, no matter what crazy things we do with it. Yeah there were tough times—for me, too. But we have come out of this knowing something that most families will only wonder about. Life is Sacred and a precious gift but it is just the tip of the iceberg. Our life is a never-ending succession of Dreams. Who knows how many or how far we can go. But we do not die. This is the gift that the Creator gave—literally, the gift that keeps on giving. Isn't it strange how people come up with little jingles and phrases like that—maybe never knowing how close they are to the truth."

Anna's eyes were filled with tears—but they were a different kind of tears now. And the spark was rekindled. "I forgot who I was. That is so...so crazy. But Shiloh—I am no longer that Spirit kind of Angel that I was seven years ago. When you healed me, I became a real flesh-and-blood girl—that was why I came to Earth in the first place anyways. Do you know that is what Angels are lined up for—to come to earth and live out the short life of tears and laughter—and experience the feelings that we can only witness being expressed from the Other Side." And then she wiped away the tears. "I guess you can't stay around?" she said.

"No—I have to go back, and live the other Dream. I have a lot to do there. Here's what we will do. Both of us need to tell mom and dad about this. Now, how will we get you back home?"

"I might be able to help with that," Mathew spoke up. "It is the least I can offer, considering the trip the both of you have shared with me. We can check out if my family is living here-abouts. My mom will help Anna get back home and see that she is safe until that happens."

Mathew's mother was just where he remembered. "I guess some people are the same no matter what the dream," he mused, when they pulled the truck up outside the shelter for homeless and abused women. "Maybe this is a good lesson for me—that when you are living your dream, everything supports it?"

"Mom, I want to introduce you to a friend that has changed the way I look at life—actually changed the way I see everything." As Mathew introduced him, Shiloh's eyebrow raised in recognition of this truth. "My friend needs help for his sister—the kind of help you do best."

"Well, Mathew, this is a blessing in disguise," she shook Shiloh's hand. "For my son to ask for help and to have him admit that we are doing something that makes a difference, you must be one special young man. Tell me what I can do for your sister and it will be done—as sure as God is my witness."

While Shiloh was explaining part of the night's happenings, a sleepy-eyed young woman entered the room where they were sitting. "Mat? That can't be you!" she exclaimed. She hugged her brother. "Are you a ghost? You don't feel like a ghost. What is going on here?" She made eye contact with Shiloh and she seemed to lose her train of thinking. "Do I know you? Somewhere…?"

Shiloh held out his hand. "Maybe," he admitted the obvious. He could not break the contact with the handshake and the eyes.

"Meg?" Mathew interrupted. "This is Shiloh. Shiloh—this is my sister, Meg."

"I know," Shiloh muttered, and then he shook her hand once more and averted his eyes.

"There is a lot more to tell," Mathew explained. "But it is crazy—and Spiritual at the same time."

"You believe in Spirit too, Mat?" Meg asked. "I am ready to believe anything. The last time I talked to you, four days ago on the phone, you were ready to…do anything… you were so angry."

"Well, I did the terrible thing that I set out to do and I got what I deserved. No—the thing I did was beyond forgiving. Even dying will not make up for it. But maybe I can make it up. Maybe I can change it—somehow—with Shiloh's help again. Mom? I don't know how to tell you this but I can't stay. Now that I've changed, I need to go back with Shiloh and see that the evil thing I did does not happen."

Mathew's mother hugged him and sat in the nearest chair. "OK, I am all ears. Who are you—an Angel? I know that my son died. I heard it on the news and I got a call from those terrorists who claimed responsibility. They actually offered me money for what he did. First I cried, because a mother knows when something bad happens to her children. Then I told them where to stick the money and that if I had any way of finding them...well, I am not a vengeful woman but a mother will do anything to protect her child. I guess you know that?

Shiloh sat in a chair beside the woman. He explained: "my sister Anna is an Angel. I am a simple man who remembers where he came from and who he is. I am the Son of the Creator. When so many children forget at birth, I did not forget," he paused to let this sink in.

"Mother Mary!" the woman exclaimed. "How can I believe this? Do you believe this?" she asked her daughter.

"Yes, I do," Meg answered. "At least I know that he would not tell a lie. Beyond that—I am open to listen to the rest of the story."

So Shiloh recounted the rest of the story.

"So I am asking you to see that my sister gets back to Kansa—to our mother and father. Their names are Mary and Joseph," he sat back and folded his hands in his lap.

"Mary and Joseph?" Mathew's mother sighed., "And are they Red People—are they Natives this time around?

"My mother is a full-blooded Ojibway, my father, Joseph, is Portuguese," Shiloh explained. "I was born to help bring about forgiveness and help heal the past. Also, I am here to bring the message of Peace again. The true message has been changed to suit those who are full of fear and wish to keep other people from moving on. There is a belief that Religion is a bridge to Spirituality. This can be true. But many have stopped on that bridge and will not cross over. They have stopped and are too busy judging and fighting darkness that they have given it a name. In doing so, they make this darkness strong. To fight something that lives on war and fear is much the same as worshiping it."

Mathew's mother raised both her hands and shoulders. "This is beyond me. I have been taught another truth and I cannot change. But it is part of my belief that the children and the young women that I help might change the world. And I do so without knowing if this is true. I do this because it is the right thing to do. Both of my children have my colour—I am a Red Person first but I have embraced my former husband's religion. He was an Irish man who loved the brew more than God. And I can only say: may God forgive him."

"My Spirit father does forgive him—but will he forgive himself?" Shiloh answered. "I have been given a gift from the Spirit. I have an Arrow called the Arrow of Truth. I can see the truth but my Spirit Father has sent me to say that compassion is more important. That is why I helped your son and that is why I gave my life to save the children and the innocents that are slaughtered in the name of someone's misguided religious beliefs. Your son and I need to leave soon. We need to return before the morning sun changes this Dream. You have not lost your son—he will return to you in that other dream. I think I will also see you again," he managed a smile upon catching Mathew's sister's eyes one more time.

"OK, what now?" Mat asked when the tearful good-byes were said, and the two young men were back in the truck. "This is why our People do not have a word for good-bye," Shiloh said. "This is why we always say: see you again."

"I have a feeling that you were right before. We need to be in the same place we left. Either nothing will change or we won't make it back," Shiloh reflected.

"That might be a bit difficult. The guards know us and I don't think they will let us pass," Mat said exasperated.

"Everything worked for us 'til now," Shiloh reminded him. "Just drive us back there and we will think of a way to convince them. Meanwhile, what are you going to do with this truck and all the explosives?"

"When we get back, I will turn the truck around and drive it back to where I got it. I can't be sure if the catering company is in on this so I will leave it locked about a block away from the office with a note on the windshield warning about the explosives. Then I will disappear. I will try to make it back to Kansa and hide out. My mother and sister have not heard from me in awhile—except for the one call to Meg. I will phone my mother when it all blows over and tell her I am sorry for all the grief I caused her."

They rode on in silence. The sky was beginning to lighten a bit in the East when they neared the University. "OK, it's now or never," Mat whispered when they were parked in front of the barrier by the guard shack.

"Hi," Mat rolled down the window. "We want to have another look at the place where this explosion took place."

The guards looked very dubious. They did not draw their guns, but waited, with hands on the gun butts. "I can't let anyone in here," one of the guards explained sharply. "You should have gone back to the shop like you said."

"But can't you just let us have one more look? We won't touch anything. There is nothing left in there anyway."

The other guard stepped forward. "Let me call our superiors and maybe the captain will say it is OK," he motioned with his head to the other guard. They both stepped back into the guard shack talking at a level that Mat and Shiloh could not hear. Then one of them glanced back at the truck and took out his cell phone and began to dial.

"They are probably calling the police," Mat whispered. "Get out your rattle and get ready to shake it. We are going thru."

Shiloh did as requested. He disliked the idea of crashing the barrier but was forced to admit there might not be another way.

The guard had made his connection and the other man turned his head to listen in on the conversation. Mat slipped the truck out of gear and floored it, crashing through the barrier and pushing the wooden gate off its hinges. For a moment, both the guards were stunned and then one stepped out of the shack and fired at the speeding truck. The bullet passed through the back window and thudded into the panel behind the two young men.

"It's now or never," Mat yelled. "Either we go back or we go to jail"

Shiloh was gently shaking the spirit rattle, calming his mind and recalling the sound of....then he heard the sound in his mind, in sync with the rattle in his hand. The truck lurched and seemed to halt in mid-air. Mat hit the brakes as they almost collided with the car directly in front. It was broad daylight and they were back in the line-up as if no time had passed. Mat breathed a sigh of relief.

"See you again," Shiloh said in Ojibway and opened the passenger side door. He got out of the truck, and explained to the marine that came running that the truck needed to be taken back to the shop. Shiloh asked if they could have help in turning around. While the marines directed traffic, Mat turned the small refreshment truck around and waved to Shiloh as he disappeared out the main gate by the guard station.

Shiloh walked calmly back and regained his place in the pickup with the two other boys.

"What was that all about?" John asked.

"I just saw a friend and had a short talk with him," Shiloh explained.

"That was a pretty brief conversation," Mark said. "You barely had time to get in and then you got out and he left."

"Yeah," Shiloh confirmed. "He had to go. But sometimes you can talk to a friend and a moment will be worth a couple of hours."

"Whatever," John chuckled "James did say that his brother could be a strange bird. I am sure he meant it in a good way." All three boys shared a laugh while waiting for the line of cars to begin inching toward the main gate of the University.

This young man called Shiloh was indeed a bird of a different kind. Some would say that he was a true Shaman. A Shaman, in the way of the People, is not someone who declares him or herself to be. A Shaman is one who will be recognized by the People as having been a protector and healer—sometimes within their dreams. Once within the compound walls and having parked the pickup, the three boys distributed the Peace placards to anyone who would join their quiet demonstration. Then John and Mark waited with the rest of the crowd for the Vice President of the United States of New Rome to make his appearance. Shiloh made his way over to where the children were disembarking from the school bus.

"Look," one of the children exclaimed and they gathered around. It seems that they had shared a disturbing experience while waiting in the bus. "It's the man who protected us in the bad dream."

Later when the address by the Vice President was over he shook hands with all the children in front of the TV cameras. Shiloh and the other boys got back in the pickup and slowly made their way back past the guard shack at the main entrance. There was a crew working to repair the gate. Shiloh simply observed and smiled as they drove by. He had already decided that it might be prudent to put off visiting Mathew's mother in this dream. When the refreshment truck was found and the explosives were discovered, someone would come looking for the driver. No matter who was eventually blamed—even though no actual harm had been done—it was a good possibility that the home for Abused Women would be watched to see if the wayward son decided to return to his mother's home. The repair to the gate was a confirmation for Shiloh. He recalled that many times when he dreamt parts of the dream will show up in his waking world, including the people's memories. He could not chance being under scrutiny by the law or otherwise in the public eye, until he chose to be.

It was quite later that evening that John and Mark let Shiloh off at the family cottage in Bethany. The lights were still on and his father and mother were sharing a tea by the open fireplace.

"I saw the van outside," he said in a low voice.

"Yes," his mother welcomed him home with a kiss and a hug. "James is back. He is sleeping it off. Did you have a good day?"

"Mom and Dad," he said excitably "I had one amazing time. And you will never guess who I met."

Chapter 4

MY DESTINY?

The next morning, Shiloh was awake early but just coasting—enjoying not having to get up. He heard the bedroom door open and his mother stuck her head in. She smiled and he waved. With the door still ajar, she called out:

"Everybody—dad and I are going for our morning walk. See you at breakfast in about an hour." He heard James' muffled voice answer from the other end of the sprawling cottage, and the door was closed. The house was silent as Shiloh got up and threw on his tattered housecoat almost by reflex. Only James and he were there, so he didn't have to worry about making any good impressions. Then he made his way down the hall toward the bathroom. He almost reached his destination when the door to his brother's room opened and a tall, blonde girl clad only in a bra and underpants stepped out and froze like a deer caught in the headlights of a car.

"Who the fuck...?" she blurted out.

James' voice answered: "Pet—I asked you—please don't use that language in this house."

"Soryeeeee!" she responded, still not attempting to hide her near-nudity. "I think I just met your brother. Hello—she said: "I gotta run. When a girl's gotta pee, a girl's gotta pee," and she slipped quickly into the bathroom.

"Sorry, Shiloh," James came to the bedroom door. "That was Petra. I kinda thought mom or dad would have told you last night?"

Shiloh shrugged in amazement, attempting to hide his embarrassment. "I guess there was so much that I had to tell them and it was late, that it slipped their minds. James—I saw Anna yesterday!

Just like she was alive—and she is—only now she is almost grown up."

"No guff. That is so...un-Rude," James was astounded at his brother's statement but had learned to take Shiloh's spiritual revelations almost as a natural occurrence.

The toilet flushed and the next sound was: "OK you two. Enough with the reminiscing. You can catch up on the brother stuff at breakfast. I am coming out and if either of you are going to be embarrassed, well tough shi…, I mean—just look away." She slipped quickly out the bathroom door and into James' bedroom while managing a quick smile in Shiloh's direction.

"See you at breakfast," James had a big grin. "Put the kettle on will you brother? I feel like a bear until I have my morning coffee."

When James and Petra (now dressed in a pair of torn jeans and a tee shirt) came to the breakfast table, his brother made the more formal introduction. "Shiloh—Petra. Petra, this is my little brother, Shiloh. Petra is the lead singer in the band—I think I told you that before?" But James had not mentioned that he was sleeping with her, Shiloh mused, and in our parent's home. But then his mother was open minded and didn't judge. She had her own standards and lived by them and wouldn't question even her children's friendships—so long as there was no abuse. It was no mystery where Shiloh's teaching originated. He was sometimes amazed how Spirit picked the two perfect parents for his birth.

"Shiloh is a Shaman," James stated mater of factly. "Oh man—you made real coffee. Gimme—gimme."

Shiloh poured for his brother and his girlfriend. Petra raised her eyebrows when she made eye contact with Shiloh as though she was sharing a private joke and set back to sip her coffee. Her eyes twinkled.

James told Shiloh a bit about the members of *The James Gang* nearly a year ago over the phone but Shiloh hadn't met them. Petra was the lead singer. She was Russian-born and moved to Australia to go to university. She was going to school to be a lawyer and then quit. Then she moved to New Rome and began singing in a small club. That was where she met James. James told him that she was hired for her looks and they did not really appreciate her talent. James said: "She is as brilliant as she is beautiful.". And now Shiloh couldn't help but notice that all that James had said was true—even though he hadn't heard her sing.

Shiloh was sharing his story about seeing their younger sister, when Mary and Joseph came back from their walk.

"Oooops," Mary put her hand over her mouth, "did I forget to tell you that Petra was here?"

"No harm done, Mrs. Renauldi," Petra said. We met in the bathroom."

"She means that…well everything worked out OK," James looked skyward, turning his eyes. "Women—will I ever understand them?"

"Probably not." Joseph answered, "But the mystery is half the fun."

"Since you young folk seem to have everything under control, you won't mind if Joseph and I take a drive into the city for some groceries and a bit of a look around?"

"Mom!" Shiloh kidded. "Don't you already have more shoes than the wife of that dictator that was disposed? What was her name?"

"I know the one. She had about a 1,000 pairs," Mary laughed at her son's remark. "I only have 10, I'll have you know. It's the shopping I like. And so does your father. Right Joseph—I said. Right, Joseph?"

"Oh, yes dear," he winked at the same time. "And on a not-so-serious note. You young people should know that this is what makes a marriage work. A little give and take. I look at the shoes that will fit those pretty feet that I adore and your mother comes along to the hardware and lumber stores with me."

"And we balance this out with our walks in the woods," Mary advised.

"About the trip into the city?" Shiloh asked. "I was hoping dad could get me started on a wood-working project. The Shaman business doesn't pay very well for a person that just wants to help people find their own way. And I'd like to learn a trade that's creative and keeps me and my maybe-future wife in the means that I'm accustomed to."

"Hmmmm? Future wife? I haven't heard that one before—Joseph maybe we should put this trip off until tomorrow morning while you have a serious woodworking discussion with your son?" Mary sounded pleasantly surprised.

"We had that talk," Shiloh reminded his mother. "I just want to learn to be a carpenter."

"Sounds good to me," Joseph replied. "It's out to the workshop we go after breakfast." In both of Joseph and Mary's homes, Joseph had added on a full woodworking shop, so that he could continue his well-paying business of custom renovations on both sides of the Red River.

The next morning, after an early breakfast, Joseph and Mary got into the new Jeep and headed for the city. "We will be back when we come back," Mary affirmed. "Sometime in the afternoon I'd like to pay a visit with Jake and Jenene before he goes to New Rome. He and his band have a gig starting at a country western bar and Jenene is pregnant after all this time."

"Holy Willy Nelson!" James exclaimed. "Congratulate Uncle Jake for me." After a moment, he said: "I need to go to Bethany to meet with a fellow that may be our new drummer."

When his mom and dad left, Shiloh went out to the workshop to continue on the woodworking project that Joseph helped him get started yesterday afternoon. After awhile, he heard James' van start up and leave. The cottage was silent except for the small sander that Shiloh was running to pre-sand his project before completing the rest by hand. And then the door to the workshop creaked open.

"Hi. What are you working on?" Petra asked.

"Hi, yourself. I thought you and James went to interview the new drummer?"

"I'm not interested in that," she explained. "The band's problem is not going to be solved by getting a new drummer. The problem will only be fixed by getting rid of another person—our lead guitarist. He hits on all the drummers. I can't understand why. Only the drummers. But that's for another time." She came and looked over his shoulder.

There is some truth in Aikido that drew Shiloh to study it. All living things have a circle—some might call it an aura but Shiloh found it to be more. It is the respectful circle that only a person that you trust is allowed within. At this minute, Petra was within this circle and her presence was unnerving—and not in a bad way.

"I am making a birdhouse," he explained. She continued to watch over his shoulder. He could feel her breath on his neck. "My father said I should start simple and when I've mastered the easy things to the extent that I'm making art, I can graduate to the more complex." He had not turned to face her but concentrated on his sanding.

"I can understand that," she said. "A young man who has no experience should start slow. Sometimes a good teacher is all that is needed the first time." She laid a hand on his shoulder.

"You shouldn't touch me," he looked up over his shoulder into her eyes.

"And why is that?"

"Because for you and I it would be wrong to be touching—alone out here." He turned to face her directly and gently removed her hand. "I am not saying that there is any wrong intended by either you or me. I am a Native man and I have no belief in the White man's sin. But let me tell you about what my People do believe." He sat back on the nearest tall stool and motioned for her to do the same.

"A long time ago, before the White man came, some of our People thought it was right to have more than one wife. This seemed to work for a while but they noticed that there was a problem. At first, it was thought to be a matter of jealousy between the women but as time went on, a few men that were open to ask, began to question their wives. "Something is missing," they said. "Do you know what it is?"

"The thing that is missing is in the beat of your heart," the woman answered. It is something that only one man and a woman can share at one time. It is this sharing that connects us to the Earth. It is part physical and part spirit. But the important thing is to have this open heart. The trust must first be felt like the beat of a drum. Trust is the key that will open our hearts to share Love with one man and one woman."

"Awesome!" Petra exclaimed. "I wish I could find that. So how did this change your People's relationships?"

"That is the point," Shiloh said thoughtfully. "My people are open to change when Spirit tells us. This is because we are following the teachings of a Spirit Father that is alive and speaking to us through our hearts. I am not meaning to judge but for us there could not be a book of written laws."

"Like the part in Genesis that tells about Eve tempting Adam into sin?"

"Yes—like that," he smiled. "I have HIS memories when I need them. And the One that came before did not write this. It is an inspired book—that is true. But for me, and most of our People, this book is one-sided. It is all about a male view of Life. That does not make it wrong, but there is no balance. To be balanced, there would need to be more of Women's teachings. The book called Genesis is mostly about the fear that a man is responsible for his own feelings for the woman he loves. The Spirit Father that I know wouldn't have cursed Eve—he would have given her a blessing to be able to share love and bring children into this world. That is how I see and respect the woman with whom I will one day share this mystery. And that is how I respect the woman who shares my brother's bed."

"Well said, for a man so young," Petra leaned back on her hands. "But what about your feelings that you have minute-to-minute? The story you told us at breakfast the other day was about how our thoughts create realities. Am I right?"

"You are as intelligent as James said you are," he laughed. "I am learning to channel my thoughts into creative projects like this birdhouse. I am not about repressing or controlling. If there is a world in which my thoughts concerning a certain woman in the hallway yesterday morning are being enacted—I will let it be and respect that which is beyond my control."

James returned a bit after lunch. He stuck his head in the door of the workshop. "Hi, Pet. What's up?"

"James!" she exclaimed with the exuberance of a child. "Shiloh and I have been making a birdhouse."

James cooked the late lunch. He made an omelette with fresh mushrooms and threw together a side salad. Freshly brewed coffee for Petra and him and a tea for Shiloh was on the table when he called him to come in from the workshop.

"Great dinner, hon," Petra congratulated James. "You could be a chef."

"Yeah, I could be a lot of things," he conceded. "But right now I would like to be a member of a successful hard-rock band. My drummer is threatening to quit and it's becoming a bitch—sorry Shiloh—to find a replacement."

"The 'B' word's appropriate though," Petra noted, as she dove into her salad with gusto. "And you know I'm right."

"So—if I admit you're right, where does that get me? To fix the problem, I might need to give up on a long-time friend." James poked at his food.

"What's this all about?" Shiloh asked. "Is there anything I can do to help?"

"No, I don't think so little brother. I have to admit that you have a knack of finding ways to heal people—that's your Shaman thing. But this is something that I take personal responsibility for. Jude and I go way back. I have stood behind him through thick and thin and I am not giving up on him now."

"But that is the real problem, love," Petra finished the salad, pushed the bowl away and sipped her coffee. "You are like a dog with a bone when it comes to something like this. Maybe you're not a bear totem after all?"

"Bears are born healers," Shiloh noted. "They store up all that energy and take it into a long winter's healing Dream. When that bear comes out of his cave in the spring, he's thin and hungry but his Dreaming has helped Mother Earth get ready to birth a new world."

"Whoa! I think there might be something Shiloh can do," Petra exclaimed. "He has a different way of looking at things and when we were talking earlier this morning he helped me see something in a way I might not have."

"What kind of something?" James had a faraway look in his eyes.

"Just something. But maybe this is about healing…Jude definitely needs help. It's either that or someone's gonna put him down when you ain't there to protect him."

"What's this about Jude?" Shiloh asked.

"Jude is our lead guitarist. He plays a mean Hendricks—you gotta admit that, Petra. I've known Jude from high school back on the Rez. We had a small band then—or thought we did, anyways. And, well, Jude was always getting picked on and I did the big brother thing when my real brother was away touring the world. And oh, Shiloh, in case I didn't tell you—Jude is gay."

"So?" Shiloh waited for more. James was not one to judge. Being part of the Renauldi family had helped him gain a strong sense of who he was. James was not gay—could never be gay—bordering on macho, but he was so centered in his maleness that it did not faze him to be the friend of someone who saw the world from another perspective.

"So Jude is not just gay," Petra supplied. "He flaunts it and he goes out of his way to hit on every drummer we've had to date. He won't let up until they quit."

"Maybe I am missing something," Shiloh queried. "If someone were allowed to—let's say—put him in his place, then the problem might not exist."

"See! See!" I told you," Petra grinned. "But there is the slight problem with big brother—who is the leader of our band. Sorry hon. I love you fiercely but the truth needs to be out."

James shrugged and leaned over to kiss her. "Shiloh!" he exclaimed. "That from a pacifist Shaman? Little brother, you do surprise me to no end. Is this like what they call tough Love?"

"I don't really like that term. Love is not tough. It is soft and gentle like water, but strong like a willow tree. Love is also truthful and compassionate. I am a strong supporter of Peace," Shiloh explained. "No—more than that—I am Peace at all costs—except when it comes to the lack of mature self responsibility. I will protect the children and the innocent with my life—literally. But there is a point when we need to be responsible for our actions. That point comes when I make a choice to live my life in a different way—walk a path that is 'less travelled' to quote a certain author. It is not about the choices we make, as much as that we live from the Heart and give up the role of the victim."

"Yeah," James agreed. "But there is a belief among the gay community and their supporters that it is not a choice, as much as that it might be something that is part of their DNA. I don't know what to believe, honestly. What do you think of this? This seems to be up your alley little brother. Kind of the Shaman's expertise—if I may be the eloquent one..."

"Honestly, I am neither for nor against a gay person living the life he or she chooses. The life of a Shaman does not seem to be a choice, but it is. It could be said about what might happen to me and those I love or I can make the most of the gift of being different. I learned something from Anna about Angels. She said that the Angels are lining up to be born here. This is part of the Circle. Angels are creatures that are balanced—they are neither male nor female but can communicate with those of us in this world in a way that is right for us. Our People saw that two-spirited men and women were powerful Shaman. Before Anna was born—and after—she expressed pure female energy. Is it possible that some so-called Gay people are the way they are because of circumstances that involved abuse early in life and other Angels may have been simply misconceived? They may have been prepared to be born as a woman and through an act of Coyote Spirit be born as a man?"

"What is Coyote Spirit?" Petra asked.

"Our People talk about the Coyote as being a trickster," James explained. "The Coyote is a mischievous creature that helps you learn by leading you down the wrong path or by showing you the reverse of the truth."

"But isn't that lying?" Petra looked puzzled. "Isn't the reverse of truth a lie?"

"That's up to us to discover," Shiloh replied. "Maybe we are meant to make the most of what we have and find a truth where there seems to be none? Either way—it is not about the judging of your friend's lifestyle. It is about helping him to respect those who are different than him."

"Well, I'm willing to admit that Petra may be right as she generally is on many things," James winked. "So...little brother, are you up to practicing your healing skills on the members of *The James Gang*?"

"You could begin with me." Petra suggested.

"How so?" Shiloh recalled how the shared woodworking project began.

She smiled in a familiar, womanly wise way. "I mean—when I sing I get tightness in the back of my neck. The minute I step up to the mic in front of an audience, I get a feeling like it is my chance to 'finger the man'. Not men—the Man—you know—the establishment. That is why I packed in the horse manure of the legal system. Wow—I am feeling intense just thinking about it." Her voice changed as she spoke, becoming strained.

"Ho—hold on there!" James urged. "Save the hot stuff for the bedroom." He gently squeezed her shoulder.

"Yeah! That's better," she sighed. "A bit to the right," her voice softened once more.

"I could help but it looks like James is more of a healer than he gives himself credit," Shiloh observed.

"I think you might be able to help," James said. "I've tried this a few times when we are on-stage. It works for a while but Pet just pours it on like Janice Joplin. She has real soul. Sometimes it sounds like she is hurting so much that I want to stop it all and carry her off the stage." A tear welled up in his eye and he turned his head to hide it.

A few moments of silence filled the kitchen.

"Maybe I can help," Shiloh agreed. "People need to express their feelings. We can't stop that—or we shouldn't anyway. And we are all unique in that. Your friend Jude might need something different than the rest of the band but that is his choice. If it is OK with you and Petra, I'll come to your next rehearsal and see what happens. If I do my healing thing, as James puts it, who knows what might happen. I don't doubt that I can heal—oh but you need to understand that healing is not meant to be an *I'll do it all for you* thing. It's about helping you get to a place where you can let the Spirit flow and let the healing happen naturally."

Later that week James asked everybody to get together for a rehearsal. Despite early insinuations that he was leaving the band, Lucas, the present drummer, agreed to attend since James promised that Jude would mind his manners. Shiloh had learned that the couple of previous drummers had simply moved on—declaring that they had some personal "stuff" to work out instead of saying up front that they were hassled by Jude. Lucas had walked off stage during their last performance so James almost had to finish the show without a drummer. Lucas agreed to return one more time by stating that the first time Jude came near him, he would "stick his drumstick where it would do the most good". But then even after a talking to by James, once the music got loud and angry, Jude sidled over toward the drummer and was menaced by the proposed drumstick. The performance ended on a sour note—which seemed to add to the "enjoyment" of the paying customers. "We give them a show and allow our fans a chance to blow off a bit of steam," James explained to Shiloh that it was meant to be all for show but it was too much reality. "They should put us on TV," he half joked. "We are a traveling reality show."

The rehearsal was arranged in a local farmer's unused barn. The farmer was the father of Mark—one of the young men that Shiloh had hitched a ride with to the Peace rally in New Rome the previous week. The barn was far off from the main house but had the electricity that the band required. As it turned out, the band had a following of some of the local teenagers and to make things more "realistic" James allowed a few to attend. The rustic nature of this kind of rehearsal appealed to James since it was his desire to put on a show that was more impromptu than staged.

"This is my brother, Shiloh that I told you about" James introduced Shiloh to the other three members that he hadn't met before. "Lucas is our drummer, Simon plays bass guitar and last, but not least, this is Jude, on lead guitar." All three of the young men gave Shiloh's hand a reasonable shake—including Jude. The more reluctant hand shake was from Simon—just quick and to the point and he backed away.

"Well, let us be at it," James suggested and in no time at all, the band filled the vacant barn with sound. Shiloh sat on a small milking stool near the drummer. He had brought his hand drum, explaining that he just wanted to drum along to get the feeling of the energy that they created together. Gradually, the volume grew and as they cranked it up, Shiloh became aware of energy that threatened to burst the walls of the barn. Right away, it became apparent that Petra was the focus of that energy. Her voice was raspy and energetic—similar to Joplin, as James had said, and soon she was screaming in a way that sent shivers up and down his spine. The rest of the band took up the cause and an angry mix of rap and blues came alive like a tortured demon.

They were good—as Jake had said—or could be if they weren't so damn angry. Meanwhile, James was in never-never land. He was tripping out on Petra's voice. It was not a surprise to Shiloh, at this point, that the leader had little interest in keeping the rest of the band in line. Shiloh mused with the thought that it might be a good thing to practice a little of the healing he promised with Petra. But for the moment he wanted to see where this was going. Also, he was amazed at his brother who was momentarily caught up in her intensity. And then he noticed a peculiar action by the lead guitarist—or was it part of the rock scene act? It was almost like a re-enactment of the energy of Hendrix and Joplin—and everyone knew where that ended up, for both of them. Between riffs, Jude became agitated. After playing like a demon, he would lean the guitar in the stand beside him and shuffle around like a calypso dancer.

"Great! Here we go again!" Lucas' voice drifted to Shiloh's ears over the music. Shiloh kept drumming and turned his head to catch the rest of the conversation. Lucas just shook his head. "I'll kill that little freak if he comes near me!" he threatened.

But Jude had other ideas, or so it seemed. When the music and Petra's voice reached its crescendo, it must have touched some memory or something else in his heart," Shiloh wondered. "Then, since the drum is the connection to the heart it literally turned him on." Soon the lead guitarist was being drawn like a flame to the nearest man with a drum. Shiloh just kept on drumming, seemingly oblivious to Jude's advances thinking that there was no harm done—unless he attempted to get personal. Soon, though, the guitar was forgotten and Jude leaned over to the object of his affection.

"I would be careful about how close you get—unless your intentions are purely respectable," Shiloh said, not turning his head. But his warning went seemingly on deaf ears as Jude stood behind him and leaned over…and…in the next instant, the lead guitarist flipped in the air and landed with a thud on his backside on the barn floor. Shiloh scarcely missed a beat on his drum but Jude ended up sitting stunned—wondering what had happened.

"Oh yeah," James offered a hand up with a huge grin on his face. "Did I forget to mention that my little brother knows kung-fu and a few other good Japanese words?" A slightly bedraggled Petra glanced back and smiled her approval. Then James said: "Can we take it from the top?"

Everyone resumed their places—more or less. Jude, rather grudgingly, picked up his guitar, muttering something about: "I didn't mean any harm." Lucas had trouble settling down—he was laughing so hard. Shiloh resumed his drumming, hoping that the tension had been broken and that some sort of point about respecting each other's space had been made. Soon everyone was cooking and Petra came alive. The energy began to build again. Jude began his act. "What will it take to wake him up to see that there are more people in this barn than him and his personal wants?" Shiloh waited for the stalking part to begin, because that is what it was in its most primal form. "Maybe he can't help himself?" Shiloh wondered. He stood and met Jude face to face. "Wake up," he suggested. "Or I won't be responsible for what happens—again. Is the drum bothering you—or what? I have stopped drumming." He stood eye-to-eye. "In the old days, the White man outlawed our dancing and drumming. I think they were afraid that it made the People lose control. But our Dancing and Drumming is Sacred to us," Shiloh explained. "It does excite our emotions but there is something else that is present. This is called Respect. We drum so our heart can communicate with all of the other creatures—in a Respectful way."

"Yeah—sure. I understand," the other man insisted. "I didn't mean to be disrespectful—I just want to share. I just want to be friends—you know…"

"Friendship is a good thing," Shiloh agreed. "Let's let this pass and get on with…" He went to return to his milk stool but the moment he turned his back, Jude reached out his hand. Whether it was truly meant to be the gesture of good will, as he would claim later, the result was the same. The moment after his hand made contact with Shiloh's shoulder, his behind made contact with the ground.

"Hey, man," Shiloh held out his hand to the man on the barn floor. "This has got to stop—or you could get more than your pride hurt. I don't want to see that happen and I will not be the one to cause it. You need to see that Respect means giving some thought before you act—of whether your actions involve another person." Jude refused the hand up. Shiloh shrugged and this time backed up to his seat on the stool in the manner of the martial artist—bowing but keeping his eyes on the other man. He was about to say that he had nothing against Jude's lifestyle choice if that was his truth, with another consenting adult but Jude had resumed his guitar—playing like nothing had happened.

When Petra's voice escalated to painful heights, Shiloh saw an opportunity to demonstrate his words and to do—more or less—what he had come to do. Still drumming, to make his presence known, he had walked to her side. Having caught her attention, he hung his drum on a nearby empty microphone stand. Then he said in a calm, even voice: "I am going to put my hand near the back of your neck. I want to sense your energy and then I will touch your shoulder and neck. Is that OK?"

She kept on singing but nodded: "Yes."

He did exactly what he said he would do, step by step, until he had both hands gently massaging her shoulders. Even before this point, he was aware that he did not need to touch and that simply balancing her energy would have worked. But there was an element of expectancy—a different kind of respect—for another person's belief. And there was the matter of Jude and the rest of the band watching and listening. When he moved both hands from massaging her shoulders to the back of her neck, Petra's voice lost its pain. The power and emotion were still present but the pain was audibly absent. In fact, her range increased with a sweetness that was intoxicating. She was singing from a clear heart unblocked by hurtful memories. "Some people might think that it was the pain that gave the song the authentic sound," Shiloh mused. "But I would be happy to do without that and obviously so would she."

When the song was finished, Petra hugged Shiloh with gratitude. "I feel so much better," she said. "But will the pain come back?"

"Not if you are done with it," he answered truthfully.

"This changes the way I sing," she said to James. "I might not fit in with the direction that the band is going."

"Then the band will need to make some changes," he assured her. "We've tried to accommodate the feelings of the rest of the band but maybe the problem has been the kind of music we're playing. Maybe we are ready to loosen up a bit."

"That move you did when Jude got a bit close," Simon asked Shiloh "That looked like Aikido. Are you an Aikido master? I have never seen that done so smoothly."

"It is Aikido," Shiloh confided. "But the man that taught me did not call himself a Master. My teacher told me that there are only teachers and students. And sometimes the roles are reversed. He told me that the best teacher is always ready to become the student. Before I left Japan, my teacher gave me something. Rather—he helped me to create a tool to be used by a student of Zen. Let me show you—see if any of you can guess what it is for?"

Shiloh took something from the pocket of his arrow quiver that carried his flute. He showed it to the rest of the group.

"Looks like a plain piece of rope or string. A bit thicker than string." Lucas suggested. "Can I touch it?"

"Sure," Shiloh handed it to him.

"It's not a normal hemp string," Lucas held it and drew it through his hand. "Is it some kind of sinew?"

"What's a sinew?" Jude had gotten over his hurt pride and became curious. He didn't seem to hold a grudge for very long. Shiloh noted.

"A sinew is made from animal tissue," Simon stifled an outright laugh. "Where have you been hiding all your life, Jude?" And then he asked Shiloh. "Can I see it?" Shiloh handed him the sinew. "Yeah. That's what it is. But it's too thick for a guitar string. What's it for?"

"The Shaman, who helped me get this, called it Trust—and Respect. I think if I show you what it is used with, you will understand." Shiloh reached into the quiver and drew out a wooden staff about three feet long that was tapered on both ends and had a hand grip in the middle, covered by a similar cord (or sinew). "My Aikido teacher was also a follower of Zen—he helped me make this part on my last week in Japan."

"A bow," Simon exclaimed. "And the cord is the bow-string."

"Why didn't your teacher give you the bow-string or help you to make one?" James asked.

"He was a wise man and he wanted me to know the value of the components of a Zen bow and his last lesson was about Trust," Shiloh explained. "He said that a bow is more than a weapon. It is a way to know about Trust—and Respect."

"What does Respect have to do with it?" Petra enquired. "I know that Respect is important," she eyeballed Jude. "But what is the connection here?" She watched as Shiloh attached the cord to one end of the bow and bent it with one knee—to attach to the other end. "Where are your arrows? I can't imagine what a man like you would use arrows for anyways?"

"I didn't have my arrow then," Shiloh smiled. "I do have an arrow now—just one arrow. I'll tell you about that some other time. Right now—the connection is made. This bow and cord begins with Trust and together they represent Respect." A baffled look passed around the group. Simon just shrugged.

"It's a Zen thing," Simon offered. He was a long time practitioner of the martial arts—a black belt.

"That's true," Shiloh admitted. "My teacher left it up to me to find the bow string. He said that in the Zen way it couldn't be given to someone. He said that Trust and Respect are things that we need to earn. He told me Zen is a thing about the moment, so he could not say when or who would help me get the bow-string."

"So where in the world did you get the bow-string?" James reached out and Shiloh gave him the bow. He pulled on the string, enjoying the "twang" sound when he let it go. "Not much difference between this and a guitar—except this can kill."

"Very astute," Shiloh agreed. "That is part of how I came to get the cord. One day near the end of the seven years of studying abroad, I came home to Kansa for a brief visit during the summer break. I went to see Sarah—the lady Shaman—and she asked me to come with her to visit her Grandfather. Her Grandfather lived way out on the plains. He was a former member of the Sons of Soma who left to live in a more traditional, peaceful way. The rest of Sarah's family live almost the same way as our ancestors. They put down roots—long enough to grow crops. And to make a long story shorter, Sarah's grandfather suggested that I go with him and the younger men to hunt Buffalo."

"Like I said before," James handed back the bow, "little brother—you surprise me to no end."

"I surprise myself," Shiloh said. "I think we should always be ready to walk our talk. We should not be quick to judge unless we have walked or rode on horseback, the proverbial miles. I have to say that I reserved the right to stop at any time—if the hunting party became something I could not be a part of. I did not do any killing—but I accepted that being part of the hunting party was the same as if I had shot the arrows that brought down the Buffalo. The braves were quick and sure. I watched from a nearby ridge while they rounded one Buffalo out from the herd—a bull, not a cow and ended its life with their arrows. When the Buffalo was dead, the Grandfather did a ceremony—to thank it for the gift of life. Then they cut up the animal in the ways that our People have done since the dawn of time and nothing was wasted."

"During the cutting and packing of the Buffalo meat, the Elder instructed me to make the bow-string. This is not the kind of cord that you can buy in any store," he said: "This comes from a living creature that sacrificed its' life so we may live. The name of this bow-string and our Relationship with the Buffalo is Trust—and when it is used to bend the bow—it is called Respect."

"But how could you be part of it? The killing I mean?" Petra shuddered.

"All things are sacred. All creatures are sentient in their own way," he answered. "I was part of this so that I will never take for granted the food I eat was once alive. I am mostly vegetarian—but even the fish that some vegetarians eat and the birds that others eat are conscious. So are the vegetables and even the rocks. The Earth herself is alive. I will not be using my bow and arrow to kill. It is all about Respect."

"But I am not here to lecture," he passed around the bow for the group to test. "And I am not here to start another religion. There are enough religions and Spiritual teachings to last us many lifetimes. What we need here is to be open to ask questions and respectful enough of each other and Spirit to listen."

"Do you think I need healing?" Jude asked. "Am I wrong to think the way I do?"

"It's not anyone's right to judge how a person chooses to Love—or how they think," Shiloh accepted the bow back. "It is how a person acts, in the expression of what they call Love, that might be in Question. There is a Mystery that we call Spirit. The expression of this can be Love. Without Trust and Respect—Love is just a word. In the White man's book, they write that the WORD was made flesh. Here I am—and here you are. We are more than a word—our actions will speak for us."

Later on during the drive home, Shiloh sat in the seat behind his brother, who drove the van. "You seem too wise for someone so young," Petra remarked, turning her head to speak. "And if you really do have some of the memories of Jesus, as you say, or if you are somehow his reincarnation—his second coming—then aren't you a bit apprehensive about your future?"

"I am one who remembers," Shiloh answered. "The second coming story is from the White man's book. It is true that the four riders spoke about a prophesy being fulfilled, and the events of my birth were more than co-incidental. But there is more to the Mystery than can be written in any book. Prophesies are about a future that has yet to be. They are both warnings and insights—they are not written in stone. And another thing about that—even stone can be changed by water. My destiny is to walk in the Way—the Beauty Path, as my People call it. I will do my best to walk in the Way of the ONE that came before. I will do my best to tell the truth that needs to be told and be responsible for the outcome of my actions. The Great Spirit would not ask much more from anyone in this world."

Chapter 5

THE PATH OF BEAUTY

"The birdhouses are becoming works of art." Joseph went out to the workshop to see how Shiloh was spending his time. The band was on the road again. "What are you working on now?" Joseph asked Shiloh.

Shiloh held up his latest project for his father to see. It was a tree branch—as straight as a pool cue and almost as long as his unbent bow.

"Good choice," Joseph smiled. "How are you going to put the hole in the middle?" Shiloh had sanded it smooth except for one end where he was going to carve an eagle. It looked almost like another flute but Joseph could see what it would actually be. He could see that the stem was part of a traditional pipe.

"I asked a couple of the Elders how they made it," Shiloh explained. "Then I thought the best way would be to cut it right down the middle, make a grove in both sides, then glue it back together. Then I will finish the carving and decorate it with feathers. What do you think?"

"I could help with that—if you want me to?" Joseph suggested. "I have a saw that will do the job—clean and straight with very little waste. Tradition is a good thing but I think a bit of help from modern technology would be a good thing—for a modern Shaman. You'll be doing the most important part by hand."

Shiloh agreed to his father's help, especially since he is a professional carpenter. He looked up from his carving to say as much—and the knife in his hand slipped. "Whoa. I didn't plan that," he held his left thumb to stop the bleeding. "Just the same—it's a strange co-incidence. Don't you think?" He had the bleeding under control but his pipe stem was now stained in a way that would now make the pipe very personal.

"Any idea where you will get the stone for the bowl?" Joseph knew that most true native pipes had a bowl carved from something called pipe-stone. This stone was almost the same colour as the young man's blood.

"I guess the pipe bowl or the stone will appear when I am ready?" There was an unspoken meaning to his words that both the father and son understood. The joining of the pipe stem and the bowl is significant of a different type of completion. As the story goes, the pipe was one of the gifts that the Buffalo Calf Maiden gave to the young warrior who she chose as her husband. "It's a matter of respect for the balance of Spirit. Many religions believe that the Creator made us complete in Spirit, yet in the body we seek to find our other half. They often teach that it is our goal to seek purity in Spirit and that the natural "urges" of the body are wrong. The White man's religion has invented a word for this—they call it sin. Our ancestors knew different before they were taught about sin by the black robes. We respected the natural way of life and respected the women who would complete us."

"So what happens to what you call the White man's teaching?" Joseph asked. "You are also my son and therefore you are part White."

"A good point dad," Shiloh agreed. "I acknowledge the truths that are in the teaching of the Bible. It is an undeniably inspired book. And if it were taken from the context as being about the One called Jesus, as the followers of Christianity proclaim, then it would be the Word that they claim it to be. However it has been written from a place of non-balance, and so tells us that the relationship between man and woman is somehow wrong. And because of this, children are not created through the expression of Love but are deemed sinful from birth. How could this be?"

"In my younger days, I was told something by Spirit or by the Sons of Soma—I still am not sure," Joseph said. "This teaching was that the Truth cannot be changed or hidden. This is why I returned to reading the Bible as a reference—knowing that although the book was written and altered again and again by men who were fearful of their natural urges and feelings, there is a way of reading it if the person who is looking for inspiration will find the Truth that he or she is seeking."

"True. The story about the life of the One who came before is in those pages, even though He was misunderstood. I believe that those who follow the Man and treat the Book more like a work of fragmented Spiritual history will not go wrong. My father is a good example for me to follow."

"Which father is that?" Joseph joked. "The Spirit Father or the flesh and blood one?"

"For me, they are both the same," Shiloh patted his dad on the back. "I hear the call to lunch—we had best not keep mom waiting. By the way, how did you know that mom was the one for you? Did you see her in a dream before you met her?"

When the pipe stem was completed, Shiloh was not in a hurry to find the mystery woman of his dreams. "All in good time—in the Great Spirit's time," he told himself. He hung his completed work above the head board of his bed and immersed himself in his "apprenticeship" with his father as a carpenter. By making a pipe and becoming a carpenter, he was following his bliss—the Path of Beauty in an outward way so the inward path was given the freedom to create.

* * *

"Are you really Jesus?" Petra's question was open and clear. She was without bias or thoughts of religious condemnation. With Shiloh's help, she had found and liberated that part of herself that many of the "new-agers" call the Inner Child. Petra, James and *The Gang* had returned from a very successful six months on the road. "We are becoming a family," James had told his brother during a phone call a few months into the tour. "Yeah—there are still things we disagree on but when you start with respect as you said that night in the barn there's nothing that can't be worked out."

When James and Petra returned, he told his younger brother about the ongoing situation with Lucas and Jude. "Only once has Jude tried the old act and Lucas stood up and gave him the eye. It took just a look and they both began to laugh. Afterward, they talked—Lucas began by saying that if Jude wanted respect that he would have to show it himself. Simon is still distant but I can see that he is letting his guard down a bit, as well. Sure, Lucas might still go his way but I don't think it will be the nasty split up we've suffered in the past. I am all for letting go—if someone needs to move on. You, too, honey"…James winked at Petra, "but I really hope that is not your plan for awhile?"

"No such luck," Petra punched his shoulder and kissed him on the cheek. "You just try to get rid of me, you big lug, and you will have a real fight on your hands."

"Whatever you just said does not make sense," Shiloh looked on in wonderment. "I can hardly wait for my chance at this fight-and-Love relationship thing."

"Your time is coming," James said with certainty. "How about getting your drum out and singing with us?"

When the three of them had sung and drummed for about an hour or so, Petra asked the question: "Are you really Jesus? Since the last time we saw you, James and I have been reading a bit of the Bible. That's pretty heavy stuff. I never got into religion before 'cause I was too logical for that Spirit stuff and, you know what? It is still way out there as far as I am concerned."

"Me too, little brother," James added. "There is way too much judgment and war in that book for me. I would not want to think about my brother looking forward to that kind of future either."

"Here's the thing," Shiloh responded. "It doesn't have to end that way. It is a book that contains stories and prophesies. It is about things that have happened and things that might happen—that is, if something is not done to bring about a change. And that is why I am here. I have His memories but in answer to your question," he addressed Petra. "I am Jesus—.and I am also every messenger that came to earth…and so are you."

She looked puzzled.

"Every child that is born, is born from the Divine spark. Every child is a son or daughter of the Creator of All Things. And then they forget. Some remember for a while until the memory is replaced by the teaching of their parents and their tribes. All too many are taught that they were born in sin—or some such belief that judges them as being less than worthy. Then the Creator—the Mystery—sends someone to earth who will not forget. I am no different than you—or James—or any other person for that matter. You might have read or heard that everything that I can do, you can do—and more. This was true when spoken by the One and the others who came before. And it is true now. I am still learning what is possible—more like remembering actually. And it would blow your mind if you only knew."

James and Petra were silent for a long while. Then James spoke. "It makes sense—in a crazy Spirit way," he conceded. "With the right parents—a Mary and Joseph like our mom and dad—the kind of parents who this man called Jesus was born to. And the right circumstances—the right surroundings would help."

"All that being equal," Petra mused, 'why aren't there more Jesuses—more messengers being born?"

"There are," Shiloh explained. "Like I said before—all children are born from the same Spirit. But then there is the Gift of free will. Free will makes this Earth the Path of Beauty that our People say it is."

"Or the path of Fear," James concluded. "Depending on whether your parents teach you a way of Love and that all life is Sacred and connected…or if they convince you that you were born through sin—into a life of sin?"

"Exactly—kinda," Shiloh agreed. "So many people on the Earth today are not living the Gift that they were given at birth—free will. Instead, they are living other people's lives. Now, that includes many of our People, too. Many of our People have forgotten the Ways of our ancestors and live only for Revenge.

Or they are trying to live the way of the White man as it was taught to them through abuse in the residential schools. There is an old psychological story—truth or fiction—that innocents who have been abducted may, for some reason, begin to love their captors if they aren't rescued for a long time. And they begin to relate to them no matter how despicable the person is who abducted them. Think about this in the context of angry, misguided parents who have been granted the birth of a Divine child. The scars may never heal because when the child grows up, he or she has forgotten who they are."

"So how are you going to change this?" Petra asked. "It seems a big job for one young man. And look what happened to Jesus for all his teachings."

"The Way of Jesus and Buddha and the messengers that came before, was right for their times. They did what they were sent to do. The rest was, and still is, up to free will. It is not my job, nor was it the job of any who came before, to force anyone to wake up. The Gift of Life is Sacred in that way. My Way is related to the People who are my tribe and my ancestors. It is about living the best example that I can. I only have to figure out how to appeal to the best in people without preaching. The time for talk is mostly done. What we need now is to walk the talk. This is what the Traditional Native Way is all about: Singing and Dancing and Sharing, with Respect for all life."

"I just had an idea," Petra exclaimed. "I remember a song that fits the occasion. James? How would you feel about your brother joining our band?"

"That would be great," James agreed enthusiastically. "We could use another drum—a Native drum. How about it Shiloh? The direction for *The James Gang* has changed since that night in the barn. I think it's time for us to change again—and evolve."

"As both of you are aware, I am open to new ideas," Shiloh was excited. "What's the song you have in mind Petra? Can we start working on it now?"

Shiloh joined *The James Gang* on the road in a minor role at first. He played a second drum as James had suggested. In the meantime, whenever they could, James and Petra introduced new songs that became the trademark for the evolving band. And as Shiloh's drum became more prominent James started calling their new music *Spirit Rock*. It caught on and the fan base changed and their following grew. Then on the fourth month on the road, in front of a cheering crowd, James changed the way he introduced the band. Before, he would quietly introduce them, saying their names, which instrument they played and finishing with: "and this is Shiloh, on the Spirit Drum." Shiloh played a large new Native drum that he had made with the help of his father.

On this night, after the first round of songs to get the crowd warmed up, James went through the regular intros and finished up with: "and playing the Spirit Drum is Shiloh, who was the inspiration for our new sound. Please welcome my brother! He has a song he wants to share with you and we might get him to say a few words about what *Spirit Rock* is all about."

James motioned Shiloh to come up front—to stand beside Petra and the mic. Shiloh made his way, bringing his hand drum that was a gift from the riders from the stars. Rather tentatively, he tested the mic and said: "hello—I am here tonight to tell you something—not about me but about you." The crowd hushed in anticipation. Previously they had just heard his drum, but now they were eager to hear a few words from this young man who helped create the music that they so enjoyed. "I am here to tell you that you are the inspiration. You are all children of the One Creator and the reason I am here is to remind you of that truth."

There was a moment of silence and then a growing, thunderous applause. Shiloh looked at Petra and James and they both nodded, as the applause subsided. "I have a song that this beautiful lady will help me sing," he motioned to Petra, and she returned a sweeping bow to show that she was ready. "This song was not written by me. It was written by a couple of men called Burt Bacharach and Hal David and it was beautifully sung by Jackie DeShannon. The main reason I am telling you this is that this band has created a new sound. *Spirit Rock* is not entirely new however; it is a combination of Rock and Native Music. Both of these sounds have been around for a long time—especially the music of my ancestors. I am saying this because we do not need to create a new Religion—we have everything we need. We just need to start Dancing and Singing and living the Gift of Life that we have been given—from our Heart." He lifted the hand drum and began to play. The Crowd responded and then became quiet as Shiloh and Petra began to sing:

"Lord we don't need another mountain,
There are mountains and hillsides enough to climb,
There are oceans and rivers enough to cross..."

And when Petra and Shiloh reached the part about: "What the world needs now," the crowd was singing—a thunderous echoing of voices joined in.

"Love sweet Love—it's the only thing that there's much too little of."

* * *

"How is it coming along?" Mary went to the workshop to find Shiloh attaching the feathers to his pipe. Two years had passed and the band had gained a dedicated following of fans and were being noticed in the media. They had also briefly toured Kansa when the family moved home for most of a year. Now they were back in Bethany in their second home, and Shiloh had taken a break to apprentice his second job as a part-time carpenter, working with his father.

"It's about finished," he answered. He didn't need to add that the pipe bowl was still absent. "Mom?" he asked, as he held the pipe up for her approval. "There are a few things that are troubling me?"

"Do you want to talk?" she asked, after accepting the pipe, and admiring it, and handing it back like a talking stick.

"I feel different," he said. "I know—you will say that I am not like any other boy but that is my mother talking. I need you to help me with some things that have been bothering me—with the truth that I know you can give."

When she was silent, it meant that she was listening. She sat at the work bench and sipped the tea that she had carried out to the workshop with her.

"I am different. I have always known that. I am different than any other man or boy. And I am different than the man they called Jesus even though I have many of his memories. I am like the One who came before, but I am not the same. My purpose is the same but different as well. This is the Mystery that our People talk about. I am here to tell the truth about him but I will do that by living his life in another way. And I have my own thoughts and urges as well. This is troubling me now. How can I do what is right by Him, when I think about…?" He lowered his head to hide the blush.

After a few minutes, she accepted the pipe back as a sign that it was her turn to talk. This was a respectable way of talking—when someone will tell you their truth as they see it, a mother to son, heart-to-heart, and as one trusted friend to another.

"I have read a bit about this man called Jesus, in the Bible—with your father's help in the translation," she smiled. "Even though he was beyond reproach, he was also a man. He made that very clear, although the people who wrote about him painted a picture of someone who was a God and beyond mortal feelings. He was a living example of how a man or woman can be. In his culture, however, it would have been right for him to take a wife. I believe that this part of his life was ignored by the men who wrote about him because it would have made him too mortal in their eyes. I think that was the result of their personal fears, as you have said before. But I believe that he would have been open to live the life of Love that he talked about. He was not about saying something and living another truth. He would have walked his talk."

Mary hesitated, as though remembering something, and instead of handing the pipe back, she began to speak again. "I will tell you a story about a young woman, a girl who had the same doubts that you might be feeling. This is a story about the Ghost Dance."

"If you remember, the best known use of the Ghost Dance is the role it played in bringing about the massacre at Wounded Knee 1890 which resulted in the deaths of over 150 Lakota Sioux. Before that terrible incident at Wounded Knee, the government of Rome broke another treaty by adjusting the <u>Great Sioux Reservation</u> of <u>South Dakota</u> into smaller reservations. Once on the reduced reservations, tribes were separated into family units and forced to farm and raise livestock. Their children were taken away to <u>boarding schools</u> that forbade any use of Native American traditional culture and language. And then our People were moved again to new reservations—prison camps, we call them—along the northern banks of the Great Red River. At that time, Native Dancing was declared against their law and punishable by a prison sentence and/or death. This law was never removed from the books and, as a result, I was once kicked out of the States for Dancing. Now, I am a full citizen of Rome as a result of marrying your father. I wonder what would happen if I danced here the way I dance at the Pow-wows back in Kansa?" She smiled broadly and continued with the story/poem.

Why do we Dance?

A child asked her Grandmother:
Why do we Dance?
Her Grandmother answered:
Did you not hear about Wounded Knee?

But why do we Dance?
I have head our People say:
Today is a Good Day to Die.
And they all died.

This is not about Death,
This is about the Celebration
Of Life.
We Dance to Celebrate Life.

But I have also heard that
If they had quit Dancing
That they would not
Have Died?

This may have been true.
But many promises
Were broken
So we chose to Dance.

So why do we Dance
Today?
I am not a good Dancer
Like my sister

Do you fear not knowing
The Steps?
Do you think you will
Look different?

Steven WinterHawk

I see my sister Dance
She floats like a bird.
I am afraid that I will
Trip and fall

This is why we Dance
You will not Dance
Like your sister
You will Dance your Dance

But there are Steps
To this Dance.
What will happen
If I forget?

At Wounded Knee
There was a Fear
But not by our People
The Dance was the Fear.

How could they Fear
A Dance?
My Dancing will not harm
Anyone but myself.

And how could you be hurt?
By Dancing your Dance
You might find out
Who you are.

But that is my Fear
I might not be good enough
I might make
A mistake.

That is why we Dance.
To learn to let go
To make mistakes
And Learn to Love.

Are you saying
That I might be hurt?
If I learn to Love
If I learn to Dance?

No—that was the Fear
Of the Dance.
We Dance to find
Who we are.

And will I like
Who I am
Will I love her?
How can I be sure?

You can be sure that
If you Dance your Dance
You will be like
No other one of the People

So I will be different?
You said that before.
I am beginning to understand
That this is not a bad thing?

This is a Good thing!
You are one of the People
Of the Earth
But you are unique.

Steven WinterHawk

I will Dance then,
The best I can
I will let go of my fears
And discover who I am

This Life is the Ghost Dance
This is the Dance of Spirit
Dance to your own Drum
The Drum that is in your Heart!.

(WinterHawk—Ghost Written by Mary)

Mary then handed the pipe back to her son.

"That is a beautiful poem, mom!" he exclaimed. "But I didn't know that Aunt Millie was a Pow-wow dancer?"

"One of the best. You should have seen her. When she danced the Fancy Shawl, she floated like a bird. But before my first dance on the Pow-wow circuit, I was like a little mouse. I just wanted to hide away. I wrote this poem later, so I would remember how important it is to Dance and live my life the way my heart tells me. Our People call this the Path of Beauty."

"And now you are the Dancer that everyone looks up to and wants to imitate," he chuckled. "And Aunt Millie is dancing in another way. No offence meant—she still has a beautiful smile."

"Millie has more than a beautiful smile," Mary agreed. "She has a beautiful heart and she is dancing the dance that she chose. She got married to your uncle George who, by the way, was a dancer, too. And she had eight children so close together that she did not have time to lose the weight. George, as you know, is a long-haul truck driver and I have not seen two people more in love to this day. This is the Creator's wish—as I see it. He did not put us on this Earth to deny the expression of Love. You will find your own way. I can't tell you how to live your life but as my Grandmother told me: this is the Path of Beauty. Dance to your own Drum. Dance to the Drum that is in your Heart."

Chapter 6

THE PIPE

James and Petra returned home to Bethany to announce: "We are getting married! I want you to be my best man little brother and we need you to join us on the road again. The fans like the music we are making but they miss your little inspirational messages. At the end of every one of our concerts, they start chanting 'Shiloh'—'Shiloh'. I am beginning to get an inferiority complex."

"Yeah, sure," Petra kissed him. "Don't believe him—about the inferiority complex thing, I mean," she laughed. "But we do need you and the fans do to. Please come back on the road with us—after the wedding?"

Shiloh agreed to be the best man at his brother's wedding and to join the band on the road again. And then the plans went into full gear for a big wedding back at the family home in Kansa.

"Six months? I can't wait six months to be married to this angel," James complained to Shiloh, as they were out jogging in the countryside in Kansa.

Shiloh stopped running and bent over in laughter. "What are you waiting for?" he said. "If I am not blind, you are already sleeping with the angel of your dreams. What more do you want? A man can't really own a woman. The purpose of marriage is just so that you can both agree to share your lives with each other and promise not to be intimate with anyone else."

"Yeah, yeah that's the story. But let me tell you little brother, and don't let this get beyond us, I don't have an inferiority complex or anything like that but I envy the way you can say that—and mean it. It scares me to think of my life without Petra—so much that I have nightmares of her being lost somewhere and I wake up in a cold sweat. In the middle of the night, I have to hug her just to know that she is really there. And then one thing leads to another...and you know—I am not getting much sleep to tell you the truth," he smiled broadly and then frowned.

Shiloh nodded and neglected to share his personal envy of his brother's problem. Instead he said: "I can help you with the dreams. Dreams are as real to me as this life and this forest path. In fact, I know that they are a path that our Spirit has takes. If we are not afraid to go the distance, there is a way to solve the challenges in these dreams."

"Just tell me," James pleaded. "I am getting worn out because of not sleeping and other more pleasant happenings," he blushed—an uncommon thing for Shiloh's big brother. He set off running again.

Shiloh ran to catch up and when they were jogging side by side again, he suggested: "The next time you have that nightmare, don't let the fear get the better of you. I suggest that you go to bed with the belief that you love her so much that you know that she does not belong to you. Keep telling yourself that she is free and you love her the way she is—even if there are secrets that she has that she has not shared with you."

"Secrets?" James took a deep breath. "We share everything. What secrets could she have that I might be afraid of? I would love her no matter what."

"Just be ready to live up to your words," Shiloh advised—all the while wondering what right he had with his lack of experience to advise someone who has experienced the pain and pleasure of a physical relationship. Then he recalled that the one thing he had the greater knowledge of was Dreams—and the worlds that existed beyond the curtain of human awareness.

"We all have secret fears and doubts. Some may be real and others may only come to life in our dreams. Petra has a right to her personal fears and secrets that she may not be ready to share—just yet. Your job—if you wish to accept it," Shiloh said imitating the famous *Mission Impossible* voice, "is to follow your fears. If you keep telling yourself that you are ready to face your fears of losing, then her you will actually find her. You will wake up in a dream—when both of you are ready—and you will be ready to help her face her secret fears. This is the real commitment that marriage requires. And don't think this is a small thing. You might in fact lose her—even though you end up helping her to find herself. That is the fear that you need to overcome."

"Little brother, you are scaring me," James admitted. "But I love her too much not to try."

No further mention was made of the subject and the wedding plans became the focus of the next few months. The actual ceremony was a blur of "I do" and "I do". And then it was complete, and the family and friends gathered for the reception at the Renauldi home. The reception was a great mixture of all-coloured skins. There was representation by both sides of the family, including Joseph's aging, but spry, mother who flew over from Portugal. She brought along a couple of large bottles of the famous Renauldi homemade wine to celebrate the occasion. Joseph had planned to have everything catered, but Mary's sister would have nothing of the sort. Mary's family prepared all the food and Joseph's friends and family supplied the liquor—and the water. Jenene and Jake brought more Portuguese wine, and Jenene was the first to remind Joseph that most of her Native cousins would only drink water. "Spirit has always been our greatest help and our potential downfall. Just remember, Spirit can be the Coyote, the trickster for People of Native blood," she said to Joseph.

The party was in full swing when one of Mary's cousins asked Joseph: "My Grandfather asked me if you would turn on your TV?" he shrugged. "He is spry, but a bit too elderly to continue to dance—and he lives way out in the wild without television or electricity. He is also very curious about what he calls White man's toys." This was the Elder who helped Shiloh get the sinew for his bow-string.

Joseph has a TV and when he was in Kansa he had a few science fiction shows that he liked to watch. For any news, he used the radio instead, because the news from New Rome was too full of graphic violence. Kansa only had one TV station that broadcasted from Vega and the content was what most called the "blue movies". Joseph turned on the TV for the Elder and selected a channel that had mostly nature and geographical themes. Then he handed the converter to the older man's grandson. The younger Native man then began to translate because his Grandfather did not speak any English.

A bit later, Joseph took a break from dancing and sat at a small table beside the Grandfather and the grandson who had given up the converter so his Grandfather could channel surf. "He is amazed," the young man explained.

"Yes, there is a lot to watch," Joseph agreed. "We get a satellite feed that picks up stations from Rome which are bounced off the Friendship Tower. You can even watch bull fighting if that's your thing."

"Actually Grandfather did watch a bit of that and a program about how cars are made. But the thing that amazes him is all the advertisements—especially for pills." The Elder made a remark that Joseph could not understand. He only spoke a form of Cherokee that eluded Joseph's grasp of Native languages. He could make out a few words but that was about it. It appeared that the reverse was actually true because the Grandfather appeared to know what his Grandson was telling Joseph.

"Grandpa just said again, that he cannot see how anyone could take all those pills. He also told me that his good health comes from only putting natural things in his mouth and on his skin."

"How old is your Grandfather?" Joseph asked.

"He is over 90, I think. He won't tell anyone his true age. He just laughs at us if we ask and says that he quit counting and that is why he is still around."

Just then, the Grandfather paused his channel surfing to feast his eyes on a young beauty in a swim suit. He smiled in Joseph's direction and wistfully changed the channel. It was obvious to Joseph that his mind was still interested—if not his body.

"Grandfather said that there is still one thing that a pill will not replace," the Grandson smiled. Joseph agreed and then as true to Spirit playing the trickster, an ad for Viagra appeared on the screen. The Grandson translated and the Grandfather shook his head in disbelief. The elder man laughed long and heart-fully. "Grandfather says that he will no longer envy the White man's toys or his way of living. He says that the day he needs a pill to enjoy time with his woman, he will think it is time to pass on to the Spirit place."

Joseph agreed, holding out his hand for the Elder man to shake. "That calls for a drink," he proclaimed, as he held his glass up and the older man did likewise and promptly downed his glass of spring water. The Grandfather held his glass out to his Grandson and said something Joseph could understand—at least by the gesture.

"Grandfather says that he likes your water. And he can tell that it was not created by the hand of man."

"True," Joseph said. "It is bottled at a natural spring. But we still have to buy it at the local grocery store because our well has dried up. Mary would you please pass me another bottle of water?"

"Sorry dear," she replied. "I will need to send one of the boys to the store. It won't take more than a few minutes. I guess, in all the hustle and bustle that is the one thing we forgot to stock up on?"

Mary ventured out to where the younger people were dancing and tapped Shiloh's shoulder as he danced with a cousin.

"Mom? Do you want to cut in?" he joked.

"Not this time, son, I need you to go to the store for some water. Be a dear will you? The keys for the Jeep are on the peg by the door."

He nodded and excused himself. On the way to the door, however, he passed the box of special Portuguese wine that Joseph's mother had shipped over for the occasion. A memory surfaced. It was a memory of a different place and time—it was his memory and yet it was not. He did not consider distrusting the memory in the least. It was something that would prove (if that was still needed) who he was. He took one of the remaining three bottles of his father's wine from the box and walked to the table where Joseph sat facing the Elderly Grandfather who had his back to the dance floor.

"You wanted a drink?" he asked his father.

"Not me," Joseph answered. "Our guest would like a refill of his glass of spring water but I was told...what are you doing?"

Shiloh was using the corkscrew on the large bottle of wine. He seemed in another world, so intent on his task. When the cork popped, he reached over and poured crystal clear water into the Elder's glass."

The older man smacked his lips in appreciation. "Good. Good." he said, using the few English words he knew.

Joseph's eyes grew large. "What just happened?" he asked in disbelief. "Son—I love you, but I would appreciate if you didn't empty out one of my prize bottles of wine."

"I didn't do that, dad." Shiloh came alive—or at least seem to snap out of the trance or whatever had come over him. "Would you like a refill?"

"I—I guess I would. At least I want to see what comes out of that bottle you are holding."

"Wine—what would you expect?" Shiloh chuckled and refilled his father's glass. And when he poured it this time it was just as he had predicted.

Joseph rather tentatively brought the glass to his lips. He smelled and then he took a sip. "It is wine," he said with a great degree of surprise.

The elderly Grandfather spoke to his grandson who translated: "Grandfather says that this is a much greater trick than Viagra—any day!" And the Elder laughed heartily at Joseph's amazed expression. Then, with the aid of his grandson's translation, he said: "I know this young man. I met him before. Do not believe anything is impossible when he is around."

Joseph was overcome as the story began to make sense. He stood and hugged his son mightily. "Son," he said, "I will never doubt that you are who you say you are—ever again!"

"What?" Shiloh asked. "Who am I? I have the memories of the One that came before, but I am your son."

Later that evening, James and Petra packed up and said good-bye to everyone. "We are off to Portugal," he pronounced. "We will try to find that beach that mom and dad told us about. If not—well, I won't be looking at the stars anyways."

At the front door, James gave his brother a good-bye-for-now hug. He smiled like the coyote in the stories that Shiloh had read. "Your time is coming little brother," he said with a knowing wink. "I had that dream that you suggested and it worked. There is a gift for you there." That is all he would say, no matter what Shiloh asked, except: "Your time is coming." James and his new bride were on their way. James had promised to take a month off the road to set up housekeeping. He had requested that Shiloh rejoin the band in his place for a couple of local "gigs" before the family moved back to Bethany.

After enjoying a few months in Kansa with the band, including a couple of new members—the two young men whom Shiloh had hitched a ride with to New Rome. John played keyboard and Mark filled in on lead guitar. John's girlfriend, Simone, was a good singer so she shared some songs with Shiloh. This gave Shiloh a bit more exposure and a chance to bring his message to appreciative fans. He felt that enough had been said by the One who came before. So he taught: "this is about you." And reminded them that "this is about the music—we are here to sing and dance together and find inspiration in our new and old friendships."

Shiloh and Simone sang *What the World Needs Now* every night to kick off the concert. And they finished with John Lennon's *Imagine*. In-between there was a lot of good *Spirit Rock* the fans could dance to, interspersed with a number of inspirational soft Rock songs that Petra and James had practiced with the new members and the rest of the band a month or so before.

When the Renauldi family moved north again, the band followed. John, Mark, and Simone lived near Bethany. The band had become like a family, as James said and each member was allowed a vote in choosing their fate or otherwise known as their touring schedule. "We are no longer serious about this," James liked to say. "We are in this in the Spirit of fun—and money too."

Shortly after the first break and back in Bethany, James told Shiloh that he was not ready to return to the road just yet. "Petra and me are thinking about a family," he confided to his brother. "If it feels right for you, just carry on without us for awhile. By the way—did you have any good dreams lately?"

Shiloh told his brother "no" and that he had not been dreaming much lately and asked why he was even interested.

"Just asking," Shiloh could sense a smile, even over the phone. Shiloh called a meeting with the band and they all agreed that they wanted to carry on no matter how long it took James and Petra to return. So, one evening when Shiloh was getting together a proposed

new touring schedule he received a phone call. Thinking it must be one of the band members, he was surprised by a voice he didn't recognize.
"Hello, is this Shiloh?"
"Yes, who is this?"
"I guess you don't remember me from the *Back to the Future* trip?"
It was Mathew. "I have been in hiding," Mathew admitted. "Seems that after the van was discovered abandoned by the road, the authorities questioned the catering company and the company knew nothing about the explosives. No surprise there but they found my fingerprints all over the van and no one else's. One thing lead to another and when the licence plate of the van was recorded as having been at the Vice President's address a couple of days before, well, they put two and two together. And guess what? I am a wanted man."
"What can I do to help?" Shiloh asked.
"I was wondering if it is possible to go back?" Mathew said.
"Back?" Shiloh responded.
"I have no life here. I will be a wanted man the rest of my life. I could turn myself in but I really did nothing wrong—this version of me, anyways. Yes, I did plan to commit a terrorist act and that desire for vengeance caused a terrible thing to happen in that other dream. But I am sincerely sorry that I even had the idea and I am a changed man. The only place I can do some good and the only place I will be allowed is in that dream where I am legally dead. Do you get my drift?"
Shiloh began to understand. "If I can get you back there, what do you plan to do?" he asked. He was not even sure that it would work. It seemed the only time this happened was when there was a good reason for Spirit to make it so. He had wondered about making that trip back, if not just to meet again with a certain young woman—Mathew's sister. It seemed a bit presumptuous to show up at her door in this time and space and say "hello—did I meet you in a dream?" Still he was on the verge of doing just that—before Mathew contacted him.
"If I could get back there," Mathew said, "I think I could write a book about our experiences together—a book about you. I had tried my hand at writing in high school before everything fell apart and I believe I can do it. I have been following your band—went to almost

every concert—and your messages are inspirational. I have seen how you can heal people, too—even though you try to play that down. OK—you can say that I am clutching at your coat tails and reaching for your answers, but with great respect. I could not do that here and I would not do anything to endanger you or your mission. I can see who you are and I believe in you. If I write my story in another dream world, maybe I can be of some help. The people who dream here must remember some good things—don't you think?"

Shiloh wanted to say that Mathew was a bit crazy but he didn't. He did not want to be the focus of a book. That had already been done. Written mostly by another Mathew, no less! And it had been turned into a religion. His focus here and now was to keep it as simple as possible. *Lord We Don't Need Another Religion*—was his theme song. He decided to help Mathew—with the stipulation that Mathew promise that any book he writes would be clearly labelled as a work of fiction. And, of course, there was another good reason that Shiloh wanted to return to that dream.

And so, after having discussed the idea over with his parents, Shiloh left Bethany late one evening to meet Mathew in New Rome. They planned to meet at a designated location near the University where they had made the "jump" to the other dream world. Mathew was waiting by the road side, just where he said he would.

"How do we do this?" Mathew asked when he was in the Jeep beside Shiloh.

"I guess the best way is to repeat as much as possible everything the way we did before. When we are near the University, we'll change drivers. You'll drive as before through the gate. Hopefully, the guards won't recognize us. It was a couple of years ago and it was also in their dreams—remember? I also brought my rattle—my Spirit Shaker."

When they were near the University gate, they stopped and Mathew took the driver's seat. In a stroke of luck, the guard shack was empty. "Of course, I should have known this. There's no reason for the guards when there is nothing special going on inside," Shiloh gave a sigh of relief. "We'll just do the *Back to the Future* thing. No need to shatter the speed barrier, either. This will happen, or not, only through the help of good old Spirit energy."

As they neared the place where it happened before, Shiloh advised: "Think about how much you need to be in the other dream and I will too. Just like we did when we came back." And when Shiloh began to shake his rattle there was a familiar sound that seemed to come from inside his head, and...

"Damn it—Sorry," Mathews said in a dejected voice. "It didn't work."

"How can you be sure?" Shiloh responded.

"Everything is black. There is not a light on in the University. Not a light anywhere. We could be in limbo for all we know?"

"Look behind," Shiloh suggested.

"There is a light on at the guard shack—I think we made it!" Mathew exclaimed. "Now we just have to come up with another story for the guards."

They did a U-turn and headed out toward the light at the other end of the driveway. There were no guards—just a newly erected sign that said: "University of Frederic Chaney—dedicated to the memory of Vice President Frederic Chaney in the year 2010."

"Good thing I am dead here," Mathew made a bad joke. "I will need to change my last name but no one can come after a dead man—can they?"

"Not if that man is a Ghost Writer," Shiloh suggested back at him, "and writes a fiction book to inspire while not putting down the religion that is the flavour of the day."

They drove in silence to the place that Mathew's mother had lived. She was still there—at least the home for wayward women was still there, as the sign above the door declared. Mathew pulled up in the driveway and the two men exchanged glances before exiting the Jeep and proceeding to the front door. There was only a small welcoming light on in the window. Mathew drew a breath and put his thumb on the buzzer.

After a few minutes, a woman's voice called out: "Who is there?"

"It's me, Mom. It's your son, Mathew."

"Go away. My son is dead. He died over five years ago."

"No, really. It's me," Mathew pleaded. "Just look through the window."

The two young men heard the blind click against the window pane and then the door was flung open wide. Mathew's mother hugged him so hard that she literally lifted her son off his feet.

"On my God, it is you. Please tell me that you are not going to have to leave again soon?" Tears ran in torrents from her eyes.

"No, mom, one way or another, I am home to stay," Mathew gasped.

"What do you mean—one way or the other?" She released him abruptly and then asked: "And who is this other young man. I think I recognize you from before?"

"This is Shiloh, mom. He was here before—about five years ago. I had to leave then but I'm back this time for good. Shiloh helped to bring me back."

"Are you some kind of miracle healer?" she confronted Shiloh. "How else could you bring my son back from the dead?"

Shiloh was momentarily stunned. There was some truth in what the woman said—from a different perspective. He recalled that Jesus had been able to do this—or so the Bible said. He had never disbelieved that the One who came before could perform the miracles that were written about him. It was simply a miracle and that was that. Well—it was still a miracle, no matter how you saw it.

"Mom is having a bit of trouble remembering," another voice broke Shiloh's train of thought. "Else she would not have forgotten the reason you needed to go away." Mathew's sister, Meg, opened the door wider. "I was just drifting off when I heard you at the door," she explained. She hugged her brother warmly, all the while not breaking eye contact with Shiloh. "Won't you come inside?"

"Another strange thing happened a couple of months ago. As if our life was not continuously full to the brim with miracles." Meg sat on a chair in the small living room. She motioned Shiloh to take a seat next to her. Mathew and his mother were reliving old memories in the kitchen. "My mother and I see miracles and heartbreaks nearly every day. It has become our job to rescue women from a life on the street. I guess I told you about that the last time you were here?" And when he nodded, she continued: "Lately, the torch has been handed to me. My mother is losing her memory, so it is up to me to carry on as best I can," she paused and clasped her hands in her lap, as though summoning her strength. Shiloh was in awe of her courage and he told her so.

"Thank you," she said at length, "But the thing that happened was not really about me—it is more about you."

Shiloh looked confused. "But I have not been to visit you for years—although I have wanted to. Especially these past few months. If Mathew had not asked me to bring him back…well I was about to make the journey… well for reasons of my own."

"I can understand," she smiled. "Anyway—what happened was I had a visit a couple of months ago by a relative of yours. His name was James. A cousin of yours, I believe," Shiloh nodded again, letting this pass. He wanted to tell her the rest of her story. "James showed up at our door—looking for you at first. He said that he was looking for a connection and that your family back home told him that this was the last place and time you were seen. I told him about our friendship and how I had known you since you came to New Rome on a personal healing mission. In those days—your goal was to heal the world—single-handedly."

"Yeah. That would have been one of my dreams after my sister, Anna, died."

"I told James about how tough it was for you then 'cause you found that a lot of people did not want to be healed. They were stuck in their life of hurt and victimhood. Some, you confided in me, wore the label like a badge. And eventually you came to realize that it was not your job to save the world. It was your job—you told me one evening—to be the best example you could be, to offer encouragement, and to be there and reach out to them and pick them up when they fell. But only if it was their wish to be helped. That was a hard lesson for you."

"And I shared that with you?" Shiloh exclaimed. "Sometimes, even for me, the dreams seem to be unreal and I think I am alone even when this is not true."

"That is far from the truth. We are never alone. We only have to open our hearts and minds to another truth. This is what I shared with James. I told him in confidence of how precious and close my friendship had been with you." She turned her face away to hide her tears.

"We were that close?" Shiloh wondered about his memories of this dream that had somehow been hidden from him until now. "Then how could I have left?"

"You did not…really. See—you are here now."

"But I did not know that then."

"True—but it is about the sacrifice. It is about Love that is so strong that you will give up your life to save another. You told me this before going with my brother that night. You had a vision about what would happen—about the children in the school bus that you could not save. You told me that you would have to be there for them if you could not change Mathew's mind. That Mathew was full of hate and revenge. He saw his father become an angry alcoholic who graduated to abusing his wife and children. I never told anyone this, not even James. But Mathew—our Mathew—shot his father to protect his sister. He did not do time because the jury called it self-defence. He was only 13 at the time and he carried that scar to his grave—or wherever he went. He blamed the White man's world that caused his father to become what he had become. So he was an easy recruit for the Sons of Soma."

"And the rest I know," Shiloh added, to spare her the re-telling. "What about James? What brought him here?"

"Oh yes, James. He came here for a different reason than he thought at first. It seems that our world—this dream as you call it—is a place where hurt and deep feelings are worked out. While James was sitting here with me—in that chair where you are, a young woman woke up and puttered around in the kitchen, fixing a coffee. Just that week I had convinced her to leave the street and stay awhile with us. She was the usual—I almost hate to say that. Abused by her parents growing up and ran from home at the age of 12. Her father was a lawyer and had it in his mind that she would follow in his footsteps even if it killed her. And it almost did—on the street."

"Petra?" Shiloh whistled.

"Yes—how did you know?"

"A long story—with a happy ending," he smiled. "In my dream, James is my brother and he and Petra just got married."

"Wow! Then we are doing some good here," Meg exclaimed.

"I'll say. More than good. I used to think that you were the Angels—the ones that deal with the deeper emotions—and now I believe that may not be far from the truth. I think this is the world that the Angels come from first. I have dreamt about you, you know?"

"Oh? What kind of dreams?" she reached to clasp his hand.

"How close were we—the other me that died—and you?" It was his way of changing the subject.

"We were about to become more than friends." She did not let go of his hand or the train of thought. "I have something for you that I was saving for him. She reached up to the mantle behind her and handed him a stone that was slightly larger than his fist.

"A piece of pipe-stone," he recognized it at once. "Did you tell James about this?"

"Yes—I asked him to take it back to your dream and give it to you. But he said that he thought that I needed to give it to you personally. So here it is."

"I've been carving a pipe—actually, it's finished. I was only waiting for this stone—so I could complete it."

"Sometimes, waiting is not enough," she smiled broadly and squeezed his hand. "Sometimes we need to go after our dreams."

"I am honoured," he was chocked up. He had to wait to regain his voice. "In my world, in my dream, the pipe has a multi-use symbology. It stands for the Joining of the Spirit and the Physical. It is the joining of the male and female elements that make up all of creation. When I put the tobacco in my pipe I will be smoking the universe and all creatures. I will be smoking my dreams and prayers and see them rise up to the Great Spirit."

"In this world, too," she conceded. "In this dream that is deep and strong in emotion this symbolizes Love that cannot die."

"You must know that I cannot stay here," he said.

"Of course but I am asking you to find me—the other me, the dreamer that is in your world. I know her, this other me, she is as real to me as I am to myself. Sometimes I can feel her thoughts. I must caution you. She is more timid than I am, but I am her deepest dreams—I am what she dreams in her deepest heart. I am telling you because I know you more than I can say. When you treat her with respect, you will find me waiting within." She withdrew her hand, and placed it on his shoulder, in a gesture of friendship.

"Yes," he rose to his feet. "I need to go."

Mathew and his mother were in a world of their own. Shiloh did not need to say good-bye and as Meg walked him to the Jeep parked outside, he hugged her, and said: "our People do not have a word for Good-Bye. I will say (Giga-waabamin minawaa)—I will see you again."

"And I will see you again," she answered in the language of her People. "This is so I will remember you—in the other dream," as she kissed him warmly and lingered in his embrace.

Chapter 7

ANOTHER ARROW

When Shiloh made the transition back to his own time and space, his first idea was to do as Meg suggested. He was determined to find her. It was late, perhaps a bit too late, to call upon someone who does not really know you. But he had been down that road before—literally. He checked his watch. It was more than late—it was early the next day as he drove toward the part of the city of New Rome that Meg and her Mother would live, that is, if they lived in the same place in this world. When Mathew had come asking to be taken back to the other world, Shiloh had learned that Mathew had not dared to go home or even call, fearing that the phone lines would be tapped.

"Just around the next bend," Shiloh told himself. And when he rounded the bend in the road he was devastated at what he saw. The house that he had visited only an hour before—in the parallel world—was deserted. The windows were boarded up and so was the door. He stopped, parked the jeep on the road and walked to the front door. There was a faded sign on the door that read: "Scheduled for Demolition: This dwelling had been declared to be connected with a known terrorist and is a home of ill repute. It is hereby closed and scheduled for demolition by the Department of Home Security and Moral Injustice of the United States of New Rome and further authorized by the High Roman Empire."

"Sheesh!" Shiloh made a hasty but cautious retreat to the Jeep, and drove away. "They sure covered all bases. Terrorist and Prostitution all in one nice tidy package. I can see why Mathew needed to disappear—but it was a bit too late by the look of it. I wonder what happened to Meg and her Mother. I am sure that the law could not pin anything on them personally. They were definitely not running a house of ill repute. And you can't put someone in jail for being related to a suspected terrorist—can you?" Nothing would surprise him from a country that had kicked his mother out just for dancing. Well, he was not about to give up on finding Meg and her mother. Even if it meant just seeing that justice was truly done. After all, that was the reason and the purpose of his life—as he saw it. He was born to help the innocents and children. The journey that he had just returned from had been a result of putting his life on the line to do just that. He vowed to return the next day and begin his search. In the meantime, he needed to get back home for a bit of shut-eye.

Shiloh was fully awake—or so he thought. It was early morning and he recalled getting home as just as the sky was beginning to brighten in the East. He went straight to bed and to sleep. "This must be a dream?" He stood on a street that resembled the City of New Rome that he had left only a few hours before, yet it was different somehow—something he couldn't put his finger on. The typical tall buildings, just as he would expect but…? He was standing at the corner of a street he recognized and a place he had passed many times. This was where his father had helped to complete the Tower—the Friendship Tower—just across the street. He looked up—something was really wrong! The Friendship Tower was not there! In its place stood two identical towers—both as tall as the one his father had worked on. "This is really a dream," he confirmed to himself. "But what is the purpose of it?" He sauntered over to a familiar news stand, and picked up a paper. The date jumped out at him: September 11, 2001!

"What the hay does that mean? He turned the paper over in his hand seeking out the familiar banner of the *Tribune of New Rome*, but a loud noise distracted him—people were shouting. He looked up in time to see a plane crash into the second tower. The other tower was already on fire. And then the air was filled with dust and ash, as both towers crumbled to the ground…

He sat up in bed…and found it impossible to go back to sleep. Finally, he gave up and just lay there, letting it all mull over in his mind.

Later at the breakfast table, it was a sleepy-eyed Shiloh that recounted his dream to his parents. "This is related to that other dream that I have every month or so—since I first saw the Friendship Tower. I know that for sure but I just can't put my finger on it."

"How could it be?" his father asked. "The other dream, as you told to me, was about a clear flat land where there are no buildings whatsoever. And this dream is about buildings all around you falling down."

"Not every building," Shiloh replied. "Two buildings that are on the same site as the Friendship Tower. And in the other dream that I have there are no buildings at all. It's like I am a bird, flying high above a countryside that has no evidence of humans living there, maybe even no human life at all. I don't want to be negative—but it could be the end of the world as we know it. I need to think—what would cause this? What would bring this about? Am I here to stop this from happening? Otherwise, why would I be shown this?"

Joseph and Mary exchanged looks.

"What? Mom—Dad. I need to know."

"Before you were born, the same riders from the stars made a visit to the Emperor of Rome and issued him a warning. The gist of the warning foretold of your birth as being a chance to change things. And if the wrong choice was made—at a time of reckoning—then the world as we know it would come to an end."

"OK, I did hear about that and IF I am the one in the first warning by the riders, then I am not understanding the warning about what will happen if we don't make the right decision."

"Not we," his mother corrected gently. "I think the message was given to Rome for a reason. It is more about them making the right choice—doing the right thing at the moment of reckoning. We need to think about what THEY would do if the events of your dream were to take place."

"They would strike back in revenge," Joseph answered. "And the result of their revenge might be missiles and warheads that are probably already aimed at Kansa as we speak. Well, that's guessing that the Native People were the perpetrators of the carnage in your dream. And that is hardly possible. The Sons of Soma don't have that capability. What would they do? Shoot an arrow at the Friendship Tower? Sorry—I am not trying to joke but the idea is unthinkable."

"Maybe not," Shiloh sighed. "I think I know what the dream is about—at least I believe I do. I may have been shown it all along and didn't put the pieces together. Remember the news story a few years ago about the Concord—that supersonic jet that was built in the States and then ordered to be scrapped by Rome?"

Both Mary and Joseph nodded in unison, wondering where this was going.

"Well, it was supposed to be flown out and dumped in the ocean but the conspiracy theorists say that this never happened. They say that it was never destroyed but flown to a remote section of Kansa, out in the waste lands. And it is in the process of being rebuilt."

"I followed that crazy idea in my younger days," Joseph replied. "It leads nowhere."

"I would not have put 2 and 2 together myself, unless I was shown that they equal 5, Shiloh replied. "5 being the inverted pentacle, the so-called symbol of evil and the shape of the redesigned concord renamed *The Arrow*. But the problem is that this shape could be seen from any direction. An arrow can be a symbol of Truth or a weapon used for killing; it depends on who is pulling the bow string."

"I agree with your symbolic logic," Joseph smiled grimly. "But I think we are safe on this account because the mythological *Arrow*, as you call it, does not exist."

"But it does," Shiloh sighed in resignation. "I have seen it."

"You did? Where?" his mother enquired.

"You remember when I went out hunting Buffalo with the Elder Grandfather and his family? Well on the way to the Buffalo hunt, he asked me if I wanted to see something interesting. I guess he was wise enough to know this was something I should see. We went out to a ridge overlooking Roswell. Yeah—I know what you'll say—crazy place for UFO nuts. But do we or do we not believe that we were visited by a group of four riders from the stars?"

Joseph held up his hand. "Guilty—I not only saw them but I talked with them. And your mother and I kept the gifts they brought for you until you were ready for them."

"OK, here is what I saw. The Elder and his sons and grandsons set up a camp on a ridge overlooking Roswell and we waited for dusk. No campfires. And just about when it started getting dark, the old Shaman pointed to the sky—out to the west. He has eyes like an eagle or at least had then. Soon, four lights appeared and whatever kind of craft they were, they approached too fast for any plane that I have ever seen, stopping in the sky right over Roswell then took off to the East. I am sure now that they were waiting for the chase planes to scramble at Roswell because they moved away at a slower pace than they arrived. Pretty soon there were what must have been jet fighters from Roswell that gave chase. They took off to the East as well and soon it was quiet again."

"That's it?" Shiloh asked, but the Shaman shook his head.

"Wait a bit," he replied.

"Soon I heard a swooshing sound—not like a jet or plane engine—and another plane passed overhead going to the West. It was going almost too fast for me to see in the dim light but I could make out a wedge shape—like an arrowhead—as it passed over. Then it was gone from sight."

"What was that?" I asked the Grandfather.

"That was an *Arrow*," he answered. "Once a *Concorde* now an *Arrow*. With some rebuilding help from the People from the Stars, they were there to draw away the Roswell jets."

"Do they do this often?" Shiloh wondered why the Roswell Air Force didn't get wise to the tactics, so Shiloh asked the Grandfather.

"NO," he answered, "that was a test. I heard about it from one of our People at the other airport. That plane belongs to Kansa. It is the only one we have. When the Concorde was ordered destroyed, one of our People who was in New Rome flew it out here and they started to rebuild it. Then one night a man who looked like one of our People showed up and offered to help."

"It is remodelled," the old Shaman's Grandson spoke up. "And the engine is upgraded. We've heard that it will run on water. The engine is a super-modified Hydrogen hybrid. It will run on regular fuel if necessary but really does its stuff on water. And no one knows how fast it can go. Just in case you are wondering—the man from the stars installed a failsafe that can be triggered to explode, if the plane is discovered on the ground."

"So what's the point?" I asked. "What do we do with a plane that we can't fly without Rome catching on?"

"I imagine that is part of why Roswell is in action," he answered. "That, and to track the visits of the men from the Stars. *The Arrow* might be a bit of a diversion but who knows. There must be a reason we've yet to discover? For now, we have it and we don't know why."

"When you put this all together with the dream I had last night, I think it is important that I get back to where that plane is before it makes its maiden voyage," Shiloh suggested.

"God—son," Joseph exclaimed, "Do you think this is some kind of test that was arranged by the People of the Four Riders?"

"Whatever it is, I need to be on that plane so that the dream I had does not come true here. With the experience that I have had with dreams lately, I guess that this awful thing has already happened in that parallel world and, if that's so, then it is irreversible. They are probably dealing with the backlash."

"Which is? What do you think is happening there?" Joseph wondered.

"Who knows! If the government there is like the one north of the Red River or the one we know that is actually in charge of Rome, then a counter-attack will be swift. For all we know they may already be in the midst of a global war."

"Or they are counting down the minutes to Armageddon," Joseph replied. "Especially if they have the same Bible and Holy books as we do and if they believe it word for word. The ones that believe that their God is the only God may be preparing, as we speak, and not taking any steps to change it."

First, Shiloh had to settle the minds of his parents that this was one of the reasons that he had been born and it was part of his destiny to be on the plane that might be preparing to attack the Friendship Tower. Then, with their blessing, knowing that their son might not return, he proceeded to contact the members of *The James Gang*. "I need to put together a tour of Kansa, as soon as possible." This was all that he dared to share over the phone. It was July and if the time sequence was like he had experienced in past dreams, then that only gave him two months to be near Roswell. When he reached Dallas, he planned to get in touch with his Cherokee friends and learn the location of the plane they had appropriately called *The Arrow*. The old Shaman had told him: "If you ever need to know where *The Arrow* is, just come to see me. If you never need to know, then all is well." The older man must have suspected that it would be something important to Shiloh or he would never have said that.

The tour went off like clockwork even though at the back of his mind, Shiloh was keeping track of their progress across Kansa. James and Petra were still setting up home. Shiloh began to doubt that his brother would ever return to the road. When he talked to James, he said that they were seriously working on starting a family and he was considering a temporary job doing high steel construction. It was all he knew except for music. "It's all yours now—the band I mean. If I don't come back, you might want to change the name? How about *The Disciples* or—*Shiloh and the Disciples?* That sounds catchy…"

"Been done, before," Shiloh chuckled. "I don't want that kind of name anyways. I want to put out a simple message remember. A few words of encouragement for them to find their own path and the music will do the rest. Besides, *The James Gang* has a following and the name is just right to keep the focus off me. This is not about me. It is about The People—our People and all the colours that make up the Spiritual rainbow."

Following the concert in Dallas, Shiloh left them with nearly the same message he said to James. Beginning with: "This is not about me. I have said that before. It is about you. It is about all of us finding our inspiration and knowing that we are all related. Then he and Simone finished with a heart-filled rendition of *Imagine*. And even as he left the stage, he was planning his next move.

When he finally tracked down his Cherokee friends, he found that the Grandfather had passed on, about two months ago. He guessed that the Elder had helped to send him the dream, the warning of things to come. He talked briefly to the Grandson and said only that "he wished to go hunting again." The other man understood and asked Shiloh to meet with him at the family ranch.

"I am going to meet with a friend," Shiloh said when everyone was together in the main van. "He lives way out in the wilds on a farm. There is no electricity or things that we take for granted. So if anyone wants to, they can take the other van and head home. This is the part of the reason that I came this far. I can go on alone but if any of you want to come along, you can. I need to warn you, though. After I meet with my friend, I will begin another journey and I might not return."

There was a clamour of voices and many questions. When there was silence again, Shiloh spoke: "Sorry, I can't tell you anymore right now. This is mostly about why I have been born—everyone must wonder that sometime or the other but I have known about this most of my life. I just didn't know the details, I still don't except that I need to be in a certain place at a certain time."

"We have come this far with you," Jude spoke over the incoherent chatter of everyone talking at once. "I say that we need to go as far as it takes. I am with you." He waited until everyone else joined in. It was unanimous. Then he said: "I just hope we don't have to do the horseback thing. I tried it once and all I got was a sore bum."

Jude did not need to suffer as he feared. There was a good dirt road to the home of the Cherokee family in the wilds. The band of seven, including Shiloh, Jude, Simon, Lucas, Mark, John and Simone, all crammed into the one van that did not have the electrical equipment. They left the loaded van in the care of a mutual friend and chose to bring only their most portable acoustic musical instruments.

When they pulled up in front of the dilapidated shack which Shiloh's friends called "home", Jude gave out one more statement of dismay: "Oh My!" he cried in mock terror. "Let me guess. No indoor plumbing. Just when I need to pee so bad that I am about to burst. OK crew—It's going to be a race to see who is first out back behind the cactus." And he laughed but was sincere just the same. Shiloh had become thankful for Jude's sense of humour—it had lightened some of The James Gang's more difficult moments on the road.

The Shaman's Grandson was standing outside and when the cloud of dust that showed their arrival had died down, he invited them inside. "I have an idea of what you're hunting," he whispered to Shiloh, when the two were relatively alone in the kitchen of the three-room dwelling.

"When my Grandfather passed away, he told me to expect you. He told me that you would ask where *The Arrow* was to be found."

"There is no need for secrecy at this point," Shiloh informed him. "I trust all of these people. But, I think, the less anyone knows about why I am here, the better. It will be for their own good later. I will tell them all that is necessary now and the rest when, or if, I return."

As the tea water began to boil, the Grandson told Shiloh: "*The Arrow* is in an abandon hanger in the Phoenix airport. Appropriate don't you think—the Phoenix rising from the ashes?" There were only three airports in use in all of Kansa: the Dallas, the Vegas and the Phoenix. The one that was previously located in Ottawa was closed down when they stopped using the city as a place of leadership for the People of Kansa. "I have something that my Grandfather thought would be of use to you." The young man, who was also known as Mathew Voice-of-the-Hawk, handed Shiloh a faded piece of paper. As Shiloh carefully unfolded the sheet of paper, he mused to himself about the young man's name. "Everything is appropriate in our People's ways. Especially the naming of a child that will tell of his path on this earth. This Mathew had willingly become the English voice, the translator for his Grandfather, who chose not to learn the language of the White man.

"What is this about?" Shiloh asked, as he scanned the words.

"This was given to my Grandfather's Grandfather. It is said to be a copy of the first draft of the letter that Chief Seattle sent to the President of New Rome. This is in response to the treaty of "Free Trade" that resulted in the government of Ottawa being disbanded. Chief Seattle did not read or write English. He composed this letter in the language of his People. This was translated and written by another young man whose job was like mine. We are the bridge between the Old and the New and I am happy to have served as best I could. Also, I have been blessed with spending time with my Grandfather—especially his last days on this Earth."

Shiloh carefully read the letter that the Shaman said would help him in the days to come.

"What do you think?" Mathew Hawk asked.

"It is definitely inspiring," he carefully folded the paper and put it in his vest pocket. "I will need to think on it. I must come up with something that will change the minds of men whose actions could result in the destruction of all that we hold Sacred. If the prophesies are to believed, this may even lead to the last war and the end of all life."

"Phew! That is a pretty heavy thing to place on the shoulders of one man. If this is true maybe you should share what you just told me with your friends. The state of the world is the result of more than one thought. We are all in this together! My grandfather taught me that every action, everything we do or think of doing, has some consequence. It may start small like the movement of the butterfly's wings and be felt on the other side of the world. He told me that our People named this the Path of Beauty."

"I agree. It is like the way we dance," Shiloh said. "And this can also be true of unexpressed anger. It can build up inside, and if it is not given an outlet, someone may come along with a personal agenda that will light the fuse. There have been religious cults who used the same tactics to attract their followers this way. This is what has happened with some of our People known as the Sons of Soma."

Mathew Hawk and Shiloh joined the rest of the band around a rustic coffee table in the main room of the dwelling. Mathew brought a tray of tea and cups and sugar. The group sat on the floor and soaked up the atmosphere.

"I have something serious to say," Shiloh began. "What I am about to share should not leave this room. I will start with saying that I must go on alone from here." There was a murmur of disbelief from the group.

"No way!" Jude was the first to speak. "I am with you no matter what. What is our famous Native saying—today is a good day to die." He gulped but it was evident that he meant what he said.

"Before you, any of you, make a commitment," Shiloh explained, "I will give you a bit more background and I will tell you a few things that have happened to me that may seem far-fetched." The group listened intently as he told them about his dream journeys and about the last dream he had.

"If it were not you telling me this, I would be ready to say what a crock it sounds like," Simon shook his head, "but I am ready to be convinced."

"That's just it," Shiloh said. "I cannot convince you without showing you. You will need to be there, if that is still your choice. We will be going to a hidden place where an experimental plane has been built by our People, with the help of some men from the Stars. Don't laugh yet. I am not joking. We will then ask to be aboard for the maiden voyage of *The Arrow*. Mathew has assured me that his Grandfather's contacts will make that possible."

"Doesn't sound so bad," Lucas replied. "I am guessing that there is more?"

"There is. The men who will be flying the experimental plane believe that the purpose of this *Arrow* is to fly over the ocean and taunt the jet fighters of the Roman Empire. Much like our ancestors might ride into battle with the intention of "counting coup", you know, not harming the enemy but touching him with a hand or stick, so defeating the enemy and bringing honour to oneself. The goal was that no one would be injured. *The Arrow* is thought to be much faster than any plane in the Roman Empire. What was to happen after that? I have no idea, but I have come to believe that the Sons of Soma may have different plans. Mostly because of my dream, I believe that sometime during the initial flight, members of the Sons of Soma will take over the plane, turn it around and fly it into the Friendship Tower in New Rome."

"So our job will be to kick the crap out of them to prevent this from happening," Simon suggested. "You could probably do that all by yourself with your Aikido training."

"No. It can't happen that way. The men and women from the Stars helped to make this possible. They are showing us a way to change the prophesies. But it can't be done through violence. That will only delay the inevitable. There will not be a Judgment day, there will be a reckoning. We will need to take responsibility for what happens then. I would not want to be responsible for starting a war that leads to the extinction of our People or the ultimate end of all life."

"But according to what you just told us, there is no death—only another Dream," Simon interjected.

"True but all Life is Sacred. I believe that is what we need to learn here. That is the basic truth in the Native Traditional Way."

"So how do you suggest stopping the Sons of Soma?" Lucas asked.

"First I need to ask you again to put up your hands if you are coming with me, because where I am going, I might not return. This is not a fairy tale and yet it might be, but for the moment try to believe that I am telling you the truth. Think again before you decide."

After the show of hands to agree to go with him, it was decided that John, Mark and Simone were staying behind. They would drive the van back to Dallas, and if the others did not return, Mathew would let them know to go back home. Simon, Jude, and Lucas—three of the original band members—were resolute to accompany Shiloh no matter what happened.

When the other three band members left, Shiloh revealed the rest of his plan. "I will try to change the minds of the men who are bent on committing this terrible act of terrorism."

"And if that fails, then we kick butt," Simon suggested. "Just remember that you are here to protect the innocent, too. There will be hundreds of innocent people at work in the Friendship Tower and we are not at war with them."

"Correct, but if I can't change the way they think, I have another plan. Remember what I told you about being able to open a doorway into another Dream world?"

"You will wave your wand, rattle your rattle, and send us all into another Dream," Jude guessed.

"Right," Shiloh agreed.

"But if you don't know for sure where we will go," Simon queried, "what is wrong with my butt-kicking idea as a backup?"

"We will most likely be in the sky over New Rome or very close. If we take over the plane, it will crash and kill everyone aboard. There may be a lot of innocent casualties in the city below. My plan is the safest for everyone, unless one of you knows how to fly a jet plane. There is still time for you to stay here!"

Simon sighed. "OK I am up for doing it your way. No backing out. But as much as I believe in you, I have never seen you work this magic. So please tell me that…?"

"Yes—plan 'C' is we kick butt, find a way to turn the plane around and live or die with the consequences."

"Yeah!" Jude stuck his hand out to Simon for a high-five. Simon's eyes went big with amazement and he reluctantly returned the gesture.

Mathew Hawk had been listening quietly to the discussion. "It might be good to eat now and get on the road," he suggested.

"One more thing," Shiloh said. "Whenever I have been able to make this trip happen—I mean to another dream—there was a setup to it. One part is a strong desire to make the trip and another is to change the minds of those other men. Yet another part involves the destination—the dream worlds I have ended up in had meaning for me and the people on both sides of the dream. Before we go, I suggest we make a commitment about the result of our journey. This will help to make our ultimate destination more favourable."

"We need to make a mission statement. I think it would be good to say what we intend to do when we return. Mathew can listen to our statements as a sort of witness."

"Oh God no!" Simon again. "Not a witness. I have almost destroyed my front door from slamming it in their faces," he grimaced.

"OK, how about calling Mathew our Dream Keeper?" Shiloh smiled. "I don't believe in confession either. This is not about the wrong things I think we've done. It is about the good things we are doing now and in the future. What do you think, Jude? Lucas?"

"I'll go first," Lucas proclaimed. "If I come back, I resolve to make an effort to finish things. In the past, before Shiloh came along, I gave up too easy. I was ready to walk out on the band before making a stand about what I felt was right. That is why I am here today."

"Me next," Jude chipped in. "I found someone who I like to be with. Hey—a guy like me, what's wrong with that? I am not stalking some boy. He is an adult like me—no comments Simon. If I get back, I will try to start up a respectable relationship. Simon, what are you laughing about? Shiloh? Is there something wrong with my wanting to Love?"

"I don't see a problem with a relationship that is about Love and Respect," Shiloh conceded. "What you intend, however, would not work for me. I have to say that up front. The only thing that is right for me is a man and woman relationship but it is not my right—nor anyone's right—to judge how someone expresses Love. The important word I heard was Respect."

Simon sighed and leaned back on his hands. "You got me Shiloh," he said. "If I return, I will try to be more tolerant. My Zen teacher told me that was my biggest thing to work on. I will work on shutting the door ever so gently—and saying a polite NO when the Bible thumpers come around. I might even get over my urge to wring the neck of a certain gay fellow that I know. At least I will be more open about it," he reached out and held out a fist for Jude to punch.

"Great work guys," Shiloh exclaimed. "I think we are ready to choose our dream."

"Wait," Simon said. "What about you? We want to hear about what you plan to do if we come back." And the others nodded in agreement.

"Oh yeah—me," Shiloh responded. "When I come back—not if—I will go looking for a certain woman that I met in that dream that I told you about." There followed a resounding: "Whooooo!" from the other three men. "When I looked for her in this world, I found that she had moved. Her home was boarded up. But I will not give up until I find her—so there!"

"And then what?" Jude replied.

"Well—you know."

"Yes, we do," Simon whistled. "I guess we had better see that you get back in one piece then. OK team. Let's get this done so Shiloh can find that girl of his dreams."

The ride to Phoenix was in the back of a beat-up pickup that belonged to Mathew Hawk. Right off, Jude began asking if it wasn't against the law—without seatbelts and all. Mathew responded that yes it was but out here they pretty much let you decide how you wanted to die. Either by smoking or being bounced out of the back of a pickup in the middle of the desert—he had best sit low and hang on. Jude hollered that he would prefer the slow death by smoking to riding in the back of this torture wagon. All in all they eventually arrived in Phoenix and Mathew found a truck stop where they could clean up after the dusty ride.

Mathew Hawk made a phone call to his Grandfather's friend. The man expressed his condolences at the Elder's death and asked that Mathew bring the group right over for a look-see. He evidently believed that was all they wanted to do—was to have a look at *The Arrow*.

Once inside the hanger, Mathew explained to the man called Yellow Feather, who was the head aeronautical engineer, that Shiloh and his band wanted to be on board the maiden flight. Yellow Feather was refusing them until he met Shiloh.

"You are the Shaman that Grandfather talked so much about. I have all of your band's CDs. I have listened to the messages that you include. It is just as Grandfather said: <u>Important and amazing things happen in the way you describe them.</u> We would be honoured to have you on board the maiden flight of *The Arrow*. I will warn you though; this is a taunting flight—just to show the Romans what we can do if we are pressed. We know that we can leave them behind like sitting ducks... and when we have proven that the Arrow is many times better than anything they can build, we will send a message requesting to land at the airport in Rome."

"And then what?" Shiloh wondered.

"And then we will give-away the Arrow to the Emperor of Rome in the Spirit of Friendship to make a gesture of Peace between our people. The Give-away is one of the most powerful ceremonies that our People have practiced. Now it is time to use this to change the world."

Shiloh agreed but he felt that there was something that the man called Yellow Feather was not telling him. "I had a dream," Shiloh told him. "And in that dream there was a terrible catastrophe due to an act of terrorism, involving a plane, well, more than one plane. That is why I am here—to make sure this does not happen."

The man's face changed. "You are the man that Grandfather said you are," he conceded. "I didn't want to alarm you and your friends. But there was going to be an attempt to hi-jack *The Arrow* once we were airborne. We discovered the plot and took the four men involved into custody. We have since replaced these men with people we can trust. Now it is even more important that you and your friends join us—and take part in our give-away to Rome.

Chapter 8
A DREAM WITHIN A DREAM

"I wonder if the Emperor will appreciate our Gift for what it is?" Shiloh wondered. They were safely strapped in and waiting to take off. The rest of the band was in high spirits, following his telling of the capture of the terrorists and the halting of their plot. Shiloh thought to himself that they had a right to be relieved and he looked forward to touching down in Rome. None of the band members, including Shiloh, were guilty of any acts that were against the High Roman church or the laws of Rome, as decried by the Emperor. The message in their music was about brotherhood. There was nothing against any church or specific religion. They were about finding and living the Spirit in their hearts. "Who could fault them for that?" Shiloh mused. It was true but known to few that the Emperor had tried to find the child that was prophesized to change his world—just like in the Bible story. There was no way of knowing if that man had connected Shiloh with that prophecy. Shiloh didn't have any fear of this—he decided he would face that when and if it happened.

The take-off was smooth and quiet. In a matter of minutes they climbed into the clouds and were on their way over the ocean. A while later, Jude, who had a window seat, called out: "I think we are turning." It was hard to tell because the flight was so smooth. If this was true it must be a wide turn, if at all. "I saw land again," Jude exclaimed. "And we should not be on the other side of the ocean yet."

A short time later, Yellow Feather appeared from the cockpit. "There has been a change of plans," he informed the group, at the point of a gun. The band members were searched and passed through the metal detector before boarding. But for someone in charge of the flight, it would have been easy to smuggle on weapons. Another man appeared from the back of the plane with a handgun. "We did charge the four men that were removed for acts of terrorism," he said. "But the men I replaced them with I hand-picked and trained for this occasion. Just be quiet and this will be over before you know it. No one can match the speed of this plane and, as you guessed," he indicated Shiloh, "we intend to take down that ridiculous fake they call the 'Friendship Tower'. You are on board, because we couldn't leave you behind—you knew too much. We are fast but they just might get lucky with a rocket if they were warned."

Shiloh was immediately aware that he had very little time to change the outcome of their destination—one way or the other. He unbuckled his seat belt and stood with his hands in the air. "I have something that I need to say."

Yellow Feather smirked, "you think you can change our minds? I don't think so. But amuse me. We can use some entertainment—even if this is going to be a short flight."

Shiloh walked slowly toward the other man until he was told to stop. He carefully removed a piece of paper from his vest pocket and unfolded it. "This is a copy of a letter that Chief Seattle sent to the President of the United States of New Rome. If I may, I would like to read it to you."

"Go ahead," Yellow Feather sneered. "I have heard about this letter. Chief Seattle was a weak old man. He was ready to give our land away—just like they planned with this plane. The men of his tribe were not warriors, like the Sons of Soma—they were cowards."

Shiloh realized that he would have his hands full trying to change the minds of this man and his companions. Still there was always plan "B" or "C,"

and he did not want to see his brave friends face severe injury or death. With his mind resolved, he began to read aloud:

CHIEF SEATTLE'S LETTER

In answer to the Last Proposed Treaty

"The President of this country that is called New Rome sends word that he wishes to buy our land. But how can you buy or sell the sky or the land? The idea is strange to us. If we do not own something, how can you buy it?

The Earth is our Mother. Every part of this Earth is Sacred to our People. We are a part of the earth and it is part of us. The ground beneath our feet is the ashes of our grandfathers. Whatever befalls the earth befalls the children of the Earth.

The shining water that moves in the streams and rivers is not just water but the blood of our ancestors. If we sell you our land, you must remember that it is Sacred. If we sell you our land, remember that the air is precious to us, that the air shares its spirit with all the life that it supports.

Will you teach your children what we have taught our children? That the earth is our mother? What befalls the earth befalls all the sons of the earth.

This we know: the earth does not belong to man, man belongs to the earth. All things are connected like the blood that unites us all.

One thing we know: our God is also your God. The Earth is precious to Him and to harm the earth is to heap contempt on Her Creator.

Your destiny is a mystery to us. What will happen when the buffalo are all slaughtered? The wild horses tamed? What will happen when the secret corners of the forest are heavy with the scent of many men and the view of the ripe hills is blotted with talking wires?

When the last red man has vanished with the wilderness and his memory is only the shadow of a cloud moving across the prairie, will these shores and forests still be here? Will there be any of the Spirit of my people left?

As we are part of the land, you, too, are part of the land. This earth is precious to us. It is also precious to you.

One thing we know—there is only One God. No man—Red man or White man—can be apart. We are all brothers after all."

When he had finished reading and replaced the letter in his vest, Shiloh said: "This does not sound like words of a coward to me. It sounds like the words of a man who loved his People and their connection with the Earth and all of the other creatures—including the men that we might call our enemy. It sounds like the words of a man who knew that the time for change had come and the only way his People would survive would be to be part of that change."

"Phaaat!" Yellow Feather spit. "We have another saying: Today is a good day to die. This is in our Sacred book—as written by the prophet Soma." Still, Shiloh did notice a very slight quiver to his voice—it was hard to tell—was it just anger or something else?

"I acknowledge the Sons of Soma," Shiloh spoke clear and decisively at the point of a gun. "They have good things to say. But the book you quote was not written by Soma." He was taking a great chance here but he was aware that they were smart, even beyond their anger and need for revenge. "This book was written by a Man called Iron Hand. He was a close student of Soma and wrote this book about the life of Soma and the truths that the Elder told his people."

"Just be careful!" The gun shook in the other man's hand. "I should kill you for speaking these words of blasphemy."

"And I know you would do this," Shiloh continued, "if you did not know that I am speaking the truth. We share something—your People and mine. We respect a person who speaks from his heart. This is where the truth of our life on this Earth can be found. Our People have always known that there are things that change—but our connection with the Creator does not. Remember when the black robes first told us that the book they had contained the words of their God? They said that all of the answers were in that book. And at first our people were in wonder. They asked if the God of these people was dead. The God of our people—the One Creator is alive—and answered our prayers.

We did not need a book to know about how to live. The answer to something that is right or wrong is in our Hearts. The Prophet Soma knew this and this is how he lived. He took his people into the desert to find themselves again. To find the Path of Beauty that they had lost. Soma was not lost—he gave his life and his teachings to his People. And a man called Iron Hand wrote down what should not have been written.

"Our People," Shiloh continued earnestly, "your People and mine would know the truth of what is intended here today. It is not honorable to kill innocent people. This is not the way of our People. When we fought the White man in the past we were like the Wolf. A wolf is a noble creature that will live in harmony with all life, only killing as part of the Circle and not killing for sport or in revenge. But when the wolf and his pack are backed into a corner, he will fight with a fierceness that is terrifying to protect his family. And a wolf could not be what some people have falsely called a martyr. A martyr is not someone who takes his Sacred life and the Sacred lives of Innocents—especially for revenge. And you speak of a Warrior. As our People have known—a True Warrior will meet a man face-to-face on the battlefield and become the wolf, when this is required. This is all I have to say. The rest—this choice is now up to you."

The gun slumped in Yellow Feather's hand. His dejected voice said all that Shiloh needed to know and did not want to hear.

"It is too late to change course. We are on autopilot now and the Tower is only moments ahead."

"There have been planes tracking us," one of the men shouted from the open door to the cockpit. "I saw them far off just after we reached land again. But they aren't contacting us or shooting us down."

"It might be in the best interest of someone who wants the excuse to start a war," Shiloh said to Yellow Feather and his men. "Quickly now—tell me that you want to change this?"

"I told you—it is too late. I would if I could but look—the Tower!"

Through the door to the captain's cabin, the Friendship Tower loomed large. Shiloh took the Spirit rattle that he had stuck in his belt and began to shake it. The sound reverberated throughout the plane and in the hearts and minds of everyone present as *The Arrow* passed through the Tower like a ghost—in slow motion. This was different than any "jump" into a different dream that Shiloh had ever experienced. All of the men on the plane saw and looked into the eyes of the men and women who sat typing or talking on their phones. There was something that was passed—a memory or a prayer and the plane was through—into another place.

"What is this place?" Yellow Feather demanded to know. "Did we die and go to Heaven? The land is barren and flat. I do not see the streets of gold that we were promised."

"And you will not find the seven virgins, if I miss my guess," Shiloh smiled with resignation. Simon joined him at the window. "Where do you think we are?" he asked.

"This is a dream. It is another dream that is not like the place we came from," Shiloh said with a whisper. "I think, in this dream, the moment of reckoning that the riders from the stars spoke about has already taken place. We are still traveling over the land that would have been the outskirts of the city of New Rome but there is no evidence of there ever having been tall buildings or of human habitation. I can see nothing but flat desert stretching all the way to the horizon."

"We are off autopilot." Yellow Feather came from the front of the plane. "But we do not know where we should be headed. Do you have any insight about that?"

"Continue straight ahead," Shiloh instructed. "I have been experiencing something—a gentle pulling in that direction."

"What is this about?" Jude enquired.

"This is a dream of someone who will meet us—somewhere over the horizon," Shiloh explained.

"I don't think this is Kansas, Toto," Jude replied the obvious. "You said 'someone'—is it God?"

"No—we came into someone's dream. This dream that he or she is having is in keeping with our thoughts and beliefs at the time we made the journey. This is not God—but might be—since we are all the co-creators of our dreams and our lives."

"There is a large body of water ahead," a voice from the cockpit called out.

"Continue on," Shiloh answered. "There is an island. I don't know how I know but the pull is from there. There will be a place to land the plane."

In a short time, an island appeared just as Shiloh predicted. "There will be an old landing strip—that way," Shiloh pointed. This island was mostly rock, but here and there was a cluster of trees and green grass, making a new start after a catastrophe of world-ending proportions. Luckily, it was broad day light, because the overgrown landing strip would not have been visible at night.

"How did you know this was here?" Simon asked when they came to a stop after a rough landing.

"I saw through someone's eyes," Shiloh explained. "We have a connection I can't explain. "He saw us coming down over those trees. This is odd—even for a dream."

"Is that him?" Lucas asked. There was a small group of men running toward the plane.

"No," Shiloh answered. "These people must live here." A number of women and children followed. They waved frantically and appeared to be happy to see the visitors. "Something I know, from my connection, is that he does not know he is dreaming. He thinks this is all real."

"This feels pretty real to me," Simon proclaimed. He stomped on the rocky ground to prove his point.

"It is," Shiloh assured them. "Every dream we have is real but most people remember so little because they have been conditioned. They have been taught since birth to disbelieve anything outside a certain logical viewpoint. I should mention that this person—who is sharing this dream with us—has not learned this. His mind is open, so certain things that might seem magical to people in our world will be possible here."

"What kind of things?" Lucas asked, but he did not receive an answer at the moment because the men and women who lived here clustered around talking all at once—asking so many questions.

"Where did you come from?"

"How is it that you're all still alive?"

"Where did you get that plane? We have not even seen a boat from the mainland since the big shaking."

"What do you mean—the big shaking?" Shiloh asked one of the men.

"My grandfather told me about something that happened in his Grandfather's time. One day the Earth began to shake and it continued until everything was smooth and flat. There were only a few mountains still standing. This story was told by someone who survived—someone who made it back from the mainland. We have a few boats that we built but trees are precious. There is nothing left. I guess that this island is here because it is mostly rock. In the old days this island was called *The Rock*. So my Grandfather told me."

"And what about this place here—this landing strip?" Shiloh asked.

"I saw the name written in a book. That's how I knew about a plane," the man explained. "I am a teacher—the only one here abouts. This place used to be called Saint John's. The harbour is over that away," he pointed.

By the time Shiloh and his friends and the men from *The Arrow* had made their way to the harbour, a large group had formed, attracted by the plane and the news of the visitors. There was a small single-masted ship not far out in the harbour. A teacher introduced himself to Shiloh, then cupped his hands to his mouth and yelled: "Are you catching anything?"

A voice came back: "No—the fish are gone again."

"For a while there were no animals or fish," the teacher explained. "This was not due to the earth shaking. My Grandfather told me that the fish were pretty well all gone—fished out by large boats from the mainland, way before we were born. It was hard going for awhile; we lived on roots and whatever we could find. Eventually, the fish began to return, because the earth was healing herself, I think. But the fish have not returned in any great numbers yet. Sometimes they are there and sometimes not."

"It is about balance and respect," Shiloh said. "Tell them to throw the net over the other side."

"He is a Shaman," Jude explained. "He is able to talk to the animals and birds." Simon gave Jude a look but Jude just shrugged. "If they have faith, maybe this dream will come through for them."

The teacher cupped his hands and yelled out Shiloh's instructions. After a bit, they could see the men on the boat complying with the suggestion. The net that they pulled back in was full of fish.

"How did you know?" the teacher asked Shiloh.

"Something I remembered," he replied.

"We will et well tonight," the teacher said.

"What did you say?" Simon asked. "I mean et—it. What kind of slang is that? Where were your ancestors from?"

"I come from the Cape, bye," he replied.

"Where is the Cape? And did he just call me a boy? A bye?" Simon asked Shiloh and no one in particular.

"Great tunderin' jet engines!" The man seemed to be lapsing into an unknown dialect as he was not able to communicate. He paused and drew a breath. "Sorry," he said. "The Cape is way over yonder—by the bay, bye. I mean, it is over that way," he pointed and continued. "Our books say that we come from a place called Ireland and we mixed with the Red People that were ear-before—I mean here before we came. We do not have many books either because we burned near everything we could get our 'ands on just to keep warn at the start. We are better now that the trees and the animals are comin' back."

"What is your name bye the bye?" Simon said chuckling.

"My name is Peter," the man replied. "What is he laughing about?" he asked Shiloh.

"Simon is laughing with you," Shiloh explained. "Simon is our Public Relations Manager. We are a band. Isn't that so Simon?"

"Right, boss," Simon was still smiling. "Where is the Cape that you mentioned? Is that Cape Breton?"

"Sure—I have heard that said," Peter answered. "There was a small plane that survived—by some kind of miracle. And my Grandfather, who was a young man at the time, was found over at the mainland. He was one of the people who were rescued. Everything over there was leveled—or so I am told. Seems we had a limited supply of fuel that survived and it was needed to keep us warm."

"Great tunderin!" Simon smiled while imitating the local dialect. "You people burned jet fuel to keep warm?"

"We did—or so I am told. None's left by the way."

"Yellow Feather," Shiloh asked, "will saltwater work?"

Yellow Feather, who had been tagging along and listening in, replied with a nod of his head. "I am pretty sure it will." The men from… I mean the men who helped us build *The Arrow* said it will burn any kind of water—better than regular jet fuel."

"Well that about covers the how. At least the physical part," Shiloh said. "How did you come to be the teacher, anyway?" he asked Peter.

"My Grandfather was a preacher. He schooled me on all the books that were left—before we burned them. We had to choose between keeping Bibles and text books for the children to learn to read. And by that time, my Grandfather was an angry man. He was particularly angry at a God who he said let our world die—or was responsible for what happened. He burned all the Bibles first. I heard it said that there are a few to be found somewhere in land. Do you think that was wrong?" he asked Shiloh. "Do you think there is a God who did this?"

"I know that there is a God—a Creator of All Things," Shiloh answered with complete sincerity. "And I know that He did not do this. We are still attempting to find out how this happened and who caused it. But it was not God. The God that I know is a Loving Creator who gave us the gift of free will, and it seems like someone made use of that gift to destroy most of the world as we know it. As for the Bibles, I can't judge that either way. But the One who came before—you called him Jesus—was to have said: "when two or more gather in my name—I will listen. I have found that a simple prayer by one person in the quiet of his mind will be heard by the Creator and answered. We just have to be still and listen."

"Speaking of Creators," Simon said in a low voice. "Shouldn't he be along soon?"

"The dreamer you mean," Shiloh replied. "He is close. He is the one who dreamed this dream—he is not the Creator. We dream the dream, and the Creator who hears our thoughts Creates through us. Remember the saying: 'be careful what you wish for'? Well here it is in all of its physical reality. When there is a crisis, there is always someone listening and wanting to help. Also remember the saying that you are God's eyes and ears? None of this is due to idle talk."

The small fishing boat came close enough to shore that people could walk in the water up to their waist. They formed a line and began to unload the catch using metal buckets. "We will et well tonight," Peter repeated, and went to help clean the catch.

Shiloh pointed to a figure approaching along the shore. "Here comes our dreamer."

When the person got close enough, Simon remarked: "It is a boy—a young man at most."

"Don't be deceived," Shiloh said. "All it takes is a mind not fearful to ask questions, to dream the answers." He went to meet the boy.

"Ahniin—Hello!" He called to the boy. And when he was close enough to extend his arm and hand in the traditional greeting, he said: "I am Shiloh. What are you called?"

The boy shook his hand and clasped his arm. "That is why I am here," he answered. "This is part of my quest—to find my name. I can see that you are a Shaman, maybe you can explain my dream?"

"Tell me about your dream so far?" Shiloh urged. "In the dream before this, did you see an animal?" he listened quietly and then said: "The Eagle whose cry began this dream—that opened the door—he is not your personal Totem. Though Eagle will never send you somewhere you are not meant to go. Your Totem will be a four-legged that you have met. Our ancestors were wise to look at their animal brothers and sisters to find their way on this Earth Walk. His eyes shone and he gazed toward the sky. "What did you see, just before this Dream?"

"I saw a cloud person in an animal shape!" he exclaimed.

"Now think back to your first dream," Shiloh instructed. "Did you see this four-legged in that dream?"

"There were two dreams before this, I moved from one dream to another and then at the point of the first dream, after I said goodbye to my friends, I came to the entrance to the valley, and… turned back to see… the tail of an animal disappearing into the trees."

"Draw this cloud animal as you remember it—and with the tail that you saw," Shiloh suggested. There was a patch of sand on the beach at this point.

The Boy put down his large carrying pouch that was around his neck and shoulder and began to draw in the sand. He drew an animal that Shiloh recognized.

"Miighan—Mayingun," Shiloh said, pronouncing the syllables. "That is the name of this animal—that is the name I will know you by. We are connected. We will meet again. Do you know the meaning of this name—do you know this animal?"

"No—it is not familiar to me but the name sounds right. I know that I will learn about this animal. And you?" he said in the usual polite greeting of the Ojibway language.

"My other name is Two-Fishes," Shiloh told the boy. This was something only known by his parents. It was due to his true birth month and to a connection with the One who came before. "You can call on me any time in Dreaming."

The boy picked up his shoulder pack and followed Shiloh to where the men were about finished unloading the boat.

"We have a fire ready," Peter told them. "Who is your friend?"

"I am called Miighan," the boy answered, playing with the pronunciation the way he heard Shiloh say it. "Can I share my food with you? My Grandmother gave me this food—even though I was not supposed to eat during my vision quest," he laughed. "I guess it was to eat and share within this dream."

While they were waiting for the fish to cook in a large steel pot boiling over a roaring fire, Shiloh introduced Miighan to his traveling companions. "We are all connected he said. There is something that you will have in common with everyone you meet here."

"This is Simon. His strength is to teach about tolerance. Simon shook the boys hand and smiled at Shiloh's words.

"And this is Lucas—he is our drummer—he is about following your heart and dreams and not giving up."

"And this is Jude—he is our coyote medicine friend. He is about a boy like you who will wonder who he is—perhaps before he has met the woman that will share his life. There are many ways to share love—as long as it is with respect." Jude smiled to show that he was not offended and offered his hand.

"And you have met me. That is all I can say about this—except to say again that this is like meeting different versions of yourself. Even that man called Yellow Feather—he was instrumental in bringing us here. We all may go through a time when we are easily misled. This is about finding your truth."

"The first batch of fish is ready," Peter called out. "And there are many more people arriving every minute. We will need to feed at least 100."

"Miighan had something to share with us," Shiloh said to Peter and everyone waiting. "What do you have in your pack?"

"I don't know," Miighan admitted. "It is something that my Grandmother gave to me to share." He opened the shoulder pack and drew out fried bread. He gave a piece of the bread to Shiloh who broke it in half and passed a piece to two of the people standing next to him. Meanwhile, Miighan pulled another piece of bread from his pack and another and another—all of which he gave to Shiloh to break and hand out to the hungry people.

Soon Miighan had pulled more bread from the pack than the sack could possibly hold. He laughed until tears ran down his cheeks. "It is a good thing that this is a Dream," he said at length. "I feel like a magician with a magic hat. What should I do?"

"Keep on feeding the hungry," Shiloh suggested. "When everyone is full, then you should stop. This is a Give-away that will show you the true balance. We give with the knowing that there is always enough—for everyone. Remember this and you will never be hungry or lacking."

After the fried bread and fish had been given to everyone present, there was still more left over. "This will be for our journey home," Shiloh divided the bread and wrapped the cooked fish. Some went back into the boy's pack and the other half into a large cloth to take back on the plane. "It's good to be able to take something back from a dream." He recalled the pipe stone that Meg gave him. "This will remind us about what is real and what we should never forget."

Every one was full and the fire burned brightly. "Is there anything that the Shaman will tell us?" Peter asked. "This would be a good time to tell a story."

Shiloh stood. "There was a time that talking was the right thing to do. There is a time for everything and everything has its time. Now is the time to remember what has happened this evening and hold the memories in our hearts. We have seen some things that might be called Miracles—or Magic. This is not finished. When we gather like this as a family, we know why we have been given this Gift of Life—to Share. My friends have brought along their musical instruments. The time for talking is finished. Now would be a good time for singing and dancing. What do you think?"

* * *

Shiloh woke to feel the earth rocking under him. He suspected that there must be an earthquake happening. Men were shouting, rushing about—and tripping over him. "What are you doing here?" he recognized Peter's voice. His mind was still drowsy. He recalled going to sleep on the beach by the fire when the singing and dancing was dying down. "I don't understand how you got here," Peter asked again. The earth rocked beneath him and when Shiloh attempted to sit up, he was covered by water. He could see that the men around him were panicking.

"Be calm," he said in a quiet voice. And when no one seemed to hear him, he repeated a bit louder with a firm tone to his voice. And the earthquake slowly subsided. "That's better," Shiloh said to no one in particular, as the men quit milling about. He attempted to stand and Peter offered him a hand up. "Careful," Peter said. "You don't seem to have your sea legs yet."

His head cleared, and he stood beside Peter and leaned against the mast of the boat. "Whoa? How did I get here?" Shiloh asked.

"That was my question," Peter answered. "He looked at the other men who gathered around. "Did you see what happened?" one of the men asked.

Peter nodded in amazement. "We were in the grip of a nasty storm and he just told the storm to be calm and it did!"

"I didn't order anyone or anything—I asked everyone to be calm," Shiloh replied.

"Well it seems like the Wind and the Ocean must have been listening," Peter chuckled. "Because right after you said 'be calm'—the storm obeyed. What kind of man are you that nature listens to what you say."

"I am a man who knows that nature and all of creation—as you call it—are our relatives. If you treat nature right, you will be treated the same. How is it that you are out here when everyone else is sleeping on the beach?"

"The catch was so good last night that we decided to come out to where the men pulled in the full net of fish and get more while they were available. But when we got out here, a storm came up—and you know the rest."

"I am not at all surprised," Shiloh sat down with his back against the mast. "The fish provided us with all that we needed—but that was not enough for you. If you learn to trust the animals and the fish, they will give back to you but there is a balance. When the fish and the animals have returned to the numbers that were present at a time in the past, before we over-fished and slaughtered them, then we will eat better. We need to be aware that we are not the only creatures on the planet."

"A lesson well learned," Peter agreed. "That still doesn't answer the question about how you came to be in the boat with us."

"I have His memories when I need them," Shiloh winked. "Maybe I sleepwalked out here."

"You're kidding!" one of the men suggested. "We would have seen you, if you somehow learned to walk on water. He's kidding—right?"

"Maybe not," Peter replied. "It would have boggled my mind to see someone walk out to this boat. Maybe something happened that our minds and our eyes simply can't accept. He did calm the storm after all."

"I think I'll just ride back to shore with you," Shiloh said. "There is no need for me to prove anything—now that it's no longer required."

When they got out of the boat onto dry land, the sun was beginning to come up. Lucas came running. "We were wondering where you went," he said. The boy that you introduced us to yesterday was gone this morning, too. We thought for a minute that you both had gone back..." he smiled sheepishly,

"...without us."

"I wouldn't do that," Shiloh answered. "We are in this together, but you may be right about Miighan. He may have woken up—or moved on to another dream. He is on a Vision Quest.

"But, if he woke up, why is this place still here?" Simon asked. "You did call him the dreamer. You said that this was his dream."

"Miighan was the dreamer who asked for this meeting," Shiloh agreed. "But these people here are not his creations, nor are we. When we dream—especially a powerful dream—we give it life. And the dream lives on and the other people who have been part of the dream keep it alive. That is what happened, I believe, when the Creator had the First Dream—and he Dreamed the Universe and the planets and the Earth with all its creatures. He put his spark in us and gave the Gift to create."

"So what happens now?" Lucas asked. "I am inspired to share. When do we go back? Or is it even possible?"

"Can we fuel up the plane?" Shiloh asked Yellow Feather. The group from the plane were seated in a small circle near *The Arrow*.

"I asked Peter about that yesterday, shortly after we got here," the other

man replied. "He says it can be done. He was amazed that we could use water

for fuel. Water is plentiful here but not the drinking kind. That has been another

challenge for them, but they were up to it."

"And what about you and the other four men who took over the plane?" Shiloh asked. "There is something about going back that requires the reason we came here. And it can't be faked."

"I have worked that out in my mind and for the betterment of this place," Yellow Feather said. "I will come back and so will the pilot. We need him to fly the plane. He is right in his thoughts about the purpose of our journey. His name is Andrew John Flowing-Water. He is also a friend of mine and of Grandfather, and I convinced him to fly the plane. His heart was very troubled about the state of our People living in the desert, so it was not difficult to sway his mind."

"And what about you?"

"After much thought about all that you said on the plane and especially the Give-away that I witnessed last night, my mind is right, too. The way the people have come together, this is the true teaching of our People being lived out. This may be the result of something that happened, something that I could have helped to happen. I am ready to go back and I am ready to offer my skills to the Roman engineers who will accept *The Arrow* as a Gift. That is, if the Roman Air Force doesn't shoot us down the moment we appear in their sky. I am ready to accept that, as well. I could never agree with the way the Emperor runs the world and the part he played in the near extinction of our People. But I can see that it is not for me to judge the past. There is a time now for forgiveness and healing—for the White man and the Red man."

"They will not shoot us down," Shiloh smiled a wry smile. "That is, until we slow down to offer *The Arrow*. This is where a bit of faith comes in. When we are doing the work of the Creator, we will be protected. Remember what happened at Wounded Knee. We will not die. That is the promise and we may wake up in a better place."

"So be it!" Yellow Feather agreed. "The other three men still have some anger to work out. They would sooner remain here for that to happen. There are two other men who have lived here and would like to go back with us. Phillip, who seems to remember Andrew as a friend from another life or dream.

Thomas, who had become an angry doubter that there was a God—before he met you. And now he is prepared to go with us, even if it means that we will all die. He wants to believe and he is open to be shown more. And by the way, he plays a Native flute very well. He might be a good addition to your band."

"So when can we leave?" Shiloh asked.

"As soon as we are fuelled up. This evening I believe we will be ready."

"I am ready now," Shiloh agreed. "But I must speak to Phillip and Andrew about a goal. Something that they should be looking forward to in the other dream state. You, Yellow Feather, have a purpose on the Other Side, as you have told me. And all of our band members, including myself, have talked about what we will do when we get back. We will focus on that at the moment we are ready to pass over. This will, in effect, pull us to the Other Side."

"Like the pull of the dreamer to get us here?" Yellow Feather asked.

"Yes—without that we might have gone somewhere else. It would have been somewhere that we needed to be, in relation to our problems and desires, but this was the best place for us to be."

"It is interesting that you mention the phrase 'in relation to'," Yellow Feather was a learned man—schooled in physics and engineering. Perhaps this was the side of him that had helped Shiloh effect the change—in the plane. "This reminds me of the Einstein theory of Special Relativity. I have thought much about what happened to us and, by all theoretical laws, it should have been impossible."

"I never studied law," Shiloh chuckled. "So I guess that is why I tend to follow my heart instead of doing what someone says is impossible—or wrong—by their point of view."

Yellow Feather laughed. "The basis of the theory of Special Relativity, as I understand it, is that it is impossible for any object that has mass to be accelerated to the speed of light. Special Relativity also sets aside the regular notions of time and space. Einstein's theory was that the speed of light is the same for all observers, no matter how they moved, relative to the light source."

"He was a brilliant man," Shiloh conceded. "He also said that imagination is more important than knowledge. So he was able to theorize scientific laws and at the same time realize that they were indeed theories until proven otherwise. And then the scientific community took Einstein and Newton's theories and treated them like a religion. They act today, as if the theories are indeed laws, in the logical sense. Even with Quantum Physics, there is a need to prove the laws and theories using mathematical equations. There is another way of looking at this that explains both religion and science. If I have a need to prove something—a way will show itself. In other words, if I seek answers that I already believe I know, my belief will be validated."

"Is this discussion leading somewhere?" Yellow Feather queried. "Is it about realizing that we create what we believe to be true? Or is this about how we will be able to get back home?"

"Right on both accounts," Shiloh replied. "We found ourselves here regardless of our relationship to the speed of light. Or how this relationship is to Spirit and not to a logical physical thing that we experience with one of our five senses. Quantum physics is close to explaining it by saying that whatever particles we are made of is not in just one place, but only seems so because that is where we focus our attention, something to that effect anyway. We—you and I and the rest of the men that came with us—now know that we are not limited to living one dreamtime space. There is a problem, however, that we will need to face in order to get back to our other reality."

"What would that be?" another man, Thomas, asked. "You told us the story about how just before you hit that Friendship Tower; you did something that sent you here instead. Can't you just do that same Spiritual thing that you did to take everyone back?"

"Yes, I can," Shiloh answered. "I have no doubt about that. But anytime I have done that in the past, I have gone back to the exact moment and place that I left. There will not be time to turn the plane around. I think the gift *The Arrow* represents is more than we first imagined. The man from the Stars that helped to rebuild the Concorde from the ashes gave us the chance to see how they fly to the Stars. The ships that they use are probably an improvement on *The Arrow*, but the engines are not the secret to the way they go beyond the speed that would be required. I believe that they fly their ships with a Spiritual relationship that I was telling you about."

"So what about the prophesy? The one based on their coming back at certain times. If they can come any time they want, what is the point of saying this?" Simon asked.

"There is something else related, there is that word again, to the prophesy that is beyond the scope of our knowing at this time," Shiloh admitted. "Sometimes, even though I have his memories, I need to trust in the Mystery. This logical brain will never be capable of knowing all of the Mystery. Trust is the key to opening our hearts to Grace and thus to the Mystery."

"So back to the problem at hand," Yellow Feather insisted. "How do we avoid crashing into the Tower and killing thousands of innocent people?"

"I believe that is where the real speed of *The Arrow* comes in—and our Spiritual connection. Remember, just before we traveled here, there was a moment of slow motion. I remember looking into the eyes of the people at work in the Tower, just before we passed over. That is the moment when Spirit is asking us for our destination. This is what we call free will. I believe that if we had consciously chosen a destination, we would be there now. Instead, we let Spirit choose the best place. Our pilot will get us to the place we need to be in this dream—the co-ordinates just before we were about to hit the Tower. I believe that Andrew John Flowing Water was hand-picked by Spirit to do just what his name implies. Then I will do my thing. I will take us to that place between worlds—where we will be like ghosts. At that time I will ask Andrew to accelerate *The Arrow* and take us home."

"How do you know that we will not simply become real and crash out on the other side of the Tower?" Thomas asked.

"I know that we will exit the tower into a real place—and do so safely," Shiloh replied. "I have faith in Spirit and my ability to make this happen. Just where we will be at that time will depend on our collective choosing. The worst thing that could happen is we come out in another dream and not the place we envisioned. We may be like the fabled Flying Dutchman—the ship that roams the seas—turning up now and then only to disappear again. I do not believe that this will happen. If there is anyone who wants to change their minds about coming along—just say so now."

No one, including Thomas, changed their mind. In fact, Thomas declared; "I am prepared to follow you wherever you go because that is the place I will need to be."

"Be careful how you say that," Jude smiled. "If I said that everyone might get the wrong idea."

Everyone laughed except Thomas, who didn't appear to understand the meaning behind Jude's statement. "I was a fisherman," Thomas replied. "Now I will become a pied piper", he raised his flute to his lips and sounded a clear note "—and a fisher of men and women."

Chapter 9

RETURNING HOME WITH A PURPOSE

"In a few minutes we will be at the exact co-ordinates before we were about to crash into the Tower," Andrew informed Shiloh. The destination had been recorded by the computer that controlled the autopilot. This plane was not dependent on satellites or any man-made device for its navigational system. The man who had trained Andrew told him that it got its guidance directly from the stars and planets. He did not elaborate, except to say, that the head piece also responded to the pilot's built-in sense to compensate. This held up Shiloh's belief that *The Arrow* could be flown in a similar way to the circular crafts belonging to the Star visitors. "I think that the pilots of Rome will have a bit of a learning curve, if they even discover what this is all about," he had confided to Shiloh before taking off.

Shiloh was in the co-pilot seat and the other men were in the small passenger compartment behind them. "There will be no mistake when your help will be needed," Shiloh informed them. "We will be in a ghost-like place—within the Tower."

"Now!" Thomas shouted and Shiloh began to create the sound with his Spirit rattle. The sound reverberated within *The Arrow* and the plane, like before, changed into a ghostly presence passing through an equally ghostly tower.

"Go for it!" Shiloh shouted back, and Andrew accelerated out of the other side of the Tower into…

"We are back," Shiloh exclaimed. The City of New Rome in all of its skyscraper majesty lay below them. Just for a moment, Andrew slowed the plane to get his bearings and to appreciate the view.

"Here comes the jet fighters," Andrew announced. And in a blink of an eye *The Arrow* was beyond the horizon. "Phew!" he exclaimed. "I have flown this plane near that speed before but it takes my breath away every time. And no G-forces. I wonder how they did that? It's almost a crime to give this plane to the Emperor."

"I would agree," Shiloh sighed. "But it is tied to the prophesy in some way that we have yet to discover. I suspect it is about the Gift—given as brother to brother without attachment. And it may also be about their needing to Spiritually evolve, to take full advantage of the Gift."

"Where to now?" Andrew requested.

"Time to do what we came back to do—at least the first part. The rest will depend on the reaction of the Emperor," Shiloh replied. In scarcely the time it took to say, they were across the Ocean in Roman airspace—too fast for the Roman radar to register.

Andrew decelerated *The Arrow* again to give the Roman planes time to get into the air and then he repeated the vanishing act to the next curve of the horizon.

"Anyone following?" Shiloh asked.

"Are you kidding?" Andrew replied. "They were lucky if they saw us leave. This is more fun than I thought it would be."

"A couple more demonstrations should be enough," Shiloh suggested. "But be careful, they will be waiting for us this time."

After three more passes for Andrew's sake—he was enjoying this—they cruised to the edge of Roman airspace and broadcasted a message on a frequency they knew the other planes could intercept.

"You must be aware by now of the superior speed that this aircraft is capable of. The reason we put on this demonstration was to show your Emperor the Gift that we are offering in the name of goodwill between our people. Please respond."

After a few minutes, there was a reply on the same frequency. "This is the high commander of the Roman Air Force—you are trespassing on our airspace. Please state your intentions or leave."

"We are here to offer this aircraft to your Emperor as a Gift." Yellow Feather did all the talking.

"Let me get this clear. You want to give this aircraft to the Emperor of Rome?"

"Yes. As a gesture of goodwill between our People. Please inform your Emperor that we are willing to fly it to any place of his choosing."

There was a long pause. "I will deliver your message."

Almost a half-hour passed. "Maybe they are hoping our fuel will run low," Yellow Feather wondered. "Have you noticed any movement?" he asked Andrew. "Are there any planes on our long range radar? Is there any indication that they might be trying to trap us?"

"Nothing yet," Andrew responded. "They must be aware by now that we could easily outrun their best jetfighters."

"Attention unknown plane," the loudspeaker from the cockpit radio came alive. "I have discussed your offer with the Emperor of Rome. His answer is to decline your offer and to inform you that if you are not gone from Roman Air Space in the next few minutes, we will have no recourse than to treat you as an unwelcome intruder and commence firing upon your ship. That is all."

Shiloh and Yellow Feather exchanged puzzled looks. "Get us out of here ASAP," Yellow Feather urged Andrew, who already had his hand poised over the throttle. In about an hour, *The Arrow* was on the other side of the Earth.

Andrew eased back on the throttle. "What now?" he asked.

"We could try to find a safe place to settle down, and hide the plane again," Yellow Feather suggested to Shiloh. "Or we could become the Flying Dutchman that you mentioned before. Neither is an option as I see it. They will come looking for us, and will not stop until the plane is captured or destroyed. And any place we stay for any length of time will put ourselves and our hosts in grave danger. Any ideas?"

"I guess we should not be surprised at the answer that the Emperor gave us. He would suspect that we are carrying a bomb, at the very least."

"But he must have seen video footage of the Friendship Tower? He must know that if we wanted to blow anything up, we would have done so," Andrew said.

Shiloh shook his head. "Anything I have ever heard about the Emperor of Rome is that he is extremely paranoid. With great power comes great fear. And the greater the power the more fear there is of losing it. The only true power is found in Trust and I guess the men from the stars were hoping to find that—somehow. I am really not sure the reason behind their plan to offer the Arrow as a Gift."

"Maybe they wanted the Emperor to be confronted with his truth. It might be some future action from Rome or the Emperor that will trigger whatever happens to make the Earth like the Dream that we returned from."

"How long do you think we have before they come looking?" Andrew asked.

"At their top speed? The jet fighters should be on our tail in about 10 hours if they can do over Mach 2," Yellow Feather estimated. "At the time the Concorde was ordered to be scrapped, because it was too fast for them. Ten hours would have been the Concorde's best time. I heard that the newer Roman jets can do Mach 2.5 now—maybe Mach 3. That is three times the speed of sound."

"And we got here in about an hour," Andrew whistled. "The lack of G-force blows me away along with the speed. I don't care what anyone says, I am glad the Emperor was afraid to accept our Gift. Rome is not ready for this kind of technology."

"And that is why they will not give up. I am not sure what is stronger—the Emperor's fear or his desire to capture one of the ships that come from the Stars? Maybe if he had *The Arrow*, this might be possible for him," Shiloh replied.

"Think again," Yellow Feather smiled. "The men from the Stars would have to travel faster than light—or know some way to get around the space time barrier as we know it. Remember we talked about that? Special Relativity and all? Their home planet must be light years away. And here is a thought that will blow you away, Andrew. The speed of light is about 540 times the speed of sound. We might have done 8 or 10 Mach getting here, but 540 Mach is beyond my logical thinking."

Andrew's eyes grew large. "But there is no evidence of G-forces while traveling in this plane. The man from the stars that helped to work on the engine must have done something else—don't you see?

Isn't it possible that it is capable of more than the logical mind can imagine?"

"I think that you have discovered the real reason that the Gift was offered to the Emperor of Rome," Shiloh mused. "It is not about the bomb that Yellow Feather dismantled while we were in the other dream. But *The Arrow* is a "Trojan Horse," so to speak. If Rome and the Emperor—or anyone for that matter—were to want to join the People from the stars, they would need to change the way they think. To bypass the barrier that is represented by the speed of light, a person or race of people would need to evolve into Spirit. Not necessarily die—but evolve to think with the Heart and not the logical mind. Einstein's theory of Special Relativity is based on a thinking that includes solid material things being unable to accelerate beyond the speed of light."

"So, you are saying it is possible for a person who cares about his neighbour or his enemy as much as himself to go beyond the speed of light?"

"The logical thinking involved says that we are all separate. This is the true barrier that stops us like a wall. There is a scientist named Planck that has a theory about a wall that is not physical but stops us from accessing other dimensions. But think about where we went and returned from. *The Arrow* was not the method—it was the vehicle of inspiration. For some people, this plane will take them to the boundaries of their imagination. To make that step beyond to the stars might seem like a small step, but it will be a mighty step in the evolution of humankind. If the people of Rome were to make the step beyond their fear and need for power, then the war or whatever else that will devastate this Earth, will not happen."

"I would like to see how fast this plane will go," Andrew exclaimed.

"Then let me off first," Yellow Feather replied. "I've been changed by our experience. I want to go back to my People in the desert and do my best to help them change. I just want to help them to re-capture the Traditional Ways that Soma led them to discover. We are not about revenge—we are about living in harmony. We have become worse than the people who drove us into the desert. My vote would be to program the autopilot to take this ship to the moon or some place beyond for the future travelers to claim. Kind of like a prize for their efforts."

Andrew shrugged. "I know that you are right but I would still like to try the speed test first. What do you think, Shiloh?"

"Personally, I don't have a problem with that but how about a vote that includes all of us? We can find somewhere safe to fuel up—at least hours before the Roman fighters can catch up and take a vote on who gets off now or after the joy ride?" he smiled broadly and patted Andrew on the back. "This could get serious pretty quick. The Roman planes will attempt to surround us and we cannot go on forever. We are quicker but even the fox needs to rest. How about a pass around the globe—nothing beyond Mach 10 or so—and ask to land on that island called 'The Rock' where we landed in the dream. I have a thought that they will allow us to fuel up there. They are not part of the Roman Empire. Rome did not find anything yet that the Rock had that required that they be 'saved' from their evil ways. Back in the dream, Peter mentioned the discovery of oil in his Grandfather's time, so it probably won't be long before they are the New Found Land."

The people living on 'The Rock' were as friendly and gratuitous hosts as their counterparts in the other dream. They asked, however, that the men aboard *The Arrow* not bide longer than it took to fuel up as they did not care to attract the interest of Rome. They also agreed that those who wished to disembark and find another way home could do so with their blessing.

"Just take as much water as you please," said a man who bore a remarkable resemblance to Peter who the travelers had met before. He laughed heartily at the fuel they were taking in and shared a chuckle when Shiloh and the other men looked strangely when he asked them if they had et.

"We brought our own lunch. But we will be happy to et with you tonight," Simon informed the man, who was also called Peter, like his great grandson to come.

The travelers had agreed to share the fish and bread that they had brought back from the dream to solidify the memory of the experience. "We need to eat this food—so that we will know that this was not just a dream," Shiloh suggested. "And I will be the first to tell you that there are no insignificant dreams—they are all real. It is our memories that become coloured and sometimes distorted because our logical mind refuses to believe that there could be more than one reality."

They also took a vote and only Andrew and his new-found friend, Phillip, would board *The Arrow* for one more "test" flight before sending it to the moon and beyond.

"Who knows what might happen if we get this physical airship near the impossible speed of light," Andrew said, looking forward to the adventure.

When *The Arrow* was fuelled up and the Native version of 'goodbye' was exchanged, Andrew and Phillip boarded and were soon out of sight—but not out of mind.

"Now," Shiloh enquired of Peter. "Do you know of any cruise ships that would like to hire on some members of *The James Gang* for a trip to the Cape?"

There were no cruise ships to Cape Breton but Peter was able to help them find work in a local pub to help earn their way back home. Shiloh made calls when he was able. The first was to a certain telephone that belonged to a relative of Mathew Hawk. This was to leave a pre-arranged message that they had indeed returned safely. The second phone call was to his Father's and Mother's home in Kansa. He left a short message that all was well and he would be seeing them in a month or so. No need to draw attention. As far as anyone outside the collective families was concerned, the band was on an extended vacation following a brief tour of Kansa.

Shortly before leaving the city of St John's to crossover to the mainland, Lucas was in touch with a family member who had received a return call from Mathew Hawk. The family member had tracked down John and Mark and Simone who had driven the van back to Dallas. "John gave me a phone number where the rest of the band was staying. They were waiting for a call, so that they could meet up with us. Talk about positive thinking," Lucas smiled. "You don't know how big your family has grown unless you do something like this—I mean travel on the road with them like we have. We can give John a call and they will meet us in Cape Breton."

The friends had many things to talk about—many adventures to share so the drive back to New Rome with the two vans went by quickly. Shiloh phoned ahead so when he dropped off Mark and John on the way from the city to his family home in Bethany, his parents were waiting up past midnight. They talked until Mary noticed that it was nearly two o'clock in the morning.

"You must be tuckered out," she ruffled her son's hair. "Get some sleep and I promise not to wake you up in the morning. "Oh—did your father tell you? A young lady called while you were away."

"Who?" Shiloh asked. He was imagining someone looking to join the band.

"She said that her name was Amanda," Joseph replied. "She also said that she was a sister of Mathew and he had told her to call you if she was ever in need of help."

"Mathew? Do you mean Mathew Hawk? I wonder what that could be about?"

"No—I think she meant the other Mathew. She gave a New Rome phone number where she could be reached. It sounded urgent," Joseph handed his son a scrap of paper with the number from the coffee table.

"You didn't mention that he had more than one sister. Megan—wasn't that her name?" Mary asked.

Shiloh smiled through sleepy eyes. A young man's mother does not miss much, he thought. "No mom. Only one sister—that I know of. I'll call Amanda, whoever she is, first thing in the morning. We can't let a lady in distress go unanswered now, can we?"

Chapter 10

AMANDA
A ROSE BY ANY OTHER NAME

Shiloh woke up after lunch the next day. It was a Saturday so his parents were up and out for their daily walk in the woods. His mother's note said: "Coffee is ready to make—just push the button. Don't forget to phone Amanda—Love you, Mom." He smiled and turned on the coffee maker. While the coffee was percolating he punched in the numbers that Amanda, whoever she was had left with his father.

"Catholic Mission for the Homeless," a business-like voice said on the other end of the phone "Hello?"

"Oh—hello," Shiloh answered. "I'm sorry I expected…I mean, a young woman left me this phone number to call. Do you have an Amanda working there?"

"There is no Amanda working here," she replied. "There is an Amanda that drops in occasionally though. But we only put homeless people up for the night and feed them…what's that?" She was speaking to someone else. "I'm sorry sir, could you please hold a moment?" she said to Shiloh. After about a minute, she came back on the line. "The person who looks after this desk in the afternoon just arrived. We don't usually do this but she allowed the young woman that you mentioned to make a phone call and promised to tell her if someone named Shiloh called. She was in a very distressed state of mind. Are you Shiloh?"

"Yes. Did she say where she could be reached?"

"I don't know if you are aware. She hangs out in one of the seedier parts of the city—near Baker Street—where the prostitutes frequent.

That's about all I know. She usually comes back here to sleep but we did not see her yesterday. That is all I know."

Shiloh asked where the mission was located and said goodbye. "Two sisters that have common interests?" he wondered about that. Mathew had never mentioned his other sister but this sister is a prostitute perhaps. The key for the Jeep was on the table by the telephone. "Mom—you are always one step ahead of me." He wrote a note to let his parents know where he was going and when he might be back. He turned off the coffee maker after pouring hot coffee in a thermos, and then he headed out the door.

It was late afternoon when he reached the outskirts of New Rome. Baker Street, not surprisingly, was not too far from where Mathew's mother had lived. He drove around but did not see any young woman who looked like he imagined this Amanda might. It was too early for the streetwalkers to be out as well. "I wonder what Amanda is doing hanging around here." He did not want to think the worst. Megan and her mother would not have let that happen. But where were Megan and her mother now? The old drop-in centre for women was still boarded up—no sign of life there. He parked on a side street near Baker and decided to search for Amanda on foot.

He met a woman on the street who was dressed the part to ask if she knew anyone called Amanda.

"No, I don't, son. Are you sure it's Amanda you are looking for?" she replied.

"Yes, I am sure," he answered and quickly walked away.

"There is a church down that way," she called and pointed. "Maybe she needed to be saved?"

Shiloh somehow doubted that but decided, just the same, it wouldn't hurt to check it out. He took the shortcut that the woman told him. That street was in worse shape than the street he just left. It came to an end at a courtyard and the only way to the spire of the church was through a back alley. He sighed and soldiered on. Abruptly he heard shouting and then he saw a group of people standing a couple of yards from a tall fence. Cowering against the fence was a young Native woman. The people, who were shouting angrily at the young woman, appeared to be led by a man in a long black robe and black hat.

"What is going on here?" Shiloh asked.

"She is! But no longer," the leader replied. "She is a whore—a prostitute who had the nerve to darken the door of our church. We have seen her hanging around on Baker Street—selling her body. This is a sin that will not go unpunished."

"Whoa? Wait a minute," Shiloh replied. "What do you mean—unpunished? If she is doing what you say, there are laws to deal with this."

"The law is not enough," the man retorted. "The police arrest these women and the next thing you know they are back out on our streets. We believe that this is for the people of God to deal with. She will be stoned for her crimes."

Shiloh could hardly believe his ears. In these days! In broad daylight! It was like a scene out of ancient times—Biblical times! At that moment, as it often did, another part of Shiloh "kicked in". Memories that belonged to someone else.

"If there is anyone among you who is free of sin—as you call it—let him cast the first stone." The words came from his mouth like lines from a play that he was re-enacting.

"I am free from sin," the black-robed leader of the mob stepped forward and held up his Bible. "Jesus has died for my sin and washed them away." He drew back his right arm and hurled a fist-sized rock that hit the young woman in the side of her head. She collapsed weakly to the ground.

As the other people began to follow suit, Shiloh moved quickly to stand over the quivering woman. He then caught and deflected all of the stones that were meant to hurt or end the life of the woman at his feet. Eventually the mob ran out of stones and began to throw tin cans and whatever refuses that they could find. Shiloh stood his ground.

The crowd finally halted behind their leader. Their eyes began to lose their wild look and their breathing slowed. In some, Shiloh imagined a bit of remorse creeping in. But the leader was unmoved.

"I recognize you!" he pointed at Shiloh, "You are that blasphemer that claims to be the second coming! You and your band of false prophets! You are as bad as the whore! You are the beast—the anti-Christ. And she is the whore of Babylon! We know you know. God will deal with you and your kind in his own way. Judgment Day is coming!" The mob began to back away, all the while shouting: "Judgment Day is Coming!" over and over again. Shiloh noticed that not everyone was as enthusiastic as when he had first arrived. Shiloh wondered that there must have been something in his words that touched a memory within these other people as it had for him.

When the crowd disappeared, Shiloh bent down to see that the young woman was still breathing. She had an angry bruise on her temple. He brushed aside her hair to see the damage. Then he realized who she was. This must be Amanda…? And, if so, she was the twin of the young woman called Megan that he had met in the Dream. He touched the bruise to heal her and the brief contact confirmed what his eyes had told him. A memory arose—a warm kiss from a young woman with fire in her eyes and her hair. This was the same woman! She had long black hair, braided in the traditional Native way. But she was Megan!

Her eyelids fluttered. "Who…who are you?" She looked around abruptly to see that the crowd that had pursued her were not there anymore. Then she tried to sit up but could not do so without Shiloh's help. "Here—let me do more. I am a healer," he told her. He reached out and she flinched at his touch. "It's nearly gone. There will not even be a bruise—I promise." But there was something he sensed, that might not heal, except with time. Her beautiful brown eyes melted his heart.

"I am Shiloh." There was no hint of recognition. "You left a message with my father. I am a good friend of Mathew."

She stood rather meekly. "Mathew did not have any good friends—that I am aware. The problems I have now are mostly because of the company my brother kept. I don't know why I called you—but it was a last resort. I didn't know what else to do."

"I am not one of those kinds of friends—they were not friends anyway. I helped Mathew get to a place where he will be safe. A place where he can change his ways and pay back for his wrong doings," Shiloh said quietly, all the while searching for any change in her eyes. Nothing.

"Whoa!" she staggered and he caught her. "When I was under—down there on the ground—I remembered that you said something strange. Or was it my imagination? It was something like being part of a play or something. Right after that, everything went black."

"Yeah. Sorry. All I can say for that is that it worked so well the first time. The One who came before—Jesus—spoke those words in a much darker period of time—or so some think. I guess that we are not all as civilized as we thought we were!"

"Did it work so well the first time?" She inquired and managed the first smile he had seen. It lit up his heart. "I hope you won't judge them too harshly. We are in tough times now as we were then. People are looking for answers and some are clutching at straws. Sometimes they end up like the song *The Eagles* sing: 'Following the Wrong Gods home'." She was speaking the way he would have. The person he had promised to come looking for was there but hidden away somehow. The best he could do—the only thing he could do—was to put away his personal feelings and to offer the help she needed.

"When did you eat last?" he asked. "Can we go somewhere and get a bite to eat. Then you can tell me about Mathew and why you phoned?"

They found a restaurant in another part of the city. While Amanda was eating, she filled him in on what had happened in her life to leave her homeless.

"I am not a streetwalker—in the sense that I would not sell my body. I need to make that clear. My mother and I only wanted to help the young women who were trapped or tricked into prostitution." He nodded to indicate that he believed her—otherwise he just listened. "Then one day a person that said that he was from Homeland Security came looking for Mathew. He looked around and said that we were a threat to national security, thinking that we operated a common body house. We were convicted before going to trial. My mother, bless her soul, was put in a home and I was sent to prison for prostitution. I spent six months in jail and then they let me out on the streets. Whatever money we had always went toward keeping the drop-in center working. Our home was boarded up and is scheduled for demolition. And here I am living hand-to-mouth—begging on the street." Tears formed in her eyes but she squared her shoulders and wiped them away.

"How can I help?" Shiloh asked. "I will do anything I can."

"Somehow I believe that or I would not have made the phone call. I just need a reference or a hand in getting a paying job. I am not someone who will take advantage of a person's goodwill. I will pay you back when I get on my feet. I just didn't know where to turn. I am getting a first-hand look at how hard it is for the women who are branded—whether they have done the act or not. I am at the place where it is difficult to trust anyone—you should know that." She held her head high despite her state in life.

"Let me call my brother. He may be able to help in the short term," Shiloh suggested. He went to a nearby payphone and came back with good news. "My brother, James, and his wife have a spare room and can give you a place to sleep and eat for a couple of months. They are hoping for a baby but that hasn't happened yet, so they have a room available. Petra—that's my sister-in-law—says she will help you find some kind of work, maybe a waitressing job. She has some friends in the restaurant business. James and Petra have been checking out buying a franchise. James and Petra and I have this band called *The James Gang*, though, and I don't think it is out of their blood."

"I heard of *The James Gang*," she replied. "So you are that Shiloh? I had a feeling there was a reason to trust my intuition enough to phone you. I am willing to do any kind of work that is legal—no matter what the pay is just to get back on my feet." She hesitated in reaching out her hand and then quietly withdrew to sit demurely and through her demeanour, he could tell that she meant all that she said.

Amanda moved into James and Petra's spare room and in a week she was employed as a waitress in a part of the city that knew nothing of her false reputation.

"Who is she? I mean really?" James asked Shiloh. "You know that I do not dream the way you do but I saw her in that dream. Did Megan give you the rock?" he smiled his broad knowing smile.

"Yes, she did," Shiloh replied with a nod. "And I brought it back with me. But something happened—actually a lot happened—and Megan, I mean Amanda does not remember me. There were things that almost broke her trust in life and she needs time to gain that back. She speaks a good truth but she needs time to see it in action. As far as we are concerned, her name is Amanda—and I will keep calling her that for as long as it takes—for her to find herself. I have nothing but her best interest in my mind and heart."

A month went by and Petra called Shiloh to say: "Amanda is a gem. She can stay with us as long as she wants—at least until we have a baby, and I've told her so. There is no sign of a baby yet. We are not giving up but we may have to adopt. Meanwhile, James and I are eager to get back on the road part-time. And guess what—something else we learned about your lady friend. She is musically inclined, to say the least. Jake and Jenene came over last night and brought a couple of friends to jam. One of Jake's friends brought along a violin—a fiddle is what Amanda called it. She picked it up and she plays like a trooper! Seems her father was Irish and taught her to play when she was barely old enough to walk. Amanda is her middle name; she changed it when she was in prison. She is Megan Amanda O'Riley. But is not about to admit to Megan—there's a story there, something about her father that she won't even share with her new sister.

"I am happy for her. I really am," Shiloh said.

"There is something else," Petra said, bursting with information. "James wants to get together with you and the band to suggest two bands—both called *The James Gang*—or whatever, which we can work out another time. We want Amanda to join us part-time on the road—she is more than good enough. She is great. You should see how she is in her element when she plays an Irish jig. How about that—an Irish Native! And Shiloh—It is not only James that is asking when you will be visiting us—if you get my drift?"

Shiloh agreed to come over to talk about the new band idea that weekend. And it was no secret that he wanted to see Amanda. He sat in on a song or two with his drum—attempting to imitate the Irish bodhran drum that needs a two-headed drum stick. This gave Amanda no end of enjoyment. He was treated to a side of her personality that only came out during music and laughter.

"I am thinking that we have enough for two bands," James suggested over a coffee. Our music is good with about six people max. It is Earthy and Spiritual, as you know. I think we lose that homey feel with 10 or more. What do you think?"

Shiloh agreed and all the while, he noticed that Amanda was watching him. When their eyes met she would look away. "I think a rotating group would be best. That will keep everyone fresh. What do you think, Amanda? About playing for crowds on the road, I mean?"

"With a group of at least six, I like the idea. I lose much of my shyness when I start to play. I could never be out there in front like Petra but I'd really like to try—if you want me along?" Her eyes sparkled for just a second.

"When James and Petra asked you, you were already part of the band. And I would really like it if you would join us, too," he added eagerly.

In the weeks to come, Shiloh and the rest of the band would meet regularly at James' house. Then they would practice at the barn. And then a three-month mini-tour of New Rome and Kansa. Amanda picked to go with Shiloh to Kansa—for more than obvious reasons. She was not ready to be recognized in New Rome and no one could fault her for that. Petra suggested that there was an ulterior motive but then Petra was a romantic at heart—and Shiloh told her so. "But I hope you're right," he confessed.

As the three months came to an end, a good friendship had blossomed. And when Amanda returned to her part-time waitressing job back in the suburbs of New Rome, she and Shiloh had a regular weekly movie night arranged. "Almost a date," he confided to his parents.

Joseph smiled and suggested in a *Star Wars* kind of voice: "Use the flute Luke—I mean use the flute, son. That is how I captured your mother."

"I was waiting for you to ask for a date," Mary chuckled.

"What would you have said?" Joseph played along.

"I would have used my feminine wiles and not given you a no or yes. I would have blinked my eyes and smiled my smile—the one that says ask me another time."

"Son—listen to your mother. She knows the way of the Heart." Joseph leaned over to request a kiss from his wife

"Your father is right. A Native woman likes to be wooed with music and dance."

"Mom—Dad!" he exclaimed. "I am not sure I want to get married anytime soon. I am ready to be her friend for life. But a little kiss good-night might be nice," he retorted, blushing.

Shiloh had to come to grips with the fact that he was in Love. But he was in love with a dream and that may not be the woman that had become his best friend. Amanda could be happy, quiet and withdrawn at any moment. There were times on tour with the band that he almost thanked his lucky stars that he was not ready for marriage—yet. And then, one night at the movies, he realized that this was not a test. This is real life. Even he—who spouted words about unconditional Love—needed to live it. During a touching scene on the big screen, Amanda reached over to clasp his hand in the dark. And at that moment, he realized that he was right in accepting her the way she was. And that is what a true expression of Love requires of us. Anything more is about Sharing and that is each individual person's gift of Free will.

And then came the day that Amanda asked him to come along to see her mother in the home for the aged. One of the things that Petra and James were impressed about Amanda was her dedication to her mother. She admitted afterward that the hardest thing about being on the road with the band was not being able to visit her mother as much as she would like. "Even though my mother probably doesn't remember that I am not there every day," she confided to Shiloh in the car on the way to the nursing home, "her memory is strange. She doesn't remember things we talked about yesterday but she will tell me about something that happened when I was a child—which even I don't remember."

The nursing home smelled musty. That was something Shiloh noticed right off. That was enough to bring up old memories for him. It gave him shivers.

When Shiloh was a small boy, his father and mother took him to visit an aunt in a home like this. And the aunt passed away shortly thereafter.

"We need to come again," he said to Amanda. "We need to break the cycle of forgetting. Family is important, you know?"

She looked at him quizzically. "I come here quite often," she assured him that she did not forget her mother, and then she stopped dead in her tracks. "I came here when I was a small girl with my mom and dad. I came to see an aunt—I don't even remember her name. And that was the last time I saw her. I made that promise to myself as a young girl that I would never forget family again."

Just then, they came to an open room, where a number of elderly people were watching television. An aged Native woman smiled and waved. "There is my mom," Amanda pointed out.

"She seems pretty aware," Shiloh remarked.

"Maybe this will be one of those times that she remembers," Amanda said hopefully.

It was Shiloh that the older woman remembered. "Oh this is that nice young man that brought Mathew home to me," she hugged Shiloh like a long lost son.

"No, mom," Amanda sighed. "None of Mathew's friends were very nice. This is my new friend, Shiloh. You have not met him before." She gave her mother a kiss on the cheek. "See what I mean?" she whispered to Shiloh.

"What are you whispering about?" Amanda's mother asked. "I won't tell. Mandy—when is your father going to come to see me?" She seemed to have changed realities. "Her father liked to call her Mandy you know? He taught her to play the fiddle. She was his favourite. Not Mathew. Mandy—you should introduce me to this nice young man."

"Mom—this is Shiloh," Amanda introduced him the first time to the woman in this reality. He hugged her again.

They visited for about an hour and then Shiloh wandered out to the garden to let Amanda and her mother enjoy some private time. When he returned, Amanda's mother side-stepped and said. "I can't thank you enough for bringing Mathew back. He is so much help to me—isn't he? Mmmm… what is your name today?" she whispered to Amanda. "I can keep a secret."

"Amanda—I am Amanda," she assured her mother. "And daddy will come another day. Is that ok?"

"Your father? I guess not. He can't be trusted you know. You should not let your father back in this house. Oh, I like your new friend. You can trust him, that's for sure. If you ever need anything just ask Shiloh. Mathew told me that. He said that Shiloh will look after you now."

Amanda sighed and turned her face away to hide the tears. There was a story here. And Shiloh was not an outside observer. He was beginning to understand more than he could share with Amanda. "Maybe another time?" he said to himself.

* * *

And later when her mother's part of the story was complete, Amanda did not cry. She allowed Shiloh to hold her hand through it all and she went inward. "She is safe now," Amanda repeated over and over. Shiloh wondered if she was talking about her mother—or herself. "She is in a place where no one can touch her." And that was partly the truth—good enough for the moment—for both mother and daughter.

They walked back to a car that smelled of roses and Amanda fell asleep in the back seat with her head on his shoulder. "I am so tired!" she whispered and was out like a light. He carried her into the house and she slept for more than a day. When she woke, she was bright and chipper as though nothing had happened. She announced: "I am ready to join the band on the road again!"

Chapter 11

SUNDANCE: THE FIRST DAY

It was one of those dreams like the falling of the Twin Towers. Shiloh was a ghost in the dream—partly there and not. He was at a Sundance. How he got there was a mystery. No one seemed to be aware of his presence except one man. This man was familiar but he could not recall the name—it was the face that wasn't clear...

"Can I give you water?" he asked the man but neither he nor the other two dancers acknowledged him.

"No. Only they can give me water." And as he danced, another man came around with a gourd and poured some of the contents into his mouth. "Bitter!" the dancer shook his head and spat it out after rinsing his mouth. This was one of the old-style Sundances that had been banned by the people from Rome and was no longer done by most of Shiloh's People. The people of Kansa still danced in private places but they chose to fast as a form of sacrifice and tied themselves to the Sundance tree rather than by piercing. This dancer was tied to the tree by two long ropes that were attached to his chest through the piercing of his skin. Sometimes he danced back and pulled against the ropes. He had an Eagle whistle that he blew as he danced.

Shiloh was able to talk to the man but could not touch him or the two other men—one on either side of him. There were brief periods of rest when the dancer kneeled on the earth and talked. He was able to hear Shiloh but the other two men seemed oblivious.

"This is no longer necessary," Shiloh urged. "Our bodies are our sacred gift from the Creator. We should not inflict harm on ourselves in this way."

"What do you mean we?" the man may have believed that he was talking to himself. "I am dancing in the tradition of my People. This is my choice. This is my sacrifice. Is there any other thing that you do not like or disagree with? This is the way it was passed to me—the teaching. This is the way that Soma taught our tribe. What else do we have?"

"I cannot find fault with your beliefs," Shiloh conceded. "But I have found the way of change within our teachings. Some of the old ways are harsh but they worked in their time."

"There was a time for war. Now is the time for Peace. You said that—did you not?"

"Yes, I did."

"There are some things where the ways of our People might still be correct."

"Perhaps," Shiloh agreed.

"Nature's way may still be best."

"I agree that Nature is a good teacher and is always fair—even though some do not see this." Shiloh really wanted to understand what the purpose of their conversation was.

"You have the arrow?" It was more a statement than a question. "You are the one who was chosen to carry it, but it once had a different purpose. A different use—you may think. I still wonder about the rightness of this. Our ways are dying, his way is winning. Even though his life has ended—he won."

"Custer you mean." Shiloh knew this was so. "We honour change. Nature is about change. Nature is about Respect. I respect your sacrifice even though it is not my way."

"Be careful about judging. Sacrifice is the way of the One who came before—is it not? This may be your way, if you follow in his footsteps."

"It may," Shiloh agreed. "But I am about Peace. I am about telling his story differently. The people who wrote his story lived in violent times. They told the story the way they remembered it."

"And what would you call these times today? There was a man who captures a woman and her sister helps to rape and torture this woman to death. Where is the respect for the sacredness of life? And what is the outcome? The sister is set free. And the man will live out his life in prison. Where is the justice there? How can the Arrow of Truth help make this right?"

"And what else can be done," Shiloh asked in shock. "Will revenge make things right?"

"In the old way it was not about revenge. Even some stories that the White man tell have some rightness. There was a story about a boy who had a dog. This dog was his closest friend. This dog helped protect him from a wolf that was infected by rabies. This boy's dog was put to death. It was not about revenge. It was sad but the dog was mad with a disease. In the way of our ancestors, this man who was mad would be sent to the Spirit place. No revenge—but it was the right thing to do. How can the arrow help now—today? Can you tell me how Truth will make things right? How can it protect someone like this woman? Are you here to save me? What can you do? I will continue to dance in the way that I have been taught…"

The dream faded as the morning light crept into Shiloh's room.

"Old Yeller," Joseph said.

"Old what?" Mary asked.

"It was a sad story about a boy and his dog," Joseph explained. Shiloh had told his parents about the dream—at the breakfast table that morning. "What does this mean to you?" Joseph asked his son.

"I have never had a dog," Shiloh mused. "Sometimes I thought I would like to but the wolf has always seemed more of a companion to me. A wolf is the dog's relative—maybe a dog that has not been domesticated. Yet in the story, it is a wolf that attacks the boy and infects the dog which protects the boy and his family."

"And the dog must be put to death because it has an incurable madness as a result of the encounter with the wolf," Mary shook her head. "This dream is deep. And so is the story. I wonder if the writer of the story was aware of what he was saying about Nature?"

"It is about Fear," Shiloh said. "The fear that our connection with our inner Nature may infect us and drive us insane. There is a truth to the story that the man in my dream tells. But the wolf is not insane—at first. The wolf is maddened by man's encroaching on his territory. A terrible madness comes upon the wolf and it does things that it would not normally do—to protect its family—its tribe."

"But a wolf would not kill or torture one of its own. The wolf is a noble animal. The wolf is a totem of trust and respect," Mary said.

"I know this man—in my dream," Shiloh sighed. "He has matured but I know his face. This is about his fear. He is dancing a forbidden dance—one that inflicts pain. But it is his choice. He is saying something—the dream is speaking to me. He either will not or cannot accept water from me. I cannot touch him in any physical way. I have only words—but words will not save him. The teaching of our People that has been passed down is a better truth than that which would drive us insane. In our insanity we lose all respect for the Sacredness of Life. He refuses my help—I cannot save him or heal him with words. There must be another way."

Chapter 12

THE GIFT OF TRUTH

"Everything is connected," Shiloh conceded. Parts of his dream about the Sundance and his friendship with Amanda were about having a lack of control, and not being able to change or help someone that did not want help.

"When we dream, everything and everyone in the dream is part of us. This is a well-known truth by our People since the beginning of time." Mary hugged her son before going out the door for her morning walk in the woods. "What does the dream tell you about the woman you love? I know that you love Amanda and you will do the right thing."

Amanda claimed her independence. She thanked James and Petra for the hospitality then rented a small, but posh, loft in the west part of New Rome.

Next came an environmentally-friendly sports car—red. She seemed to infer what she preferred not to say vocally. But the message was clear: "I am an individual—I have reclaimed my power and my right to be free." But had she really? Whether or not all of this was true, Shiloh recognized and respected her right to privacy. With this in mind, he was surprised when she invited him over for a cozy meal and to watch a video on her tiny 15-inch television. She was very friendly and offered her back and shoulders for him to massage while they cuddled on the wicker love seat.

The movie ended on a touching scene and Amanda stretched. "I am tired," she yawned. "Be a friend and let yourself out... I don't even feel like moving. I am going to curl up here and nap for a while. I will call you tomorrow."

Perhaps the message was clear but they were close when she turned her head to gaze into his eyes. Call it instinct or the after-effects of the movie—or just nature taking Her course, but without thinking, he kissed her.

Amanda's eyes went big. She moved to the other side of the love-seat and hugged herself. She smiled but said: "Goodnight" in a low voice—almost a whisper. Shiloh took his queue and exited stage right.

On the drive home, he was amazed—at himself but hardly at her reaction. Amanda did not get angry. That would not be the Amanda that he had come to know. Their friendship had grown over more than two years on and off the road with the band. But she had not expressed any other emotion. Nor had she indicated that until tonight with the back rubs, that she wanted their relationship to change. He turned it over and over in his mind. Perhaps he had misinterpreted the situation? No, he did not have ulterior motives. He loved Amanda who was his friend. Kissing her was true to his heart. If this had been their first date, then he would have been premature—for he was a quiet young man who still lived at home with his parents. But not for the so-called normal 20-plus man and woman who might be sharing a bed on their first or second date—if you believe the hype of the movies and videos. But when he really thought about it Amanda and he had not even dated. They were simply two friends who liked to spend time together.

"Tonight might change everything," he pondered, as he quietly slipped the key into the front door lock. It was past 1:30 and his parents would most probably be fast asleep. When he passed the phone on the small table by the front door, the light on the answering machine was blinking. "Hoo boy! That was quick," he sat down on the chair beside the phone and it occurred to him that a bit of anger would almost be good. At least it might break the ice. It was Amanda's voice: "Shiloh? Please call me when you get in—don't worry about the time." Short and to the point.

He dialled her number. It rang only once. "Shiloh?" she asked. "Yes."

"About tonight—think I gave the wrong impression. Can we go back to how our friendship was before? I am not ready for this—maybe I never will be.

I am just getting my life together. What do you think?"

"Of course," he replied. "I am here to support you as a friend—no matter what—that will never change."

"Thanks. I will go to sleep now. Can I call you tomorrow? We can go over to visit James and Petra."

"OK," he replied. "Afternoon?" She had already hung up the phone.

"Amanda?" His father's sleepy voice. Joseph made his way to the kitchen. "I heard you come in and thought that a coffee might be the right thing. What do you say?"

Shiloh chuckled. "Dad—between you and mom...I don't know? It's like you guys can read my mind. And if that's true...well what do you think about a man over 20 who doesn't go on dates and still lives at home? Don't answer that if you don't want to."

Joseph smiled and pressed the button on the coffee maker. "No tea for us tonight. We need something a bit stronger. So—no dating. Are you talking about something that happened—or didn't happen tonight? Back at—uh, you do not have to answer if you don't want to."

"I have no secrets and I do not feel trapped or coddled living at home." Shiloh got two cups out of the overhead cupboard. "Sugar?"

"Yeah—the works."

"But sometimes I wonder if I am normal. I have all the normal urges—I admit to that much. But even in the Native culture, young people are...coupling... and enjoying deeper relationships at my age. Is there something wrong?"

"Nothing is wrong except some of that 'coupling' can be without any concern for responsibility or respect for each other or their actions. And what is normal? The term only applies to people who need to fit in to someone else's idea of how we should act. You are different and, as your mother likes to say, everyone is equal and unique. I am proud of how you handled yourself as Amanda's friend. Someone else might have let their feelings of 'love' take over. There was a time that Amanda would probably have agreed to marriage. Am I right?"

Shiloh nodded. "But I have a sense that if we were married prematurely, we would have fought. And I don't want that kind of relationship with someone I love. The astrological crowd say that people are drawn together to work out their challenges. That is how we grow and learn to love unconditionally—but we might not see that until after the divorce. That is all good for those who need that kind of growth—and need another person to help them find out who they are. Bless them!" he held up the coffee cup. "But I know who I am and I might even know who Amanda is—even though women will always be part of the Mystery."

"Amen to that!" Joseph clicked his coffee mug together in agreement. "I can only add that you are way ahead of where I was at that point. I only knew that your mother was the woman who I wanted to spend the rest of my life with, no matter what. And I mean no matter what—once I even thought that your mother's brothers, Bart and Simon, were going to kill me. But nothing—except an all out "NO" in reply to my proposal by the woman I loved—was going to sway me from my goal."

Shiloh laughed aloud. "But when you think of it—mom and you were not your average couple meeting in a bar or something. There is a destiny there. Don't you agree?"

"Yes, there was. And now I see that destiny sitting across from me."

Shiloh blushed—although his skin was becoming so dark that it didn't really show. "Maybe—but it is sometimes a heavy cross to bear—oops—wrong choice of words. I have a feeling though that even if I had not come along, you and mom would have done just fine—more than fine!" He downed the last of his coffee with a broad smile.

"I think I need a little shut-eye—without the dreams," Shiloh stretched and yawned. He gathered up the coffee cups and deposited them in the sink. "Oh—after what happened tonight—I have been considering something. While I was at Amanda's, she paused the movie to go to the bathroom, and I picked up a newspaper that she folded up on the coffee table. There was an article—another in the long line by that man who writes under the name Skeeter. You know the one I mean?"

"Yeah," Joseph agreed. "Trash—don't let it bother you."

"Trash it is," Shiloh conceded. "And Amanda called it that when she returned and saw me with the paper. But just the same, she had been reading the article. I am almost sure of it. He is getting way beyond personal now. He is writing smut about my choice in friends. I am wondering if I should do something?"

"What can you do?" Joseph asked.

"Non-coincidentally, I got a call earlier this week from the director of that late night talk show *Truth or Dare*. He asked me to come on his show and confront this man Skeeter. Well you know that I am not interested in confrontation but I didn't say no. I told the director that I would think about it."

"What would that accomplish?"

"Nothing for me personally but it is about my destiny. Remember that? My path is about protecting the innocent. I am not concerned what this Skeeter thinks about me and, for the most part, what he thinks about my friends. I know who they are—decent people who think a bit different than the rest of society—like me. Part of that dream I had was about this. It may be telling me that I need to find a way to bring about real justice—in a non-vengeful way. And guess what, Amanda's life has been a great injustice. I think I need to do something to help make it right. Until tonight, I wondered if she was strong enough to face the truth but I can see that she is now. She will see the truth as she chooses. That is probably what I feared."

"What can you do? Talk is…just talk. This man Skeeter is a mosquito in the truest sense of the word—it's not so surprising that he picked that name. He is all talk and rumour and gossip. He doesn't believe anything that is written except what he makes up. A self-made agnostic he calls himself. Writes in his column that he is the only true, self-made man. You would have to go a long way to change his mind."

"I don't want to change his mind," Shiloh replied. "I accept people the way they are. He has to live with himself—that is enough," Shiloh shrugged and chuckled. "I just think it may be good to present the truth—another, kinder version for his readers to look at," Shiloh thought for a moment. "I think I will sleep on it. I mean a good eight-hour deep sleep. Good night, dad. Thanks for listening."

The next day, Shiloh met Amanda at a restaurant for lunch. In the midst of a philosophical conversation about death and dying and the how and why Jesus would have raised Lazarus, he changed the subject. He told her partly what he was intending, including the bit about clearing up her reputation."

She shrugged. "Don't care either way. I know who I am and what I did or didn't do. Go for it—you are a big boy now. You kinda proved the other night that you are not afraid to take chances. Do what you need to do" Her eyes were clear and her voice as well. Almost immediately she returned to the discussion about Lazarus.

The next day, Shiloh phoned the director of the *Truth or Dare* program. "I am not confrontational," he explained. "I really have nothing to prove but I would like to set some things straight. I will agree to come on your show if you will provide a couple of props." The man agreed to get together the two things that Shiloh asked, even though he was puzzled. "They will be ready if you agree to be on the show in about a month. I'll phone you back with the confirmed date. Any hint as to what you need these things for?" the man asked. "If you had requested anything that could be used as a weapon, the answer would have been no—for sure! And all of my guests are required to be searched for dangerous objects before coming on the set." Shiloh declined to say what he had planned.

Afterward Shiloh did not have second thoughts. He did not worry about being thought of as crazy—although one might wonder about most of the guests on the show. A lot of television did not interest most of the people Shiloh knew—on and off the reservation. Many people in Kansa had a TV but it was more of a status symbol. They were also curious and liked technological toys. The so-called reality shows were more of a joke—something to laugh about, the way Mathew Hawk's Grandfather had. Shiloh thought about how the sight of people eating worms and doing things that might disgust most middle-class white people. But he sure that this was nothing more than a joke for an Aboriginal person who would not think twice about eating grubs or many other natural animals and plants just to stay alive. And the same goes for ridiculous acts that might be part of everyday living in the outback of Australia. Or have them try an old-fashioned Sundance! "I don't think so," he smiled to himself. "What kind of reality has a camera crew filming your intimate seduction of the woman in the next hut on a desert island? Or has a helicopter ready to whisk you away to the nearest hospital in case of an accidental injury? Still, people want to be entertained. So If *The James Gang* and I can do that and still give them something to think about—all the better."

In the beginning, *The James Gang* was dismissed by anyone who was not interested in good heartbeat music that made you want to move. Then people in the Roman Empire and Kansa started to listen to the songs and the occasional gentle message by the young man named Shiloh. He said quite simply; find your own path to Spirit. I am not trying to convert anyone. If you already have a religion, then learn what it is really about. Do not be afraid to ask questions. The balance of truth about Spirituality is not black or white—it is about Love or Fear. A religion that has even the smallest bit of truth is not afraid of questions and the closer the religion is to truth and God will be known by the encouragement of open Hearts and minds. That was his and the band's message almost in its entirety—for going on six years now of toe-tapping, foot-stomping body moving rock.

Somewhere about the second year of the band's growing popularity, it caught the interest of another kind of following. This group of people thought that highly regarded positions in various churches were threatened by the little band that could rock. And this fire, strangely enough, was further fuelled by a weekly column written by an agnostic and atheist called Skeeter. "Who is the band of rag tag upstarts that say that they have found God?" he wrote. "Not only that, but they claim that they have the Son of God as part of their band. He plays a Native hand-drum, no less. And sings old soft rock and folk songs from the hippy days. Who is he kidding? The second coming in a band that named itself after one of the blackest villains that roamed the wild-west. *The James Gang*! Give me a break."

Skeeter's columns went on and on and got closer to suggesting a lynching with every passing month. Mostly, the fans ignored him and the turnout for the concerts grew. He began to try other venues. The latest was a full blown, scaling exposé of the individual members of *The James Gang*. This ended with a question about the kind of man Shiloh could be to call himself a Son of God and still fraternise with people of known criminal pasts and Gays. Perhaps he was Gay himself—or bi-sexual because now he has a close relationship with a woman who was in prison for prostitution. And maybe, just maybe, this was part of why the Church found itself losing clientele. That would not bother the writer of this weekly column, being a non-believer, but it must really cause headaches for religious groups. This last article was the trash that Amanda read and threw aside.

Shiloh showed up at the front doors to the television station RBC—a government-sponsored and regulated station. Was there any other type? The only other type was triple XXX from Vega in Kansa. He wondered how a Roman Broadcasting Corporation TV station got away with the content that they pumped out into the airways. Maybe they hoped that these so-called reality shows would warp the minds of the general population so they didn't realize how much their daily life was actually controlled. Lately there was a new law created by a puppet government in New Rome and the department of Homeland Security every day that restricted some basic rights of the people.

Shiloh's train of thought was interrupted by the arrival of the security guards. They had been informed of his visit. He was then willingly subjected to a complete search for dangerous weapons. He had brought along the long deerskin shoulder bag that contained his flute, as well as his dismantled bow. This carrying case was part of his carry on luggage when he boarded a plane—it went everywhere with him. After all, an arrowless, unstrung bow and a flute could hardly be considered dangerous weapons.

"OK, you're safe," the head security guard proclaimed. "Escort him up to studio A. Make sure he doesn't pick up anything along the way and stay with him until he leaves this building." Shiloh wondered if every guest received this preferential treatment. It was no consolation to Shiloh that Skeeter would get the same scrutiny. We would not want a guest on a reality show actually causing damage to each other—would we? Like everything in New Rome, reality was closely controlled. He chuckled inwardly thinking that "when reality is so micro and macro-managed, and every technological technique and device is used to insure that everything is in its place—then this makes it that much easier for that which is not logical to pass unnoticed.

Skeeter was already seated on the right hand of the moderator. Shiloh was shown to a seat to the left of the host, and his personal entourage of two guards moved off-camera to sit in the front row with the small, studio audience.

"Where should we begin?" the moderator whose name was Donald Baker suggested. "Call me Don for starters. And you are Shiloh. Any other name that you go by? Son of God or what do your friends call you?"

"Shiloh is good."

"And you Mr. Skeeter? Your real name is Thomas Bartholomew? I do my investigation you know."

"My name is not a secret," Skeeter snapped. "I put it on everything I write—just below the name on my column. Could we just get on with this? You can call me whatever you want to. I am not the one who is telling lies and pretending to be someone I am not."

"So this is to be the focus of our little discussion today?" Donald Baker was enjoying this already. "It seems that Mister Skeeter thinks you are lying. Are you?" he addressed Shiloh directly.

"I could not lie if I wanted to. It is not in my nature," Shiloh replied. "I follow the Native Traditional way. The basic Native teaching is that everything is Sacred—including the words that come out of our mouths because they originate with the air that we breathe and pass through our Heart. I speak from my Heart—I do not lie."

"You don't lie!" Skeeter hissed through clenched teeth. "Your whole life is a lie—including those stupid messages that you preach at the rock concerts to thousands of screaming teenagers. I am the son of Joseph and Mary!

I am the living son of God. What a load of horse…manure!"

Shiloh sighed and waited for the other man to calm down. He did not, so Shiloh replied in a calm, reserved tone: "Which of this—how much is a lie? My father and mother are most definitely named Mary and Joseph. Is this a strange co-incidence? You may call it that if you wish. But it is true. As for the screaming teenagers? Not only teens come to our concert and they do not scream. They sing with us—naturally. It just seems the right thing to do, when you hear a song about the sharing of Love—of course it causes a reaction. People start to clap and stomp their feet to the beat of the music. Soon they get up and dance and sing. We don't encourage it—it happens naturally."

"You are evading the real question," Skeeter was vehement. "Do you, or do you not, claim to be the Son of God?"

"I am A Son of God—a Son of the Great Spirit is how I say it—naturally and rightfully from birth. And so are you and you, Donald! We are all the Sons and Daughters of Spirit. Born without knowing that there is a word or a belief called sin. That is taught to us by our parents and our religious leaders or those of us who have them. Or we learn it on the street—by word of mouth. Before the black robes came among my ancestors, the Red man did not have a word for sin. Did you know that? We still do not speak a word like this in the way the church preaches it to be—like the ones who taught our children in the residential schools."

"So—this is all about revenge?" Skeeter laughed diabolically. "You think you are the second coming of Christ—to save your People from the wrongs of the White man?"

Shiloh smiled. "On the contrary. By the way, my People call it coyote medicine—the contrary way only seems that way. It is really about dealing with difficult situations in the opposite way. I am about Peace and Love. This is my Path. To remember the true teachings of the One who was wrongly accused—and who responded with Love and Forgiveness. His teaching is not at question for the Red man. It is the actions of those who pretended to talk for him. No one can talk for him—not even a man called Shiloh. I can say words but truth is only known by the actions I take."

"Fancy talk," Skeeter responded. "It is just the kind of talk that you say and do not do. You talk about teaching us to look for the best in ourselves but you spend your time traveling and sleeping with criminals and Gays and prostitutes."

He finished with a look that said "so there!"

Shiloh smiled serenely. It was as though the universe, the Great Spirit or the angels had sent this man when he needed him. And he knew that this was the truth. "I am guessing that you have not read the Bible that you say you deny as containing any truth. Do not put something or someone down, just because you don't agree with everything they say, or the way they say it. It is not my way to dwell on what is written in books—any book. But that does not mean that I do not like to read a good story. And every story that I read has some truth. I have traveled the world and heard many people tell their stories. And guess what—the story that comes from the heart is the purest sharing that I have found."

"What is your point?" Skeeter shook his head. "Preaching and Preaching. That is all I hear. What is the point of this?"

"There is a story that amazed me about the One who came before. My father told me about it. It seems that this Jesus spent time in company with friends like mine. Real people. That's what they are and I love them all for who they are. Mostly though, when I was offered the gift of friendship and really got to know the men and women that I travel with, I have found that they were wrongly accused. It is no co-incidence that the symbol of your justice system is a blindfolded woman. My People's way of arriving at the truth may be considered harsh but it can be painfully open and just. One of these ways is to sit in a circle with the person who is accused and the person who is doing the accusing and work out something that is best for both."

Shiloh paused and saw that Skeeter shrugged and looked to the moderator for...? "I am getting there," Shiloh said. "Let us look at the crimes that you say my friends are guilty of. And this is my take. Just because a person is found guilty by the high court of this land, does not always mean the judge has arrived at the truth. Sometimes it is true but often lacks the compassion to look beyond things as they appear. Horse manure is something that, if thrown against a wall, will stick. But is the wall guilty of creating the mess? One of my friends is guilty of assault—of physically throwing a person out of his home when the person stuck his foot in the door declaring that he was there to 'save' my friend from his sins. Is he guilty?"

"Yes," Skeeter replied. "But I guess I might have done the same. But your Gay friend is breaking the law and should be made accountable for his actions."

"I know the saying: when in Rome...." Shiloh replied. "My friend is not alone in his actions. Yes—it is against Roman church law—based on someone's interpretation of the Bible. But who is the Bible written about? The man that the Bible is supposed to be written about cannot be quoted as being against a man loving a man nor a woman loving a woman. And if there are quotes that you think are saying this, then look further. Look at the man in question—the man who spoke about Forgiveness and Love. In the Traditional teaching of my People there is an answer for me at least. All Love is good. It is the Right action and Respect that we teach. But we cannot—I cannot—and I believe the One who gave me his memories would not—judge a person who is doing no harm, but is loving in the best way that he knows."

"And the prostitute?" Skeeter was calming down just a little. "I guess you will say that she was put in prison unjustly? You seem to think you have an answer for everything."

"I do—have an answer, I mean. Or I could not sleep as soundly as I do at night. My friend—who by the way I love very deeply and with great respect—is innocent of the charges she was convicted of. She and her mother ran a home for wayward women. Out of their own pockets and with the help of donations, they provided a place for women who were selling their bodies to live. And my friend is guilty ONLY of spending time on the streets with these women. She is not a prostitute and, even if she was, I would know that there were reasons that drove her to this. I know her as a friend—a close and trusted friend and no more. I do not really care what anyone thinks about me—but it troubles me to see a woman with a heart that full of selfless love judged so wrongly."

"Ah ha! We struck a sore point did we?" Skeeter was gleeful. "You and your religion or non-religion—whatever you call it. You are just like the rest of us. Except you think you have the answers. But you don't, anymore than I do—or anyone else on the street. At least I admit it but you go on and on about Truth and Lies and protecting the innocent. Well, tell that story to a mother and father of a child that is abducted and murdered late in the park at night. I have been there as a reporter when they find little girls floating in the river. I am not crazy, but if I were, how would your words about truth save a child if it were my intention to harm? You cannot save a single one—no more than the man who you claim to be in Spirit!" Skeeter was agitated again.

"There is an answer," Shiloh replied gently. "Or at least the beginning of an answer. And it is in making People responsible for their actions. This begins with the awareness of Truth that you mention. We need to be accountable. And we need to be taught that we are divine Sparks of Spirit from birth. That is the start. And we need to know that Spirit sees everything that we do or think of doing. But, I can see that you're ready to ask, 'how does this happen?' Start with the Truth—not judgment. We cannot escape the truth but it is not our right to judge without compassion."

"Sure—sure, good words again. But how do you stop me from doing what a psychopath will do? I am the man who is following that little girl. How do you stop me? Especially when you are a pacifist—a peacenik whose only weapon is forgiveness?"

"Vigilance, to begin with," Shiloh squared his shoulders. "Also, I do have a weapon. It is more than the finger-pointing of sin. When my People knew that they would be defeated, they created an arrow. This arrow was pulled from a man called Custer and given to me. This is the arrow that recognizes and honours change for my People. But it is appropriately called the Arrow of Truth."

"I don't believe a word you are saying," Skeeter laughed. "Who do you think you are talking to? I am the original show-me man. I only believe what I can see."

"Then perhaps a demonstration is needed?" Shiloh turned to the moderator. "Can you bring out the things I asked for now?"

"OK," Donald Baker replied. "I still don't see the point either." And he motioned to a couple of stage hands to comply with Shiloh's request.

"Let us go along with your story about being the evil man who is stalking a child," Shiloh suggested. The other man just shrugged. "You see before you a large sheet of steel. It looks about an inch thick, at least," he turned to the moderator again.

"Actually it is just more than an inch—closer to two. Even a bullet from a rifle could not penetrate it. I hope you don't have a gun in the bag." He noticed that Shiloh was reaching into the long deerskin pouch that contained his flute.

"No. I was searched remember. There is no gun in this pouch. But here is this." He pulled out his bow and bent it with his knee to attach the bow-string."

The guards made a move to get up. But the moderator motioned them to remain seated. "He does not have an arrow. Remember that you checked him out personally." The guards nodded uncertainly and sat back down. "Are you going to tell us that you have this invisible Arrow of Truth that you spoke about?"

"Yes," Shiloh replied. "Please place the apple on a chair behind the steel wall," he instructed the stage hands. "Or would you agree to a bit of William Tell?" He asked the man called Skeeter in a playful voice.

"No bloody way!" the other man exclaimed. I don't trust him," he yelled at the moderator. "If he pulls an arrow out of that bag of his, I am going to sue you and your station for allowing me to be put in harm's way." He squirmed in his seat.

"I am sorry to inform you that I already did—pull an arrow out of the hat—so to speak." Shiloh tested his bow and smiled. I have the Arrow of Truth that I told you about—or weren't you listening? Strange thing about truth—if you are not looking for it or if you are not open to it, you will not find it. This Arrow of Truth cannot be seen or grasped by someone who does not expect to see it. Here—let me show you." He placed an object on the moderator's table.

Everyone gasped. It was an arrow.

"You can see it now because I told you to look for it. But you should not always believe that the truth is what anyone else says it is. In this case I am not attempting to lie or make a fool of anyone."

The guards leapt to their feet and rushed to the front table. Shiloh moved out of the way as they attempted to pick up the arrow, but to no avail. He shrugged. "Truth cannot be grasped by anyone who is not open to understand it," he explained. "This arrow that you can now see is not a weapon. If you would open your minds, you would know that."

The guards addressed the moderator. "Do you want this person escorted to the front door?"

"No—I am interested in what he has in mind." Shiloh guessed that it would be a big boost to his ratings if what he thought could happen, did happen.

Skeeter shouted in fear. "Are you crazy, too? He could shoot me with that arrow. It is real! Don't you see it?" He tried to grab the arrow but came up with air, just like the guards.

"Would I be able to pick it up?" Donald Baker asked, rather hesitantly.

"Of course—if you are open to what it is about," Shiloh replied.

"I don't think I need to try, then." The moderator sat back in his chair. "I am only here to listen to both sides. "I admit that I do not understand what this Arrow is all about."

"You fool!" Skeeter appeared to be ready to bolt for the door. "He is going to shoot it at me—can't you see that. He came here to get revenge for the things that I said about him and his friends."

"No," Shiloh said in his most comforting voice. "I do not want revenge against anyone—not even you. But—if someone were to threaten a child or an innocent person, or someone were about to physically hurt the woman that I love, I would not think twice about drawing this bow and sending this arrow into the place that would do the most good in stopping what they had in mind. This may be the only difference between the One who came before and me—I don't know that for sure. And I hope I am never called to find that out—but that is my truth."

While he was talking, Shiloh slowly picked up the arrow up and gently rocked it in his hand and then in one fluid movement, too fast for anyone present to have moved to stop him, he fitted the arrow to the bow and sent it on its way to its destination. A solid "thunk" was heard behind the steel make-shift wall.

"God!" one of the stage hands exclaimed. "He hit the apple right through the steel plate." He stepped forward and held up the apple with the arrow in it.

Shiloh just calmly resumed his seat.

"Give it to me," the moderator requested. He was not about to give Shiloh a second chance. The man handed Donald Baker the apple and the arrow. "I can touch the arrow now," the moderator said. He broke the apple and took a bite. "Pretty good—don't you think?" he handed a piece to Shiloh and Skeeter. "It's time for us to go to a station break."

When they came back from the station break, Skeeter had taken his leave. Shiloh and the moderator were eating the last of the apple.

"Kind of appropriate, don't you think? The apple I mean?" Shiloh chuckled and began to eat the apple core.

"You mean like the Adam and Eve thing with the apple?" The moderator was enjoying the moment. "It certainly fits I want the viewing audience to know that there was nothing planned and I didn't know anything about this beforehand."

Shiloh nodded.

"We are about to wrap this up," Donald Baker smiled broadly. "Are there any last words you want to share?"

"I would like to say something about truth—as I see it," Shiloh replied. "There is a truth that I see that puzzles me to no end. This is about justice in our world. War is never a good thing. As a result of war, many innocent people suffer. But sometimes, when our Hearts will not let us look away, we need to take the right action to protect the innocent and those who cannot protect themselves. There was genocide in a far-off African place that all the people of the world watched and only a brave group were sent there to only observe—so they were denied the ability to defend the helpless being butchered. This happened, I am told, when I was a small boy. Perhaps I dreamed it—but I do not think so. All I can see is that this African nation did not have resources like oil or gold. All that they had were Sacred lives that needed protecting. Where is the truth in this?"

This program called *Truth or Dare* was one of the few that still used a live feed with a 20-second delay that wasn't used at the end of this particular show. In the days to come, Shiloh learned that the show had been cancelled—the reason given was lack of commercial support.

Chapter 13
ANOTHER GIFT OF TRUTH AMANDA'S

The day after the television show, Shiloh and the band were scheduled to play a local concert. No co-incidence there. He had discussed this with the other members—including Amanda—and they all agreed that it was a good idea—no matter how the TV show turned out. They were a family first and could see that Shiloh would be true to his beliefs. The show in the park was about their support for his ideas and beliefs, no matter what fall out resulted from the Television show the evening before.

When he showed up, the band members stood in line to thank him, except for Amanda who was nowhere to be seen. When they were all set up, and the crowd had gathered, Shiloh took one last look around and Amanda was unpacking her violin.

It was a clear, starry night when Shiloh stepped to the microphone and said: "Hello New Rome—we are *The James Gang*." A loud resounding applause followed that seemed to never end until he held up his hand. "Before we get started," he said "I want to thank all of the fans that have supported us. You are the reason we are here. You are our inspiration." Another deafening round of applause. "All of *The James Gang* could not be here tonight," he explained. "We are two Bands now, as some of you know. Some of the original band—founded by my brother James and his wife Petra—are doing a concert like this in Dallas." He looked at his watch. "Unless they are on a different Indian time, they should be starting now as well. We agreed to these two concerts to show the kind of family that we have—on both sides of the Red River. To show that we are all connected by music. Music is the universal language of brotherhood." There was applause and whistles of agreement.

"I will now introduce the members of this *James Gang*—in reverse order of their names." There was reason to this bit of theatrical madness that those who were true fans could guess.

"This is our newest member, Thomas, who plays the flute." The applause began, and continued until he held up his hand again.

"This is Simon—on bass guitar." Another good round of applause as Simon bowed and played a few notes. And so it went with long and thundering applause for each member as they were introduced:

"I am Shiloh." he said. "I do the talking, a bit of singing, and I play the hand-drum." He held up his drum and sounded a few notes. Again the applause until he signalled them that he needed to speak.

"And way back there, beside that pretty lady, is Lucas on the regular, but essential, drums. Lucas is also one of the original members. Give us a few of your essential drumbeats Lucas."

"And up here again, by my side, is my good friend Jude, who as you know, plays a very mean lead guitar." Jude got one of the loudest applauses yet and he played a few riffs of *All Along the Watchtower*—like Jimmy would have done.

And then when there was absolute silence, Shiloh introduced: "And way back there beside Lucas, you remember, the pretty lady who will win your heart over with her Irish fiddle—the way she has mine—my best friend: Amanda." Amanda bowed gracefully and played a wee jig. When she finished, the crowd would not stop and they started a chant: "Amanda—Amanda—Amanda." They would not stop until she came forward to stand beside Shiloh at centre stage. It was their way of telling her that they recognized her as one of their own. She played a full round of the Irish washer woman and bowed in appreciation. Then, before joining Lucas at the back of the stage, she turned and thanked Shiloh with a kiss—much to the loud approval of the large crowd in the park.

While she was hugging him, she whispered in his ear: "Thank you for the support. But who is this woman that you said that you loved on national TV—the one you think you might need to protect?" And as she left his side, she winked a sly Irish wink. "I might want to meet her someday?"

* * *

In the months to follow, some things changed, most things remained the same, including Shiloh and Amanda's "friendship at a distance". They went nearly everywhere together, while apart. And seemed to enjoy the way things were—like an old Streisand song—until a summer day when the band was off tour. Actually, they just ended a long drawn out tour of Kansa and when everybody else had packed up the vans and headed back home, Amanda hung around. She asked Shiloh if he would be a dear and drive her home later or if he was not up to it, could she bunk in James' old room at the Renauldi ranch until he was up to the drive. Mary and Joseph were more than agreeable. They both liked Amanda. "There is a young woman with a purpose—even if she doesn't understand it yet," Mary told her husband as they were returning from their walk. "I trust our son," Joseph replied. "He has a level head on his shoulders."

And then, when they came in sight of the ranch house, they were greeted to an amazing sight. Shiloh was sitting on the back porch with his feet in a basin and Amanda was washing and massaging his feet.

"Hi" Shiloh greeted his parents, "my feet were done in by all this time on the road and Amanda thought it would be a good idea if I soaked them."

"Hi," Amanda looked up from her foot massage and said: "I had this bottle of oil that I carry for just this kind of emergency." Her long black hair was upbraided, hanging partly to her waist, getting entangled in the wash basin. All in all, they had obviously been enjoying an almost intimate moment, laughing and joking together.

"Carry on," Joseph suggested. But once inside he whispered to his wife. "Do you see what is going on?" He seemed surprised, and almost in shock.

"Of course—I can see love taking its natural course," Mary replied.

"Yes—that too, but there is a passage in the Bible you might not have read. Some people call it the story of the Alabaster Woman—or the Woman with the Alabaster jar."

"I don't see the point. What is this story meant to signify?"

"Well, you know how we wonder; at least I do, about the coincidences between our son and Jesus? I can see that there is a connection between them—but sometimes it scares me," Joseph shook his head in wonder as they watched the two interacting on the porch.

"I firmly believe that we make our own destiny," Mary stroked his head and shoulders. "Even if there are many things that seem the same—a prophesy is only as good as the outcome. And that is the choice of all that are involved, especially Shiloh. What is this story that has you all worked up?"

"I am not worked up, well, yeah I guess I am. I am blown away! The story goes that Jesus was visiting someone and a woman came in. She was a known prostitute—some even say she was Mary Magdalene. It's complicated because you know that Mary Magdalene was not really a prostitute, just falsely accused...."

"Like our Amanda whose name is not really Amanda?"

"Yes, well, this woman got a basin and started to wash his feet with her hair. When did you ever see Amanda without her hair in braids?"

"Never," Mary replied. "And my name is Mary—and yours...? But there are important differences that you are missing. Like the little fact that his mother is a Native American. And although our People believe in prophesies and visions, we believe that they are a warning or a message from Spirit of what is to come. And the reason for these prophesies is to help us change the way things might turn out if we do not live in a respectful balanced way. As I said before, I can only see love taking its time. It will all work out with or without our help. I have faith in our son, too."

Mary started to prepare supper when Shiloh and Amanda came in from the porch. "Can I help?" Amanda offered.

"Of course—I would be happy for the assistance but what are we going to do with these men who are milling around and underfoot?" Mary winked at her son.

"Well, if this was a different household, we men might grab a place in front of the TV to watch football or some such sport. But my hobby is woodworking. My job is my hobby," Joseph announced. "And I have a project on the go that you might give me a hand with, if you are up to it?" he suggested to Shiloh.

"Sure, dad." I am invigorated now. The healing touch of a woman never ceases to amaze me."

"It was the water and the oil, smart ass," Amanda apologized. "Oops sorry folks that just slipped out."

"We are not in the dark ages here," Mary answered. "My ears have heard worse—much worse. Now you men have been told—scat."

Soon the potatoes were peeled and the salad was ready. All the time Amanda worked in relative silence, humming an Irish ditty but refraining from talk. When they were finished the preparation and waiting for the food to cook, Mary broke the silence.

"I have never seen you with your hair down," she remarked. You certainly do have beautiful hair. Must have taken you a long time to grow it that long?"

"Yes, thanks—most of my life. I mean since I was a little girl. Funny thing, though. When I visited my mother in the hospital, sometimes it was like she was another person—but still my mother. She asked me: "When did you change your hair? I liked it down." And one time she asked me why I coloured it. My hair is naturally black. I take after my mother. My father was Irish you know—so I guess there was always a chance I could have been born with red hair. But no such luck. I upbraided it just now because I need to wash it when I have time."

"How about now?" Mary suggested. "I can help you wash it in the sink?"

"Oh thanks Mrs. Renauldi, but it would be too much of an imposition."

"Mary—please call me Mary. And it is no trouble at all. I miss having another female around. I had a daughter. I guess Shiloh might have told you. She passed away when she was small. But that's what's gone by. Anna will never be gone for any of us living in this house. Now how about the hair?"

Mary checked on the food and joined Amanda at the sink. Amanda really did have long hair—down to her waist. But with Mary's help, it was soon washed, rinsed, and towel dried. Light conversation led to: "I really like Shiloh, Mrs…I mean Mary. I like to be around him and he is so supporting—almost like a brother but more."

"Do you love him?" Mary was someone who led with her heart.

"Wow—I…I guess I do. When I think about it."

"Love is not something we need to think about," Mary suggested. "It is something we feel in our heart. But I guess the trick is to figure out what kind of love it is that we feel for a person. I am not about match-making—especially for my own son. I care about both of you and friendship is never a bad choice."

"That is a great thing for you to say," Amanda wrapped the towel about her head. I have an admission—just between us. I do love Shiloh but I know in my heart of hearts that we could never be married. I am strong—on the outside—but I have things—I can't really put my finger on them. They rise up inside me when I get emotional and they scare me. I could never honestly marry someone I love and deny my emotions. It wouldn't be fair…" she trailed off in thought. And then something attracted her attention.

"Is that Shiloh's Pipe?" Amanda asked. "He told me about it once."

"What did he tell you?" Mary brightened at the direction this conversation was headed.

"Only that he decided to carve the pipe bowl. He seemed satisfied that the time was right. What do you think he was waiting for? Shiloh told me that the pipe stem was one of his first woodworking projects. That was years ago. I wonder why he waited this long to carve the bowl?"

"Things happen and we need to honour our growth," Mary replied. "You know the thing about there being a right time?"

"I am of the belief that we make our life happen—that we choose the right time ourselves. What do you think?"

Mary was about to make a rather guarded reply about knowing when the time was right in our hearts. But Amanda had already stepped up to the mantle where the pipe was resting. "This is beautiful," Amanda said. "Did he finish the bowl?"

Mary thought for a moment. "Yes—just about a week ago. But he has not smoked it yet. You know that there is a ceremony involved—concerning the joining of the pipe stem and the bowl? They are not to be joined except when you are going to smoke it."

"Can I see the bowl?"

It was on the mantel beside the pipe and Mary almost said no—that it might not be a good idea. But instead, she urged: "Be careful, it is fragile. And if you don't know, our People, the two-legged, respect the Stone People. They are our Grandfathers and Grandmothers. They are the keeper of memories."

Something inside Mary's head cried out but she recognized this as a logical fear and she chose to say nothing as Amanda picked up the pipe bowl.

Amanda turned from the fire-place with the carved pipe stone cradled in her hands and she began to say: "It is Beaut...iful" and her face changed. She sat down in the nearest chair, clutching the pipe bowl to her bosom and she began to sob. It was a deep, uncontrollable sobbing, accompanied by tears that streamed down her face.

Mary ran to the screen door and called out: "Shiloh please come in here—quickly." Then she returned to comfort the sobbing young woman.

"Mom?" Shiloh appeared at the door. "What's wrong?" And then he joined his mother, kneeling by Amanda. He put his arms around Amanda and said softly: "Amanda? Amanda what is wrong?"

"Nothing is wrong," she sobbed and gasped hugging him with all her might. "Everything is right. I am crying because my mother is gone. Like I should have done before. Even though I remember now—that she is not really dead. And I remember where she is. And Shiloh—I remember so much more than that." And saying this, she drew him closer and kissed him deeper than he could ever remember—except it was exactly as he remembered.

And when the kiss was done, they both were out of breath, and he held her, still sobbing and now laughing, in his arms.

"Mr. and Mrs. Renauldi—I feel like I need to re-introduce myself. I am Megan Amanda O'Riley," she announced while attempting to stop the tears. "I changed my name while I was in prison, and I forgot everything I didn't want to remember. It didn't help getting that whack on the side of the head. Shiloh healed the bruises but the rest was up to me with his help and support. You don't know how close I came to remembering. Sometimes I was this close but there was a fear—like a wall or a curtain that I did not want to look behind."

"Why didn't you say something?" she asked Shiloh. "You must have known all the time. How long would you have waited?"

"You are healthy and strong—that is all that was, and is, important to me."

"I suggest a bit of a walk in the woods," Joseph said with a huge smile. "It is clear that you both have a lot to talk about. Come back when you need to eat and supper will be waiting for you."

They walked into the woods in silence, their hands entwined. After awhile, Amanda stopped and holding onto both of his hands she faced him with a twinkle in her eyes. "What name would you like to call me now? I am really the woman you met in the dream. I remember asking you to find me."

"I did find you," he replied. He kissed her tear-stained eyes and then her mouth and he whispered in her ear.

It was nearly dark when they returned to the ranch house. They were slightly flushed in the face and the tear stains were gone. "We found a stream," Shiloh explained to his parents who were sipping a coffee and relaxing on the deck. "Man—am I famished. I'm ready for that supper now. How about you, Amanda?" Mary shared one of her patented smiles with Shiloh's father as she got up and opened the screen door to go warm up the food.

"Let me help," Amanda requested. "You men can enjoy being waited on—but just be warned it won't always be like this way." She gave a friendly kiss Shiloh's cheek."

"Looks—and sounds—kinda serious," Joseph commented. He stopped himself from tousling his son's hair the way he did when Shiloh was a small boy. "You grew up fast. And there is nothing like the company of a fine woman like Amanda to help do that around."

"Dad! Good grief—nothing happened that would be unbecoming for a son of the Great Spirit—or a son of Joseph Renauldi, for that matter."

"You don't have to explain to me," Joseph chuckled. "I can't think of anything that could happen between a man and woman who respect and love each other that God would not approve. Are we looking at an early marriage?"

"I haven't asked Amanda. I still need to get to know her. She is like a new person. But I can't fool you, of course. I will ask her. I'll take my flute along and propose in the Traditional way."

"Well—don't wait too long," Joseph suggested. "Nature has a way of taking Her course. If your mother would have agreed to skinny dipping, you would have come along a bit sooner than planned," he chuckled, standing up and offering a hand to his son. "C'mon in—we mustn't keep the women waiting—that is my first rule in a good relationship."

The next day, Shiloh took Amanda shopping in the nearest town. "What are we looking for?" she asked, being intrigued.

He parked outside a store that sold bathing suits. "Precaution," he suggested with a broad grin.

"Precaution? For what reason?" her eyes twinkled. She didn't have to guess. "There are other kinds of precaution, you know?"

"I know but I love you and there is something—a moment that I want us to save until…"

She replied quickly." "I don't want to play out the Adam and Eve trip—even though there was a bit of that the other day. I mean I don't want to seem to be tempting you but it seems to me that if we love and respect each other, it is the same to me as being married in the eyes of the Great Spirit. I trust you and I have lost that fear of you being like my father."

"It's not about guilt trips," he reassured her. "There are still some things we need to talk about—things about me that you might not know—that is, if we are going to be married. You have not said yes, yet."

"You haven't asked me—yet. So if you are thinking that this is a round about way—I am waiting for the real thing and then I will give you my answer. It is a big commitment—to think about living with someone your whole life. Don't you think?" Amanda was no longer afraid, like she said, to talk openly about any subject—especially relationships and emotional baggage.

"Exactly my point," he replied. "So here we are—*The Surf Shop*. What is a store with that name doing in a desert town?" This part of Kansa was just that, with sections that included acres of old forest—somewhere between an Oasis and a mystery of times long past. "First, we learn to communicate and then we learn to love," he said.

Amanda laughed out loud. Her laughter reminded him of fairies somehow? "You have been reading too many religious books," she chided him. "You and I are Native at Heart. Love is part of everything, especially communication. OK—let's play Adam and Eve after the skinny-dipping—which some prudish people might call the fall. Do you remember your own words? To think about something with passion will trigger a reality—therefore in some dream place, we have already made love." She was teasing him with his own words, but she was also right.

"Humour me," he suggested as they entered the store. It wasn't long before he found out that being this close to the "born-again" Amanda was going to be both a challenge and a blessing. She insisted on him accompanying her into the change stall to see how the bathing suits looked. "What do you think? A two-piece or a full-body? Itsy bitsy teeny weeny or the seductive Loren Bacall ensemble?"

He was trying to explain to Amanda that he had never seen a movie where Loren Bacall wore a bathing suit, when the woman who ran the shop came over and suggested: "Can I rent you two a room? Or do you not read?" she pointed to the sign over the change stalls. "Two articles of clothing and one person only allowed in the booth at one time."

"Sorry," Shiloh stepped out. "She is really buying the suit for me…"

"Of course she is," the woman agreed. "But there are reasons we have these rules that I should not need to explain."

Eventually, they exited the shop having purchased the polka-dot number for Amanda and the plain boxer type for him. "I used to like the old movies," she explained. "But now I am more outgoing—you will just have to get used to that." She kissed him on the cheek, and slipped her hand into his as they strolled off to find an ice cream shop.

Days became weeks and Shiloh and Amanda spent most of their time in the woods by the stream. Compared to the Amanda he had known for almost three years, she could be an emotional roller coaster and the experience was new—to both of them. She laughed and cried many times in the course of their getting to know each other and by the time they were ready to return home, they had made up from numerous tiny squabbles or had agreed to disagree. When he thought about it, it was a somewhat similar relationship to how he envisioned—had they have married before she regained her memory.

"I disagree," she said promptly. "If we had gotten married before, I would have been on the defensive about my emotions. Any discussion could easily have turned into an all-out war. I know why I feel like I do about different things but now I won't be blaming those hurtful feelings on you."

"What about the good feelings?" he enquired.

"I take responsible for the good feelings as well—but I might admit that you being close to me, has had an ever-so-small influence." He could not see her face because she was resting her head on his chest, but he could sense a smile in her voice. "When are you going to start telling me your secrets? The ones that you think will change the way I think about you?" asked Amada.

"I have been doing just that," he said running his fingers through her hair and caressing her face.

"Do you think that knowing you are the son of the Great Spirit will make me love you less?" She inclined her head so she could look into his eyes. "If anything, I know that you are more tolerant and loving than the run-of-the-mill man—and not of just any White man, but even of our People. You really live the traditional ways, like our Ancestors before the White man came along and messed with our minds, filling them full of stories that they want us to believe so much so that they will kill anyone who questions them."

"That's just the point of why I am here," he explained. His mind went back to the beginning of the day. His mother and father had awakened early as planned and, after a quick breakfast, they packed the

Jeep and set out for their second home in Bethany. "I have some work contracts that need clearing up in New Rome," Joseph said. "You have a few days of holidays left. Hang around and close up… and behave yourself," he winked at his son.

"Dad!" Shiloh admonished while he was helping him pack the jeep. "I am a grown man and I have the memories of the Son of the Great Spirit—the One who came before. I have to live up to his name. I love Amanda and respect her. Even though I am tempted to follow my natural urges, I will do right by her."

"Who is to say that the natural urges are not right?" Joseph smiled. "Follow your Heart and you cannot do wrong. Don't get caught up in someone else's judgments—you told me that. I think that if you listen to the true teaching of the One my White relatives called 'Jesus', you can't be led astray. You have the advantage that the people who wrote about him did not. They wrote through the filter of their fears. Most likely they misquoted and misinterpreted his actions. Look at what they did with the Garden of Eden story. Both you and I know that it was man's own natural urges—given to him by God—that tempted him. Not Eve. She was just being the best female companion she was created to be. In your mother's words: 'face your own fears—dance to the drum that is your Heart. And if she is that important to you as she seems to be, ask Amanda to marry you'."

* * *

"Have you listened to anything I said?" Amanda's voice brought him abruptly back to the reality of the woods and the stream. "Cripes! You are his own self—you are! And from what dream did you just return? I know for sure that you are not the beast that some people north of the Red River fear in their hearts." She had heard different religious people on talk shows, discussing the young man called Shiloh, who might be the second coming or something else.

"Being a beast is not as bad as it might seem," he chuckled. "You and I know that we can learn a lot from watching the animals."

"True enough," she answered. "And what do you see the animals doing, may I ask?"

"They are disappearing—some becoming extinct, so it seems."

"But you know better, I'll bet."

"I have been dreaming," he admitted. "Not just now—I was remembering this morning. But in my dreaming I have seen where the animals are going. I was once awake in a bright place where the green and the blue were not a graphic image. The grass the trees the sky and the water are beautiful beyond most people's memory. And the buffalo were roaming free. There were People there—all colours—and they were living in harmony with the animals. Spirit spoke to me and said: "Do not be sorry for the animals that man is sending away—instead be sorry for the people who will be without the company of their four-legged and winged relatives."

"You are certainly a strange bird, my love," she rolled over to kiss him.

"There are parts of animals and birds in me," he admitted. "But my totem is the fishes that live in the ocean of spirit—Two-fishes. My Shaman name is Shiloh Two-fishes. There! Now that you know that—you can summon me at any time of the day or night."

"Really? I do like that idea," she laid her head back on his chest. "And what about me? Will you be asking me to commit to you in this way?"

"If that would be your choosing."

"I will think on that. Maybe you should play a courting song? Until then, I am one of those hard-to-catch fishes." She jumped up and dove into where the stream was its deepest.

Chapter 14

Is This My Destiny?
Sundance (The Second Day)

Sleep came quickly to Shiloh. One minute he was alone in his bed—and the next he was back at the Sundance.

"So, you returned?" The dancer acknowledged his presence.

"I cannot let you dance alone," Shiloh answered. "I would help you, if I could. I would give you water."

"You cannot help me." The man paused just long enough for one of the men from the big teepee to offer him water from a gourd. "Bitter—still bitter," he spat it out and resumed dancing. "I will dance alone. It is my choice—it is my dance. No one can dance for me."

"But why do you dance?" Shiloh asked. "What is the purpose of this painful sacrifice?"

"You will know when the time is right," the dancer replied. And then he said: "You need to change your beliefs. You need to change your memories. Look deep inside and learn what HE was about. Was he able to save even one person? It is written that he performed miracles. It is written that he healed many people—even raised the dead. Will this be your destiny? Or will you die in vain?"

"No!!!!"

Amanda's voice woke him from the dream.

"Are you OK?" he shouted in a hoarse sleepy reply.

Slowly his door opened and Amanda appeared. She had been sleeping in the empty bedroom next door. "No, I am not OK. Can I come in?"

"Of course. Is something bothering you?" he asked. She sat on the end of his bed.

"You can't believe this can you?" She thrust a Bible in his direction. She had been up late—reading in bed. He checked the clock. It was nearly 1:30 in the morning.

"Believe what?" he enquired. "All of it or just part? What did you read that bothered you?"

"Nearly all of it—I jumped to the last chapters. It is violent and scary. I thought this book was supposed to be about love? It is about wars and judgment. And the part about Jesus? That starts out great. He is a saviour—they say. He has come to change the world. But they don't want to listen to him—so they torture him to death. How can that be about love?. And the worst part is that you believe you are re-living his life!"

He sat up and Amanda collapsed, sobbing in his arms. He just held on, until the shaking subsided. "Better?"

"NO. How could it be better? I lost my mother—even though I know that she is not really dead but she is not here either. And I lost my life—I was accused and convicted without evidence—and now I might lose you, just when I was beginning to think life was fair and good and full of love!" She began another bout of sobbing again.

"A lot of people, Red and White people—all colours—believe in this book," he said when she had calmed down again. "A lot of people claim to find hope in the words—but I agree with you. You have to look hard—beyond the war and the judgment and the prophesies of the end of the world. You have to find the real man—the real Spirit of Jesus is in there somewhere. According to my memories, he is misquoted and his actions mostly misinterpreted. But that could only be my take. Sometimes I wonder but then I find myself in a situation similar to something written about him, I have feelings that go way beyond the things that were written about him. His was—and is—more than the sum total of any book. I remember the story about how our Native ancestors—yours and mine, Amanda—were surprised when the black robes said that all of their God's knowledge was in this one book. We wondered if he was dead. Before the ideas of sin and guilt were forced upon our People, we were able to talk to the Creator of All Things and he answered our prayers." Shiloh sighed and hugged her close. "No. I do not believe that this book holds all of the answers. Sometimes, I see it as an historical account of the life of someone that they did not understand."

"And what about you?" she whispered in his ear. "Do you believe that it is your destiny to be tortured and put to death for your beliefs?" she sniffed back the tears that threatened to come again.

"I believe it will be part of my destiny to stand up for the truth, to speak for those who cannot or are fearful to speak for themselves. And to answer the question that I hear you ask from your heart—yes, I am prepared to sacrifice my life, for you and everyone who needs to be protected from false accusations and injustice. That is my destiny—and that is my choice."

The room went silent. And eventually Amanda spoke again. "I don't know if I can live with that." Her voice was raspy after all the crying. "At this time, I can't think of living without you—especially if you were to die, as you say, to protect me. This is too much for me to imagine. Can we just forget and spend this one night together? I am not suggesting sex—all that aside, I want to wait until we are married, too. Just hold me and we will think about this in the morning."

The morning light was streaming in his bedroom window. Shiloh rolled over to find Amanda gone. He jumped out of bed in alarm and found her talking on the phone in the kitchen. This was the morning that they planned to meet with Mathew Hawk in Dallas. It would be a pleasant drive—they would stay over and drive back to close up the family ranch before heading back to Bethany.

"I need time alone," Amanda announced. She was almost the Amanda from before her memories came back. "I need to think. Please? I just phoned and made arrangements to take a plane back to New Rome from Dallas. It will give you time to think as well. Then, after you have had your time with Mathew, you can drive the van back and I will meet you in Bethany."

He agreed. She had already made the plans and seemed resolute. He had to respect her right to her own thoughts, at the very least. The drive to Dallas was pleasant enough. Amanda was quiet but not unresponsive. And he was kind enough not to bring up any of the conversation that they had the night before. She promised to meet him back in Bethany. Whatever needed to be resolved would be accomplished then. "True Love has its tests and I am prepared to accept the outcome," he said this over and over to himself, as though he sensed something was coming—but he was still in for a major surprise.

He saw Amanda off at the airport in Dallas with 'meenawa'—'see you again'. Then he met with Mathew Hawk to share and bring Mathew up-to-date about the journey of *The Arrow*. He had talked to Mathew over the phone but due to the suspicion that the phones might be tapped, he was never able to tell the whole story. Then he was on the road again, back to the Renauldi ranch, to close it for the winter—or maybe forever. Somehow that feeling pervaded.

When he arrived at the family home, he opened the door to see the light on the answering machine blinking. "Amanda? Already?" he smiled and pressed the button. It was not Amanda. It was James. His voice had a quivering sound to it. "Shiloh—phone me as soon as you hear this. Something has happened. James." That was all but the feeling that had been troubling him rose from his stomach to his heart and stuck in his throat as he dialled James' number in New Rome."

"James?" that was all Shiloh could say.

"Shiloh, it's our mom and dad! They are gone. There was an accident and they are gone!" James broke down over the phone.

"Tell me what happened?" Shiloh said in a low voice when James had finished crying.

"The other day, just after mom and dad got back from Kansa and went for their daily walk they got in the old jeep to pick up groceries in town." James paused to compose himself. "They had just turned that corner, I guess—you know the one that leads to the freeway. Then were hit head on by a transport truck coming the other way. The policeman who showed up at our door and said that they were most probably killed instantly. Oh man, little brother, what are we going to do now?"

Shiloh took a moment to let the reality of it all set in. "Where are they now?" he asked.

James gave the name and address of a funeral home in Bethany. "How long before you get home?" he asked.

"It will take me about a day and a half," Shiloh answered. "I need to make one stop. I need to go up to that place in the Black Hills where Soma built the medicine wheel. It is something I need to do. Have you seen Amanda?"

"Yes, Amanda is here right now. Let me put her on."

Amanda was quiet. She said simply and with great sincerity: "I am really sorry. With all my personal fears that I cried on your shoulder about, I could never have guessed this was coming. Please forgive me. I will be here for you when you come home."

"There is nothing to forgive," Shiloh assured her. "Both of us knew that something was about to happen but we did not know what. And your personal fears and feelings are important. I need you to know that. I told James that I will be home as soon as possible." Then he explained about the stop he needed to make along the way. "I am the One who came before—I have his memories and feelings. I need to go to a quiet place—a place Sacred to our People. I need to talk to my Spirit Father about this. There is a part of this Mystery that waits for me there. That is all I can say…except that…I love you."

He closed up the ranch house—the family home—and said a heartfelt good-bye in his native tongue. Then he set out in the van in the direction of the Black Hills. It was late afternoon when he pulled off the road just before the sign that said: "Welcome to Vega—a Star in the Desert". The sky was clear and cloudless, as he searched out the overgrown path that Soma would have used. There were a few footprints in the sandy soil—leading upwards and back down, no doubt left by a seeker or seekers—someone questing answers that the mortal world could not provide. Perhaps among those footprints were those belonging to his very own mother and father?

It was quite a hike up the mountain and the only signs of life were birds. There were small birds—chickadees that accompanied him at the beginning of the climb. But as he neared the peak, he saw one lone hawk circling overhead—as though waiting—to deliver his questions to the Sky Father.

At the peak, he found the Medicine Wheel that Soma had built—respectably undisturbed by time and travelers. He walked once around in a clock-wise direction to show his respect for this Sacred place and then seated himself on the stone that marked the West. This direction signified the end of life's journey and the beginning of another cycle. The West is the place of remembering, as the East is the beginning—with the Gift of Life. Both directions are sacred to the Dance of Life.

He had decided that the respectable thing to do would be to wait for an answer—wait for a sign. The Great Spirit would know all about him and his questions about the mystery of the life and death of his parents. He did not need to wait long—a couple of hours by the movement of the sun—but the answer came in the form of the Coyote. He recognized the sound immediately. It was out of place in these Sacred Black Hills. A great black bird that would have been invisible to any other eyes came to rest on the far western side of the plateau. Even as the engine died and the swirling winds reached his back, he knew the name of the visitor. "Emperor? What brings you to these Sacred Black Hills?" Shiloh did not move even when the man stood a few feet from his back.

The visitor circled until he stood beside the Eastern stone of the Medicine Wheel.

"I won't sit." The man wore a protective suit, with his face hidden beneath a black hood. Shiloh recalled reading that this suit would protect the Emperor from anything but an anti-tank rocket—or so it was boasted. He wore this the few times he appeared in public.

"I will not sit—not that I do not respect your beliefs but I expect that you will respect mine. These are just rocks in a circle to me. There is only one rock that is my salvation and demands my respect." He did not explain and did not need to. Shiloh was well aware that the Emperor of Rome was the head of the Church—even above the Pope.

"So be it." Shiloh stood behind the Western stone, in respect of his guest. "Why are you here?" he asked. His voice was without expression.

"You get right to the point," the man replied, "I am here to console you in your moment of grief."

"What do you know of my grief?" Shiloh asked. He walked the circle and stood looking out to the South East at the vast sea of lights that were the City of Vega. The sky was slowly becoming dusk and the shadow of the Black Hills already stretched out over the city below.

"You must know by now that I watch you and your family's every move." The black-robed figure moved to stand a respectable distance to his right. "And you must be aware that there is a connection between our fates—you and I? The only question that I find amusing is which one of us is the Beast, and which is the true Second Coming of the Son of God."

"I will admit that has given me a few smiles in the past," Shiloh replied. "But at the present, it is the least of my concern. I tire of this religious play—the one that opens its arms to the end of the world and the downfall of all life. I love this Earth and all of the creatures that are my relatives. I do not live to fulfill some future prophesy of doom. I live now—this very moment—in the grief that is the passing of my mother and father. In this way, I am just a man. If that makes me a Beast—then so be it."

"But you have proclaimed yourself to be the Son of God," the Emperor said at length. "I am aware that none of what you see below you is more than a passing interest to you. If we were actors in this play that you speak of—one of us would offer the other to be King of all that we see below. But, as I said, I have heard your noble speeches about how the Red man does not own the land. Is this because you cannot own the land? I, however, could take this country below you any time I want. Therefore, it is of no interest to me, either."

"So why are you here?" Shiloh asked again.

"I am here to remind you of your boast. If you are the Son of God, then you are the master of life and death. Why do you not bring your mother and father back to life? Is it because you are not the true Son of God? The One who is written about in the Book of Books could raise the dead. Who are you?"

"What is the fear that you have hidden in your heart?" Shiloh replied.

"My fear? What does this have to do with anything? You are evading my question."

"Not at all," Shiloh said. "I have to thank you for being the one who brings this answer to me. The question you asked is the question that brought me to this place. I am the One who knows that life is Sacred—and so is the acceptance of death. Our life has a purpose and no one can decide when that purpose has been completed—or if it ever will be. But there comes a time—only known by the Creator of all things—the Spirit Father and the person who is living in this dream. There will come a time when this person will awaken to a greater knowing—and they could chose to move on. This may all seem like an accident. Isn't it strange that some accidents are called "acts of God"? I am here to tell you that there are no accidents. My earthly father and mother have gone to their reward. Do I, in my grief, have a right to bring them back?"

"Are you trying to convince me that you could, if you wanted, bring them back to life?" the Emperor's voice hinted of a smirk.

"I could bring them back to this dream. If they were to ask. But without this request, it would not be the respectable thing to do—no matter how much I miss them," Shiloh sighed.

"You keep talking about dreams—as though your parents were dreaming. You need to come to the reality—they are dead and that is that."

Shiloh paused before speaking: "Read your Bible. Although it has been edited and re-written, there are truths to be found by those who are open to see.

When the One who came before—the one you call Jesus was about to bring someone back to life—a little girl and Lazarus—he said to those who stood near: 'she is sleeping—he is sleeping'. This was not a figure of speech. There were times that he spoke symbolically, but this is not one of them."

"Oh come on—you are not talking to one of your star-struck fans. Sleeping? And next you will tell me this is a dream? If you believe that then jump off this cliff and I will see if you wake up at the bottom."

"All of this is real," Shiloh conceded. "But it is also a dream. Every time you think passionately about what might happen, you create another life. This is the truth of your fear. Somewhere there is another life—where you have lived as a mortal—not someone who can extend his life almost indefinitely."

"How could you know this? You are guessing. Get back to the question at hand. If you cannot bring your parents back to life, then let me. I can do this. I have the secret of eternal life."

"Do you think you can tempt me?" Shiloh faced the other man. "There is nothing that could make me violate the Sacred trust, nor will I allow that to happen."

The Emperor backed away. "Are you threatening me?"

"No. And I am aware that there was a gift that was offered to you and your people in the form of an aircraft called *The Arrow*. If you had accepted this gift, it would have given you the opportunity to advance to another level in technology and Spirituality. This step forward is needed to address the prophesies that include you and I. We have yet to see what you and I and our People will need to do to change what seems inevitable. One thing I know for sure—we will need to face the challenges before us together. This is what the riders from the stars are saying. But they can't do it for us. We are all in this together, whatever the outcome. Think about this: I will extend an offer to take you to the place of your fear without harming you in the least. If you will face your fear, you will be free to think and live in a better way."

"I think I'll pass on that." The man in black backed up, and made his way to the helicopter parked at the far edge of the plateau.

The craft that was invisible to any eyes other than Shiloh's departed. Shiloh sat down again on the stone in the West of the Medicine Wheel to pay his respects for the passing of his mother and father.

Much later, after a long drive back to Bethany, Shiloh joined James and Petra and Amanda and a throng of friends and family at a local funeral home. There were many people that Shiloh did not recognize who attended and Shiloh was not surprised to hear many of them remark about how peaceful Mary and Joseph looked. "It seems like they are just sleeping."

A traditional Portuguese funeral followed at a church in Bethany and Mary and Joseph were then taken back home to Kansa where their earthly remains were cremated then scattered throughout the forest where they had enjoyed so many peaceful walks together.

Chapter 15
SHARING ON THE MOUNTAIN

The world changed after the video footage of *The Arrow* passing through the Friendship Tower was aired and discussed on every television in the Roman Empire. It might be more correct to say that it split. There were two distinct views of what it all meant. The people whose hearts were filled with fear saw this as a near-disaster and empiric evidence that nothing was safe. These people saw the potential for a disaster that did not happen. These people called for tighter security and the President of New Rome quickly complied. It became more difficult than ever to gain access to the USNR—especially via the Golden Gate Bridge. And all air travel became one endless line-up consisting of lengthy personal searches and laws that prohibited anything that might be turned into a weapon—from aerosols to toothpaste—from being carried onto a plane. Slowly and surely, the paranoia grew until the country was one step short of declaring martial law.

And then there was the other side of the coin. The people who were working in the Tower that day came home with a memory that would not easily be denied nor explained. They had a memory—like a dream of being closely connected with the men on the plane. Just for a micro second, *The Arrow* and The Tower occupied the same space in time. It was a crazy idea, to be sure, but it changed everyone who was in the Tower that day. They became believers of something that they could not explain with a logical mind. These people were interviewed over and over and not one of them expressed a feeling of fear—their lives were changed for the better. And these people joined a growing fan base that flocked to the concerts of *The James Gang*. And they brought their family and friends. Other rock bands jumped on the band wagon and the USNR was rocking with Spirit.

Two countries mourned the passing of Shiloh's parents. A day of grief was declared on both sides of the Red River—not by politicians but by the common folk. And it seemed that the people, however, left on the side of fear were those in the higher government positions.

Six months after his parents' passing, Shiloh brought out his flute during a mid-break of a concert in Dallas. The song he played and the way he played was recognized by a large Native contingent—and Amanda. When he finished playing, her answer was a very warm kiss. When the applause subsided, Shiloh promised the audience that he and his bride-to-be would let everyone know when the date was set. "You are our family—you are our inspiration," he reminded them.

Six months passed quickly and then came the news coverage of the greatly anticipated wedding on the news feed from CRN—the official voice of the Roman Empire:

"On a side note, but not to be ignored, CRN was there at the wedding, and the reception of the leader of the rock band The James Gang, Shiloh, and his girl friend Amanda. Although the official line is that they had no carnal knowledge of each other prior to this wedding, we find that hard to believe. Amanda is, after all, a former convicted prostitute and he is a Red-blooded Native "Shaman" from a reservation in Kansa. We all know about the Pow-wows and the ceremonial fertility dances that take place south of the Red River. As this reporter and any Church-abiding citizen of the Roman Empire knows, the temptation to sin is part of every man and woman. We are very sceptical about the claims of abstinence outside the Holy Roman Clergy. And this gets worse and treads on dangerous grounds. This display has gone far beyond the blasphemy of the Christian Bible.

Look at this video from the reception. In this footage, Shiloh and his 12 proclaimed disciples are seated at the head table. Amanda is at the leader's right—leaning on his shoulder. She is now claiming to be a re-born Native princess. He has just filled the wine glasses of the members of The James Gang—appropriate name don't you think?—including his prostitute wife with water from a nearby spring. And now he waits while the glasses of everyone at the reception are filled with the same water. We will not bore you with the rest of this pagan ceremony in which he says something about the water being the 'Blood of the Mother Earth' that is in his body and the bodies of everyone present. What we at CRN hope that you, the people of Rome, won't fail to see. Look at the head table—does this look familiar? Think of the Last Supper? This is dangerous. The President of the United States of New Rome believes that the time to act is now. Cut this off in the bud. It has gone too far. The official word, however, from our benevolent Emperor in Rome, is to wait and see. In his divine wisdom, the Emperor has a plan. We at CRN will wait to see how this plays out. For now, this is your CRN news reporter—sending you over to our Sports Desk."

And then there is the coverage of the wedding and reception by Kansa's only television station.

"This is CU-PID. The home of the Baby Blue movies in beautiful uptown Vega in the Heartland of Kansa. Your news reporter Shirley Many-Feathers was present at the gala event of the year—the marriage of our local and well—known Shaman called Shiloh to his beautiful Princess Amanda. As you may be aware, Amanda was recently pardoned by the mayor of the City of New Rome. In a televised interview—skipped by CRN—the mayor issued a pardon and a wish for forgiveness for having wrongly judged and sentenced a young woman who was simply in the wrong place at the wrong time. After a number of free concerts in the park in New Rome, Amanda and Shiloh and their Spirit Rock *band, called* The James Band *were unofficially named part of the family of New Rome. In case you wonder—yes the mayor is at the end of his term, and will not be running again. No surprise here.*

And now, on with our video coverage. The actual marriage ceremony performed first by a local Catholic Priest in Dallas, and then with personal vows from Shiloh and Amanda. All this took place in a Catholic church and no cameras were allowed—strange, don't you think? Anyway, here is Shiloh and Amanda exiting the church, dressed in their traditional Native regalia. Beautiful couple, don't you think? It is this reporter—Shirley Many-Feathers'—personal opinion that it is amazing how two young people, so much in love as they obviously are, could endure three years of courtship without physical intimacy. I commend them. It would not be within the beliefs of CU-PID, our Baby Blue station, to conceive of such an idea. The policy of this television station, however, is freedom—of speech and action. Therefore, a roving reporter like me can admire and express romantic thoughts that a relationship like this is possible. As far as I am concerned, it is a great thought but I guess I am a little too liberated (she winked). *They make a beautiful couple but, speaking candidly for CU-PID, they are a bit too Nice—prim, and proper—if you get my drift?*

And oh? I need to mention that the reception really touched my Heart. When Shiloh offered the water for everyone to drink—saying that it was his blood and the 'Blood of Mother Earth' well, he had me there—for at least a heartbeat...

....and now on a much lighter note—I will send you over to our sports desk to Miranda White-Tale. Miranda is the official reporter on the scene for the segment we call 'The Nude Sports'. Miranda has been on a two-week holiday on a beach in sunny Portugal where nude bathing is not allowed—what a bummer! Miranda—how about showing us your white tail?

OK. Miranda here—and here: (she did a pirouette for the camera*). And now...the Sports scene was down-right Naked this week with a major turn about for our favourite Lacrosse team. There have been major changes to our "beloved" Maples. The whole team has been sent down and the farm team from that strange country called the Rock—the St John's Rock, will take their place for the rest of the year. I have seen a few of their practices and I guess you know that I am a good judge of Lacrosse men* (she winked). *I can tell you what the men from the Rock will show the rest of the NLL—they will send a clear message: 'Et this—ehh!'*

...wellllll! Miranda! This IS prime time you know? The kiddies are still awake and might be sneaking a look.

...This is your station: CU-PID, in Beautiful uptown Vega—the only station in Kansa—returning you to our early evening programming of Baby Blue soft porn."

* * *

Shiloh and Amanda honeymooned in Portugal and then rather than go straight home, they took a number of connected flights to circle the globe in a northerly clock wise direction. This was a flight that honoured the Medicine Wheel beginning in the West, to the North and to the East, and back home to Kansa in the South. The time of the turning of the Earth was Spring—the time of new beginnings and birth. This was not a co-incidence. As the plane circled the Northern hemisphere, the sky came alive in the right window where Amanda sat. The Northern Lights—the aurora borealis—filled the sky with Mystery and wonder. "This is a good sign," Amanda whispered in awe. "We will name our daughter Aurora."

"Our daughter?" Shiloh asked. "We don't even know when you will be pregnant—much less that the child will be a girl."

"I am pregnant." Amanda answered with certainty. "If your mother were here she would tell you that a Native woman knows the moment when life is created within her body. A woman of the Earth does not need to wait for a test to confirm this. That night on the beach in Portugal—just like you were conceived. Perhaps it was the same beach. The reason is to bring the people of the Earth together. Our daughter will be like her father—Aurora will be a bringer of light. This is what I know."

"And what of her mother?" Shiloh snuggled close to share in the wonder outside and inside the plane. "None of what you talk about would be possible without her Mother. This much I know for sure."

Three months later, Jack and Jenene held a birthday party for their twins. Jack and Jacqueline were seven. During the course of the evening, Amanda was playing dolls on the floor with Jacqueline when the seven-year-old reached to put her hand on Amanda's stomach. "It's a girl," she proclaimed with her big smiling eyes.

"Yes," Amanda agreed.

"What?" Petra asked in amazement. "Amanda? Shiloh? You didn't tell James and me."

Amanda nodded her head. "She will be called Aurora."

"Man!" James slapped his brother on the back in congratulations. "You sure don't waste any time. How long have you known?"

"About three months," Shiloh explained. "Amanda told me on the plane back from our honeymoon."

"How could you know?" Petra asked. "Oh, yeah—the Native-mother thing. James? Does this work the same for Native fathers?"

James shrugged. "If anybody should have known, I would have bet on my little brother the Shaman."

"Women are part of the Mystery," Shiloh replied. "Together we create with love. That is the way of the Creator of all things. What the hay do we men know about these things? I am blessed to part of it—that's my feeling."

"Don't you think it would be a good idea to check in with a doctor?" Petra asked. "Just to be sure that everything is OK?"

"Jacqueline just confirmed what I already knew," Amanda smiled. "Children are the best teachers because they are still close to the Mystery. When they get older, society will try to teach it out of them, like it did me. But now that I have this little one inside of me, it's like I am plugged in again," she glowed, her radiant smile spread over her body.

Still, Shiloh suggested a trip to the doctor in case of complications and Amanda complied. "Three months," the doctor confirmed. "Give or take a few days. And the baby is in good health—and growing. And now, how about the mother to be? You look a bit pale—anaemic—undernourished? What are you eating? I have a small diet I'll prescribe."

"My mother was borderline haemophiliac," Amanda replied. "When I was born, she had to be rushed to the hospital and she just about didn't make it."

"Amanda," Shiloh asked. "Why didn't you tell anyone?" He really meant it. "Does this mean Amanda's life will be at risk by having the baby because she is a bleeder?"

"Not to worry," the doctor insisted, "I will check her out for the risk and make sure that she comes to see me regularly."

After a thorough check up, the doctor declared Amanda fit as a fiddle, which she found quite appropriate. "She is a bit anaemic, as I suspected, but there is no sign of the haemophilia being passed on from her mother. Make sure she keeps on her diet and bring her back to me in a month."

The West Mountain Hospital of New Rome was on the borders of the city and within a 10 minute drive from James and Petra's home. The lady Doctor had a long and tough last name to pronounce, beginning with Hazz...something or other. She told Shiloh and Amanda: "Just call me Sam—or Hazz. Most of my patients do."

In the months to come, Amanda would not miss an appointment—Shiloh promised that to himself. And when the time got close, he asked James and Petra if they would rent out their spare room again.

The best laid plans—as they say, sometimes go astray. "Whatever the reason," Shiloh wondered, "maybe there was a truth about the hand of fate."

"Maybe we should take a holiday from touring with the band?" Shiloh suggested.

"It is too early for that. Besides, I would be bored. Music is in my blood," Amanda replied.

"OK—then a compromise," Petra suggested. "Let us juggle the members around. John and Simone are eager to see more of Kansa, so let them team up with Jude, Simon, Lucas and one other, and that version of *The Gang* can do the summer tours south of the Red?"

"That sounds like a plan," James agreed. "We will put it up to a vote at next Friday's get together. That way Shiloh and Amanda can stay close to home in Bethany until the baby gets close. What think you little brother and wife?"

"OK with me," Shiloh replied, "Amanda?"

"Sure, and just so you all know—our baby will be part of some good rocking before she is born. Music is an important part of a healthy life. She needs to get a good start."

During the next week, James phoned everyone to remind them about the Friday get-together. Everyone agreed to be there and the weather was so perfect that they decided to hold the meeting outdoors.

"How about that park across from the Mountain Hospital?" Mark suggested. "It's almost the half-way point for most of us."

"What do you think about a picnic?" Petra asked James. "I will phone Simone and ask her to organize the people in the east of New Rome."

When Friday afternoon arrived, all of *The James Gang* members—the East and West members—showed up at the park across from the Hospital with food to share. Conversation was slow at starting as everyone sat in a circle of blankets and passed around the sandwiches.

Jude was sitting facing the hospital across the park on the hill. "This is kinda like the story of the Sermon on the Mount," he quipped.

"How so?" James replied.

"Well—there is the mountain," he pointed to the hospital. "And here we are all gathered, waiting for the leader to give us the latest good words."

"Oh yeah," James appreciated the joke. "Just don't let Shiloh hear you. He does not see his job as some kind of preacher, you know."

"But he has said that he has the memories and that he is the Son of God," Mark pointed out. They watched Shiloh who sat on the other side of the circle. He was too busy doting on Amanda to hear any of this.

"What my brother said," James corrected the other two young men, "is that he is A Son of the Great Spirit. He also says that all of us are the sons and daughters of the Creator of All Things. It just so happens, according to Shiloh that he remembers who he is—and all that he does—any one of us can do it too."

"Well, that sounds like the One who came before speaking," Mark replied. "That is what Jesus said to his disciples and anyone else who he thought might be able to understand. Now I see the picture. Jude, my son, do you think that you could be one of the disciples? A gay disciple? Now that's a thought!"

"I know about love just as much as the rest of you," Jude stuck his chin up. "I could be a disciple, so long as Shiloh is the leader and the teacher."

"Right you are." James was enjoying this. "Shiloh? Little brother? What do you think? Are we your disciples?"

"What???" Shiloh appeared to have caught just the last part of what James was saying. And then it sank in. "I don't see myself as having disciples. No matter what those crazy newscasters say. You know that the media likes to stir things up. They will create a story even when none exists. But—if anyone were to be disciples. I think Jude could be one as easily as anyone else. When Jesus was around he did not judge anyone. Everyone was equal in his eyes. Jude is right—anyone who is not afraid to love could have been a disciple of Jesus. But as for Shiloh—I do not have disciples, thank you very much—end of story."

"James started this band," Simone piped up. "And the name sticks. We are *The James Gang*. But the real leader now—the one who gives us a purpose—is Shiloh."

"I agree," James nodded. "We were like a ship without a rudder before my brother stepped up and sang that theme song. Hey? I just said something poetic. Did you hear me, Pet? A ship without a rudder—wow. Maybe I could be a disciple, too?" And then he gave them his patented grin. "Shiloh is right you know. Any of us could be more than we think we are. But we don't need to repeat what somebody else has done. We are doing it our way—like the old crooner Frank Sinatra—and Elvis—yet not like one of them. We are doing our part with our music and I can tell you that I am proud to be part of it."

"That's all true," Simon shifted and stretched. "But I have seen Shiloh do things—using the quiet mind, that I would like to learn to do. And the strange thing is, it is a lot like the Bible story. I have personally seen him heal people that had no right being healed—they literally threw down their crutch and walked away."

"First, Simon my friend, no one is healed that does not rightfully deserve to be healed," Shiloh said. "They are healed because of their faith—I help it along by telling them the truth—that they are as much a child of the Creator as I am. But, in the end, it is between the Creator and the person who believes. My job is not to do it for them; my job is to be the best example I can be. And as for it being like the Bible story, our ancestors knew a truth called the Circle of Life. This is a Circle that is also a Spiral that we repeat again and again. And each time we do it a little different—and each time we get closer to that inner memory of what is right and possible. I think it is a good thing to have someone that came before as an example to follow."

"I hope you aren't saying that the way that Jesus and his disciples did things was not right—or good enough?" Thomas spoke up.

"The way that Jesus taught the people and his followers was right for the times and the place," Shiloh replied. "And there is still a lot of inspiration to be found in what is written about his teaching today. But if he was here today, he would probably just need to clear up the misinterpretations. The spirit and the man that he is—is timeless. We just need to give ourselves a shake and not be stuck in believing that the written word is all there is. There is the famous quote: and the word was made flesh. I am here—and you are here. We are in this together."

"OK. I accept what you are saying." Simon shrugged. "But since we are here now—whether we call it a Sermon on the Mount, or whatever name. There is more to what we are doing or could be doing than meets the eye. I for one would like to know more."

"The more that you look for it, it is already yours," Shiloh sat back down.

"When we accept who we are, we need to accept that we have been given the gift to grow. We talked a bit about this in the dream place called the Rock. Look at what you might have troubles with—and you will see the Wall. The wall is that logical belief about something we cannot overcome. Spirit does not know walls."

"So that's it?" Thomas asked. "That is the sum total of your secret teaching?"

"That is not the sum total of anything," Shiloh smiled. "There is no limit and total nor a sum. The Traditional Native Way is about simplicity. The simple truth of this teaching is that everything is Sacred—and it is in Respect that we acknowledge the right to see each other as a separate and Loving person. The rest is in living your truth instead of just talking about it. One of the main teachings of the One who came before was that you cannot serve two masters. He said this in reference to anything that you place in higher esteem than your true Spirit—and the Spirit of all other creatures. You my friends have moved beyond that wall without thinking about it. We do not share our music and the message of family and brotherhood because we need money. Just think about this—has either of you had a concern about money or food since we started this?"

"That is right on," James agreed. "I think what Simon is saying is that we sometimes have a hunger for more than money and whatever fame it means to be a *Spirit Rock* band. I guess the main question might be related to how accepting and peaceful you are, brother of mine? We do not have the memories that you have—we have only our faith."

"But the next step in faith is to be able to extend that foot and take the next step. This is usually related to Love—like the dream that you had—because you loved Petra so much you were ready to do whatever it took. And as it is written to inspire us: 'Faith can move mountains—which may be a kind of Spiritual segue',"

"I was just thinking," Shiloh said. "How there are no co-incidences. You know well before I knew about my parents' accident, I took a trip to see Mathew Hawk in Dallas. Mathew Hawk is true to his name. He is a messenger and a Dream Keeper. He is also someone who was selected to pass on the Traditional teachings. His Grandfather was chosen before him and his Grandfather before that. When Soma returned from the Black Hills, he passed this teaching onto a boy called Seattle. This boy did not go to a White man's school. He lived the teachings of the Medicine Wheel and when Soma led his People into the desert, he was seeking something that he already had. To make a long story short, when I visited Mathew Hawk he saw this as an opportunity to pass this on to me."

"So what happens now?" Simon asked.

"Just like Mathew Hawk, I can see that Spirit is asking me to share this teaching," Shiloh replied. "Our purpose is not all about me. I do see that I might have to make a choice that will affect all of you—maybe the fate of the world as we know it. And because of this, I am prepared to share the teaching that Soma received, so that it will not be lost. Mathew Hawk does not know, who other than his Grandfather, was given these teachings."

"We are all ears," James replied. "Here we are at the foot of the Mountain. What better place could there be?"

"Actually, there is a better place for this. This is not logical teaching that I have learned from Mathew and it has already come to mean something personal for me. None of the Traditional teachings of our People have been written down. The reason for this is that someone who learns must see this as a live, breathing and growing knowledge. Like our Relationship with the Creator, everything we teach is through action or a story. It is not like gossip though because these stories are shared from the Heart. The best place to do this would be in the Black Hills where the Medicine Wheel that Soma constructed still is—after all these years!"

"I have an idea," Lucas spoke. "How about if we all take part in the first concerts of the new season? I mean everyone here. What I am suggesting is that we do the first concert in New Rome together and then to support those who will be doing the tour of Kansa, we all go to that first concert in Buffalo. Then we can go to the Black Hills together and, if everything seems right, we can go through the Traditional Medicine Wheel teachings together?"

"It sounds good to me," Shiloh agreed. "How about if we put it to a vote?"

A show of hands followed and 14 voices echoed around the circle: "Let's do it!"

Chapter 16
ANOTHER MOUNTAIN—
THE WHEEL OF LIFE

The two first concerts of the new season were an immense success and a Spiritual boost for both the fans and *The James Gang*. The first was an open-air show in a field near Bethany along with a few other *Spirit Rock* bands to celebrate the Spring Equinox. Then a similar celebration took place a week later in Buffalo, just minutes by car over the Golden Gate Bridge on the Southern side of the Red River.

After the concert in Buffalo, *The James Gang* drove to the Renauldi ranch to prepare for their trip to the Black Hills. Before the experience of the Medicine Wheel, they would do a Sweat. Years ago, Joseph and Mary had built a large sweat lodge at the ranch to accommodate many friends and family from the nearby villages. The Renauldi ranch had often been a gathering place for seekers of all skin colours that wanted to experience the "Native Way" of rebirth that takes place in the womb of a Sweat Lodge. This night, the Lodge would be filled, shoulder-to-shoulder, with 13 members of the Spirit Rock band that called themselves *The James Gang*. Shiloh had previously made a phone call to his uncle George that lived a few minutes away. George had happily agreed to be the keeper of the fire and the person who would pass the heated stones into the lodge.

Shiloh would lead the four "rounds"—asking only that they be brief, because of the large number of people who would be sharing what was in their hearts. Shiloh gave a short explanation of the meaning of each of the four directions at the beginning of each round of sharing. And then he said: "We will start at the East—and each of you can speak into the darkness of our mother's womb. Share only what you feel ready and safe in sharing what this direction means to you at this moment in your life." At the beginning of each round George used a pitchfork to bring smouldering hot stones from the fire and ceremoniously put them into a pit in the centre of the sweat lodge. Then the door flap was closed and water was poured onto the glowing stones, making the lodge fill up with a cleansing steam. At the end of the round of sharing the door flap would be thrown open and everyone then declared their thanks and acknowledgement of "All Our Relations". At this time, anyone who found the sharing or the heat to be too much was invited to leave the lodge. No one took advantage of that invitation but after the four rounds were complete, a couple of the first-timers barely crawled out from the lodge.

When the sweat lodge ceremony was done, everyone gathered in the Renauldi home for a light but late supper—a feast consisting of contributions similar to the picnic in the park across from the Mountain Hospital. Then Shiloh offered the hospitality of his parent's home to anyone who wished to rest before the trip to the Black Hills in the early morning. "I would like to get there before the sun comes up," he grinned... "But we live on Indian time—so when we arrive will be the right time. There are sleeping bags and blankets. And this house has five bedrooms. Find a resting place that suits you—the morning will come soon enough."

* * *

The sun was not up the next morning by the time the group had driven to the Black Hills and hiked up to the plateau where the Medicine Wheel was located. Everyone had carried one small log up the mountain for the fire that was now ablaze in the center of the eight stones that made up the Wheel. They gathered around the circle of stones as Shiloh began to tell the story about Soma.

"In the beginning, the circle that Soma built was only four stones," Shiloh explained. "And he re-gained the original teaching of our ancestors by sitting at each of the four points and meditating on the fire in the centre. We know this because this is what he told the boy

Seattle when he found him waiting at the bottom of the mountain. The version of the teaching of the Medicine Wheel that he relayed to Seattle was about the four directions. Seattle told his grandfather that Soma was only able to find four good stones nearby to illustrate the teaching—the rest were small gravel and sand. This is not surprising to us now because the Elders that passed on the teachings were able to see that the correct way was meant to be this simple. When Soma told the boy, Seattle, of his meditations and dreams he believed that his haste to tell the story made him unable to find the other four stones.

Later on at the dinner table of the boy's home, Soma had told the rest of the story. After he had been given the teaching of the Medicine Wheel and the four directions, and gifted with the Four Truths, he started down the mountain path, eager to share the knowledge with his people. Half-way down, however, his logical mind began to play with the teachings and how there could be eight stones, including the cardinal directions, and how each of the original directions might represent a colour and one of the four races on Mother Earth. He stopped and began to think about the animal totems that might be in the four directions also. His head was filled with more and more new revelations until he halted again and came to believe that the teaching that he would be sharing with his people would be incomplete. So, he turned around and retraced his steps back up the mountain to craft the small Medicine Wheel and to complete his thirst for knowledge."

"This is the secret to the teaching I am about to share with you," Shiloh explained. "It is meant to be simple. It was meant to be an inspiration so that the individuals and the tribes could find their personal meaning—the colours that called out to them and the animals that became their guides. This is similar to the different religions all over this Earth. Our people do not have a religion—we have the simple inspiration of the Medicine Wheel and our Dreams to guide us. In our beliefs, in our knowing, the Great Spirit is alive and can teach us a new way to live in balance and harmony if we are open to change."

"Before I begin, I must remind you that change is the message of the *Arrow of Truth*. Our ability to learn and grow increases when we are open to change. When I was born, the four riders gifted me with four things to help me learn about who I am," Shiloh said.

"But didn't you tell us more than once that you have His memories?" Petra asked. "What more could you need to know?"

"I do have His memories," Shiloh agreed. "But so do you—all of you. You are all gifted with the divine spark that was alive in the man called Jesus along with every one of the other messengers that have been born at different times and places on the Earth. I recall his memories mostly because his teachings are important to my Earth Father's people and speak to the relationship of my Mother's people. I am a living example of two teachings, And because of the ways of my Native Ancestors, it is part of my path to show that all people—all four colours—are important and necessary to the balance of the Circle of Life."

"You began to talk about the gifts of the four riders," Lucas reminded him. "What is happening with these gifts that is so important now?"

Shiloh smiled. "You see? You said once that you have trouble completing things. That is because this is your challenge and your true talent. This is about completing the reason I was given the Spirit Shaker, the Arrow, the Medicine Wheel, and the Drum. The Drum has been my first give-away. The Drum is my Heart that I have given to Amanda. And she has gifted her heart to me." He kissed Amanda appreciatively.

"But now the sun is about to come up in the East—I need to continue. I am about to give-away the Medicine Wheel to my 13 closest friends—my family. This is all in the way that Spirit moves. When I was last here, seeking answers when my Mother and Father had passed so suddenly, I asked why I should be the One to bear this burden. And my answer was a visit by someone who could be called my enemy. But there is more—just before this visit, I gazed into the fire and proclaimed my desire to be a normal man—someone who could live in this one dream with my future wife. Spirit spoke to me in a clear quiet voice: "Your Spirit Shaker will work one last time. One more journey—choose it wisely." That was all I heard and the visitor distracted me from my quest. And now, as the sun rises in this place, I know that before this day is done, I will be called to make use of the last of the four gifts—the *Arrow of Truth*."

"Let us begin the teachings," Shiloh suggested, as the first ray of the sun in the Eastern sky touched his face.

"The first thing you should know is that the Four Truths that were given to Soma, and the four original directions of the Medicine Wheel, might be without meaning and power, if it were not for the center of the wheel. The Fire is the energy that is called Love. But the balance of this is that Love is not Love—until it is expressed. This fire is given life through the four directions.

This is the teaching of the Centre of the Circle:
At the Centre is Fire.
It is the Warmth of Friendship.
It is the Flame of Passion.
It is the Sun and the Moon.
It is like a Mirror.
It is difficult to say
Which is the Reflection
and which is the Source.
Perhaps they are One?
This is the Mystery!

And having said that, Shiloh continued: "And now, the Four Truths as they were gifted to Soma in these Black Hills. They are Life and Death. And then between those two are Dreaming and Dancing. These Four Truths are at opposite, but not opposing, directions of the Medicine Wheel and begin with the Gift of Life in the East." And when our People dance at the Pow-wow, they move in the clock-wise direction around the circle—with the Drum and the singers in the middle. The Drum, you see, is about our Heart—and our Heart is about Love."

When Shiloh was quiet for a moment of contemplation, Thomas asked: "I can understand that Life is a gift. But Death? How can Death be considered as a gift to the People by the Creator?"

"Life and Death, as I explained, are on opposite sides of the Circle, but are not in opposition. They are both about Spirit. Spirit does not die. Spirit changes. Our bodies are our sacred cocoons where Spirit is growing and becoming ready to take another form. Evolving into the next form—the next transformation—is a gift as much as the gift of birth into this Dream. It is something we earn—it is the reward that is waiting for us at what seems to be the end of our journey."

"But now you can see the problem that faced Soma," Shiloh mused. "A bit of knowledge leads us to want to understand more. Knowledge can be addictive. This is my interpretation of the warning in the White man's story called Genesis. There is a warning about trying to explain Spirit—or God, if you like. When we begin to try to explain Spirit—especially when we write it down and believe it to be the Truth or a Law, we become separated from the Mystery. We are, as the White man writes, thrown out of the Garden. But then that may have been part of the Creator's plan. Asking questions is a good thing. It is what the inspiration of a good story is about."

"Now, the way that the teaching is best learned, is through experience. With the sharing that all of you did in the sweat lodge, who will be the first? Who would like to sit in the Eastern direction?" Shiloh asked for volunteers, as he had explained, in the cabin after and before the sweat.

Simone stepped forward and John stood behind her. They were planning to be married soon. She sat on the stone of the East and gazed into the Fire at the middle of the circle of stones. "Just think about what you shared in the sweat last night or let your mind relax," Shiloh suggested. "I will recite the words that were given to me concerning the Eastern direction".

> The East is the Beginning.
> It Begins with the Gift of Life.
> It is the Moment that is Now.
> To Live Now
> is to Live in Forever.
> This is the Gift of Life.
> The Gift is to Live.
> The Gift is Now.

Everyone was silent until Simone took a deep breath and opened her eyes and looked around. "Wow!" she exclaimed. "You are all still here? I thought that you must have given up waiting. I am so sorry to hog all this time."

"Only a few minutes went by," John grasped her shoulder. "What happened? What did you see?"

"You're kidding?" Simone smiled and stood up. "My head is too full of stuff—memories and things that happened to me. So much that I can't get a grasp on it all—whoa? I feel a bit dizzy," she sat back down.

"Rest—don't try to understand it all at once," Shiloh cautioned. "Who's next?"

"Me." Amanda sat on the rock that was in the Southern direction. "But don't you think? I mean is that all there is...?"

"...For Simone?" Shiloh finished the sentence. "When Simone is ready, she will share her experience—if that is her choice." Simone continued to rest on the Eastern stone, holding John's hand and drawing on his support. "We will continue on around the wheel, until we come to the Eastern direction once again. Then, if Simone is ready, someone else can take her place. Now, if you are ready, take a deep breath and gaze into the Fire. I will speak to you about the Southern direction".

> The South is a Dance of Sharing.
> It is about One.
> It is about Two.
> It is not about a Number.
> Sharing is not One-Way
> Sharing is a Two-way
> The One that Gives is Equal
> to the One that Receives.
> They are the Same
> One.

The silence that followed was broken with a gasp from Amanda's lips. "Oh my!" she exclaimed. Tears were pooling, filling her eyes. Then she shook her head to clear her mind and reached for Shiloh's hand. "I saw..." she began, but for a few moments was too choked to continue. "I saw the result of our sharing. I saw our baby being born—or I think...? But I was outside my body like an observer...and...she will be a beautiful baby girl." She leaned back in his arms. and closed her eyes. In a moment or two she was breathing normally again. "OK. I'm OK now. Let's move on." She sat up straight and strong and repeated. "Let's move on people. Time is precious."

Shiloh and James exchanged looks. "You can take my turn," James spoke to Lucas, who had stood behind the stone in the Western direction behind James. "I need to think. This stuff is some kind of dynamite." James had shared in the sweat the other night that he would like some kind of sign that his adopted mother and father were indeed safe and happy—wherever they were now.

Lucas sat down. "I am ready, I think," he proclaimed. "I am ready to get on with my life. I am not concerned as much about what is coming for me, as I am wondering if I am as ready as I think I am."

"Breath deep and look into the fire," Shiloh said. His mind was still with Amanda. She smiled back at him encouraging him to continue.

> The West is a Spirit Circle
> The End is also the
> Beginning
> This Spirit Dance
> Is the Mystery Dance.
> Spirit is the part
> Of the Mystery
> that Remembers.
> This Circle
> Is a Journey
> of Remembering.

"Of course," were the first words out of Lucas' mouth. "Of course. It all makes sense now. I have not been able to go on—to finish anything off, because I have not learned to let go." He straightened his shoulders. "I have been forever starting new things—but never finishing one of them. I loved someone—a woman—a girl, really. We were both so young at the time. I had this crazy notion that we would get married and spend the rest of our lives together. But she had other plans. She wanted to see the world and nothing was going to stand in her way. Including me. She walked away and I never saw her again—because I was too bent on holding on. Whoosh! What a trip. I just relived all of the time I spent with her—all three amazing years. OK—I know what I need to do. But that doesn't make it any easier. Shiloh?"

"Just be easy on yourself, Lucas," Shiloh suggested, "give yourself time. When you are ready, you will move on."

James moved to stand beside the rock that was the Northern Direction. And in the synchronicity and non-coincidence that happens when we listen to the heartfelt sharing of someone else, Petra stepped back. Later she would say that her questions about the truth of dreams were best shared with the one she loved. She moved to the East direction for a different way of seeing.

James sat upon the rock in the North of the Medicine Wheel and nodded to Shiloh.

> The North is a Dreaming Circle
> Sometimes the Dream
> And the Waking seem One
> Perhaps they are!
> To Know that Both are Right
> Is to Live your Dream
> To Live your Dream
> is to Dance in the Circle
> Of Forever
> This is the Path of the Heart!

"OK—that's different," James smiled and sighed. "As you all know, my question was about the continuing existence of our mother and father after death. This was a strange dream—if that is what it was. My question was answered in a way I would never have expected. I was in an apartment home that I shared with Petra. We were not yet married but we had plans. I was woken up from a sleep by the phone ringing. I turned on the light and I saw Petra still sleeping peacefully through it all. I picked up the phone and whispered: "Hello?" It was our mother. "I know it's late," she said. 'But Anna just came in the door from New York'." It crossed my mind to ask where Anna had been," James continued. "Where is New York? Anna was Shiloh's sister, who died as a child."

"I didn't have a chance to ask about Anna or the city that I didn't recognize," James went on. "It seems that the sleeping me knew about both—although it eluded the dreaming me. Crazy! Anyway mom asked me if I had seen my cousin, Shiloh. Skip the question. Mom and Dad had not adopted me in the dream. She said that Anna had met Shiloh in New York but he said that he couldn't come home with her. She said that Shiloh had died saving some children but he came back to tell her that he was safe and he would come home when he finished what he needed to do. Shiloh? What the hay is this all about? I was just happy to talk to our mother and I got her to wake dad so that I could talk to him, too. I am content. I am happy to know that they are safe and happy somewhere. But this brought up another question. Shiloh, are you thinking about joining our parents? I hope you are not thinking about dying any time soon? This has my head spinning."

Shiloh glanced to where Amanda was still sitting in contemplation on the rock of the Southern direction. She did not seem to have heard what James had to say, or, if she had, she was keeping it to herself.

"We will all go home one day," Shiloh answered. "But it is no secret to anyone here that my fate is somehow tied to the events of this world. I will admit I do have some trouble accepting any pre-determined out-come. I believe that I—no, WE all—have been given a choice to live our lives the best way we know how. Even if there are prophesies that appear to be coming true, there is always a chance to change things. Otherwise, why would our Spirit Father—the Creator of All Things—have given us the ability to see the future? This is a Circle. And this is what the Medicine Wheel teaching is about. Even though the story and the Circle of Life continue, the story is not always told the same. This is why our teaching is passed on by action and the sharing of stories and not written in a book of laws."

"And now, the teaching of the Wheel of Life will continue from the beginning. We are back to the Eastern Direction. Who would like to go next?"

John traded places with Simone and the Circle of Sharing began again. John's sharing, like Simone, is about their life—their future as man and wife. John openly spoke about things that would not be too intimate. He spoke about beginning a new life and letting go of what had gone before. "It is so true," he noted. "New beginnings—the direction and the teaching of the East is tied to the teaching of the West. If I bring too much baggage with me into this new beginning with Simone, it could cause our relationship to be at risk from the start. To start again, I need to let go of most of my previous hang-ups and beliefs about relationships. Simone is not like any other friend—woman or man—who I have known. And our marriage need not be like either of our fathers' or mothers'."

Next, Jude had taken Amanda's place on the Southern stone of Relationships. Shiloh recited the words that spoke to this direction on the Wheel, as he had for those before, and a quiet moment followed.

"Oh my?" Jude's exclamation was not so different than Amanda—a female like emotional outburst. And to the credit of all present, there were just a couple of stifled, uneasy chuckles to acknowledge this fact. The two newer members of the band, Jimmy and Bert, were recruited just before Shiloh and Amanda's wedding. Jimmy was the son of George, Shiloh's uncle, and Bert was the son of Mary's Brother Bart. Both young men lived in Kansa so they were eager to tour with the contingent of *The James Gang* in their home country. But neither of the two had time to get acquainted with Jude to any extent. There followed another moment of silence and Jude spoke in a quivering voice: "This is too personal to share—even with a group of supportive friends. I can only say that it gives me a lot to think about."

The sharing continued around the circle. Simon took Jude's place when the Southern direction was reached,

"There was once a time that I would have been pretty positive that I would never have anything in common with Jude," Simon spoke after his meditative experience. "At that time in my life, I will admit, that even if I had a similar thought, I would have kept it to myself. But now I can see that we are all brought together because we can teach each other. I attracted this fellow into my life because of my intolerance. I could never follow his lifestyle but I will declare here and now that I would defend his right to be himself—openly, in whatever way it takes." He stood up and shook Jude's hand. "Just don't offer to kiss me—I draw the line at that." And this coaxed a friendly chuckle from everyone, including Jude.

When everyone had taken a turn at the Wheel, Shiloh began to congratulate everyone. "Well that is about it. The ceremony I mean. But it will be part of an ongoing commitment—if you make it so. I have memories that you do not have—yet. Memories about the Sacredness of the Circle of Life that will never stop, and the way the right thing happens just when I need it. This is available to you, too. It is a matter of clearing our judgments and fears. It was too bad that Andrew and Phillip could not be here. Our newest members might not know but Andrew and Phillip flew away in *The Arrow*—that airship that the Men from the Stars helped to build. I hope we will see them again but only time will tell."

"You said that anything that you can do is possible for all of us," Simon inquired. "Is that related to clearing our baggage?" Simon had often shared about his interest in the spontaneous healing that Shiloh was capable of.

"Yes—there is a definite relationship," Shiloh answered. "The healing that I do is about getting myself out of the way and becoming a clear conductor, you might call it—as a connection between the person, who wants to be healed, and my Spirit Father, the Creator of All Things. This can happen because I do not judge the person and so have no reason to withhold healing. My Spirit Father is also responsible for removing dark spirits who have taken over a person's body. It is not my way to judge any healer from any church the way they believe they need to fight the dark spirits, or use exorcism, as they call it. They say they are doing it in the name of my Father but the Creator is not about fighting of any kind. Without judgment and instigating a war, only the sincere request in my Father's name is all that is needed to send the possessing spirit on its way."

"And what is your Father's name?" Thomas wanted to know.

"I say: my Father. And the true name comes from my Heart. The name of our Father—who is the Mystery, since he is also our Mother, is found in our Heart. Our Heart is our one physical and mystical connection to the outpouring of Grace. When you live with a clear Heart, if you ask this mountain to be moved—it will happen."

"Can you prove this," Thomas smiled. "I mean right now? A simple demonstration, perhaps."

"What did you see when you looked into the fire?" Shiloh asked. Thomas did not talk much about his experience.

"It was unclear," Thomas replied. "OK—I know what you are about to say. I am the one who is unclear. I have my doubts."

"That is your right," Shiloh said. "But you asked for proof. What would it take? You were living in another dream and you boarded a plane and came back with us to this life. What more proof do you need?"

"Sorry—I guess it is just my nature to doubt. Like my namesake?"

"There is a bit of truth in that," Shiloh agreed. "But perhaps I can help. If you are willing sit across from me in the circle. I can help you to see more clearly. But be forewarned—what you see will be about the two of us."

"That is agreeable to me," Thomas replied. He took a place in the southern direction and Shiloh sat in the North, while everyone else gathered around.

"Look into the fire—and let your mind be clear. Just trust me. I will be with you but I will not control your vision. It will come naturally and be something that we both need to see."

First there was darkness and both men found it difficult to see. Also there was a loud resounding drum—like a clock marking time. After a minute Shiloh could see where he was. "I have been here before," he announced. "Thomas? This will not be a good thing to see. Do you want to go on?"

"Yes," Thomas answered. "I need to see this or I would not be here. I can make out a tall tree and a couple of large teepees. This is an old time Sundance. I can see a man tied to the tree—lying on the ground."

"There is no one else here," Shiloh replied. "When I was here before, there were two other men dancing, but even the water carriers have left. We need to see if this man that they left behind is OK."

Thomas and Shiloh bent over the man. "Check there," Shiloh noted. "He has a wound in his right side. The last time I was in this dream, his only injuries were from two ropes that connected his body to the tree."

Thomas inspected the injury in the man's side. "He has lost a lot of blood," he told Shiloh. "I think he is dead. Must have been partly due to dancing for days without food and the stab to his side that finished him off." Thomas had his hand on the man's neck, checking for a pulse. "He is gone," Thomas confirmed. "Who was he?"

"I could not see his face clearly in the other dreams," Shiloh replied.

Together, they rolled the man over—and Thomas gasped.

Almost immediately, the two men were back at the Medicine Wheel facing each other across the fire. And for Thomas, it was a matter of seeing his friend's face—a second time. "It was you!" he cried. "How could that be? Why did I need to see that? But you are not dead. You are alive!"

"The Circle is still a Mystery," Shiloh replied. "Perhaps, like Soma, we were seeing the future. But this is a reoccurring dream for me. I do not know if this is destined to happen or has already happened. This was not like the journey or *The Arrow*. This is another kind of dream—the kind that any man can have. I was in that dream before as a ghost; I could not touch this man until now."

"Perhaps, because you cannot be alive in the same place at the same time," Thomas suggested. "In this dream you were dead. But you are here now and alive. It is the story replaying. Is there no way we can stop this?"

"There is a saying: 'don't kill the messenger'." This is what happens if the message is not acknowledged. The message is the important thing—this is what the sacrifice was about. When the sacrifice is made, it may be too late."

"But can we change this?" Thomas still wanted to know.

"We are doing all that we can to change the fate of the Earth that we love. We are sharing our Singing and Dancing. A world cannot be forced to join together in Peace and Respect. There are people that believe that the messenger has not come yet. To these people I can only say: I am a man and the One who came before was a man. We are all that One man and that One woman. This Mystery cannot be contained in any book, no matter how inspirational the words may be. The Mystery is to be found by living the Sacred Gift of Life. We need to live in a Sacred Way Now! Not for the reward. The reward will come soon enough. Our People believe that the Gift of Life is the Reward and we do not appreciate its value. That is why we keep searching for more."

> It Begins with the Gift of Life.
> It is the Moment that is Now.
> To Live Now
> is to Live in Forever.
> This is the Gift of Life.
> The Gift is to Live.
> The Gift is Now.

"There is more," Shiloh said. This is not the end or the beginning. This is a Circle. This is about enjoying our Rewards as a result of Free Will. But beyond this and included within, there is a Gift from the Mystery that the Christians have called Grace. Grace is always available despite belief in our worthiness of reward. This is the true Mystery about the unconditional Love of our Creator. At any time, Forgiveness and Grace are available. We just have to open our Hearts and accept—without judgment and that which is best for us will be given."

Chapter 17

THE WINDS OF CHANGE
THE WHEEL TURNS

The fire died down and everyone helped to clean up so that the site where the Medicine Wheel was located would be ready for the next person or group of people when they arrived. Then one-by-one, they filed down the path to where the vans and cars were parked. Shiloh waited behind, talking to Amanda and gazing out at the panorama of the City of Vega below them. Shiloh and Amanda had driven there in his father's Mustang and would go back to the ranch for the evening, and close up before heading back to Bethany. Everyone else had gone but Jude remained. Shiloh walked over to see what Jude had on his mind.

"Can we talk for a few minutes?" Jude asked.

Shiloh nodded.

"I think you might be able to guess what I want to talk about?"

Shiloh nodded again.

"I couldn't tell anyone else about my vision," Jude explained. "No one else would understand." He turned his back in dejection.

"Everyone here—including Simon—would stand up for your right to live the way you choose. They would protect you with their lives."

"Maybe now," Jude turned to face Shiloh. "But that will change. If this is really a circle, as it seems to be, then I want out. I want to play a different part in this story. What would happen if I disappeared? I have a motorcycle parked down there. I could just hop on my bike and never be seen again. That should change the story, don't you think?"

Shiloh rested his hand on his friend's shoulder. "It would change the story for you and if that is what you need to do, then you have my blessing."

Jude collapsed, sobbing in the other man's arms. "Either way I will have abandoned you—I will have betrayed my best friend. Maybe you think my way of living has already betrayed you!"

Shiloh smiled encouragingly in Amanda's direction. She smiled back and turned to the view of the city in the distance. "I am not one who will judge the actions of anyone. You know that all too well. Honestly—we have had this discussion before, if it were my life I could not see myself living your choice with an intimate and physical male partner. But I can only know about how you came to be as you are by what you have told me. And it seems that you are not completely sure how it happened either. Either way, I accept you and love you as you are."

"Yes—I believe that," Jude fought back the tears. "And I love you, too. Like a brother—no kissing, like Simon said," he managed to laugh. "All kidding aside, if it were not for James and you, I don't know how I would have survived. I have fought with the idea about ending it all and I might have a long time ago, if James had not been strong enough in knowing who he is to accept me the way I was. I guess James has your Mother and Father to thank for that. And then you come along and give it to me straight." Jude laughed again at his own joke. "You taught me to Respect myself and others by treating me like any other person who needs a firm and loving hand—gay or not."

"And now you can see your part in all of this?" Shiloh asked. "It is the way of the Creator—your Father and mine—to send us a challenge that He knows we are ready for. But I am telling what is in my Heart when I repeat: I won't judge you if you choose to walk away. Here is a thought. We have a choice that this does not need to happen as the story is told. This is a problem with teaching stories that are written down. People begin to believe that this is the only Way. Our People hear a story and see that our life might be like this teaching, but the rest is up to me to decide how it comes about—even the outcome might be different. That is part of the Creator's Gift."

"So what should I do?" Jude wiped the tears from his eyes.

"Go home and rest. Think about what you need to do to live your life from your Heart. Do not be swayed by what anyone else thinks. Talk to our Spirit Father. And whatever you decide will be the right thing by me."

Shiloh gave his friend a hug and sent him off down the path. Then he rejoined Amanda where she sat cross-legged on the side of the plateau. He sat slowly and carefully down beside her in the grass.

"You should go ahead," he suggested. "I will be along directly. I have some unfinished business here."

"Everyone else has left," Amanda reminded him. "How will you get back to the ranch?"

"Maybe I will walk," he replied.

"Or maybe you don't expect to come back. I saw the future—the birth of our baby. It was like I was a ghost. We need to be there for our baby—and for each other." She clasped his hand tightly. "What are you waiting for? What could you expect to happen here that we can't face together?"

He straightened his shoulders. "Not what, exactly, who?"

"Someone is coming," she looked around, seeing and hearing no one.

"You won't see him," Shiloh replied. "But I will. If you listen close, you might hear his vehicle. He travels quietly and invisibly."

"The Emperor? I remember now. You told me about his stealth helicopter and how he came to tempt you on the day that your mother and father passed away. You expect him to come back? Is that it?"

"He has technology—spy satellites. He admitted that he kept a watch on us and all our friends. For all I know he could have been responsible for my parent's accident. Not directly—he doesn't do that. He sends other people to do his work."

"But then...?" she wondered out loud.

"Why would he come here to face me—alone? He knows that there is a connection between us—he and I. The four riders from the Stars told him about me—before I was born. And the time is rapidly approaching—the time that the Spirit of Chief Seattle called the reckoning. Something will happen that will bring an end to this world as we know it—or change it for the better. This is the way of our People. Our stories and prophesies are about a circle—that can be changed into a spiral for those who are brave and clear of heart to make the right choice."

"So what do you hope to do today?" Amanda asked.

"I hope to make a change today. But like my ancestors before me, I will respect the winds of change." He stood up and walked to where his knapsack and his flute bag lay on the ground beside the Western stone of the Medicine Wheel. There were other objects that he carried with him everywhere he went besides the flute. "I will do whatever is necessary so that there will be a future for you and our unborn child and all People on Mother Earth. You should go now. Wait for me at the ranch."

"I will not," she answered, "I will stand by my husband ".

He took out his bow and began to connect the Buffalo sinew string, bending the bow with his knee. "He is coming now. Listen to the wind. If it was not for the wind, the man who has called himself my enemy would be undetectable."

After a few moments—"I hear something!" Amanda stepped close. "Over there."

"This ship can hide him from radar and all forms of technology but not from Nature." Shiloh notched the Arrow but kept the bow held low. He could draw and fire the Arrow faster than someone else could think. He waited.

And then a man stepped into view—seemingly out of nowhere. He stepped out of the door of a helicopter that would be invisible to anyone who did not know where and how to look for it.

"Hold your weapon," the man called out. "I am unarmed and without my protective armour." He held his arms up to demonstrate. "I come at my own peril," he said. "I am here because I trust you. I am here to ask for the help that you offered when we met before."

"What do you want?" Shiloh did not release his hand on the Arrow or the bow. He was serenely relaxed and ready to do what might need to be done.

"What do you want?" The Emperor replied. "I think we want the same. We both want to bring an end to this prophesy—before it happens. I am willing to do anything I can to change what is written, if you are willing to accept that changes are inevitable. Oh forgive my manners. You must be Amanda. I am pleased to meet you—at last." Amanda held back. He shrugged. "I guess my reputation precedes me. I shouldn't be surprised. But I am here today to make amends—or at least take a step in the right direction."

"You should know something," Shiloh said at length. "Whatever you have heard about me being the second coming of Jesus or being the beast of the Apocalypse, neither is right but neither is wrong—depending on your point of view. Some might think that I am here to bring about an end to the world—or maybe an end to religion. That would be their fears talking. I am not here to speak out against religion or promote it. I am not trying to force my beliefs on anyone. If they are happy with the truth they have, then my message is that they keep it. But don't be afraid to ask questions. That's about it! The other thing? I am not here to save anyone. My message is about Respect and—I can help you take responsibility for your actions and your life."

The Emperor responded: "Everyone wants it given to them—and they want it now! That goes for enlightenment or salvation. They have been raised to believe that a saviour will come to rescue them—take them away to Heaven or some other place where there will be streets of gold for some or unlimited use of vestal virgins for others."

"That is one of the truths that I came to set straight," Shiloh replied. "We are all responsible for how our lives turn out. The rewards that come during our life and at the end are in harmony with our actions and choices. But it will also be based on what is right for all other creatures. We will not be rewarded for mistreating others by an opportunity to use women in the afterlife. Love and Respect is rewarded by the same in the next life. Everything is balanced out. The Creator is Loving and Compassionate. The Gift of Life that we were all given is about unconditional Love and free will."

"Then, I guess you could say that is why I am here today," the Emperor replied. "I have lived a long life and now there might be an end in sight. But even if this is not the end, I am tired of being fearful of what will eventually happen. My religion tells me that I will go to hell for the things I have done—especially my actions to preserve my life. And your teachings say that I am, and will be, held accountable—even if you don't call it judgment. No matter what you call it, I want the kind of happiness that I see my subjects able to achieve—even the poor ones. Even the ones that are ignorant to spiritual teaching seem to find happiness in their ignorance. Maybe my fault is my belief that it will all end one day and there will be hell to pay! Either way, I am not happy. I cannot be happy when I live in fear. So what can you do—what will you do to help me? Is forgiveness the answer?"

"Can you forgive yourself?" Shiloh asked.

"But what you are saying is that if I am not ready to forgive myself—then I can't be forgiven," the Emperor sighed and sat down on the nearest rock. It was the North, the direction of Dreams. "I am tired," he said. "I am tired of hiding away. I am a prisoner of my own castle. Sometimes I have disguised myself and I attended functions that other men who believed they had power would arrange. While they strutted like peacocks, I was able to mingle with the crowd that pretended to care about them. It was eye-opening to say the least. I also traveled to New Rome and stood among the fans in your concerts—and that was the start of a new kind of knowing. Your fans really do care—about you and each other! It was an uplifting experience. But when I returned home, it was still the same—for me. I am tired of fearing the unknown. I want this to change but I am too fearful of the consequences to take my own life. Is there another way?"

"There is," Shiloh responded. "It is called facing your fears. This is not new. This is something that has been known by Shaman, and people who are dedicated to accepting the gift of freedom that they will do anything that is respectable and honouring to attain this peace and clarity in their lives."

"I was not ready then," the Emperor admitted. "But I am now. I need the kind of help that only you can give. I am open to learn," the Emperor assured Shiloh. "I know that something happened that was not caught on the video tape of *The Arrow* passing through the Friendship Tower. I listened to the accounts of the people who were changed. I want the kind of peace that they gained through this."

"Are you willing to live the fears and dreams that have haunted you?" Shiloh inquired. "I am not talking about pretending—and saying to yourself that this is only a dream or a meditative experience. You will need to be prepared to let the dream be real. This is the difference between Dreams and Illusions."

"I thought that Illusions and Dreams were the same kind of experience—both originating from the mind?"

"Illusions," Shiloh explained, "are really a trick that has been played on the mind to bring about some kind of result in the 'real world'. This is not to say, by any means, that all such healing is done by sleight-of-hand. However, the Mystery can always be ready to be part of our waking experience."

"And Dreams? Are you telling me that Dreams are real?"

"Dreams are real experiences that we have played a part in setting in motion. Most of the time, however, we are unable to accept that we could be co-creators of our own existence, so that memory of these dreams might be distorted or just unclear. A good example of what is true here is the speech by a well-known black man called Martin Luther King, Jr. when he said: 'I have a Dream'. This dream was already becoming real.'"

Shiloh continued: "And a simple spiritual object, like this…" He relaxed one hand from his bow and took his Spirit Rattle from his belt. "…This can be used to fine-tune our beliefs and transport us to the place of our dreams."

"That rattle can accomplish something my science is incapable of doing," the Emperor said. "I find that hard to believe."

Shiloh managed a smile. "Our spiritual objects do not really do the miracles. They facilitate something in us—or the Mystery. Perfumes and sage and other things work like this. Some also have Spiritual connections though, and resonate to a higher place of being. They help us connect with another truth. But please be warned, I will not be able to come and rescue you if the fear is too great to face."

"That is not a comforting thing to know," the Emperor responded. "However, I did not arrive at this point in my life to turn back now. What happens now? Do you shake that rattle and send me to another world, or what? I feel silly even asking about it."

"I will need to shake the rattle and take you there," Shiloh responded. "And if it is like any other time when this has happened before, the place we travel to will mean something to both of us. I will accompany you and then I will return to live out my life here with my wife and friends."

Amanda nodded. "It's the right thing to do," she replied. "And I have trust in you that you can do everything you say you can and I will wait here for you."

The Emperor gave a great sigh again and stood up. "This is what I am prepared to die for. I want someone who will love me like your Amanda and trust me to do the right thing—even if it could mean losing me. This has not been a common thing in my world. But when I see it now—I know that it can be real."

Shiloh put away his bow and arrow, kissed Amanda and straightened his shoulders. "OK, I'm ready."

"What do I need to do?" the Emperor asked.

"Just stay inside the circle," Shiloh replied. "The Medicine Wheel will be our vehicle of transportation." He began to shake the Spirit Rattle. For just a few moments, nothing happened and then Shiloh heard the familiar sound that vibrated inside his body. Soon the vibration spread out within the circle of stones.

"What is that sound?" the Emperor enquired. And a mist descended on the two men until Shiloh could not see an arm's length in front of him. "Are you still there?" the Emperor's voice trembled with alarm. And then the mist began to clear, advancing down the down the mountain until the plateau at the top of the Black Hills was in bright sunlight once more. The mist halted its descent and anything below was not visible. They might be in another totally different world, for all they knew.

"Your wife is no longer with us," the Emperor exclaimed. "Did she go down the path?"

"Amanda did not go anywhere," Shiloh answered. "We did."

"But everything looks the same," the other man replied. "How do I know that this is not one of those illusions you told me about? Are you trying to trick me like you said some Medicine Man would do? You will find that I am not easily fooled."

"Walk around outside the circle," Shiloh suggested. "Go to where you left your helicopter."

The Emperor scoured every foot of the plateau but could not locate the vehicle that had carried him to this place. He took a control device from his pocket and pressed it repeatedly but the Helicopter did not become visible. It was no longer on the plateau. It had vanished just like Amanda.

"OK," the Emperor gave up. "Something happened that defies all logic. This mountain looks the same but something is different. What gives?"

"We are in the place that you go to when you dream," Shiloh answered. "I believe that the mist is not letting us see what is below the mountain because some of it is different than we remember. The mist will go away when you make a final choice and go down the path."

"Do you mean that the bottom of the path will be different than I remember?"

"I am sure of this much," Shiloh agreed. "You will descend into a world where you do not exist anymore. Most likely you died. But now you can choose to have a second chance. You can choose a different future than the one you would have in the other dream. Just remember, both dreams are real. It is a matter of which we choose to live in that makes it real for us. I might have been here before but Spirit is hiding it from me, too, for some reason. Maybe it is not my time to be here. I have learned to trust the choices that the Creator gives me."

The Emperor stretched. "I already feel better. You can go back to your wife. I will go down that mountain and live whatever life I have in a better way. Oh—about my helicopter… it runs on solar batteries, so it will stay invisible for years. But one day that will break down—maybe years from now—and the helicopter will become visible again. You and your friends might want to push it off the cliff… or not. Either way, you will have to deal with my being lost and it being found. Another thing, I made temporary arrangements should I be missing for more than a year. My son will be made the new Emperor."

"Your son?" Shiloh asked in amazement.

"My clone," he answered. "I am not too proud of that. But there it is. My son or clone—whatever, will quickly mature, not like a child being born. He will have my cellular memories to be sure but not my real life thoughts and beliefs. He would not get them until…."

"Great Spirit! How could you!" Shiloh gasped.

"I was afraid of death. But I longed to live like everyone else. I wanted a life outside the palace and my sons gave up their lives so that I could live. I guess you can judge me as the great evil one? Well, when I was doing what I did, I used my logical mind and fears to justify my reasons. And it caught up to me. Now, I am ready to make up for my past in whatever way I can. My only hope is that God is as forgiving as you say. I therefore commit my life to his mercy."

The Emperor made his exit down the path into the mist and Shiloh began to shake the Spirit Rattle one last time, to return home to Amanda.

Chapter 18

AURORA
THE WORLD CHANGES—
AND WHY IT DOES

Shiloh and Amanda returned to his parents' second home in Bethany. When their baby was close to being born they moved in with Petra and James who lived near the Mountain Hospital—no more than a half-hour drive to the hospital in case of complications. While waiting for the baby, they toured with the band in the state of New Rome. The Absence of the Emperor was nothing new since he was known to like his privacy and would sometimes disappear from the public eye for months on end. Shiloh was now aware of the reason for some of those disappearances in the past. The old stories about the Emperor not dying and having doubles or clones proved to be more than rumours. And his reputation for being cold-hearted and evil was not too far off, if someone had known the full truth. Watching Amanda's stomach grow as the miracle continued, Shiloh wondered how the Emperor could have been so heartless as to take his son's life in order to avoid his own death. He knew without a doubt that he would have given up his own life if it meant the safety of Amanda and their baby.

Months passed by quickly and after one bout of false labour pains in early November, Amanda and Shiloh's life were back to normal with no hint as to when the baby would arrive. "Aurora is already living on Native time," Amanda joked. "She will make her debut into this world when she is ready." Shiloh and Amanda had toured locally with *The James Gang* until October and then it was a case of waiting for the baby to be born. Christmas Eve came and everyone gathered at John and Simone's on the east side of the City of New Rome. Amanda was in great spirits and even managed to dance much to the disagreement of Petra, who had become like a doting mother hen. By now, Amanda could have been a stand-in for Santa with her protruding belly full of a baby. Still, she was hardly overdue. At the last trip to the doctor, she had been proclaimed on-time for late-December or the first week of January. Shiloh only agreed to attend the party because there was another hospital about half-an-hour east of the city.

At about 11:30, Amanda informed Shiloh that she was too tired to stay any longer. "I need to go home," she told him. "I am not sure who will get here sooner if we stay—Santa or our baby." Shiloh bustled her out the door after a round of hurried good-byes. "Are you OK?" he asked when they approached the freeway. I mean should we head east or west? The Mountain hospital is over an hour drive. "No, I am OK," she replied. "Probably just another false alarm. I think we should head home. The baby has settled down again. I wouldn't be surprised if she shows up sometime tomorrow, though."

Shiloh took the freeway entrance to the west. "I think it would be a good idea if we went straight to the hospital." Then, as they neared the half-way point on their drive—which would make it 45 minutes to the Mountain Hospital—Amanda announced that "the baby is coming." Shiloh's head was swimming. Either hospital was too far-off for his caring. "Can you hold on?" he asked.

"No. There is not enough time," Amanda gasped in pain. "Our baby will be born in this car...unless...unless? Where are we? What street was the last turn-off?"

He told her the name of the exit that just flashed by and as he spoke he experienced a familiar feeling, accompanied by a sound vibration that began to take over his body. "Oh Great Spirit?" he exclaimed. "Why now?" He recalled that the Spirit had told him that his spirit rattle would be capable of one last journey, and that had been used up. "How is this happening? Who is doing this?" He asked out loud but Amanda either did not hear him or she was too focused on what was happening with the baby.

"Watch for a hospital sign," she grimaced in pain. "About two more exits."

"There is no hospital in this part of the city," Shiloh sighed and drove on, his knuckles gripping the wheel. "Are you sure we can't make it?"

"The Mountain Hospital is too far," her eyes rolled and it looked like she was about to faint. "Trust me—I know this part of the city. I lived here most of my life."

He had no other recourse but to keep driving and looking out for a sign for a hospital that did not exist. The sound that he heard earlier had not diminished. It continued in the back of his mind. His body trembled. "Do you hear that?" he asked.

"What…?" Amanda replied, coming out of a near black-out. "What street was that?"

He told her the name of the exit that was now in the distance—less than a memory back down the road.

"Watch close. It should be the next exit. Trust me—I am saving our baby's life."

A chill took hold of his body at hearing her words. He wondered, at this point, that if he did see a sign for a hospital that he knew should not be there, whether he should take a chance.

"Trust me," Amanda seemed to read his thoughts.

And then…an unmistakable sign appeared: "Hospital—Next Exit."

And another sign for the turn off. He slowed down just enough to take the exit from the freeway. This ramp wound around and deposited them into the middle of the city. He followed a clearly marked route until he saw the entrance to the hospital and in a few moments they were parked at the emergency doors. A large neon sign proclaimed: "Grace Hospital". He gave up trying to figure it out. This hospital might not exist but Amanda had lost consciousness in the driver seat beside him. He turned off the car and bolted for the hospital door.

"Here is the good news," the doctor came out of the room where Amanda had been taken on a stretcher. "You have a healthy baby girl. But your wife is in a coma. She lost a lot of blood. We do not know what will happen now. Only time will tell."

"Can I go in now?" Shiloh asked.

"Yes," the doctor replied, but be warned. "Anything can happen. I have to be honest. She is hanging on by a thread. It's not a matter of life support, she is breathing on her own but her vital signs are too low to make a judgment about whether she will pull through."

Amanda was in an emergency room—number 101. There was no one else in the room. Her bed was surrounded with pull curtains. Shiloh gently pulled aside one of the curtains and stepped inside. Amanda was hooked up to a lot of machines that would monitor her vital signs and he could not hear her breathing. However her chest rose and fell almost imperceptibly to his worried eyes. He closed the curtain as he entered and sat on the edge of the bed. "Amanda, dear," he held one of her hands. "Here is where we tell how much you want to stay in this world. I can't make you stay. I can only give you into the hands of my Spirit Father, the Creator of All Things, and pray," he closed his eyes and did just that.

Minutes passed, he lost track of time and a mist filled the room. He stood in a different place. The woman who held his hand now had flaming red hair. She smiled and sighed. "Shiloh, my love, Amanda is with me now. You must know—I am Amanda, too. I am Amanda as much as she is me—more so now. She has been with me for some time—since you took that turn off the freeway. Together, we have been holding on, so that our baby could be born. You need to wake up now and let go. Amanda will be waiting for you, when it's your time to come home."

Shiloh was jolted out of the dream by a loud beeping sound from the monitor on the other side of the bed. The sound brought a team of medical personnel with paddles and more electric machinery. Shiloh was pushed unceremoniously out of the way. He turned his back not wanting to see what happened next. Yet he could not help but hear the whole valiant attempt to bring Amanda back from the other world. Finally, they had to give up. The room became silent as the machinery was shut down. A hand touched his shoulder. "I am sorry. We did all that we could."

The doctor was the last to leave the room. "Take as long as you need," he said in a voice that was full of emotion—amazingly so, for someone who must witness this many times over. Shiloh pulled a chair close to the bed and sat holding Amanda's hand for the last time in this world, at least. Her face was peaceful—you might think she was just sleeping—and if you knew the truth, well—that was the truth. But even that bit of knowledge did not hold back the deluge of tears that followed. No matter how you looked at it. No matter what he knew about dreams and other worlds—some just a whisper away—there was just one thought that burned in his mind and his heart: Amanda was gone! And just when he began to gain a bit of control over his mind, his body betrayed him and the tears could not be stopped. Finally, he did as Amanda in the dream vision had said he must—he just let go.

When he had exhausted his tears and no more would come, he raised his eyes skyward and prayed: "Great Spirit, I do not know the reason this needed to happen. It seems so wrong. At this minute, I cannot see how this could be a good thing. Please help me to understand."

And when no answer seemed forthcoming, he prayed:

"Great Spirit, please look into my Heart—see what I need at this time, and give me that."

"Young man? I could not help hearing what you said," a gentle voice called out. He had not heard anyone enter the room or pull aside the curtains. He looked around to see who was speaking. A nurse, in sparkling white uniform, so white in fact that it dazzled his eyes, stood at the foot of the bed. "This is your daughter. You need to hold her now," and the nurse handed over the new-born baby, wrapped in a pink receiving blanket. Shiloh took his daughter in his arms. The baby sneezed and, as if that was kind of a magical signal, a bright mist enveloped the bed and the space bounded by the curtains. And as quickly as it had appeared, the mist disappeared and so did the nurse.

The room was different somehow. The sounds outside the door were different. But Amanda was the same—sleeping peacefully—or so it seemed. He bent and kissed her forehead. No, that much was the same. She would not be waking up—in this world at least. He pushed his way through the curtain and cradled the baby with one arm while he opened the door. This was not the corridor where he had waited anxiously on the bench for the doctor to tell him that Amanda and the baby were going to be OK. The bench was not there. There was no doctor to be seen. Down the unfamiliar corridor, he saw a sign and an arrow. The sign said: "Nurses Station." He followed the arrow and around the corner was the nurses' station. A low radio could be heard playing *Silent Night*.

"Hello?" Shiloh stood at the desk. "Is there anyone here?" Two women in nurse's uniforms came from the back.

"Sorry, we are short staffed. Its Christmas morning, you know. What can we do for you? Oh? How did you get that baby? I didn't see you in the nursery."

"This is my daughter," Shiloh replied. "She was born a couple of hours ago—room 101. Mrs Renauldi."

The younger nurse looked through an admittance book. "Renauldi—Amanda Renauldi. Yes, she was admitted just before midnight. I am so sorry Mr. Renauldi, but that still doesn't explain the baby. Your wife was unconscious when she was admitted, and she passed away before we could do anything to help her. There is no mention about a baby, though."

"Let me see that," the elder nurse requested and took the book from her counterpart. "Sorry about your wife—but my fellow nurse is right. There is no record of a baby."

"I don't need a record," Shiloh said firmly. "I have all I need right here. This is my daughter—her name is Aurora." The baby squirmed and sneezed, as though to punctuate her father's words.

"There is no record concerning a baby," the elder nurse reaffirmed. "I don't know how you got this baby out of the nursery but she has to go back. Her parents will be looking for her." She held out her hands.

"No way." Shiloh was still not moving. And then he noticed the baby's hand and arm—waving free of the blanket. A hospital bracelet loosely encircled that tiny wrist. "Look here," Shiloh said. "This tag should convince you that I am telling the truth. It says Aurora Renauldi—Daughter of Amanda and Shiloh Renauldi. And the birth date is this morning."

"Let me see," the head nurse replied in an authoritative tone. "That doesn't even look like one of our bracelets."

Shiloh held the baby tightly but let the nurse examine the bracelet. "The writing on the tag does say what you said it did. But it also has the insignia of another hospital. See…and the words Grace Hospital…I can't make out the street or number...New York. Who are you trying to kid? There is no other hospital within two hours' driving distance. You are in the West Mountain Hospital in New Rome. I haven't even heard of a town or city called New York. Are you from another state—or another world? You should hand over the baby before I call security."

Shiloh was reluctant to hand over the baby until the two nurses agreed to blood tests—himself and Amanda and his daughter. "My wife is down the hall, in room 101," he reminded the nurses. "First check in the nursery to make certain that there are no babies missing. But please be quick. I think she must need feeding soon. I am more concerned for her well-being than ownership. I helped bring Aurora into this world but that does not mean I own her. All children are sons and daughters of the Creator of All Things."

The elder nurse's eyebrow arched at his words but she hurried out the back door to check out her list of babies in the nursery. "OK. No babies missing. But we still don't know where this little lady came from."

"I just explained to you," Shiloh sighed and handed over the squirming infant. "Do whatever it takes to convince you that the baby is from Amanda and me."

Hours later, around noon on Christmas day, the doctor on-call had checked out Amanda to confirm that she had been pregnant, and was no longer.

The nurses had already extracted blood samples. It was a quiet day in this Emerg, even for Christmas day. The two night nurses and their replacements did everything possible to enable tests that would prove or disprove the claims that Shiloh had made concerning the new baby in their nursery. "We have the most up-to-date equipment that Rome provides," the doctor explained. "There is a new DNA test that will prove it beyond a doubt. It takes about a week. I am afraid we cannot release this baby to anyone until we are sure. Do you have the medical benefits to cover this?"

"My wife and I are covered by a plan available to all residents of Kansa," Shiloh explained. "And we have an extra plan for USNR—because we live part-time in Bethany and we work in the USNR."

"What kind of work do you do, Mr. Renauldi?" one of the day nurses asked. "I located your wife's files. She has been coming here once a month for the length of her pregnancy. I am so sorry about the way things turned out."

"We are musicians," Shiloh explained. "Were musicians, I mean," he paused and fought back the tears. "Amanda and I were part of a *Spirit Rock* band called *The James Gang*."

"Wow!" the nurse exclaimed, "you are THAT Shiloh?" She checked out the names on the records. "Shiloh Renauldi? I didn't connect the last name but I recognize you. My boyfriend and I went to one of your concerts. I hope you aren't thinking of quitting? Amanda would not want you to give up. You and your band have been a great inspiration for a lot of people."

"Well—it looks like I will have my hands full now," Shiloh replied "Being a single parent can be a full-time job all by itself."

"You know this man?" the head night nurse asked. She was getting ready to leave at the end of her shift. "He really had us guessing. He walked up to our reception area carrying a mystery baby last night. We were hard-pressed to believe that he had not stolen the child somewhere."

"You must not watch much TV?" the day nurse asked. "You must have heard of *The James Gang*? This is the man everyone is calling the second coming."

"The second coming of...? Oh you can't mean...? No, I hardly turn the box on—I have better things to do with my time. But I thought that was all hype—to sell records. Yes. I have heard of him. Nice uplifting music. But I never made the connection?" And to Shiloh: "You've got a lot of nerve pretending to be Jesus. And what is the baby about? If you were who you say you are—how do you explain the baby?"

"I don't need to explain a baby," Shiloh replied gently but firmly. "Amanda and I are in Love—we got married. The rest is about nature—the Circle of Life, my People call it. There seems to be a belief that the One who came before would not be part of this. Your books have been altered. If I were religious, I might call it the sin of omission. But I am not—religious that is. I am Spirit. I am a Son of the Creator who remembers who he is and where he came from. I never said I was Jesus—or the second coming—or Jesus re-incarnated. I have been misquoted—like the messenger who preceded me. I said that I have his memories—and so do you if you allow yourself to be open enough to listen to your Heart."

"Whoa," the night nurse took a step back. "When did you sleep last? That was a mouthful. We got off on the wrong foot. I guess if I were in your shoes and I had someone I loved die and then have an upstart nurse try to take away my baby—well, I might be a bit hot under the collar, too? But look at this from our perspective. This is all a bit hard to believe. We deal in hard, cold facts—life and death situations. I try to be compassionate but let me tell you—it can harden your heart. We don't have time for tears—we need to act quickly and do the best we can to save lives." That said, she turned on her heels and departed.

* * *

When the head night nurse returned the next day to begin her evening shift, her co-worker had been there a couple of hours early.

"Julie? When did you get here? You are almost always a few minutes late. And why are the CRN vans parked in our lot? What happened here today?"

"Marg! You remember that man with the baby? Shiloh? He left when you did this morning. I guess to get some sleep. Then about four hours later he returned with his brother and some members of his band. The rest of his band members—all 11 or so, came later. This man is for real. After he and his band gathered around the baby-viewing window, they went touring around the hospital. And CRN—the TV station—sent a camera crew to cover what is happening. People are being healed! They are walking out of here healed—of everything from AIDS to Alzheimer's. And advanced cases of cancer, too."

"This is crazy," Margaret exclaimed, "are there any sick people left for us to look after? Do we even have a job left?" And then she bit her lip. "I mean—it would be a good thing if people were made well like you say is happening, but then why is there anyone left in this hospital? If he were really Jesus, all of the people would be healed and

CRN would have broadcasted it. Then I would expect this place to be overrun by the rest of the sickly in the city of New Rome."

"A lot of people were healed—by Shiloh and every member of his *Spirit Rock* band," Julie explained. "But that was not the angle that CRN reported. CRN reported the failures and told the world that this man and his group of rock musicians were publicity-seeking charlatans. The way they reported and filmed what happened today was not what really happened. It was a politically correct version of the truth—as instructed by the government."

"Careful," Margaret cautioned her friend and co-worker. She motioned with her eyes in the direction of the cameras that kept a record of everything that went on in the hospital.

"Sorry about my runaway mouth," Julie said loud enough to ensure that the apology would be recorded so she might not wake up tomorrow in a security prison charged for conspiring against her country and the "Holy" Roman Empire. Homeland Security had been beefed up following the rumours of the Emperor's disappearance. She stepped back behind a column and talked a bit calmer and at a lower level. "OK—I got carried away. But when I get a call from one of the day girls about what was going on, I came in a few hours early to see for myself. "I met Mr. Jenkins—you know that elderly man in room 303 that chemo didn't help? He was here just waiting to die. Well, I met him being wheeled out in a chair by his family. And he stood up—a bit shakily but he stood up—and got into the car with little or no help. For some reason, he was not part of the noon-hour newscast on CRN. The people that were filmed did not get healed. In fact, Joyce Johnston, you know that young girl with AIDS—she died right on schedule—like how our new DNA deterioration detection unit, the DDU, predicted. Well, Joyce was the feature of the noon broadcast."

"So why are the CRN trucks still here?" Margaret asked.

"Vultures!" Julie whispered out of the corner of her mouth as she returned to her stack of paperwork. "Just waiting for the worst to happen so they can get it on the evening news."

"I could have told you so," Margaret replied. "This is all the worst case of blasphemy. It is a crime against the Holy Bible for someone to pretend that he is the second coming of Jesus. But Jesus is coming that is for sure—and very soon. And all those sinners will get their just reward."

"I beg to differ," Shiloh spoke. He had just come up from the cancer ward and could not help overhearing the conversation. "I would like to apologize to you for my judgmental way of speaking this morning. I have no right to tell anyone what to believe—unless their beliefs are hurting an innocent person—especially a child. I am here to protect the children—like the One who came before. The Children and the Elders are our hope for the future. But—again—I have to differ about Jesus coming. Jesus is not coming because he did not leave. Jesus did not die. Look that up in your Bible. His message and my message is that the same spark of Spirit that was and is Jesus, is in all of us. Every one of us has the potential to be like the One who came before me. He said that clearly. That was his message."

Margaret shrugged, "OK. Let it go for now. But what about the people that were not saved? What about Joyce—the young girl that died of AIDS today? Why were you not able to help her?"

"You might also ask—why was I not able to heal Amanda or my mother and father—why could I not bring them back to life? Everybody knows that Jesus was able to heal the sick and raise the dead. I am sorry to carry this conversation on from this morning, but you asked this time. First I will ask you to note that the TV crew did not seem interested in the ones that walked out of here on their own power—and that is the truth. On their own power. I do not heal God, the Great Spirit—whoever you wish to call the Creator of All Things, healed them—each and every one. I only help them to re-connect with Grace."

"And about Joyce...and Amanda, too," Shiloh continued. "It is not my right to decide who gets healed or not. Even the woman I love. I do not own her. I cannot own or control the lives of anyone. I can only, when asked, help them re-connect to Grace and to the Source of all things. The young lady called Joyce did not die—anymore than Jesus did. I helped her to see her choices. And a young man appeared that could only be seen by the girl and me. He would not appear on the TV cameras. But when he reached out to her—she was peaceful. And when she went home with him, she had a smile—without fear—on her face. That would have been on the original video footage."

"You speak so eloquently." Margaret replied. "You almost convince me that you are the real thing. But I have my Bible. And it is the source of my inspiration. I find all that I need in that one book."

"So be it," Shiloh agreed. "The word is Inspirational. I am not here to preach or ask anyone to give up their religion, although it seems I am carrying on a bit lately. I guess that the illusion that I have lost Amanda has left me in a state of shock."

Margaret accompanied him to the nursery-viewing window. After a few minutes of watching him smiling, and making faces at the baby, she said: "I saw the results of the blood tests that the day nurse hurried through for you. It looks like she is really your daughter."

"Of course," he pressed his nose and hands against the glass. "When will I be able to take her home?"

"In a couple of days. All this publicity has convinced the hospital that we better not make a mistake. They have ordered DNA tests. I have another question about the people that could not be healed?"

"The members of my band and I helped them to search for the reason for the illness and to help lessen their pain. Cancer or even the common cold has a cause. There are no co-incidences. It only seems so for someone who does not want to or cannot take responsibility for their life. Even the apparent death (or abuse) of a small child has a root in Spirit. And before you get all alarmed at me, let me explain that children are Angels—Spirits come to earth. The child does not consciously put herself in harm's way but an interaction might be 'arranged' to give an otherwise incorrigible adult a chance to redeem themselves. Think of it this way: an Angel comes to earth and is entrusted into the care of an abusive adult—mother or father. This person has a chance to learn to love. But failures happen—the children and the Angels do not fail—the failure is in the hands of the abusive adult. A Guardian Angel is always ready to protect the one who is in harm's way, if necessary, by taking that child back home. This is a simple as I can explain about what could be a horrific event. This is still mostly a Mystery to me. I feel the grief, the same as anyone. I am a Spirit in a man's body but I am still just a man at heart. If I were to see a child being harmed, I would do whatever necessary to stop the abuser—including a real arrow from my bow."

"And what about justice afterward?"

"Revenge is not part of the *Arrow of Truth*. Justice is about doing all that can be done on earth to make sure this person is not able to abuse again. And an eye-for-an-eye is not the answer. We are all partly responsible for the cancer that is called evil. That cancer needs to be healed for all sentient beings before it devours all of us."

He stepped back then and said: "Now that I feel confident that my newborn daughter is in safe hands, I will pay my friends in the cancer ward one last visit for tonight. Then I am leaving to get a good night's sleep. Tomorrow, I need to complete some last minute arrangements for Amanda's celebration of life. I will come back to visit tomorrow afternoon. I thank you for being here to look after my most precious little one."

The next day, Shiloh along with the other members of *The James Gang*, returned to the West Mountain Hospital. More people were healed or at least had their suffering eased. Meanwhile Shiloh spent a lot of time by the viewing-window in the nursery.

"Why did you and your friends come back? I can understand why you are here. Your daughter is here. But there is no TV coverage. So why continue?" Margaret found Shiloh in the hospital lounge taking a breather from his "work" on the cancer ward.

"I am here to help as many as will accept help," he replied, sipping at a tea. "If you recall the story, the One who came before did not seek out people to heal. They asked for his help. They asked to be healed and he granted their wish. There was a great group that had surrounded him in the marketplace and one that needed his help touched the hem of his robe."

"And was healed." Margaret continued the story. "He felt the healing take place even though he had not consciously wished it to be done. You remember that? Who are you—really? Are you the One returned to save us?"

"I am not that same One. But I have his memories. And so do you. If you would only accept this as truth," Shiloh replied.

"No," her voice quivered with uncertainty. "I am a sinner. I need his help. I need him to save me from my sins."

"Then you do not need me," Shiloh smiled encouragingly. "But one day you will know. In your own time. That is the gift from our Spirit Father—the Gift of free will."

A long silence. "So why are you here? Not in this hospital. I mean, what is our purpose for being here?"

"This is a Circle. A Dreaming Circle. Sometimes the Dream and the Waking seem One. It is difficult to say—which is the reflection and which is the Source. Perhaps they are the same?"

"You talk…in Circles," she laughed. She could not recall the last time she had laughed. The Emergency ward had changed her, as she had said before. "I…I need a coffee," she rose and moved on, with no intention of returning to this conversation.

Shiloh finished his tea and made his way to the nursery. A couple of days and Aurora would be able to go home with him—to James and Petra's nursery that was his temporary abode. James and Petra had been more than happy to be part-time "tribal parents" for Aurora.

"You need to leave here and take your daughter," Margaret insisted when Shiloh showed up in the evening two days later. "The DNA test confirmed that she is your daughter. But the head of this hospital has had a visit from a government official that wants to keep her here. The request has been turned down but they are seeking a stay—or an injunction or something like that."

"Why?" he asked. He could almost guess. "What would the government of New Rome want with my daughter?"

"It's not the child they are after," Margaret proceeded to bundle the baby for traveling. "There is a rumour concerning the disappearance of the Emperor. They believe that he has met with foul play. And for some reason, they suspect your people to be involved—you in particular. But they have no hard evidence. Only a high official from Rome who said that the Emperor had an interest in keeping watch on you and your family. You would not have been responsible for the Emperor's disappearance…would you?"

"I do not have enemies," Shiloh replied. "Even those who believe they are my enemy—if they were to come to me for help. I would not turn down the request."

"Circles again," she shrugged. "I kind of understand what you are telling me. That is even more reason to tell you that this is the day for your daughter to go home—to her Native home."

He nodded. "If my brother James calls or shows up here today, please tell him that I will call him from my father and mother's ranch." He gathered up his daughter and headed for the door. "I bought a bassinette that straps into the car after Amanda's cremation. I had planned to take her ashes back to Kansa—today is a good day for that."

* * *

"Did you have any trouble at the border?" Shiloh asked James, when his brother and Petra showed up at the Renauldi ranch with their most essential belongings in the van.

"Not at all—you?"

"Me, neither, but I don't think I can go back any time soon."

"Good thought," James agreed. "They did a thorough search of the van at the bridge. Seemed to think I might be smuggling a fugitive. What did you do? Something happened after that time in the Black Hills when you and Amanda stayed behind." Shiloh had told his brother about the visitor but no more than the others needed to know.

"I didn't kill him. If that's what you mean. He came to me for help in facing his fears. I helped him. That's about it."

"But the question is, how did you help him? He is not coming back—right?"

"Not unless he learns to travel between Dreams." Shiloh helped unload the van. "I only hope I did the right thing. I only hope that he was sincere in his desire to change his life."

"How would you be able to tell?" James struggled with a large bag of unwashed laundry.

"Something will change here. There is a Spirit connection between worlds. It may be a subtle change, since it also depends on the people in this dream being open to allowing the change to happen. But you and I will know."

"Well, I wouldn't hold your breath," James grinned. "You are the number One Most Wanted on the other side of the bridge."

"Wanted for what?" Shiloh asked. "They have no hard evidence that I did anything wrong, 'cause I didn't."

"You and I know that. A couple of Homeland Security men showed up at my door looking for you. They said they just need to talk. Yeah sure. They know that something happened because—he is missing. Nothing more but you would be held for questioning—a long time if they had their way. Right now there is not enough evidence of wrong doing to ask for a legal what-cha-a-ma-call-it to come and get you."

A few months passed and James and Petra settled in. They transferred most of their savings, bit by bit, to the bank in Dallas just in case. Meanwhile, they organized a tour in Kansa for *The Gang* and became doting tribal parents for Aurora. Then one day James called Shiloh and Petra to the TV. "You gotta see this," he exclaimed. CRN midday news was covering a story about the Emperor's disappearance, and the young man that they were interviewing was a spitting image of the guy who disappeared.

"For those who just joined us, we are live from Rome. The man we are interviewing is reportedly the son of our Emperor. We were not even aware that the Emperor had a son but the High Minister of Internal Roman Affairs has concurred that, this man is the legal and rightful blood relative of our missing Emperor, and he is the next in line to the throne."

"My father left word with the Minister that if he did not return after one year, that I am to take his place as Emperor of Rome." The young man speaking was more of a twin than a son. He was the exact duplicate of his father and only Shiloh and a few others knew the full truth. "My father was in touch with the Men from the Stars." The son continued, "he knew of the forthcoming prophesies and he had asked the men from the stars to take him away to a place where he could do more good toward fulfilling those prophesies."

Partially true, Shiloh mused.

"A year has come and gone and my father will not be returning. He has sacrificed his life here to help keep the world that he loved a safer place. Now I will be appointed Emperor. I must tell you now that my rule—although it may be short, will be significantly different than that of my father's. You will learn more in the coming months and days. But first I will publicly declare a wrong made right. This is concerning a man called Shiloh." James and Shiloh and Petra exchanged questioning looks. "This man and his family and friends were highly respected by my father. I will now request that any possible charges or suspicions regarding the disappearance of my father be formally dismissed. It will be made known that this man and his friends are welcome to live or visit any country in the present Roman Empire. That is all I have to say today."

James breathed a sigh of relief. "Does this mean that we can go home now?"

"I think you are home," Petra suggested. "Of course, this is open for discussion my love, but I think that we should move here permanently with Shiloh's approval of course?"

Shiloh nodded. "My home is your home and Aurora will need her second parents. I will warn you though; a bit of babysitting might be involved."

This was all good—as far as James was concerned. "I was just getting the Kansa tour arranged," he grinned. "I guess Lucas and Jude will keep it going North of the Red? I don't imagine you want to take a chance, no matter what the new Emperor says?" he asked Shiloh.

"Not for the moment, at least," Shiloh agreed. "But when things settle down, who knows? I have made a lot of friends in the States and I would not be true to my calling if I let them down."

In the months that followed, the new Emperor made a number of television appearances to report the changes that he was initiating. The first thing he announced was a gradual dissolving of the connection between Church and State. "The church of Rome should not be involved in military and matters of government," he explained. "Church should be in the best interest of the Spiritual part of man and women. The logical things like armies and taxes and the making and enforcing of laws should be the concern of the men and women who will be elected to run our country."

"Did I hear him say women? In the Roman government?" Petra whistled. "That'll be a major step in the right direction as far as I am concerned."

"Thinking of running for office, Pet?" James nudged her.

"If I were in Rome, maybe," she replied. "You know that old saying. When in Rome…? Well, that may be getting a more positive meaning."

"Did you notice that he seems a bit pale?" Shiloh interjected.

"Now that you mention it," James agreed. "But there must be a lot of stress to the job he inherited. Not to mention the flack he must be receiving from the old guard."

"Watch how he looks in the next few months," Shiloh suggested. "He is on schedule for at least one interview a month. I have been keeping count."

"So what would you be intending to do little brother?" James winked. "Go over there and heal him?"

"If it were something he wanted," Shiloh replied. "And it would seem in the best interest of the world as we know it, so long as this young Emperor was to keep on making the changes that he has promised."

Chapter 19

GRACE—AND BETRAYAL?

When the rest of *The James Gang* showed up at the hospital that morning following the birth of Aurora and Amanda's untimely passing into Spirit, Jude was there. Jude just reappeared on the scene and there was no reason for Shiloh and his long time friend to talk about what came to light on the plateau in the Black Hills. For Shiloh's part, he was happy to see Jude again. There is always a chance, however, that the turn of the wheel might mean repeating something that had happened before. One can never be sure.

A couple of months after the new Emperor's first appearance on TV, Shiloh and James were convinced that the young man was progressively becoming frail. "He is ill, that much is certain." Shiloh turned off the television. This past week had seen the Emperor announce the dismantling of more weapons of war. The week before had been about the transferring of tax money to the outlying countries to help feed the hungry and facilitate the building of hospitals. "I will make a long distance call to request an audience." Shiloh was never one to let a challenge or a chance to do good pass by. "If I am turned down, then so be it. I will offer to help and if he turns it down, then so be it. He does not seem controlled by the fears of his father."

The next morning, however, Shiloh received a surprising long distance call—from the Mountain Hospital in New Rome. It was Margaret, the nurse that had warned him to take his daughter and flee the country. "I just thought you might be interested in an amazing occurrence," she told him. "You remember that hospital bracelet that your daughter had when you brought her to our station that night? Well, just today there was an announcement made that due to a large grant of money from Rome, a new hospital will begin construction closer to the City core. And the new hospital is to be called—get this—Grace Hospital. How much of a co-incidence is that? It must be some kind of sign, don't you think?"

"What kind of sign?" Shiloh smiled to himself.

"It seems to me that it is about what they say about a good deed done—will come back to us tenfold."

"And what good deed do you imagine set this in place?" he asked.

"Well," Margaret said, "I am wondering about the first interview that our new Emperor gave. He seemed to be saying that something or someone helped his father have a change of Heart. That bracelet was a sign for me—and it told me that I should not be quick to judge and I should give thanks that God does move in Mysterious ways. Oh, and another thing," Margaret paused as though considering her words. "I guess you might be seeing our new Emperor on television. I don't usually watch TV. I don't even own one. But Julie told me what he was saying on the monthly broadcasts. Well, I watched a few episodes on the TV in the lounge. He does not look well. You must see that if I did. Just a thought. It might be a good time for a distant healing, if you do that kind of thing? That's just a thought—distant healing, I mean."

After Margaret said her good-byes, Shiloh told James and Petra what she had said. "She emphasised the word 'distant'". I guess she must have guessed that I would be concerned enough to do something?"

"I agree," Petra replied. "Margaret is more aware than we first suspected. She knows that something should be done but if something mysterious should happen to the Emperor right after your intended visit—well it would be a perfect chance to kill two birds with one stone—as the old saying goes."

"Have you ever done that little brother?" James was concerned that Petra might be right. "Our new Emperor might be winning over the common folk but he will be making enemies in high places at the same time."

"If you mean, have I ever done distant healing," Shiloh replied. "I have. Sometimes with more success than others. This follows my belief that a person has the right to experience certain things of their choice. Prayer for a troubled friend or even a troubled world is the best example of this. This is what prayer is all about. Asking the Creator to help this person or send an Angel to give them a little nudge in the right direction. In this case—I think I will also send a poem that I have been working on that is appropriate. It is called: *Accept your Greatness Humbly.*"

Accept your Greatness Humbly

Accept your Greatness Humbly
You are a Child of God
Your body is a truly a Temple
It is not just a bit of sod.

My Grandmother used to tell me:
Children grow like weeds...
But she loved and accepted
all of her Grandchildren equally.
The difference between a dandelion and
a sunflower is a matter of Judgment.

Accept your Greatness Humbly
The Gift of Grace the same...
The Way a blossoming Sunflower
Accepts the Sun and the Rain

I Believe—and wonder:
We are the sons and daughters
of Spirit. The Bible says that we were
created in His Image. If that is so,
who will we be when we grow up?

Accept your Greatness Humbly
You were not born in sin
You do have a Mother and a Father
But Grace is your next of kin.

Kahlil Gibran:
Your children are not your
children.

They are the sons and daughters
of Life's longing for itself.

Accept your Greatness Humbly
Doubt may creep in through the mind
But it won't find a place in a Heart
filled with a Light Divine.

Nelson Mandela:
Our deepest fear is not that we are inadequate.
Our deepest fear is that we are powerful beyond measure.
It is our light, not our darkness,
that most frightens us.

Accept your Greatness Humbly
Stand tall and straight with Pride
A woman or man who is humble
Has nothing they might need to hide.

For Me and You:
Imagine that you were created
in His Image…
Then who do you see in the mirror
every morning?
Pride does not come before a Fall
A fall happens when we lose our Balance.

…WinterHawk

A couple of weeks passed and a third. Then came the monthly scheduled TV appearance of the Emperor. "Is it my imagination or does he look a bit better? There is a light in his eyes," Petra remarked.

Shiloh and James agreed. "He is about to speak:"

"My fellow Roman countrymen—and those who live in the lands across our great ocean. And for all of those who send emails and letters expressing concern for my health. I must tell you that the concerns were justified. But the good news is I am feeling much better. This is no doubt a result of your prayers on my behalf."

"Most of us, including myself, come into this world born of parents—created in their image—believing that we must be like the father or mother that birthed us. We are then taught that we must live up to the reputation and the teaching of our parents. And even if this is not verbally expressed to us, we learn by hearing and watching the actions of our parents. I would like to say, publicly, that I am not my father—unless you have not already figured that out by the changes I am initiating. I inherited his hopes and dreams and even his fears. But now that he is gone to someplace where he will do the most good, I will be ruling and making changes that reflect my ideas about life. At first, I was reluctant to take his place—I felt unworthy. But now I know that it was time for a change and the chance to be the one who can start the process has been given to me. I say the chance to start the process, because the changes that will be made are not entirely up to me or my Ministers, or even the individual leaders of your countries. Any lasting and real change must include all of you who hear my voice."

The Emperor went on to outline a plan that he would be putting in place—a plan already in progress. This included dissolving the official Church and State relationship in the day-to-day running of the Roman Empire. This was already being done. This did not mean that the Spiritual relationship of the two would cease to be. On the other hand, he said that this would be more important than ever. But to have one church deciding what laws were correct for all people is not true in the light of Spiritual truth. He went on to repeat that it was part of his plan to give individual freedom and self-government back to the countries on both sides of the ocean. "The world should not be ruled or owned by Rome. That time has passed. Instead, Rome will become a guiding force—a big brother or sister ready to help any who require aid but allowing the freedom of individual growth and expression. I know now that true Spirituality is not about control. It has taken this long for Rome to become aware of this. The job of religion is to plant the seed, water it, and then let it grow in the way that it will. Every seed—every creature has a part to play that God has given to him or her. I have planted the seeds, and I will be here to water and then my job will be done."

In the months that followed, the power to govern themselves was restored to the countries that made up the former Roman Empire. And the Military technology that belonged to Rome was dismantled until the only remaining missile silos were located within the borders of the USNR. The President of the United States of New Rome realized his apparent power and instead of completing the disarmament, he tightened the borders and was one step from declaring martial law. That step he did not need to take because, over the years, his family had manipulated the constitution, until it had become the third generation of the Forester clan to rule the country. The grandson was in charge of the most powerful country in the world, now that Rome had fallen—at least in President Forester's eyes. The President's message to his country and the world was: "We have prepared for this moment. Our country would have been vulnerable to terrorist attacks, if my family had not foreseen this. This is the reason that our Homeland Security was created and given its mandate to protect the citizens of the proud USNR."

President Forester went on to welcome any visitors from foreign soil…as long as they carried a recent passport and agreed to the security provisions as defined on the latest enactment of the Homeland Security act.

"Do you want to go home now?" Petra asked her husband.

"I believe that I am already home, "he replied with a wry grin.

The Northern contingent of *The James Gang* was allowed to continue its concerts. Shiloh reasoned that however strong President Forester's grip was on the country, he was still aware of the power of the people. "Our church will not be separate from our countries' destiny," the President announced. "Therefore, freedom of religion will be tolerated in as much as it does not cross the moral boundaries that keep our country strong."

John and Simone reported that it was "business as usual".

"As far as we can see, nothing has changed. There are still the secret—and not-so-secret cameras and microphones everywhere. It is a cat and mouse affair. Life goes on. We cannot give up on the people who have become family to us. We need to keep their hopes alive and our music will help them do that."

Shiloh agreed. He and James still had dual citizenship—in Kansa and the USNR. Both brothers had been born in the States, but only James was a registered birth. Shiloh's passport had a stamp of approval due to his father being a loyal upstanding Roman—on both sides of the ocean. "We can still take our music to the people—wherever they need us," Shiloh declared. "I will not be taking Aurora over the bridge, but I must support the loyal fans north of the Red River—the people who believe in another way."

Within a year, the new Emperor stepped down. His last message to the people was to tell them that it was up to them to find and pursue their own destiny. Following that, the Emperor disappeared. Rumours followed that he was seen in Tibet studying with the Dali Lama.

When Aurora was old enough to walk, she joined her father on stage, dressed in a jingle dress—a healing costume adorned with bells. But when it came time for him to venture over the Golden Gate Bridge, Aurora stayed behind with her Aunt and Uncle. He did not stay longer than was necessary—one weekend concert at a time but it was enough for the people of the USNR to see that he had not forgotten them. Jude joined the rest of the band and when the concert took place in his home-land, he came back late on his motorcycle. For a reason known only to the government of USNR at the time, Jude's new partner was not allowed a Visa to cross the bridge into Kansa.

Time passed quickly and the band became lulled into a false sense of security through their ability to come and go—crossing the bridge at will. Not all of the members were asleep to the possibilities, however. Jude and Shiloh found themselves on edge during the time spent north of the Red River. "You are making me nervous." Shiloh managed a grin as he greeted his friend back at the ranch. "Whenever we finish up and head back home, I find myself looking over my shoulder. That is not the way I want to be, but what can I say?"

"I can say that it's a good thing to be aware of the visions that we shared on the Medicine Wheel," Jude replied. "Maybe you changed the future that was to happen? Maybe we won't have to be part of a story that belongs to someone else. Nathan and I have been talking about it. I feel that my place is with you and James and the rest of the band. I owe you that. But the time is coming that I will be staying behind to be with Nate."

"You owe us nothing—except to live your life the best you can," Shiloh told his friend with complete sincerity.

And then there came a time that Jude did not join the rest of the band on the trek back to Kansa, and James remarked: "I hope he has found peace. I had a feeling that something was in the air."

The concert that evening was in the western part of the States, and the journey home would take a bit longer than usual. The band made their way down country roads following the Genesee River. The name was derived from a Seneca word meaning good and pleasant valley. It was still at least a four-hour drive home, so they made a stop by the side of the river and pitched a couple of tents that James and Petra had brought along to air out. Shiloh went for a stroll along the river to stretch his legs.

He walked in silent meditation until he came to a particular turn in the river where the trees hung over the water. It reminded him of the river that Amanda and he had discovered in the forest behind his father's ranch. He sat down with a sigh and dangled his hand in the water. His mind was at once full of memories—of Amanda and returning sheepishly that day—to the knowing smiles of his parents. His eyes were filled with tears that would not be halted. And his heart pounded in his chest. He was in such agony at that moment that his tears might have been blood! Even as the memories that were not entirely all his own began to surface, he tried to push them away—to deny the significance of the moment lost in his personal anguish.

"Oh God! Oh Great Spirit!" he cried out in pain. "Father—why must I be part of this? I have lost my mother and father and the woman

I loved more than life. I have a daughter that needs me. Is there no way that this can be completed without me?"

"There is a way." It was not a Spirit voice. He turned his head to see Jude. "There is a way," Jude repeated. "I am here to warn you. You can take my motorcycle. I parked it further down the river. Go now, and no one will find you. You can be over the bridge in a couple of hours if you leave now."

"And what will happen to you and the rest of the band?" Shiloh stood to hug his friend.

"I am here to warn you. The homeland security police will be about an hour behind me. They found the Emperor's helicopter on the top of the Black Hills beside the Medicine Wheel. We should have known that the President was not going to give up. They showed up at Nathan's place this morning and gave me an ultimatum. They need a reason to arrest you—and hold you for questioning. But you and I know that will not be the end of it."

"And what did they threaten you with?"

"It is against the law in this country to be a homosexual. It doesn't matter if there is love or whatever else. I might have been dancing for that matter—you know yourself—people have been arrested for less. The law is on the books. They were just waiting for the right moment. And once they arrest you, they can bring up the matter of the Emperor's disappearance. President Forester and his secret police didn't buy the young Emperor's story for a minute."

"But what is your part in this? Why didn't they just throw you and Nathan in jail and be done with it."

"There is the excuse to get their hands on you," Jude explained. "And of course there is the story—they are hell-bent to follow the story to the letter."

"And of course—no one is about to take responsibility for their part in the prophesy," Shiloh added. "At least not in the President's camp. The Prophesy of the four horsemen—the Four Riders from the Stars is coming due. The world as we know it will end, unless there is a sacrifice."

"But we know better," Jude sighed. "Even if as a result of you being found guilty and put to death—the end will come."

"So what did they threaten you with?" Shiloh repeated.

"You know the story. But I would not take any amount of money they offered. And I don't believe the one who played my part did either. They have Nate in custody. They said that they will let us both go if I did what was necessary to incriminate you. I pretended to go along so that I could warn you. Time is wasting. You need to get out of here now."

"I am not about to run," Shiloh said firmly. "If this is to be my fate, then so be it. I just realized here today that all that has happened would have been in vain if I ran away now. I am not guilty of anything. No court in the States or Kansa will find me guilty of these trumped-up charges. No one would believe that I am Gay—if that is what they intend. No offence meant to you."

"Of course. They know that. It is just a reason to get you behind bars. And it is almost laughable—if it wasn't so stupidly serious. They will get here in about a half-hour now and use some lame excuse to poke around. Then, I...uh, that's when they will arrest you. The rest is history—according to the Book. They are devious and so good at twisting the Bible for their own purpose."

"Let's go back to camp," Shiloh suggested, "I would have preferred not to have it happen this way, but no matter what—I want you to play along. That way no one else will get hurt. Understand? I am asking you to do this for me—no matter what it may seem to anyone else. James will believe in you and I will find a way to tell everyone that you were only doing what I asked."

Shiloh and Jude walked back to where the vans were parked, in relative silence. It was, as Jude had said, almost laughable—if it wasn't so serious. Shiloh remembered a part out of one of Shakespeare's plays. Something about "all the world's a stage" and another "the fault is not in the stars, but in ourselves." It was insanely appropriate.

The temporary camp was almost as Shiloh had left it. Mark and John were tossing a frisbee. They were joking—but there was an edge.

"What's up?" Shiloh asked James. "I would have thought you would be catching a few winks. I need to tell you something."

James shrugged. "Too late for that, I think I know what you were about to tell me," he motioned with his head. A couple of serious-looking men dressed in suits walked into sight around the tent.

"What are you here for?" Shiloh asked them.

"Nothing in particular. Just checking that you rockers have no drugs or booze."

"Did you find anything?" James was becoming irritated.

"No. But we are allowed to check just the same," the man had one hand inside his coat.

"This could get out of hand pretty easy," Shiloh thought to himself. He leaned against a tree and looked to where Jude stood at the edge of the clearing. He motioned with his eyes.

Jude read his message and sauntered over. "I never got to say a proper hello," he said and leaned close. "I am so sorry about this," Jude whispered and he kissed him.

"What are you doing?" James exclaimed.

"Yes—what is it that you are doing?" The strange man drew a gun from his coat. "Shiloh—or whatever you call yourself—I am arresting you for an indecent act. I am arresting you for fraternizing with a known homosexual. You should come quietly and no one else will be implicated."

"To hell with that!" James stepped between Shiloh and the man with the gun. "My brother has not done anything wrong and you will not be taking him anywhere." At that point, the other band members surrounded the two men. "No one is taking Shiloh anywhere. You will have to use that gun—and there are too many of us to shoot before we take it away," Simon stated in a menacing tone.

Shiloh sighed. He stepped toward the two men who were waving their guns, attempting to cover the circle of men. Shiloh held up one hand and opened it, then said in a clear calm voice. "You do not want to harm anyone. In fact this is not the kind of situation that you expected. It has been a long day and you must be tired from your trip here—down all those dusty country roads. You must be getting tired," he repeated. "I think you are so tired and stressed that you need to let it all go. Let it all go now. Let it go and rest here for a while. You need 8 hours of restful sleep. You need to rest here on the grass." He motioned with his hand and the two men slumped to the ground—along with most of *The James Gang* members, leaving only James and Shiloh standing.

"What???" James blinked as his brother touched his shoulder. "I was getting ready to have a nap. I have never seen you do that before."

"Necessity is the mother of invention," Shiloh smiled grimly. "And I remembered the rest of the story."

"Oh yeah. That story," James looked around. "Well you weren't about to find us asleep when you needed us," he stated. "This is where we change the story. But what do we do now?"

"Now I will wake up our friends and we go back home. When we are all safely back in Kansa, I will consider giving myself up."

"Bull," James replied. "Why should you? Can you think of any good reason?"

"Not right now but I will do whatever is necessary to keep peace." Shiloh went around the circle of sleeping men touching them and waking them up. Jude was last.

"Maybe you should leave him asleep," James suggested with a firm lip.

"I need all of you to know something," Shiloh declared as he helped Jude to his feet. "Jude came to warn me. He asked me to take his motorcycle and disappear. But I suspected that something like this might happen. So I asked Jude to go on with the plan. I do not want anything to happen to any of you."

"Are you forgetting something?" Simon stepped forward and placed his hand on Shiloh's shoulder. "Don't worry—I am not going to kiss you," he gave a sideways glance in Jude's direction and shook his head in wonder. "Are you forgetting that we are all in this together? We all knew that it might not be a bed of roses. It goes with the territory. We will not let you down—how about it?" he asked the others and was met with an outstretch of arms in a circle. "Now let us put these two sleeping beauties to bed in the tent, so the rain doesn't dampen their camping experience. In eight hours, we will be safely home, and no one will be the wiser."

"I need to stay behind," Jude replied. "Put me back to sleep in the other tent. I could never forgive myself if anything happened to Nate because of me. It needs to look like you believe that I betrayed you," he pleaded to Shiloh.

"There was a time I would never have thought he had it in him," Simon remarked, when they were packed up and driving away. "I guess you don't know what a man is really about when your judgment about the way he lives his life gets in the way."

Chapter 20
ONCE ON A BLUE MOON

Once on a Blue Moon
He goes down to the River
Where the teepees were gathered
But the teepees are no longer there.
The People have moved on.

Once on a Blue Moon
He goes down to the River
Where the Water ran so clear
His People drank from there
But the River is now poisoned.

Once in a Blue Week
He visits the Hillsides
Where the Forests were so dense
The Animals were at home there
The Animals and Birds have disappeared.

Once in a Blue Week
He visits the Hillsides
There are no Animals and no Trees
The Forest and the Birds are no longer there
The Trees have all been cut down.

Steven WinterHawk

Once in a Blue Hour
He goes to the broad Prairies
Where the Buffalo once roamed
Buffalo as far as the eye could see
But there are no Buffalo to be seen.

Once in a Blue Hour
He goes to the broad Prairies
The Buffalo were his Relatives
They Gave his People all they needed
The Buffalo were all slaughtered needlessly.

Once in a Blue Moment
From the top of the Black Hills
He looks out at the Valley Below
A railway track cuts through the Valley
It crosses the poisoned river and barren hillsides.

Once in a Blue Moment
From the top of the Black Hills
He remembers the Buffalo
Who Gave up their Lives for His People
And he accepts his part in all that happened.

Once in a Blue Heartbeat
He leaps to join the Buffalo
He will fly—or die like the Buffalo
An Eagle Spirit joins him in the Wind
And takes him to the Creator in the Sky.

Once in a Blue Heartbeat
He leaps to join the Buffalo
And the Earth receives his blood
And the Creator accepts his Sacrifice
And the Circle will begin again.

It does not take a Blue Moon
For People to make a Difference
Animals become Extinct in a Heart Beat;
Stop our Rivers from becoming Poisoned—Now
and Take Responsibility for the Way we Live

We must Wake up and Learn to Live
Moment to Moment—Second to Second
We need to Care for this Earth who is our Mother
And all Creatures who are our Relatives
Not just Once Every Blue Moon!

…Steven WinterHawk September 2008

Two weeks after their escape from the Security Police in the Genesee Valley, Shiloh and James learned that the bridge to the States was closed and relations between Kansa and the USNR were suspended. Shiloh paid a visit to an Elder Chief in Dallas. Chief Daniel Kicking Horse informed him that the President had issued a warning that the People of Kansa were being considered responsible for the disappearance of the Former Emperor. Furthermore, Shiloh was considered a wanted criminal. Among the charges that included the practice of homosexuality on Roman Soil, was the crime of direct interference and blasphemy on the part of the High Roman Church. In other words, pretending to be the second coming of Jesus.

"These would be dangerous charges if the Roman Empire had not been dissolved and the State and Church were still in control of most of the major countries of the world," Chief Dan explained. "As it is, The President is calling himself the Emperor of New Rome—now that Rome has fallen. He states that it is up to him now to bring you to justice. I think he knows that the end of time prophesy of the Four Riders from the Stars is upon us and he is frightened. He will do anything to blame someone other than accept that he and the citizens of Rome are also responsible."

"So what will he do?" Shiloh asked. "I mean if I don't turn myself over? That's it—isn't it?"

"That is it in a nutshell," Chief Dan acknowledged. "He has issued an ultimatum. He says that he has a nuclear missile aimed at Vega which he has judged as a source of evil and against the laws of the Christian Church. This missile will be on its way in four days, unless you turn yourself over to his Homeland Security. We are quietly urging everyone to evacuate the city and get as far away as possible."

"You know he won't stop there," Shiloh stated. "But what choice other choice do I have?"

"I can't ask you to do this," Chief Dan replied. "And part of this is that what you say is true. If getting you out of the way somehow stops the prophesy, which I doubt, then he will continue until the Red man is extinct. How do I know that? Oil was just discovered in Western Kansa. Oil is the new black gold. It is about to begin again.

Our message to him will be: 'today is a good day to die'. Our only hope will be that the people of this New Rome will not let this happen."

"I have come to trust the people of New Rome," Shiloh replied. "These people are fair. They will not let me be convicted for something that I didn't do. I did not kill the Emperor and I have never claimed that I am Jesus. I have said that I am like every man, woman and child who is born with the spark of divinity that is part of the One who came before. When my story is told in court, they will understand. They are kind and compassionate people who are ready to let the bad blood between the Red man and his White brothers and sisters be a thing of the past."

"Then go home and think on this," the Chief urged. "Maybe you can trust the people of New Rome, but they are not the ones with their finger on the button, and this President is crafty. He will have a plan to get his way."

A visitor was waiting when Shiloh and James returned to the ranch. It was Andrew who had flown *The Arrow* away years ago. The last time they had seen Andrew and Philip, Andrew wanted to test *The Arrow's* speed before hiding it on the other side of the moon. They also hoped to get in touch with the Men from the Stars.

"Is Phillip with you?" Shiloh asked as he greeted Andrew.

"Phillip is with *The Arrow*." Andrew replied. "We met with the Star Men. They are from Sirius—the Dog Star. In their Dream universe, Sirius is a planet, and when we see it on this side of the dream, we only see its light. Philip and I have learned much about stars and other worlds and things that are mysteries even for the people from Sirius. More about this another time. Philip is with the much improved *Arrow*, which is now equipped to be invisible. But if the President has the technology that belonged to the Emperor, his men might be able to track us. We can't stay too long."

"Where are Phillip and *The Arrow* now?" Shiloh asked.

"He is moving around. It is more difficult to track, if it is not in one place. There is a tracking technology available that is similar to the way some planets are found that might be invisible otherwise. It is based on seeing how an object interferes or affects other objects nearby. But someone would have to be looking for this interference to track our ship." A small blue light flashed on what appeared to be a wrist watch that Andrew wore. He held the device to his mouth. "Phillip? Is everything OK?" Then he moved it to his ear. "This is a bit primitive but it is the least noticeable of the communication devices that is available on Sirius. "OK—we will meet you there." He spoke into the device again.

"Phillip will be landing again out behind the woods. We can take your car—or Jeep," he suggested to Shiloh. "But, sorry to the rest of you. It will be less noticeable to the President's spying if only Shiloh and James came along."

"OK," Shiloh agreed. "But I can't stay long either. I need to pick up my daughter soon."

"You have a child?" Andrew was astounded. "I thought that people—a Shaman like I know you are—would not...well you know."

"Yes—I did get married. It is a natural thing for any true spiritual man or woman. Sharing love is what the Creator's gift of life is all about. But Aurora's mother is passed on and I am her sole blood parent. Still my daughter has lots of tribal parents to look after her. How about it James—want to see *The Arrow*?

"Sure," James agreed "But no unplanned trips out of this world for me. Petra is waiting for me over at your uncle's place with Aurora, and I do not want to be separated from her any more than you want to leave Aurora behind."

On the ride to meet up with *The Arrow*, Andrew began to tell his story about what happened when he and Phillip put the aircraft to the test. "At first, we circled the Earth, building up speed until everything outside the ship was a blur and then we were alone. Phillip asked me how we would know when and if we reached the speed of light. I didn't know except that the way *The Arrow* was built, the throttle—the stick that controls the speed—does not have a limit. When I had been piloting the ship before and I held the throttle down as far as it would go, the plane just kept on accelerating. I didn't know if there was a limit. That is what we were there to find out. Philip said he had a feeling in his gut that we had reached the limit of our physical bodies.

I felt the same. I looked at Philip and asked if he wanted to go on and he said:" "go for it." Then, a second later, we were in the middle of a burst of white light. And we came out into the blackness of space and the stars began to appear all around us." Andrew's face became peaceful and euphoric at this part of his storey.

"And then what happened?" James was eager to find out.

"And then a ship appeared—one of the circular ships that we recognized as belonging to the People from the Stars. And they guided us to their home planet they call Sirius."

"So the men and women from Sirius are able to fly faster than light?" Shiloh asked.

"Yes," Andrew replied. "But even at that speed it takes years to get from their planet to Earth. There is something else that is needed—a belief in the Dream, as Phillip and I have through personal experience, or the natural "bending"—the folding of Space and Time. These naturally occurring yet mysterious 'events' can be sensed by the People from the Stars and they employ them to travel distances that would not otherwise be possible."

"So you and Phillip can do something that is not possible by the people from Sirius?" James asked, all the while feeling like he was in the middle of a science-fiction movie.

"No—not always," Andrew admitted. "But sometimes. We do not know why it worked when we traveled faster than light. But it happened naturally for us. And took us to where the people from Sirius could rescue us. Phillip and I have not been able to duplicate the Space-Time jump again, and we do not have the natural ability to know when the doors in space are about to open," he sighed. "But we are learning and, thanks to our new friends, we were able to be here today."

"So, why did you come back?" Shiloh asked. He had a sense that it was something to do with the prophesy.

"I'll explain that in a bit," Andrew answered. "Stop the car here and park in the woods. We will walk the rest of the way, in case we are picked up on one of the spy satellites. I don't know if these systems are still in use with the Emperor gone, but we can't chance *The Arrow* being spotted. It needs to become visible for us to get on board. It is not like the Emperor's kind of invisibility technology. That only works for the naked eye—and most radar. This makes the ship completely invisible—I have no idea how, except it does. Some kind of trick with the spectrum of light and energy waves. Philip will meet us just beyond the next clear patch of ground."

They left the car parked hidden in the trees, and walked for a few minutes, until another clear, open space about the size of a small baseball field appeared.

"There is not enough room for a plane to land here," Shiloh noted the obvious.

"But here a plane can land vertically," Andrew explained. "I told you that *The Arrow* has been modified. See..." And even as he spoke, the hardened dirt and dust became agitated in four equal-distant places, as though some force was pressing down—a force that pushed and burrowed into the earth. Four large invisible feet settled and the dust with it. And then, the clearing was filled with a large arrow-head shaped craft.

"Quick—inside," Andrew urged. The three men raced to the opening door. Once they were inside, the door began to close. "Buckle yourself in. We are about to take off." Andrew did as he instructed, and within a few moments' time they could feel the sensation that told them that they were lifting off the ground. The nearby windows also confirmed what the men could feel. "We can still see out—the glass has been treated so that it will not reflect light—or something like that," Andrew said. "James this is my friend, Phillip. We have been friends for longer than either of us can remember. We rekindled the friendship when Shiloh took me along to the other world in this plane. Phillip came back with us. And Phillip—James is Shiloh's brother."

Philip nodded and smiled his hello. "I learned to pilot crafts like *The Arrow* on Sirius," he explained. "Don't look so worried. We will not be leaving the Earth. Once we are at an appropriate height, I will put the plane on automatic pilot and we can talk while circling the globe at supersonic speed."

At a given time, good to his word, Phillip joined the other three men in the passenger area. James glanced back toward the cockpit with a worried look on his face. "Not to worry," Andrew explained. "This plane is now equipped with an automatic sensor that enables it to avoid other planes or hitting a mountain top. And we are fuelled with a concentrated water that could last a month, if need be. Then, if we were to go into outer space a different kind of engine kicks in and we run by the power of the movement of the stars. Sort of like running on starlight. The people on Sirius call it Zero-Point Energy. We mortals," he joked, "are so far from understanding this, much less utilizing it that Phillip and I just accept that it works. But this is not why we are here."

"Exactly why are you here?" Shiloh asked for the third time. "Not that I am just glad to see the both of you."

"To begin," Andrew said. "The Men and Women from the Stars have visited us many times in the past. One such visit that is pertinent to the current state of the Earth was in biblical times. You could read in the bible about an encounter by a man called Ezekiel. The version of Ezekiel's story in today's bible is a much-changed passage than he originally would have written. In today's Bible we read what is called Ezekiel's vision. To be sure, the man would have been hard-pressed to understand what he saw and was told. The People from the Stars appeared in the skies with their circular craft, and upon landing, spoke to Ezekiel about things that the Red man have been talking about since the dawn of time. They told him about the Medicine Wheel and how each and every man, woman and child on this earth is spiritually related—to every creature that shares the planet with them. They told this simple spiritual man about a belief that we call totems—that every person is linked to different animals and that we should respect the animals to show us how to live in harmony."

"This is the part about where Ezekiel saw people with four animal faces and wheels within wheels," James explained.

"James? Brother—I didn't know that you read the Bible?" Shiloh smiled.

"Well don't let it get around," James poked his brother in the ribs and grinned. "But I have always been a bit curious about other people's beliefs. And I am pretty tolerant, you know."

"Yeah. That is what Ezekiel wrote about. And I was told that they showed him projections—3D images to help him understand. And you probably could guess that there were visits to the Egyptians. Think about the pictures of the gods with a head of a hawk or a jackal? But those were not gods that visited them—they were just men and women like me and you but quite a bit advanced in technology. And they wrote about it as a part of a warning like how the Four Riders delivered to our modern day Emperor."

"The prophesies that are about to come true." James jumped in.

"Exactly," Phillip responded. "And they told about the coming of a messenger—a son of God that would help them get their act together, so to speak. Then Jesus came along and told them that if they followed his way, they would live in peace and harmony. He also told them the true meaning of sacrifice and that it meant being willing to die for your fellow creatures—the way the buffalo gave their lives for the Red man. But they misunderstood or were led astray, by those in charge that did not want to give up their power over the people. And eventually Jesus was put to death. The one great thing he accomplished was to stop the sacrifice of animals. But the priests and those who did not want to accept self-responsibility or to give up power shifted the sacrifice from the animals in the temple to Jesus. And to this day, many well-meaning Christians still depend on the sacrifice of Jesus to save them from their mistaken ways. In a sad way, Jesus is still on that cross being tortured so that some people can excuse themselves and not be held accountable."

"That is the story as I remember, too," Shiloh agreed. "But what most people do not acknowledge is that the Creator gave us the gift of free will. The first question I would ask when I began to wake up would be if I have been praying to the wrong God."

"So why did Jesus come and why did he still go through with it? And where is he now. And better still—why do you think you can do what he did not accomplish?" James asked his brother.

"But he did do what he came for," Shiloh replied. "He awakened the people to the next level of Spirit. People cannot be forced to evolve to be more loving and peaceful. Jesus came to be a living example of the way to live. When he healed someone, he just said: "go your way and live from your heart." But what was written down by those that were mired in judgment was: "...and sin no more." And as to what happed to Jesus. He is alive today but many of the people who have chosen to live in this dream have also forgotten him. They live in a dream that he does not seem to inhabit. That is the choice that comes with free will. Grace is always available, but not to those who deny it.

"Sounds all right to me, brother," James smiled. "But you evade the question that is foremost in my mind."

"Why do I think I can do something that the One who come before did not? I answered the last first because this is important to know. There will be other messengers to come. He was not the first and I will not be the last. Simply put, I can make a difference now and at this time. How much of a difference is up to everyone who chooses to live in darkness or light. I choose to have a better world for my daughter to grow up and for her to raise her children in the way her mother was not able. I will give my life if there is even the smallest chance of this becoming real. This is my Dream that will not die."

"We came back because we learned something important about the prophesy," Andrew spoke up. "This prophesy is based on real events that are known by the People from the Stars. Our new friends are able to sense and predict where and when the shifts in time and space are about to take place—that is how they are able to travel such great distances between stars. And there are cycles to this space shifting that can be predicted. The last one that matters to this story was the moment of your birth," he said to Shiloh. "There is a plan. A reason in all of this chaos. This plan is known only to the Creator. But if we watch closely, we can see where some of it is happening, even if we cannot always guess the reason. The day that you were born, the planet that is a star, appeared in the sky over the place of your birth."

"Like the Star of Bethlehem," Phillip interjected. "No coincidence."

"Yes," Andrew agreed. "And as the Riders from the Stars predicted, they will return. The planet that is the Star Sirius will shift in Space-Time, to pass between earth and the sun, four days from now. There will be major eclipses that will last seven hours. And during that time, the earth will shake and the tall buildings that humans have built will come crashing down."

"A Blue Moon," Shiloh spoke as if remembering something.

"What is a blue moon?" James asked.

"A more, well-known example of a Blue Moon is the second full moon in a month. But I have heard it used to describe other exceptional and rare things that happen. For example, it is an eclipse of the sun by the moon. Blue is the spirit colour in our people's beliefs. It is the other side of black. It is an extraordinary Spiritual event to happen at any time, but this will be a great Blue Moon."

"This is true," Andrew agreed again. "And the rest of this is about peace and balance. The shaking of the Earth is a form of cleansing that is natural in its occurrence; however it is feared by those who see natural disasters as having no meaning. But they still call them an act of God. This is not about a vengeful God that wishes to punish his children for their sinful ways. Nature is about spirit and will seek to regain balance. Mankind needs to be more aware of the damage that they are causing in the environment and to the other creatures that live with us on this planet. The People from the Stars are aware of this. The Creator has sent his son once again to help people prepare for this. His son will be the one that will help people learn to live in harmony and love."

"And when this Blue Moon happens and the world is shaking, it will be a time to care for each other. And if anything else should happen to interfere within the seven hours of shaking, who would know the consequences?" Shiloh mused.

"I think the world that I came from was the result of how great the devastation could be," Phillip replied. "Everything—not just skyscrapers was levelled. And it was rumoured that most of the people of the earth did not survive. We wondered what could cause this, but now we know."

"In fact we do know," Shiloh agreed. "This is all the more reason that I need to do what I must to stop this from ending life on this Mother Earth as we know it to be. I need to respect the dream and fulfill my destiny."

"Perhaps there is another way," Andrew suggested. "We came here because you can do something that even the People from the Stars can't do. You can take people to another dream without waiting for a door in Space-Time to open. The People from the Stars respect that you are the messenger and if you agree to help, they will join in to take our People to a new land—a new dream."

"And what about the ones that are left behind?" Shiloh was aware of this as part of the prophesy as it was told in the White man's Bible.

"They will need to accept responsibility for the fate of a world that they created. This is their dream. It is not up to us to save them from themselves. You said that before," Philip suggested.

"I did say that," Shiloh agreed, but I include those people—the White men and women and their children when I speak about all our relations. We are all part of this dream—all of the four colours—and all of the creatures on this Earth. We will face this together. There will not be anyone left behind. This is the way of our ancestors. When I am before the White man's court—I will tell them this."

* * *

Shiloh was taken aboard a special Homeland Security helicopter the moment he crossed the Golden Gate Bridge and set foot on the soil of the USNR. His hands were bound behind his back and he was blindfolded. There was no reason given except that it was a necessary part of the security precautions. Shiloh also had a cloth tied across his mouth to prevent him from talking. The man, who was in charge, was the only person who Shiloh recognized before being blindfolded from his television appearances. This man was the head of Homeland Security and also the lawyer and judge. His name was Philip Ponte, nicknamed "The Hanging Judge". Ponte enjoyed being the one sent to pick up the offender. It was rumoured that if Philip Ponte was present at your arrest, then you were already as good as sentenced. In the helicopter, Shiloh began to wonder what the destination would be. It was unlikely that they put him in some secluded prison because the President would want this to be over in a matter of days—less than four days.

After a lengthy time in the air, the helicopter descended. With the blades still cutting the air above him, Shiloh was roughly hauled from the vehicle. "Keep your head down—unless you want to lose it," one of his guards ordered. "Better yet," another laughed sadistically, "hold your head up like the Son of God you pretend to be and we won't need to go through with this trial. Do you think God will protect you from being beheaded by a helicopter propeller?" Shiloh was jostled around until he heard Ponte's voice. "Smarten up! You are part of the Roman Air Force, so act like it. Actually, now the title would be the Royal Air Force of the USSNR. Besides, it is our job to hand him over to the big chief of the SOS where he will be tried."

"The SOS? Of course," Shiloh became grimly aware of the President's plan. No court in the USSNR or Kansa would convict him of the trumped up charges, but the Sons of Soma were another matter. He wondered at the truth of fate and how easy some people became trapped in the wheel—in the story that had begun to play out for the second time. Even the names were similar. Perhaps karma was another way to explain this. But the Red man called it the Circle of Life.

"Why is he blindfolded again?" one of the men asked.

"This chief of the Sons of Soma requested it," Ponte explained. "These people believe that our prisoner can work magic—and that his eyes might convince us to let him go. That is why his hands are behind him and his mouth silenced. You can untie the cloth from his mouth now—I don't want him to suffocate before we deliver him."

"Aren't you afraid he will cast a spell on us?" the man laughed as he undid the cloth.

"Not at all. And I want to show the Chief who is really in charge. Did these primitives really think we couldn't capture them anytime we wanted? Our spy satellites have been keeping track of them until the time came that they would be of use to us. Here—move forward," Ponte said after they had walked for a bit. He shoved Shiloh. "Chief Iron Hand—this is the man we spoke about. He is to be tried in your village—by your law."

Two men who were under the leadership of the Chief—two different, but just as uncaring, men replaced the security agent's rough grasp on Shiloh's forearms. "Unlock the handcuffs, "the Chief demanded gruffly. "I want to tie him in our way. I do not trust hands that I cannot see."

Shiloh's hands were momentarily freed and brought to the front of his body. Meanwhile, a stick was thrust between his elbows and both hands were bound at his sides by a cord that joined across his lower chest. Memories surfaced of a cross.

"I will prepare him for the trial," Iron Hand told Ponte and his men. "You can watch if you want." He led Shiloh to a small hill where the wind blew lightly on his face. "You pretend to be one of our people," he addressed Shiloh. "If this is so—then you will know what will happen next. We will test your worthiness to stand trial in our circle. If you cry out and whimper to be set free, then we will set your spirit free and you will not need to sit in our circle."

Shiloh had heard the stories—of the old ways of his People. Some tribes believed that torturing a man would give him a chance to show his bravery—and if he survived, then he might be set free—or maybe become a member of the tribe that had captured him. He steeled himself for what would come next.

"These tests have been prepared for your eyes," the Chief spoke to someone—perhaps Ponte—who must have followed. "This will remind you that your People, the White-faced, are not so different in their beliefs than the Red man. This is from your sacred book. I have prepared a headband that is wrapped with thorns. This I will put on this man." And he did so, tightening the cloth, until Shiloh could feel the excruciating pain. The hot blood began to trickle down his forehead.

"And now the true test," the Chief stated. "Stand straight and tall," he instructed Shiloh. "Now that the cloth is removed from your mouth, my ears will be open to hear you call out for mercy."

At that, another man began to apply a whip to Shiloh's back. He gasped and held his breath and firmed his lips as the Chief counted 10 lashes. And then when Shiloh did not speak, there followed another 10. And another methodical 10. And again, until Shiloh lost count. And on and on, until a merciful blackness closed in and Shiloh collapsed unconscious to the ground.

When he came to, there was still blackness, from the cloth across his eyes. He was laying on his back and the minute he stirred, the Chief spoke. "You surprise me. I did not think you would pass this test."

Shiloh was helped to his feet and supported to stand unsteadily. "Do whatever you need," Shiloh said with his head high and gasped. "In the words of my People: 'today is a good day to die'. I am Anishinabe.

I am a son of the Creator put on this Earth. I will endure it all for My People and my Mother Earth."

"This is brave talk indeed," the Chief replied. "But you have earned my respect. I do not believe that we require further testing. There is one thing that I must ask. How can you say that you are one of us? Your father was not one of our People. You claim your heritage due to being born of a mother who had Red skin. This is not enough to be one of us."

"I have heard that said," Shiloh replied. "But think of this: we look to our animal brothers for our teaching. And if a cub is born of a female Wolf, does this mean that he is not one of the Wolf Tribe?"

"You will say no more, unless requested by the Circle," the Chief instructed. "I was told that you have a magic tongue and it appears to be so."

With his hands and arms still bound and his eyes still covered, Shiloh was helped to sit, to join a circle of men who would decide his fate. He could not see the other men but he was aware of their places around the circle by their voices. The man called Ponte and Chief Iron Hand—a descendent of the original Iron Hand sat together directly across the circle. Like a Medicine Wheel or a true Native gathering, there was a fire burning at the center. Shiloh could feel the heat and he gathered some strength to help take his mind off his extensive wounds.

A deep drum was struck and the Chief spoke. "This begins the Circle that will decide whether this man called Shiloh is guilty of the charges that are brought against him this day. Who will speak about this?"

"I will," the voice was Philip Ponte. "This is the list of crimes. I give only those that pertain to my country and religion. First there is the crime that led us to arrest this man. He is to be found guilty of befriending and fraternizing with a known homosexual. If it is not a crime in the Red man's way, it is in my country. Under the laws of modern day Rome we pride ourselves in being tolerant, but we stop short of allowing the breaking of our God's most sacred covenants. A man will lie with a woman and not another man—this is God's way—it is the way God decried that children should be brought into this world. Do you agree to this charge?"

There was a murmur that passed around the circle. "We agree," Chief Iron Hand spoke. "Our people have found this not to be normal and out of balance with nature. We would ban a man for this—send him away. There was a time that this way was considered to be a Shaman's way but this was changed through the teaching of Soma."

"The next charge is possibly the most sinful and against all that Rome is about. This man has traveled our countryside claiming to be the second coming of Jesus—the Messiah, the One and only Son of our God. He has been responsible for misleading our people—claiming to save them from the fulfillment of the Prophesies. The fulfillment of these prophesies, as you know, are upon us. The fate of all of our people is at stake. The very fate of this world may be in balance as a result of this man's teachings."

Iron Hand replied: "My spies among this man's people returned today to tell me about his meeting with People from the Stars. There was a gathering of the Chiefs following this meeting to say that he could not save his people from the events that will follow—even though he has done this magic in the past. This tells us that he is not who he claims to be—or is lying. Either way, he is not the return of Quetzcotl—the Winged Serpent that our people have waited so many years to save them and restore them to the glory of the past. To pretend to be the saviour that Soma promised is a grave crime in the eyes of my people—one that must not go unpunished."

"Thirdly," Phillip Ponte spoke again, "I need to add another charge—an addendum to the second. We do not have conclusive proof of this but my President believes that this man and his teachings are in some way responsible for the disappearance of our former Emperor. I add this as an afterthought, should he be found guilty of the crimes of blasphemy, we will consider this at that time. That is all that I have to submit now. I give this over to this Circle and Chief Iron Hand.

Chapter 21

THE LAST SUNDANCE

"You have heard the charges," Iron Hand proclaimed to the circle of men who would be judging the Shaman, Shiloh. "We will now allow the accused to answer us, before the Creator of all things, if he is guilty. There is one problem, however. We cannot allow this man who is known to do magic to speak uncontrollably. I will repeat the charges and he will give a single-worded answer to each—either yes or no. Then we will decide his fate. This is how it will be done!" At that proclamation, the chief struck another loud resounding drum to signify that this part of the trial was to begin.

"You are charged with having relations with a man who is a known homosexual," he addressed Shiloh. "Are you guilty or not? Remember to answer only yes or no."

"Yes," Shiloh answered truthfully and a murmur passed around the circle.

"The other charge against you is that you have spoken publically that you are the Son of the Creator—in admitting to this you will also be telling the White men present that you are the Son of God. How do you answer? Are you guilty or not? Yes or no?"

"Yes," Shiloh replied again, and a resound of "Ho" was heard from every Native around the circle.

"Ho—so be it," Iron Hand repeated the Circle's agreement.

"At this point I would like to ask the accused an additional question," Phillip Ponte requested. And when there was no objection, he continued:

"Are you responsible for the disappearance of the former Emperor of Rome?"

"No," Shiloh answered truthfully once more—as best he could under the constraint of a single-worded reply.

"Are you aware that the Emperor's helicopter was recently found abandoned on the plateau of the Black Hills in Kansa?"

"Yes."

"We have calculated the use of the solar batteries and the time it would take under normal decay of the related systems. That helicopter has been on the plateau over three years. We have subsequently searched the satellite logs given over to us by the former Minister of Defense of Rome when this part of the government was being dismantled. The video tapes are lost but the logs indicate a meeting by you and your band on and about the time the helicopter would have landed. The rest is inclusive but I need to ask you—did you meet with the Emperor at that time and place?"

Shiloh believed that there may be more information available that the man was not disclosing but in either case his reply was the truth.

"Yes."

"But you told us that you were not responsible for the Emperor's disappearance? Don't answer again—I believe you might be telling the truth, but is there more to this than we are able to understand with the limited knowledge we have available through this line of questioning? I mean, are you involved with what happened to the Emperor in a way we might not understand?"

"Yes."

"You do know what happened to him?"

"Yes."

"Is it possible that he is not dead and that he is gone somewhere? This is a stretch of my logical belief system. Did you take him somewhere?"

"Yes."

"Let me think for a moment. This indicates to me that you took him somewhere that he asked to be taken."

"Yes."

At this point the questioning was interrupted by Iron Hand. "Did I not tell you that this man could not be trusted? This is why I will not allow him to speak for any length—and he is even blindfolded and bound. You are putting your mind and spirit in danger by leading him on in this way. He could actually be leading you somewhere you do not want to go. I suggest that we end this now and pass our judgment accordingly."

"I agree—for now," Ponte replied. "But I would like to reserve the right to pursue this again should the opportunity arise."

"There will not be another chance for that," Iron Hand said. "All that we require at this time to pass judgment on this man was his admission of guilt." A moment of silence ensued, however, during which Iron Hand asked for the members of the circle to consider their judgment. Then he spoke again: "I now will ask if there is one man present who hears these words, who disagrees or will speak out in defense of this one called Shiloh. It should be noted that anyone who would speak untruthfully or against the religion of our People, will be dealt with in a manner to fit the crime. Your friend," he addressed Shiloh, "the one that you changed and sent back to us faced this fate. The one called Yellow Feather attempted to change the ways of our People to the weak Christian ways, and he was found guilty of this. Despite that, he passed the ritual of torture. This Circle judged that his mind was possessed by a Spirit—so we cut off his head. Now—I will ask again: is there anyone who will speak for this man?"

"I will speak for this man," a voice sounded from beyond the circle—beyond the campfire.

"Who spoke these words? Step forward into the light."

"I am the one you have named Horse Thief," was the reply, now just behind where Shiloh sat bound with ropes.

"Who is this man?" Phillip Ponte asked.

"He is one of our people. He joined us about 13 moons ago. His mind and heart was thought to be clear of evil spirits and he has been awaiting a mission that would give him a name that would honour him in the eyes of the Sons of Soma. Would you give all of this up and face the fate that will be decided—to speak for this stranger?"

"I will," the man called Horse Thief replied. "This man is no stranger to me—nor is he a stranger to all Red men and White men alike—or to all coloured people. I could not stand by and see this injustice be done. If a man is not allowed to speak for himself then it is a right thing in the eyes of our Creator that someone who knows of his deeds be allowed to speak in his defense. I ask for that right."

A murmur of agreement passed around the Circle and Iron Hand replied:

"So be it. You will speak for this man and you will share in his fate—whatever this Circle decides."

"I still want to know what gives you this right," Phillip Ponte requested. "Are you just a Horse Thief as your name implies?"

"I am." the man replied. "At least I was. I was not always the man you see before you. Once I was a lawyer. I was born in your country. My father and mother earned their money fairly, living in the White ways and honouring your system. But that was all that was on their mind. Money and things and the acquiring of more and more. I grew up neglected. I had everything that a boy could want—except parents. I vowed to make a difference defending the poor and helpless. And..."

"...you snapped," Ponte interjected. "Ah, yes, I remember now. I remember reading about you. Young man with a promising future caught stealing horses. Your excuse was that you were freeing them in the name of your ancestors. And even when you were released on bail, it didn't stop."

"When my parents both died of cancer—I believe caused by the stress of keeping up with the White neighbours—I lost hope. I inherited a large sum of money. I had lots of time on my hands to feel sorry for myself. I tried booze and then tried to live like my ancestors. I was given a slap on the wrist and told to be a good Indian and behave myself. It wasn't long before I was back at my old games. I got caught and escaped..."

"It was during this dark time of my life that a friend suggested that I go to a *Spirit Rock* concert in the park. I went grudgingly and saw this man Shiloh and his band. This was when I began a long wake-up period. Eventually I hid in a horse trailer and made my escape over the Golden Gate Bridge where I believed I would be welcomed with open arms. Imagine my surprise when a Circle of local Chiefs told me to go back and face the consequences of my actions."

"So," Ponte interrupted, "to make a long story short, here you are today. Is that about it?"

"Pretty well—but I have changed. I have had time to regret the things I did and realize that I cannot blame other people for my actions. And I am a peaceful man—like the man that is on trial here today. I believe that the Creator does not make mistakes. Today I am where I am meant to be. This is my chance to make things right."

"I am willing to hear what he has to say," Ponte told Iron Hand. "As you pointed out, he has a lot to lose by coming forward in defense of the man before us."

"First," the man called Horse Thief said, "I will ask the questions that were addressed to this man in a different way:"

"You are charged with having relations with a man who is a known homosexual," he spoke to Shiloh. "Before you answer, I need to point out that in the ways of our People, all creatures are our relatives. We have a Relationship with all people, animals, and birds. And it is this relationship of love that you are agreeing to. Am I correct?"

"Yes."

"And have you ever taken part in or considered a sexual relationship with another man—especially this man called Jude?"

"No."

"But he was seen kissing this man," Ponte spoke up.

"Being kissed, and sharing a kiss are two different things," Horse Thief stated. "I need to ask. Did he kiss you on the lips as a man kisses a woman?"

"No."

"It is easy to guess that he kissed you on the cheek and that his back was to the arresting officer. Is that correct?"

"Yes," Shiloh smiled through his pain.

"Then, I might suggest to this court...sorry, I mean Circle, that this being true, then most men that come from the country that is the birthplace of the former Emperor would be considered guilty of this crime—that is, if kissing on the cheek is a sign of latent homosexuality," he addressed Phillip Ponte.

"Point taken," Ponte smiled and conceded, but it does not mean that this man could not be gay."

"It does if you know about this man as I have by attending his concerts and mingling with his friends. This man was married to a woman who died but will not be forgotten as long as he lives. His love and his faithfulness for this woman go beyond death. Is this not correct?"

"Yes," Shiloh replied and bowed his head.

"If this man were to love another man or woman for that matter, it would be like a brother or sister."

"Agreed," Iron Hand spoke this time. "And about the other charge?"

"The other charge is that he publicly claimed to be the Son of God," Horse Thief continued. "I have a question for you," speaking to Shiloh again. "Would you say that this man from North of the Red River—this man called Phillip Ponte, is a Son of God?"

"Yes," Shiloh replied.

"And what about this Chief of the Sons of Soma? Is he also a Son, a child of God—the same Creator of All Things?"

"Yes."

"It is surly not my intention to offend either the religion of the Sons of Soma or the Christians," the man called Horse Thief assured the Council. "But this charge is similar to the other charge against this man called Shiloh. Although his beliefs may be like both religions he is truly not religious. He lives by the rules that come from his heart. I know that by having been at his concerts. *Spirit Rock* is about Spirit and Rock, as in the music that moves you—not about Rock as in 'written in stone'."

"What does this have to do with the charge of blasphemy?" Ponte inquired.

"This means that as the first charge was about this man's ability to love everyone unconditionally; this charge is about his belief that everyone—every creature in fact—is a child born of the Great Spirit. We are all from the same spark of energy—we are all children of God. I believe, having heard him speak and experienced the music of *The James Gang that* Shiloh only remembers more about Spirit than the average man. He has retained that connection to all other living creatures and possesses memories that belonged to the one called Jesus. Is this true?" He looked at Shiloh. "Is this true?"

"Yes."

There was a mild uproar among the men around the circle. Philip Ponte spoke.

"If this is indeed true—I mean that if he really believes this—then he is either who he says he is or he's mentally unstable. Therefore I do not have a problem with the charges against this man. My President would like to know more about his involvement in the prophesies of the Bible and the later additions of the Men from the Stars. And we are still not clear if he is criminally responsible for the disappearance of the Emperor. I officially drop the charges mentioned at the beginning of this Circle and give him over to the Sons of Soma to determine his fate."

"Speaking for the Sons of Soma," Iron Hand replied stated, "regarding the first charge, I can let that go. But I cannot let go the preaching of any man, stable or unstable, that questions our religion. In our religion, blasphemy is the same, even if it comes from a raving, mindless person. We will not let the words of our prophet Soma be questioned—especially by someone claiming to be the returning of our spiritual messenger. It would seem that we are not compassionate. But in light of his claims, we will let the punishment fit the crime according to our laws. He claims to be a holy man—a Shaman. So therefore I will suggest to the Circle that he be allowed to dance the sacred dance—the Sundance—but he will dance to the death of his body."

A round of "Ho" followed from every Red man around the circle, except Shiloh's lawyer.

"Wait," Ponte requested, "I appeal to the Circle, as a last request, to be able to hear this man tell his side of the story. My President and I would like to know what passed between this man and the Men from the Stars when they met in secret a couple of days ago. And why, after this, he decided to give himself up, knowing that he might be put to death."

"We cannot allow this man to work his magic here," Iron Hand was firm. "There must be payment for his words and actions. Our prophesy says that a man will come like a feathered serpent to save our people and restore the land and the creatures to the way it was before. We cannot allow false prophets and false hope for our people. There must be an example set so that this will not happen again...and if there should be any truth to this man's words, then he will not die and the prophesy will be fulfilled. You can take the man called Horse Thief back to stand trial for his crimes against your country. Unless you force this circle by your superior weapons—this judgment will be done!"

Ponte thought for a few minutes, and then he replied: "My President was clear in that he wanted this man to be tried by his own people. We will respect your judgment in this matter. There is, however, what our judicial system would call precedence, an occurrence of another case that we can relate to. I would not think that I would be drawing on a spiritual answer, as I am a very logically minded man. But this is my suggestion—as much as it surprises me—I suggest a trade. If it is right for your Circle, I suggest we trade the currently accused man Shiloh, who calls himself the Son of God, for the other man called Horse Thief. In your own words, this thief has chosen to share the fate of the person who he spoke for?"

Iron hand conferred with the other men of the Circle—the men of his tribe. "Yes, this is agreeable," he replied. "By our law, someone must pay for this crime. This is a good test. If this man called Shiloh is who he claims to be, he will then save this man from the fate that was meant to be his. This is a good trade for both people."

Shiloh opened his mouth to speak out in protest but he felt a firm hand on his shoulder.

"Let it be," the voice of the man called Horse Thief urged. "What they say is true. I chose my fate by speaking as I did—in your defense. I have learned that a man cannot stand by and witness an injustice. I believe that you need to tell your story to the President. If there is to be hope for this world, all races need to put aside their differences and work together. Is this not your true message?"

"Yes." Shiloh let his shoulders slump as he accepted the truth that the other man spoke. Saving the world was not something that could be done by one man alone.

* * *

Once back aboard the helicopter, Phillip Ponte sat in the back beside Shiloh. When they were in the air flying in the direction of New

Rome, Ponte removed the bindings that held Shiloh's arms and hands. Then he took the blindfold off as well.

"I do not believe that you are capable of magic," Ponte explained. "Then again, even if you were, I do not feel threatened. I have a hunch that you are sincere about sacrificing yourself to save the people of the world from themselves. A man who would do that would not harm another person. Am I right?"

"Yes," Shiloh agreed, as he rubbed the circulation back into his wrists. "But I am not here to save the world. My job is to help people to wake up to the fact that we are all in this together. Would you like to know what I learned in my last meeting with the Men from the Stars?"

"That is why I released you," Ponte replied and Shiloh told him what Andrew had learned as a result of living amongst the Star People. The other man shook his head in alarm mixed with disbelief. "I must say that this is a bit hard to swallow, but in the event you are even a bit right, the President needs to hear this. The only thing I have to go on, if we are to believe you, is that there have been visits by men from another planet. Once I had a hush-hush meeting with the Emperor and he confirmed his meeting with men that claimed to be from the Stars. Wherever they were from, their technology was far beyond anything that Rome had to offer. The Emperor also confirmed that the Riders from the Stars, as he called them, had presented him with additional knowledge relating to the prophesies of Armageddon."

"When did this meeting take place?" Shiloh asked.

"About a month before the Emperor disappeared," Ponte replied. "He requested a contingency of us from New Rome—including myself and the President. He did not even allude, however, about his impending departure. I am not sure he even knew at that time."

"I think he had already decided," Shiloh said.

"So it is true that you had something to do with that?"

"Yes. I believe it is safe to tell you that I helped him leave this world—this Dream—for a place that he could redeem himself."

"Do you mean that he committed suicide?"

"No," Shiloh replied firmly. "He did not die. I helped him pass into another Dream. This world—all existence for that matter—is a Dream."

"I've heard that. But I thought that to be some kind of metaphor. Is this what happens when we are forgiven our sins. Did you forgive him?"

"Sin is another thing. That is the illusion—a lie told to keep the people of the world under the thumb of the religious orders. Forgiveness is just as it sounds—no trick of the word. When you are born—you are already fore-given the gift of Grace by the Creator. All you have to do is open your heart and mind and accept it."

"Whoa—hold that thought," Ponte exclaimed. "And for the moment, keep it to yourself when you meet with the President. This is too much to digest at one time—much less to believe. That old Chief Iron Hand may have been more right about you than he guessed. You have a way of talking that works some kind of magic. Let's just focus on the problems at hand. Just tell the President what you told me about the eclipse and the earthquakes that it will cause. If any of the other is true, then time will show that."

"That is just the point," Shiloh shook his head. "By the time you learn that I am right, it will probably be too late."

As it turned out, the President was more concerned about seeing that Shiloh was kept out of circulation until the days foretold by the prophesies had passed. He granted a short hearing where he promised to listen to Shiloh's side of the story. The only people allowed at this meeting, other than Shiloh and the President, were Phillip Ponte and two armed guards. The two guards were equipped with ear phones that would keep them from hearing anything that was said.

"You have 10 minutes to convince me why I shouldn't put you behind bars and throw away the key."

Shiloh would have liked to say that even in this country where this man had appointed himself King; he would still have to account for his actions one day. New Rome was, after all, considered a democracy and the public would come looking and expecting, at the very least, a trial. The President had hoped that Shiloh's people would convict him. That was how the story went if you followed the Book, word for word. He could still have his way, however, but at what expense?

"I met with a Representative of the Star People, a friend of mine, he was the one that flew *The Arrow*." Shiloh let that sink in. "The bottom line—the truth about the prophesy—is part of how they are able to cross the distance between the Stars. There is a naturally occurring phenomenon in the universe that involves the folding of time and space. The Star People are able to sense when this is about to happen, and they use it to travel distances that might take lifetimes—even at the speed of light."

"What does this have to do with anything?" the President interrupted. "Get to the point."

"Of course," Shiloh continued, "the reason I spoke about this, is that planets and stars also get caught in this shift and end up somewhere they might never otherwise be. As I said before, however, there is a cycle to this—a pattern that the Riders from the Stars are able to predict. An example of this would be the Star of Bethlehem appearing in the sky at just the right moment and just the right location when Jesus was born. The Men and Women from the stars are able to predict such happenings."

Shiloh noted that the President was shifting and becoming impatient, so he got to the point as he had been ordered. "Now I will admit I have only the Star People's word to back this up but I need you to believe me. There will be a shift within the next two days—this was part of the prophesy that the Riders told to the Emperor. If you remember, they said that they would return at seven year intervals. They really meant that their planet—which we can see and call the Star Sirius—has been visiting Earth's sky. Each time it comes, it gets closer and closer. In two days, it will appear in our sky again—between the Earth and the Sun. There will be an eclipse, but at the same time due to the proximity of the planet, the Earth will experience seven hours of major earthquakes and most of the tall buildings will come down."

"So that is the great warning of the prophesy?" the President appeared unimpressed. "Or so you say if I am to believe you, which I find hard to do! Let me understand this—a Red-skinned man who admits that he does not believe in the Christian Bible, has the audacity to stand before me and tell me he knows the truth about Armageddon. So even if you were right, you are telling me that some tall buildings will fall? That hardly seems to be the Apocalypse, the end of the world as foretold in Revelations."

"No—that would not be the end of the world as we were warned about. The reason I am here at this late moment in time is to tell you to imagine a world that is already shaking and then imagine that someone triggers a nuclear explosion, like the one you threaten to unleash on Vega. The Star People have calculated that this would set off a chain reaction that would bring about the end of most life on this planet."

"Ah ha!" the President chortled. "Now you show your true colours!" and he laughed aloud at the joke he thought he made. "Star Men! From a planet of Red-skinned people! Indeed! See—I told you he was lying! He made up this story to save his pagan friends in that city of sin! Can't you see it now?" The President's voice rose in crescendo as he shouted orders at the two guards, who could not hear a word he said: "Take him away! Get him out of my sight!"

Ponte calmly motioned to the guards that they were to escort the handcuffed prisoner out of the President's office. He accompanied them and once outside the large door, he indicated that they could remove the ear phones and asked them to wait with the prisoner in the vestibule for him. Then he pressed the buzzer near the door of the President's office.

"Yes?" the president's voice was heard over a nearby speaker.

"Could I have a word with you in private?" Ponte requested.

"Come in." The buzzer sounded indicating that the door was unlocked. The wooden surface of the door hid the actual security that was in place. Including all of the electronic surveillance equipment and this door that had a six-inch plated steel core.

When the door closed behind him with a hissing sound, Ponte addressed the President. "I am doubtful about much of this man's story as you," he began. "But we both know that the Men from the Stars are real. At least their coming to our planet in ships possessing technology that is far advanced of anything even the Emperor had. The rest of the story we can only accept at face value. It may or may not be true."

"What are you suggesting?" The President asked.

"I think it may be a good thing to take measures to protect the people in the event that even a part of the story is true. This weekend is, coincidentally, an important religious holiday. It seems that if this man were to plan this, he and his accomplices have planned well. So we might assume that something is going to happen. Something big. There was already a potential threat to the Friendship Tower that was averted—even though we do not really know how. This man called Shiloh has told us that all tall buildings will come down. This could be either as a result of the eclipse—as his story goes—or of a massive attack by terrorists. I think it would be a safe thing to announce that due to the strong religious beliefs that our country was founded on, there will be a decree that all of the people must attend church services this Sunday and all office buildings must be closed."

"I can see where you are going," the President replied. "But what about the people that live in the tall buildings in the city core?"

"We will say that 'all of the people' means—everyone. Everyone must attend church this day. And since the churches will be crowded, we will demand that the stadiums and the meeting halls be used to gather in 'His' name. My reasoning is that if something major does happen to bring down the tallest buildings, you will be seen as having great foresight. Meanwhile, we will have our Air Force ready. And most of the people of New Rome will have been saved from harm. This would go a long way to raising you in the eyes of the common man and woman."

"Personally—I could care less if the sinners got caught in the office towers on a Sunday," the President blurted out. And then he realized what he had let slip. "That is between you and me, of course. What I mean is that anyone who works on a Sunday—especially this one—deserves what happens to them. But then, there are the others who own and rent condos. Yes, you have a good idea. Get right on it as soon as you put that man somewhere he won't be found. No one must know that he is in our custody—including the guards. The men I picked are sworn to secrecy—at the peril of their lives."

"I have a thought about the Shaman, too," Ponte replied. "Alcatraz is deserted. We closed it down over 10 years ago but it is still usable. What do you think?"

"Another good idea," the President's eyes lit up. "Put him in solitary and post guards outside the door. I will decide, I mean, we will decide what to do with him when this whole fiasco is over. In a couple of days those Redskins will be too busy dodging missiles to be concerned about one missing Indian."

"So you are still going ahead with the bombing of Vega?"

"Of course," the President chortled. "Those heathens need to be taught a lesson. Can't you see what is happening—that is a city of sin and corruption. This is a chance to put those Red-faced pagans in their place and snuff out a nest of homosexuals at the same time."

"Like Sodom and Gomorrah?" Ponte suggested. He was intelligent enough not to say anything about the promise that the President had previously made to the Natives, concerning the surrender of Shiloh.

"Yes. But this time we are doing God's work." The President's mood had changed greatly. He was on a high of anticipation. Ponte, on the other hand, was beginning to see the writing on the wall and the script of the story did not look well. The name of this all-too-familiar biblical tale was Armageddon! And the President was looking forward to it. A sense of dread was like a fist to his stomach.

"And what about you?" The President interrupted Ponte's thoughts.

"Me? What do you mean?"

"I mean that you deserve to be rewarded for all of your hard work and loyalty. Is there anything that you want—money or women? Name it and it will be yours."

Phillip Ponte would have liked to say that his reward would be to still be alive come Monday, but instead: "I would like a promotion—I mean a full-time job. If it is at all possible, I would like a position in your elite personal security. It has been a pleasure having been recruited to work for you and I would look forward to more of the same."

"Consider it done," the President smiled, believing that he had found a man after his own heart. "As of this afternoon, you will be a captain of the guards for my palace," he saluted "Captain Ponte—your first official duty will be to pay a visit to the Island of Alcatraz to check out that it is still in working order," he winked as Ponte returned a salute and a wry smile.

* * *

"How sure are you that the eclipse will take place?" Ponte asked Shiloh on the boat over to the island.

"As sure as you are that your President will push the button to send a nuclear missile to bomb Vega and as sure as you know that it won't stop there. And I know that when this takes place, it will be the trigger that it will bring an end to the world as we know it."

These thoughts were running through Ponte's mind, as he closed the door of the cell in the depths of Alcatraz. His parting words to Shiloh were: "If you are who you say you are, no prison can hold you. I will do my best to persuade the President to hold off bombing your people, as he promised. I do believe that he will wait the two days that are left in the prophesy of the Men from the Stars. The rest is up to you."

"Your duty," Ponte instructed the two guards that he posted at the door to Shiloh's solitary, "is to make sure that this door in not opened—for any reason. I will return in two days. He has water and all that he will need until I return. We cannot take any chances. Just remember that the President depends on you—he is the only one that knows this man is interned here."

In the darkness of the cell, Shiloh found a bunk and lay down on his side to meditate and to nurse his wounds. He wrapped himself in the blankets provided and attempted to sleep. Sleep did not come easy, but eventually exhaustion took over and the deepening darkness engulfed him.

Time passed—how much time, it was difficult to judge. Shiloh was awakened by a noise—the sound of his cell door being opened. Light streamed in, temporarily blinding his eyes. He heard voices, men's gruff voices, speaking in a language he did not understand. Hands reached and dragged him out of the cell. When his vision cleared, he could see that he was in a courtyard of a village.

"This is not Alcatraz," he exclaimed.

The man nearest to him spoke again in the foreign language that was beginning to sound familiar. He had heard this on his journey around the world when he was still a teenage boy. And then he placed the dialect. But the words were not fully understandable. That did not seem to matter to the men who shoved him into the village centre. These men were dressed like actors in some play about ancient times. And then—he awoke mentally. This is not a play! The costumes are not costumes. The armour that the men wore and the swords and shields they carried were not for a play. It was something different. This play, this story, could only be memories—a re-enactment of the fate of the One who had come before. But the re-enactment was now for his benefit. It was his dream, and as real as any so-called dream that he had ever experienced.

As if to drive home the reality of the situation, the men, Roman soldiers, pushed Shiloh toward an object in the village square. The object that they directed him to was a rough-hewn cross! There was no mistake about their intent—even for someone who might not have read the story. As he bent to pick up the cross, he began to search his memories and his mind for a sign that he was not alone. He searched for the man who the memories belonged to. He was alone! "Why have you deserted me?" he cried out to the heavens. But the only answer was a blow from the broad-edge of a sword.

"Shut up! Or the next time I will cut you and you will die here." The soldier's laughter was joined by his comrades.

Shiloh looked for support in the village people milling about. Some refused eye contact and still others spit in his direction. He straightened his shoulders with resolve and accepted again the choice of his sacrifice. Now or then—whatever the time-space may be. If it was his destiny—to follow in the footsteps of the One who came before—then so be it!

"Move!" the soldiers commanded. "We do not have all day." And they laughed again—as though this was a joke—as though they knew what was to happen that evening and the next morning. And then Shiloh realized the truth or, rather, he remembered. Even the darkest heart is aware of the choice—to do the right or wrong thing. Even the darkest heart is connected to the light—connected to Grace, even if the mind denies it.

Shiloh shuffled along—dragging the cross on his shoulder, his mind on the destination. His eyes scanned the crowd for...no—there would be no encouraging friends and family—they had all deserted him—or passed on. But wait, as he passed, he saw everyone that had journeyed this far with him. They were like ghosts, watching from another dream, but non-the-less they witnessed him passing by and their eyes held a knowing that he had helped to inspire. And a way up ahead, he was sure he saw his mother and father waiting by the side of the path up the hill...and then he stumbled...and when he looked up from his knees, he was once more...alone...

...and then a man rushed from an uncaring crowd to his aid.

"Let me help you carry this?" said this man who Shiloh recognized. A friend and a comrade who shared the Dream. "Say the word," the man whispered, as they carried the cross together. "Say the word and I will bring 100 of our People—our best warriors—and these men will hurt you no more."

"No," Shiloh sighed, "This must be done. It is not for our People to fight a war that they cannot win. The time for War has passed. Our people will be the ones that will rebuild and heal the Earth. This is my choice—and my choice is my message."

The man who helped to carry the cross was silent, then resigned to his friend's request. And the rest of the journey to the top of the hill was a blur to Shiloh's mind—even the binding of his wrists to the cross—so that the nails that were driven through his palms would support his weight. Morning blurred into a pain-filled afternoon—into an excruciating moonless night. But the darkness that descended was not the end. There would come another day—before that fateful... eclipse—something he had almost forgotten.

"What?" There was a movement at the foot of the cross. His memories told him that this might be the soldiers returning to mock him and steal his clothes.

"Friend?" a familiar voice whispered in the darkness. "I have come to set you free."

"No—I cannot..." Shiloh began to explain again.

"Yes, you can—if I take your place. Someone must die it seems. A sacrifice is required. But it is time that we accept responsibility for our own mistakes. That is your true message—and that is your true purpose. You have told us that a loving Father would not send his Son to a painful death. I know that to be true. It is time for your suffering to end. A sacrifice once intended is already completed. I accept your gift—and I am prepared to die for you—and for myself."

Before Shiloh could protest, he felt warmth that healed all his wounds. He was no longer on the cross and as a bright light enveloped him he heard a soft and gentle Voice speak the words of Grace: "You are Fore-Given."

Chapter 22

AFTER THE SUN DANCE

On what seemed to be a day like any other day, Phillip Ponte awoke with the dawn. But this was not to be like any other day, if the prophesies came true. He went about his new duties as head of security for the President's palace. Everything was as it should be. The guards all saluted as he passed by. All was secure and there was no reason to believe otherwise—except for the prophesies and the words of one Native Shaman. He stood on the palace steps that surveyed the courtyard. It was quiet and a clear cloudless sky. "What a ridiculous idea. I was so close to believing it," he exclaimed, glancing down at his watch. The hour hand moved to 7 AM...and then the watch disappeared from his view in the darkness. "What?" He had envisioned that an eclipse, if it happened at all would be a gradual event. It was something that took place when the moon or another planet, passed between the Sun and the Earth. But this was different. In less than a second, the sun was blotted from the sky—like it ceased to exist.

And then the street lights winked on. So far, everything else was working OK, but there was a shudder that began with an audible hum and the ground beneath him began to vibrate. The natural gravitational force was being disrupted by the imposing presence of a large body—a planet so close that, in the light of the sun, they would most likely be able to see the continents with a low-powered telescope. At least this was his guess—hopefully to be verified later. He hastily drew out his cell phone but the signal was gone! Then he proceeded to run to the nearest phone booth just outside the palace gates. He made one pre-arranged phone call and then another to summon his personal Jeep. In less time than it took to wonder at the truth of what was happening, he was on his way across town to the shipyards, where there was an awaiting speed boat that would take him to Alcatraz. Phillip Ponte was quite aware that his place at this time was with the President. But there was a pressing need to know what might have happened in the solitary cell on the island.

His appointed guards greeted him with a salute as the boat pulled up at the dock. "Any problems?" he enquired as he stepped ashore.

"No, sir. None except this darkness," was the reply. "Any idea what is causing it?"

"An eclipse." Ponte gave the simple answer that might ease their minds. But he was all too aware that it was less than simple. This bordered on a miracle, that is, if what he suspected had taken place on another place on the island. The electric generators were working perfectly—so far. He was greeted by a couple of crisp salutes at the door to the solitary cell that held Shiloh.

"Has this door been opened for any reason?" Ponte enquired.

"Not at all, sir," a man replied. "The generators kicked in right after the darkness began. What...?"

"Don't worry," Ponte replied. "I need you to open the door now. I need to talk to the prisoner." Ponte, on a whim, had affixed a Presidential seal on the main bolt that secured the door to the cell. He cut it now and one of the guards handed him the key.

"See, just like you left it. He probably slept the whole time," the guard smiled as Ponte slid the bolt aside and swung the door open. Ponte then asked for a flashlight and stepped inside. At that moment, the guards who followed heard their captain's amazed voice: "Oh my God, save us!" They frantically searched an empty cell.

* * *

When Shiloh felt the pull of the living light, his mind was in turmoil. He had come to accept his fate. But now everything had been changed by the intervention of the man who took his place on the cross. And the reality of that was even a question. He did understand the symbolism of this dream—but in his experience, a dream is another form of reality. And now, a part of him rebelled.

He was not ready for heaven, if that was where he was taken. He had friends and a daughter to care for. And what about Amanda...would Amanda be waiting for him in heaven? Somehow, during his short life on Earth, he had not considered the possibility of heaven being a real place. But now?

"Father—Spirit Father?" he cried out. "Please hear me. I am not finished here." But his answer was silence and the ever-present enveloping light. After a moment, he calmed down. And he began to smile. How could he be so impertinent to believe that he could second-guess the Creator? He relaxed and accepted that wherever his destination, he was sure that this was not the end by any means. He was still alive in a way that was beyond even his comprehension. And his wounds were healed—in fact he was hardly aware that he had a body. He was clad in only a breech cloth as his ancestors had worn. This was how they had left him—on the cross. Had Christ been so attired for crucifixion? He raised his hands before his face. "Look here, Thomas," he exclaimed in joy. "This would blow your mind. There are no nail holes! Would this mean to you that the sacrifice did not take place?" He sighed and drew a pleasant breath of air into his spirit lungs. "Life is what we believe it is. That is the truth of Free Will!" Then he was standing on what surely felt like solid ground!

The mist and the clouds began to clear. And Shiloh walked forward into a familiar moon-lit scene. "What happened here after I left?" he wondered. "Did the eclipse take place? Has the Earth been destroyed?" The village was still there as he remembered it, but deserted and only the Sundance tree remained standing. Beneath the Sundance tree everything was exactly as he remembered the Dream. But this time it would be different. He bent to touch the shoulder of the man huddled on the ground who had spoken out in his defense—the same man who had danced in his place. When Shiloh and Thomas visited this village in the dream the man they found who was still tied to the tree, might easily have been himself, but now he knew a different truth.

"Maiingun? My friend? Are you still here?"

"Shiloh?" he replied weakly. The man attempted to raise his head but could not.

Shiloh gently rolled his friend onto his back and supported his head with his hand and arm. "I am here to take you home," he declared. "The pain will be gone now. This is not the way of our People."

"They said that you would come back for me." A wry smile crossed the man's face. "I guess they believed in you at last—when the darkness came. I was laughing as I danced."

"But the wound in your side? Was that necessary?"

"It was to someone who is stuck in a story that is neither White man's' nor Red man's. Our People are lost like this. They are Red men and women who are trapped in another man's dream."

"But it is not a good dream unless it is right for all living creatures," Shiloh replied.

"I will be leaving soon," Maiingun said. "But first I would like a drink of the water that you offered before."

During his other visits, Shiloh was unable to give the dancer a drink—only the men who attended him could do that and the water was bitter. He found a gourd nearby and lifted the water container to the man's lips.

"Sweet! The water is so sweet," the man in his arms whispered when he drank his fill.

And he was gone. But his lifeless body remained. And then Shiloh remembered that he had told his friend that he had come to take him home. "So be it," he declared, unfastening the man from the thongs that bound him to the Sundance tree, scooping him up into his arms. He walked toward the exit of the village. And when he stepped through the gate with the man in his arms, he walked from moonlight into a bright sunny day.

"Where to go?" Shiloh wondered. There was only desert to be seen in every direction. Looking back, he saw a deserted village—even the Sundance tree had decayed and fallen. "What happened just now? I am in a different place—perhaps a different time?" He had had stepped from one dream world to another and the transition was quick and without fanfare. Every other journey between worlds had a sense of fate, so there was no reason to question whether this was where he and his friend needed to be. He waited at the gate of the village sensing that something was about to happen. "I feel like I'm waiting for a taxi," he smiled to himself, even in the darkness of the moment. Here he was, possibly miles from the nearest town carrying a man who was, for all logical sense, dead. But again, Shiloh knew differently about the man cradled in his arms. This man was a fellow traveler—a dreamer.

"What now Maiingun?" he asked the Spirit of the man. "Is this your dream or mine? Have I brought you here—or was it the other way around? And what are we waiting for?"

A few moments passed and Shiloh heard a familiar sound—an unmistakable sound of an engine approaching from the east. Then Shiloh saw a Jeep come over the nearest sandy hillside. He shook his head in disbelief. It was not just any jeep; the licence plate gave it away. It was a personalized plate with a thunderbird crest, and the name "BWOLF". "Black Wolf" was his father's adopted Native name. The Jeep coasted to a halt and his mother leaned out of the passenger window.

"Looking for a ride, stranger?" Mary smiled and swung open the door to the Jeep. It was a slightly younger mother than he remembered who bounded out and hugged him and his friend—covering his face with kisses.

"Who is it you're carrying son?" Joseph leaned over the top of the car, standing on the running board. He, too, was at least 10 years younger than Shiloh remembered.

"A friend," Shiloh replied. "It's a long story—you remember that biblical fate I was concerned about? My friend Maiingun gave up his life for me and I promised to take him home."

"Maiingun? A man after my own Heart. No co-incidence there." Joseph rounded the jeep and hugged his long lost son. "Well, we need to see that he gets home then." Joseph opened the tailgate of the jeep, lowered one of the back seats and helped Shiloh stretch out the lifeless body. "By the way—where is home for this man?"

"I really don't know," Shiloh replied. "Maybe this is his home—it could be, because he and I have a lot in common. Can we take him back to the ranch and bury him in the woods?" This was not an unusual request for Kansa, but north of the Red River this would be against the law.

"That sounds like the right thing to do," Mary agreed. And soon the reunited family were headed back over the hills in the direction that Shiloh guessed would be his parent's ranch. The distance was unknown to Shiloh since he had originally been brought to the village by helicopter and he was not really sure how this world compared to the one he had left behind.

"What is happening here?" Shiloh asked after they had driven in relative silence for about half an hour.

"What do you mean, son?" his mother turned in her seat to smile at him. "Your father and I might ask the same about you. You are our son—that is for sure, but you are more…mature. Where have you been? Anna told us that she met you in New York but you told her that you could not come home. She said that she heard you had died with some kids in a school bus. But then she met you after that and here you are now—a grown man. This is almost too much for me—even though I believe in the Mystery."

"Anna? Is Anna OK?" Shiloh was amazed as well.

"Yes—she is back at the ranch. It was Anna that told your father and me to drive out here and look for you. We have been making this trip for about five years now—every Easter Monday. Your sister was so insistent that you would show up that we could not take the chance she might be wrong. She has been right about so many things since she came back from New York where she said that you rescued her. She said that you reminded her that she is an Angel come to earth and now she believes that completely. Her belief is not a prideful, ego thing, mind you. And she has visions."

"OK. So that explains how you showed up when I was feeling like I was waiting for a taxi. But you said that Anna came back from New York—I think you said that. I met Anna in New Rome. What is that all about?"

"Oh yeah. That did take a bit of getting use to," Joseph piped up. "The name change came shortly after Anna returned home. The story about the kids in the school bus had a twist. There was a big explosion at one of the Universities in New Rome—as it was called then. And when I checked out Anna's story, it was rumoured that a bus-load of school kids died in the blast set off by a terrorist. At least that was the original newspaper headline. Pictures and all!"

"And then," Mary took over the story, "about seven days later at the same place where it was pronounced missing, without a trace, the bus reappeared. Late one night, the security guards heard a commotion and when they investigated, there was the bus—and all of the children were safe and unharmed. And there is more. There was also a person on the bus with the children that was almost a surprise as great as the bus reappearing," she paused and Shiloh gave a deep sigh.

"Let me guess," he offered, "the Emperor was on the bus with the kids?"

"Yes," Mary replied. "How did you know?"

"More than a lucky guess," Shiloh admitted. "I will tell you about it someday, when we have time to catch up. Please go on."

"Well, the story as the Emperor tells it, was that he went to the meeting at the University in disguise, just to mingle with the crowd and see firsthand what the regular people thought of him. I guess he got an earful and a ride, and for seven days no one knew where the bus with the kids and the Emperor went. Our Emperor came back a changed man. Over the course of the next few years, he dismantled his Army and Air Force, and declared to the rest of the world that had been under Roman rule that they were free to live as they choose. But before that, he came over here, to what had been New Rome and systematically closed up all of the missile silos and disarmed the President of Nuclear Weapons. Then he declared an election, and went back to Rome without waiting to see the results."

"And the name of the city changed?" Shiloh asked.

"Well, with a new leader and government, the people north of the Red decided to drop Rome in the name and someone came up with York. New York is the capital of the free United States of the North or USN," Mary explained.

"Then I just have to say, Shiloh interjected—that there is more communication between the worlds that I visited than I first thought possible. Even if the people are not consciously aware, their dreams are bringing about changes in their waking world—and then that, in turn, affects how they dream."

"Speaking of which," Joseph chuckled and glanced at Shiloh's mother, "there is the matter of a young woman who phones every once in awhile asking for our son."

Shiloh gasped. "Might her name be Amanda?" It was too much to hope.

"Well, you are right," Mary smiled at her son. "The first time she phoned was about a year after your sister Anna returned home. And she said her name was Megan. Then about three years ago she started calling herself Amanda. Your dad thought it might be two different women chasing our son because they sounded different—somehow. So I asked the next time she called and she admitted to Megan O'Riley. But she said to tell you that you might like to call her Amanda. Son, what exactly is your relationship with this mysterious young woman?"

"Well, mom—and dad..." Shiloh was ecstatic. Tears of joy filled his eyes. "Megan and Amanda is the same person. There is so much that Amanda taught me and all it took was learning to accept and love her as she was. A woman is naturally closer to the Mystery, like the story of the White Buffalo Calf Woman. I guess I don't need to tell you that? I have also learned that we live lives in many places—many dreams at the same time."

"I agree with the part about women," Joseph interjected. "When I met your mother, I began to know my destiny."

"And what did you know about your destiny?" Mary smiled slyly.

"I knew it was my destiny to be with you," Joseph leaned over for a quick kiss.

Shiloh asked if Amanda or Megan had left a number where she could be reached.

"Yes, she did as a matter of fact," Mary replied. "It is back at the ranch in the book by the telephone. Your dad and I were sure you would need it whenever you came back home."

Shiloh let the "back home" words sink in. His head started to swim. In the midst of this, with his mind preoccupied, he barely heard his father's words—"...he is gone..."

"What? Sorry, dad, I missed that?" He looked up to see Joseph glancing in the rear-view mirror.

"I said that I see that your friend is gone. He just disappeared a few miles back."

The man, who Shiloh had carried in his arms, had indeed vanished.

"I guess he woke up—somewhere else. He's done that before. I believe that he's becoming more aware that he can do that. He did experience all of the pain and suffering in my place, or for himself, depending how you see it. That was all real. In fact everything that we think of with emotion is real, whether we acknowledge it or not. I have also found that it can become disconcerting, bordering on insanity if we are not Spiritually-balanced."

"So, if we are not balanced or focused, we could be 'tripping out' when we least expect it?" his mother replied.

"That's the danger of drugs that open our minds before our Heart is ready," Shiloh agreed. He could see the farmhouse in the distance. "I can't stay with you right now," he said with a touch of sadness in his voice. "And If I were to talk to Amanda now, it would be twice as hard. When she phones again, please tell her that I will be with her as soon as I can. She will know that I need to be with our daughter right now and there are things about the Prophesies that I need to see about—to tie up loose ends."

"Daughter?" His mother's eyebrows went up.

"It's OK mom," he chuckled. "Amanda and I were—are—married, and even if we were not, as the world defines it, our union is Sacred and Respectable in the eyes of the Creator. And 'yes' to your real question. How would it feel to know that you are grandparents?" It occurred to him that this was even more amazing since his parents in this dream world appeared about 10 years younger than he remembered. Perhaps they had come to this world in which their romance was in its infancy—choosing to relive the gift of getting to know each other a second time. This was a sign to Shiloh of his Parents' Spiritual maturity—skipping the cycle of reincarnation to meet your soul mate through free will. There is the sleep of death—where one awakens, like from a dream. And then there is the sleep that takes you directly into the dream, as his friend Maiingun might have been experiencing now.

"Grandparents?" Mary smiled. "It sounds and feels good. When will we be meeting this little one?"

"Her name is Aurora and she turned three this past Christmas—in the other world. She is with her god-parents, James and Petra. Some things are different there. James is my adopted brother who I grew up with. Anna passed away as a child. I didn't heal her in that world. I am a healer there but I have followed a different path because my destiny is to be a messenger for the Creator—to help the different races learn to work together to overcome their differences."

"And what about the sacrifice—the Crucifixion like in the Bible?" Joseph stopped the Jeep just outside the gate to the family ranch.

"I was prepared to accept that, as well," Shiloh confided. "And I discovered that accepting it with an open heart is just the same as having experienced the event. Amanda taught me an important lesson about Love and Acceptance—more than one actually. But the main one is a prayer that I live by:

"Great Spirit: look into my Heart,

See what I really need…

And give me that."

"When I prayed that with an open Heart, the Creator and Amanda gave me Aurora to love. Your Granddaughter is one of those children that the 'new agers' might call Indigo, or special children, except they are unaware that all children have always been 'special'. Everyone—all children are born with the Divine spark. They are all children of the Creator—sent to earth to experience and teach us about Love. The challenge comes if they do not have parents like mine who support this truth—they are re-programmed at birth to believe differently!"

Mary and Joseph hugged their son. And once again stood united as a family again at the gate of the ranch. "I can only say," Mary told Shiloh with tears in her eyes, "we will pray for you to come home soon. But you will do what you need to. That is all your father and I could ask."

* * *

Shiloh turned towards the Northerly direction, the direction of Dreams. Taking one step, he looked back to see that the farmhouse had changed and his mother and father had disappeared. The house he saw now had become a bit rundown, not having the care of a carpenter who had passed on years since. And there were other differences, too. His ears were filled with the sounds of voices. He saw a gathering of cars and trucks in the field just north of the house. His friends—the members of *The James Gang*—were waving and shouting and a moment later, his daughter came bounding to meet him.

"Daddy! Daddy! Where did you go?" she cried as he scooped her into his arms.

"Where do you think I went?" he asked as he hugged her.

"Auntie Petra and Uncle James said that you might have gone to Heaven to be with my mommy, but I knew that you would come back for me."

"You are so right," he agreed. "No matter where I go—I will always come back to help keep you safe."

"The next time I want you to take me along," she whispered in his ear. "Then you and mommy and me can be a family."

He stopped in his tracks and wiped away the tears streaming down his face. Then in a calm voice, he said to James who walked to meet him: "How did it go?"

James clasped his hand and hugged Shiloh and Aurora together. "You mean with this one?" he asked. "Aurora was no problem—but let me tell you something: she is wise beyond her years. Every night, instead of asking for a story, she told us about the dream she had the night before and how she would be meeting her playmate friends again, as soon as she closed her eyes."

"Where did you go while I was away?" Shiloh asked his daughter as they walked to meet the rest of the group.

"I went to a faraway place—to play with my friends. They live on a star! Did you know that? Way up there," she pointed skyward. "But you know what? My friends came to visit us—when the sky went dark and the ground was shaking. That's why I was not afraid. I tol' Auntie Petra: 'don't be scared, it's just our friends that have come to visit'."

"You know what?" Shiloh tickled her and laughed as she giggled. "I believe you—every word."

"James?" Shiloh enquired. "I take it the eclipse happened as planned."

"Sure did," James replied. "And it scared the be-Jesus out of the rest of us. We were just waiting for the President to nuke Vega and that would have been the end of the world—just like the prophesy in Revelations."

"But the missiles didn't come," Shiloh said.

"No," Petra replied. "We were packed and on our way—far away from here. We just came back this morning. How can you outrun a nuclear bomb, anyways? Or the truth of it was, as you said before the Security police took you away, it was not the bombing of Vega or the shaking of the Earth. It would have been the combination of the two that would have been impossible to escape."

"So what happened?" Shiloh wondered. "Did the President change his mind?"

"No, that was not going to happen," Thomas spoke up. He offered his hand for Shiloh and carefully scrutinized the hand that was extended in return. "Hum…no wounds?"

"I assure you Thomas," Shiloh replied, "the wounds were real. At least they were real to me—and to the One whose memories that I share. And He has been re-living that sacrifice—for too long. Do you remember Maiingun—that boy that we all met in the dream after the flight in *The Arrow*? Well, Maiingun is a mature man now and he believes that it is time for that sacrifice to end and I agree. It is time for everyone to take responsibility for their own actions."

Thomas shrugged. "Don't hold your breath," he replied.

"It only takes one person at a time to step up and live his or her truth," Shiloh smiled. "Actually there are two of us that I am aware of—unless Maiingun is another me? Or am I another him? The Elders will tell you that everyone and everything in your dream is a part of you. We just need to remember that when we're waking up. And then I am speaking figuratively. There are a great many more that follow that path, mostly Aboriginal people who have that truth in their heart. We just need to remember, to recapture our memories of the Dreamtime, and the Ways of our ancestors."

"You asked about the President and what stopped his bombs?" Lucas chipped in. "Like James said, we were waiting in anticipation and then nothing happened. Sure, the Earth shook and tall buildings—we learned later—came tumbling down. But the seven hours of darkness passed and no bombs. Later, we found out that the people of New Rome were responsible. Someone told them the truth about what was to happen. Then when the darkness and the eclipse proved to be real, they marched on the President's palace. There was a bloodless rebellion. The guards simply stepped aside and the people of New Rome walked in and took over. Everything has changed—on both sides of the Red River."

"Changed for the better," James spoke again. "Driving back here, we heard that they have appointed an interim President until they can have an election. Seems that this was in the planning for some time—at least since the former Emperor disappeared. The new President is a man named Jefferson and his wife, the new First Lady, is a Black woman that was once his mistress. He married her and his misgivings were immediately forgiven by the people of this new country—they started to call it the United States of America. They even have a newly written constitution based on freedom and justice for all."

"And a new holiday," Jude stepped forward. "It is the day after Easter Monday and is called Independence Day," he smiled wryly. "Too bad the old homophobic laws are still in effect. But who knows? It is not possible yet for a gay marriage in that 'freedom-for-all' country. But the border laws are relaxed and homeland security is said to be on the way out. Nathan was able to come to Kansa with me since he is no longer a prisoner in his own country."

"President Jefferson immediately sent a message to the head Chiefs in Kansa," Petra said. "Then he phoned to personally say that he hoped that there would not be bad blood between the people of Kansa and the USA. He promised to visit, in the near future, to bring about a treaty of true free trade. This time, he said, there will be more than a written treaty, one where when both countries have agreed on something that is good for all. And the agreement will be based on a handshake. Who knows, only time will tell?"

"Wow?" Shiloh exclaimed. "To be quite truthful, I did not know what to expect. This really goes a long way to support our beliefs that every man and woman, not to mention child, has a good Heart. Sometimes, just helping them to see that is all that is needed."

"For sure!" James slapped his brother on the back. "And our band brought the Spirit Music to the people who were in need and helped the cause a lot. Not to mention a certain little brother of mine that did not preach or judge but believed that music would speak louder than words."

"I have to admit that I did get a little carried away a couple of times," Shiloh replied. "There were a few concerts when I felt I had to say some words of encouragement, no matter how short."

"But that is just what I am talking about," James insisted. "Whenever you spoke out, it was from the heart, and it was always related to something from personal experience. You walked your talk and shared the pain, but mostly encouraged everyone to do the same—follow the Path of the Heart," James was beaming. "I am proud to have been able to be part of this and I hope that we can continue."

"I was going to say something about that," Shiloh smiled, "about the future for all of us and our friends and *The James Gang* in particular. When I came back I was not sure what I should do next. But listening to Aurora and holding my daughter in my arms was the first step. And now that I heard how everything turned out, I have come to a decision. It is time for me and Aurora to go home."

"Go home?" Thomas asked. "What do you mean—this is your home. Or do you mean…?"

"No! I do not mean Heaven," Shiloh replied. "At least not in the way I see it. Maybe it is, but whose Idea of Heaven is correct? My parents are there and Amanda is there. And you know what? I realized that Aurora was born there. Aurora was born in a hospital that still does not exist here—but is in the planning stage for this time-space. She was born in a city called New York. And that is where Amanda is now. That is not a coincidence. If I ever had any questions about what I need to do when my 'message' was delivered, Aurora gave me the answer. I prayed for that answer at Amanda's bedside, when even I wondered why she had been taken from me. And I accepted the Creator's plan. We do not lose anyone. The Creator does not take them away. They pass on to another, better place. These are not idle words to me; they are a truth that I see when I hold my daughter in my arms. And this is the rest of my message—for anyone who has the Spirit ears to hear and the eyes to see."

"One day we will awaken, like from a Dream. It's our Birth-Right that we are Fore-Given."

"Did anyone ever tell you that you talk like a poet?" James chuckled as he hugged his brother. "Let me be the first here to say that I love you and whatever you choose to do will be right with me. I will miss you, though. Do you think you can drop into my dreams and say 'hello' once in a while?"

"Of course," Shiloh hugged him back. "But don't be surprised if I show up in the flesh occasionally. I'm getting a handle on this dream-other-world-travel thing again. I discovered that if there is a good reason for me to get somewhere—I can be there without effort at all. That is how I came back here. I just knew that I needed to be with Aurora and the rest of you, and in a blink—I was here. And now that everything is in order, I feel the pull that is my relationship with Amanda. That is how the Creator made us. We complete each other. Not in the needy ego way but in a Spirit way. This is where the yin/yang concept comes from." Shiloh was hugging Petra as he said this.

"I agree," Petra said. "Although there was a time I could not have understood any of what you just said. I have a confession," she said to James. "When I first met your brother, my mind was taken by an impulse to sleep with him. Remember that morning that we did not know that Shiloh came home the night before and I met him in the hallway? Later that day, Shiloh put me in touch with respect and gave me the first glimpse of what a loving and trusting relationship might be."

"I know," James replied. "I knew about that and I felt a bit guilty in the way things came down. I admit that I am not sure if I was testing you—or I didn't mind sharing you with my brother. That is when I really began to trust you and knew that I wanted to spend the rest of my life with you."

"People seem to think that being a spiritual man or woman means that we don't have urges," Shiloh smiled as he released his hug. "Let me tell you both—that it was a difficult thing not to take advantage of the situation. Alone in a house with a beautiful woman. But in the end,

I had to remember who I am and why I was here. I came here to find someone, and to have a relationship that goes beyond the physical. I have that now, but I could have let it all slip away. I want to thank both of you for helping me to see that."

Lucas was next as Shiloh made his way around the circle of friends—saying good-bye in the Native way. There is no good-bye, since we will be forever connected—I know that I will see you again, if not in this world, then in the next.

"When the darkness came," Lucas explained, "I believed that it might be the end. And I began to go over in my mind all of the things I either didn't complete or was afraid of starting. I have always been one to back away from conflict in any form. When I first met you, I was about to quit the band because of the way Jude was acting. That was my way of handling life; it was not Jude's problem, as I see it now. And when the darkness came, it was something I could not escape by running away. One day we will all die...whatever that means. I want to learn to live life to the fullest. What is important to me now are the things I do between my birth and my death."

"For sure," Shiloh stepped back a moment. "And this could be a lesson for all of us: Another lesson would be: You do not have to do everything, especially those things that others have planned for you. All that the Creator asks is that you live your life in a respectful way that makes you happy."

"Simon?" Shiloh extended his hand. Simon was never a huggy kind of man. "Should we do the Aikido thing? Or maybe Judo? Karate? How about a little arm wrestle?" During the time that they all had spent together on the road, Simon was continually finding ways to test his knowledge of the martial arts.

"Aikido is fine," Simon bowed with his hands clasped at his heart, then extended his arm for a traditional Native handshake. He then drew his friend into his "circle" to emphasize his trust and lack of needing to prove superiority in any way. "I am you—and you are me. You will be forever in my heart." Letting go and stepping back, he said 'Namaste' once more.

Shiloh continued around the circle until he stood before Jude and his partner, Nathan. A number of thoughts ran through Shiloh's mind about the kind of relationship his friend had chosen. Nathan was a former college professor, a good number of years Jude's senior. He was well-groomed and greying at the temples, with a prominent manicured goatee. Nathan had been dismissed from his position at one of the larger universities in the former city of New Rome when he "came out of the closet" about his gay lifestyle. In the years following, before he met Jude, he had used his savings to start a new-age book store.

When Shiloh had smiled pleasantly and shook both their hands, he said:

"Even the Son of God and that includes you," Shiloh looked him straight in the eye. "Even a son of the Great Spirit has been granted the gift of Free-will. I am who I am, not because He expects it of me and certainly not because the religious followers or anyone else for that matter believe I am the Beast or the second coming of Christ. I am who I am because I believe in myself and I know who I am. This is your gift as well. And this gift will not disappear, even if you deny it—it will still be available to you."

"This sounds a bit judgmental?" Nathan commented. "Are you being critical of how Jude has decided to share his 'gift of life' as you call it?"

"It may sound that way," Shiloh admitted. "But it is not. I am stressing that Love is a precious thing. And if love is taken as a purely physical experience, even for a man and a woman, it can temporarily disconnect you from Grace. We are all learning to Love as best we can. The next question might be: Is there a right and wrong way to Love? Can a woman love another woman? Most assuredly. And can a man love another man? I am standing here today as a result of this expression of love. A man, a friend of mine, sacrificed his life for me. What greater expression of love can there be than that? It is not that we love—it is in the respect and expression of love that makes this love so right."

"So are we so wrong?" Nathan held on to the question. "Is it wrong for Jude and me to want to be married?"

"If you are expecting to have the blessing of the Church of Rome in a marriage ceremony then, as Thomas has said, don't hold your breath.

And why would you want their blessing anyways. First, they have a right to believe as they will and that might turn away some potential followers, or not? And secondly, by society's standards, as we know it today, your relationship would not be considered 'normal.' The question you need to ask yourself, and not anyone else including me, is: *Do you love each other or are you just in it for the physical experience? Either way—just be honest and try not to harm each other in your relationship that you are telling me is about Love.*"

"It still sounds judgmental, even in your poetic way of speaking, like your brother James noted," Nathan shrugged. "What about you Jude? What do you think?"

"I think Shiloh is just speaking the truth as he knows it," Jude replied. "I know that if I asked him point blank about what is right and wrong, he will say that there is the 'Arrow of Truth.' Sometimes it can kill in its correctness, but with compassion that will not be a judgment but in defence of Life. Do I understand that right?" Jude asked his friend.

Shiloh smiled and accepted the arrow back from Petra whom he had given it for safe-keeping. "This is the arrow that lodged in the heart of a man called Custer," he explained. "It was recognition of Change, an honouring of the person who helped bring that change, even though his methods were beyond reproach. The Arrow is not the Truth, it points to the truth in our hearts. These are the questions. The Great Spirit created us, man and woman, male and female. He created our bodies in a certain way. It is a mystery that is both beautiful and enlightening; in how the physical joining of male and female is a sharing of the Love that is the Creator. The truth of the Arrow and the Traditional Ways is that to change this way of sharing is wrong. But that same Arrow is about change, with compassion. It is about Grace. We need both Change and the honouring of the Traditional Ways of the Heart. Some things change, as they must. But what does not change is Respect"

"Point taken," Nathan replied. "And I understand that you care enough about Jude to want the best for him. I hear so many people in Kansa talking about the Traditional Ways but those beliefs seem about as scattered as the numerous Christian sects. Is there a simple explanation of the tenents that make up the Native ways? In as few words as possible?"

"Yes," Shiloh replied. "Three words: Everything is Sacred."

"And now there is this Arrow," Shiloh turned and held it aloft. "When I left it in the safekeeping of my friends I left it in the hands of someone who understands that justice and compassion must go hand-in-hand. I realized that this must stay with you." And he presented it to Petra once more. "This is not the ONLY Arrow of Truth, every dream and every world has one. The problem arises when one nation believes that they have the only truth and they are the chosen people. When this happens, the Arrow is corrupted and becomes a weapon, instead of an instrument of Compassion and Love. Think, if you will, about the story of cupid. The true use of cupid's arrow is the intent of Love. Not Love that controls or harms another but simply says, in its purest form of intent, 'Please Share with me'. When we release that Arrow, the universe will respond in kind."

"And now," Shiloh said, "the time for talking has passed. My Heart is sensing a tug that is pulling me Home. It's time for Aurora and I to go home."

With his daughter at his side and holding his hand, Shiloh proceeded in the direction of the ranch house. It had to be her choice. He could not carry a child to the other world, no matter how right it seemed to him. And, at a point where the tug of his Heart seemed the strongest, he looked skyward and said in a low voice: "Maiingun this is your Dream. I pray that your quest will be successful. And that you will discover who you are."

And then father and daughter stepped forward into the Mystery… and disappeared.

Chapter 23

WHERE THE VISION QUEST LEADS

Coming down from the mountain, the dreams were beginning to fade from my mind. There was too much to remember. It was as though I had lived another life. The valley looked the same as when I had left. That should not be surprising, considering that I was only gone four days and nights. It was serenely quiet. Smoke rose from the teepees, and one smoke trail in particular led me to Grandmother's fire.

"You received your answers?" Grandmother looked up from her morning meditation as I approached.

"Yes," I smiled and hugged her. "My head is full. How could there be so much? I have lived a lifetime—or more. I went up to that mountain a boy and now I feel like a Man."

"Well, don't let all that go to your head," she joked. "A lot of what you experienced was for your Heart. Come, sit down and tell me about it. Did you learn about your name?"

I asked her for some soup—and some of her special bread. Then I sat beside the fire to tell her about my dreams. "Yes," I began. "I met a Shaman who told me that my name would be Myangun. Do you know what that means?"

"Do you mean Maiingan?" she asked.

"Yes—what does it mean?"

"It is the name for an animal that is much like our People. The White man called them Wolf. They gather together in tribes called packs and mate for life. If any animal still lives outside this valley... well, I would guess that they would be one of the first to return."

"White man?" That brought back a memory. "I have never seen this White man—but I dreamed of him. How is this possible?"

"It is possible because our dreams are more than they seem. Do not be concerned if you do not remember all of your dreams. When you need them they will be there. One thing you should know, however, is that our People believe that everything in our dreams is a part of us. This is a good teaching that we need to bring back with us into this world. So, now, my grown-up Grandson who is called Maiingun, *I liked the way she said it this time,*" what will you do now? What will you do with this knowledge?"

"Although I am still remembering some parts of my dreams, there is one particular memory that stands out," I replied. "My dreams were mostly about sharing. I have been happy with the company of my Grandmother. You have also been like a mother and a father that I did not have. But there is another kind of companionship that a young man or woman feels drawn to seek out."

"I knew that this day would come," Grandmother smiled. "When will you be leaving our valley?"

"Perhaps I will not need to leave this valley after all. At least not at first. There is someone that is calling to me—across the water that divides this valley. I have felt this calling before but until I dreamed, I did not know what this voice was about. There is someone who stands waiting—over there."

I pointed to the mist that covered the large body of water in the centre of our valley. As a curious youth, I had attempted to journey around this water. I tried both directions but with no success. I journeyed to the west only to find an impassable waterfall that was the source of the water. It emptied into the valley from a tall plateau. In the opposite direction, there was a path—one that I had used to enter the valley as a younger child—but the path that leads to the outside world ran along dangerous rapids where the water left the valley. Many nights under a full moon, I had sat on the bank of the water and gazed out to the other side. There were times I believed that I could almost see the other bank and imagined someone standing—reaching out to me. And then the mist would close in and I would be alone with my thoughts. Until now, after the experience of my Dreams—my Vision quest—I would sigh wistfully and give up. But now, with the dreams urging me on, I knew that I must find out the truth that waits on the other bank or leave this valley.

"How can I cross this water?" I mused out loud. "It is too far to swim. There must be another way?"

"Perhaps the tree people can help?" my Grandmother suggested.

"How can a tree help me?" I asked. "A tree cannot travel. It is a prisoner of the Earth."

"None of the Creator's creatures are prisoners when they are being true to their spirit form," my Grandmother reminded me. "Our ancestors learned of different ways of sharing with the other creatures. In the past, our ancestors were able to build a canoe and with the help of the tree people, both tribes shared journeys that would not have been possible without this respectful relationship."

"Can you show me how to build this canoe?" I asked.

"Yes," my Grandmother answered at once. "You only had to ask. When you have a need, our tribe living in this valley will help. We will ask the tree people for their help also. This is the way of our ancestors. When you respect all life, then all of the creatures who are your relatives will do whatever they can to make your life better. They will even make a sacrifice for you if it is in the best interest of all things. Even though we do not kill and eat meat—even though we in this valley do not eat our winged or four-legged relatives—the plants that we do eat are to be respected, as well."

When I asked at the tribal fire, all of the people offered to help me build a canoe. And when I asked why this was not done before, they all smiled and told me that they were happy as they were and did not have a desire to travel over the water. I began to wonder if I was doing the right thing. Grandmother replied that this was not a bad thing to be curious. It was the next logical step in the Vision Quest to follow your dreams. It seemed so simple the way she explained it but there were still questions in my mind about how this might affect the lives of the people who had accepted me as one of their own.

"This is the Way of the Creator," Grandmother explained. "When the people are ready to grow or to move on, an idea will come to them. Sometimes this idea is in the form of a man or woman who comes to them who is different. They still have the right to say 'no' to new ideas but even an idea has its time. If it is a good dream, it will be good for all creatures, and will happen in the right time."

"But how can I know if this is a good idea? How can I know if this will be the right thing to do?"

"Does this feel good—does it feel right in your heart?" Grandmother smiled and placed her hand on my chest.

"It feels like my heart will burst if I do not do this," I replied.

"Then we will do the ceremony to ask the trees and if they agree to give up one of their tribe to help you, the canoe building will begin tomorrow morning."

"And if the tree people do not agree," one of the other men of our tribe replied, "you will need to practice your swimming."

That night we danced around the fire. The dance that Grandmother taught us was called the Eagle dance. She explained that the People who were our ancestors did the Eagle dance to ask for answers or for something that they needed. "The Creator will give us what we want—if it is the right thing for us and all creatures involved. Since the trees are part of all there is, the trees will make their wishes known to the Creator."

And when the dancing was finished late that night and everyone was exhausted, we slept to the sound of rain on our teepees and a powerful wind that would cause a tree to fall just outside the circle of our village.

* * *

The water was clear and calm and the mist was lifting, and it was lifting from my mind as well. This is just a dream! It has to be. The only sound was the paddle as it dipped into the water. I looked back and Grandmother waved good-bye from the bank, silhouetted against the fire—the fire that she kept burning for as long as I can remember. Perhaps she was the fire-keeper since the dawn of time? Or at least since the beginning of this dream. And I waved. She was not saying good-bye. Our people do not say good-bye. Instead, in our language we would say "see you again". And this meant so much more to me at this moment…if this was a dream, I didn't want to lose it.

But even as I turned my mind back to the paddle in my hand, I was aware that I was losing my connection to the world that Grandmother inhabited. I began to question so many things and at the heart of these questions was Grandmother. She tended this fire—she kept it going. Or did she? Yes—now I recall her feeding the fire with branches and bark that she gathered—all of which fell from the trees in the small forest beyond our camp. She did not cut down any trees for the fire but there was always enough wood to keep it going. And here was the beginning of my questions—the root. The amount of wood that was available to Grandmother could never have fed a fire for the length of time that I was living in this valley. And I have no way of knowing how long she was the fire-keeper before I arrived as a naked child from the world outside the valley.

And then there was the way the storm, the lightning and the trees gave me the wood to make a canoe. In the morning, a tree was down—just the right tree to make a canoe. Grandmother proclaimed: "It must be the right thing to do." She thanked the trees and the fire and we spent the next while building a canoe. Even though none of them had made a canoe before, everyone in the village helped and they all seemed to know what was required. And after the canoe was built, they were perfectly happy with their lives and had no curiosity about what or who was on the other side of the water—or outside this valley, for that matter.

"Am I doing the right thing?" I asked myself and Grandmother once more. She simply smiled and replied again, "does it feel like the right thing to do?" She placed her hand on my chest. "In here? If it feels right, you should not question what other people might think—including all of your friends." And she waved her other hand to show that this included all of the people who had helped to build the canoe. "When you have a Dream that comes from the Heart, and not your head, it will be the right thing for everyone and will live on. That is the test of if it is right."

"But how...?" I stopped short of asking. "How can I know if this would turn out right for our tribe?" They were happy with the life they shared in this valley. And that was it. They had a life that involved a sharing that I did not. And this was what my heart was telling me. The curiosity that tugged at me—to see what or who was on the other side of this river came from the dreams of my Vision Quest. This was somehow part of my purpose—part of my being in this valley and my friends were aware of this. Our lives would change as a result of my curiosity and they, being the true friends that they were, did not pressure me either way. They were more than friends, especially Grandmother. They were teachers of how to live the Good Life—moment to moment.

"Was there ever anyone that you shared your time with—like the other people of our tribe?" I once had a child's curiosity and innocence to ask Grandmother.

She rocked back and forth with laughter at my question until tears filled her eyes. Still, she smiled. "A Grandfather? Yes there was a Grandfather. On our way to the safety of this valley, he was lost in a great snowstorm. I will tell you about snow at another time. It is like rain, but more. Anyway, we were traveling with our tribe, including the children and me and we came upon a Wolf. This Wolf had an injured leg and Grandfather stopped to care for it. "Go on ahead," he urged us, 'I will catch up'. But he never did. I waited at the entrance to this valley for some time, but my duty was the safety of the children. And for many moons I expected to see him. But time became lost to me as well and I cannot say what had happened in the world outside."

As I continued to paddle in the direction of the faraway shore I thought about Grandmother and her love that she lost.

When the shore came into sight, my heart was pounding—louder than the heart of the Earth that I had listened to before my Quest. It beat stronger with every stroke of my paddle because I saw someone waiting, just as I had imagined. As I drew nearer, she waved excitedly. I leapt from the canoe; she met me with open arms. At that moment I believed that all of my dreams had come true.

The young woman who hugged me so tightly was not like any person I could recall meeting before. Her skin was pale in comparison to any of the members of my tribe on the other side of the river and her hair was ablaze with the colour of the setting sun. All of our tribe, including Grandmother and me, had hair that was the colour of the night, and skin the colour of the earth that we shaped into pots and dishes. Grandmother said that our People were the true children of the Earth and the Great Spirit. Our skin, she told me, is red like the skin of our true mother. This woman, who I held in my arms, was like a ghost—a ghost from my dreams. But if she was truly a ghost, then she showed that a ghost can be warm and inviting to the touch.

And then just as quickly as she had come into my arms, she let go and stepped back. Her pale skin began changing colour and I thought for a moment that she might be one of the mysterious people called shape-shifters. I thought that she was about to change into one of our tribe. But then only her face changed colour and slowly began to go pale again. She smiled.

"I am Eva," she said in a language I did not understand. And when I opened my hands to show that I did not understand, she repeated, "I am called," she pointed to her heart. "I am called Eva Marie Peters. That is my name. What is your name?" And she pointed to me.

Grandmother once told me that I was quick at learning to speak the language of the People. "You have an open heart and mind." She told me that I had a mind like a certain four-legged relative. I did not know what this creature might be—and she laughed. "You will—one day. One day you will."

When this young woman repeated the motions with her hand while repeating the words "Eva Marie Peters", I began to understand that this was her name and she was asking what I called myself. Since I was quite new to having a name, it made me feel happy to tell her who I was."

"Maiingun," I said, and pointed to my heart

"Gun? Are you saying that you are called 'Gun'?" she laughed. Her eyes were the colour of new grass as she spoke. "What a funny thing to be called." She held out her hand. "Well, hello Mister Gun, I am pleased to meet you."

When she reached out to me, I thought that she wanted to share another of the hugs that I enjoyed so much the first time. I took hold of her hand and pulled her into my arms.

"No—no," her voice shook, and she stepped back. Her face was coloured like one of my People again. And then she smiled again. "Oh? You thought I wanted to hug again, didn't you? OK—but we will need to learn how to be... more...civilized...more respectful—you know? No—you don't," she held her one hand out again, but held the other hand up to show me that I was to keep my distance. I took her hand in mine and she made a strange movement, shaking my hand up and down. I understood. With the respect of my tribe, I gently released and adjusted my grip further up her arm—in the greeting of my People.

"Maiingun," I said, pointing to my heart again. This time I made sure that she knew that this was my name—as a complete word. Why this mattered, I do not know, but it did at that time."

"My-an-gun," she smiled. We had at least understood that much. She was called "Eva-Marie-Peters" and I am "Maiingun". It was a start and there was a respect in the beginning of this relationship.

Eva asked me to shorten her name when I continually called her Eva-Marie-Peters. "This is my full name," she explained. "My friends just call me Eva." I was happy to know that I was considered her friend so soon. This came after I met the rest of her tribe. Eva's friends and tribe were made up by many different coloured people. They were mostly Grandmothers and Grandfathers. Later, when we learned to talk the same language, Eva explained that her tribe had found her, rescued her and brought her with them to the safety of this valley when the Earth began to shake. I did not know about this shaking, since I was only a boy when I came to this valley and the shaking had happened long before I was born. I had only a memory of a story that my Mother had told me about a time long ago. When I told this to Eva, she shook her head in wonder.

"Then it is true—what the old people tell me. Time does not happen in this valley the way it does in the world outside. If we were in the world outside, I would be old enough to be your Grandmother—or probably dead and gone. But here we are—as the Lord would have us—the same age, living in the Garden of Eden, like Adam and Eve meeting for the first time."

When she told me about this, her face became like one of my people again. I later learned that this was called blushing. But I could not understand why this happened until much time passed—until we were to become much closer friends. Our friendship grew quickly as we had this in common: there was no one else our age on either side of the water. To be sure there were young people our age that still lived on my side of the water. But they were couples—they were "married" as Eva called it. I had not heard that word before, but her explanation of it sounded right. At which I said "I came here to find someone to be 'married' to. I came here to find a mate like the people in my tribe. I know that now. Will you be my mate? Will you become married to me?"

This was one of the times that Eva's face became even deeper coloured than any of my tribe. But she did not tell me 'no'—so I began to believe that it was something she wanted as well. "You will need to give me some time," she replied. But she smiled and told me that it would seem that it was part of God's plan.

When she said the word "God", this caught my interest. It was something I had heard before. And when she sighed and began to tell me about God, I recognized that this was another name for the Great Spirit that Grandmother talked about so much. And I remembered the name from my dreams. Eva quickly shook her head.

"No," she said firmly. "If we are to be husband and wife, like the original Adam and Eve, then you will need to know about the real God—not some pagan Spirit." This began my education about Eva's God—through a book that she read to me called The Bible. This book, she explained, was the absolute Law considering anything of a spiritual nature. As she said this and read to me, I began to remember more from my dreams, but I learned to keep quiet about this previous knowledge for fear that Eva might no longer want to be my friend and refuse to be mated with me. And so I hid away everything that Grandmother had taught me and held back the dreams that attempted to surface as Eva taught me to read using her Bible. Pretty soon I was able to speak and read the language Eva called English and I continued to read from her Bible. She looked upon me with glowing approval. She began to call me a Christian and I hoped she thought of me as her Adam. Eventually, Eva took me to meet the other people of her tribe but she asked me to refrain from reading the books and studying the religions that they followed. I was at that time a true convert to Eva's religion. Later, I had to be honest in my Heart, as Grandmother had taught me, that it was Eva that was my sole interest. Like her Bible story about Adam and Eve, I might have converted to the religion of "Trees of Good and Evil", if she had asked me, but in my Heart, I accepted my responsibility for my part in this. In my Heart, I was in love and, at that time, I believed with a certainty that Eva was the young woman that appeared in my dreams.

In the beginning, being truthful to Eva's religion, I stayed in a hut that the people of Eva's tribe built for me. Until the time I learned to read and speak the languages of the people, the Elders visited me, giving me food and friendship. Soon, however, I began to learn that they spoke other languages—not everyone spoke the same as Eva. At that point, Eva did not discourage me with finding other friends but cautioned me about listening to their beliefs—as there was only one God—and only one true religion. Later, however Eva began to think that my mind was in danger by spending too much time with her friends who had different beliefs. I wondered if she must have led a lonely life before I came. She assured me that she was strong in her beliefs, that sharing with these people had not been a problem for her. They had rescued her and brought her here to the safety of Eden. That aside, I learned that some of the Elders had different names for this valley. Some called it Shangri-La—and they all seemed to agree on something that Eva told me. An Elder told me that Eva was a descendant of a holy man called Jesus. I am not, to this day, sure of how they knew this, but they had searched her out and rescued her from an abusive father who had adopted her. Eva's "father" was a traveling "Spirit man"—a preacher. She was his possession, to be displayed to the public at-large as evidence of the truth of his ministry. He had found Eva wandering alone in the wilds as a child. He was instantly taken by her innocence—and something about her that caused a man to want her and at the same time to be in awe at some kind of "light" that surrounded her. I did not speak about it to Eva but having heard about her treatment at the hands of this man made me want to be closer—to protect her.

Eventually, while we were still reading daily from her Bible, Eva felt it would be best if I shared her hut. She wanted to protect me as much as I wanted to be close and protect her. She explained, like before, that

I should only hear the truth, as she understood it—as it was written in her Bible. This truly did lead to an understanding of the story of Adam and Eve. It happened so naturally, that I was surprised. And after we had shared, I understood what she had said about guilt and sin. Before this evening, we had read the Bible and Eva had told me about sin. "My People do not know about this word in this way," I proclaimed. "We do not have a word for this sin. For my People, there is Love and there is sharing—we have a word like this, but it is about the sharing of food with good friends." And I continued grappling with memories from my dreams. "Until the White man came to our land, we did not know there was such a belief."

And then, while I was holding this sacred woman who I had vowed to protect, I felt my first pang of guilt. One minute, we had shared Love and the next; she was the source of my knowledge of sin. It was not simply, as she weeped later, that we had sinned. It was more. I was awakened to knowledge about myself and my dreams that I could no longer hide. I could not blame Eva for naming what had occurred. She was only voicing her beliefs. In a flood, the dreams returned to me, and I knew, too late, that I had been drawn here to help and protect her but, in her eyes; I had taken advantage of her in the same way as the man who found her wandering in the wilderness. In my Way, I loved her and would until the end of known time, but I did not know at that moment if I could make this right.

"I love you," I said with all the truth I could manage. And it was not a lie. "I believe the way to make this Right is for us to be married in the way of your people?"

"Yes," she sniffled in my ear. And after a long, quiet moment, "but though we will be man and wife in the eyes of God, we are like the original Adam and Eve. We have sinned and will always be guilty. Only the blood of Jesus can save us."

"Can we pretend that this did not happen—until we are man and wife?" I was looking for a way to make this right. But even as I spoke, I was aware of the ignorance of my words. In the eyes and in the truth of my People, when two share Love, it is natural and beautiful, as this had been with this woman of my dreams. But those two people must be able to live those truths. I would need to discover how this would fit—in the Way of the Dream that is right for everyone that lives within it. "We cannot pretend," I conceded. "We will live the best we can—with Love." The truth of this was that the sinning did not end with that night—nor did the Loving.

Chapter 24

TO SEARCH FOR THE WHITE BUFFALO

Eva and I were married in her custom of her People. I used my canoe to bring Grandmother and some of my friends from the other side of the water and took them back when the ceremony and the celebrating were complete. When I dropped off my Grandmother on the other side, she hugged me close. "See you again—soon," she whispered in my ear, and I could feel her breath tickling as she chuckled from her private joke. And she was right—in the way that time in this valley could only be measured by the things that were shared and not by a passing of the moon. My mind was only on the sharing that was to take place with Eva—for the rest of eternity.

And the sharing was beautiful. It was always beautiful but it did not continue as I imagined. Eva and I journeyed to the great waterfalls at the western end of the valley. We planned to camp there and let nature and the Loving take its course. But the time there became measured by the moon overhead. The moon appeared overhead and the moon disappeared four times. And then Eva said: "Let us return home and get ready to raise a family. It is time for us to start the world again. That is part of God's plan."

I asked her what she meant. "Are you ready to have little ones?"

"I am ready," she smiled. "As soon as God helps this to happen."

I was not sure what God had to do with this. But Grandmother had told me in a story how children came into the world. And when I asked why there were no children being born as a result of the sharing of the young people of our tribe, she replied, "I cannot say. Perhaps the Creator has a plan?" So Eva and I returned home to wait for God to work his magic. But the children did not appear, even though Eva and I did our best to make this happen—much to my continuing enjoyment.

"Something is wrong," Eva exclaimed one morning. I was not about to complain. As far as I was concerned, everything was right. Eva, I had discovered, believed that the plan of God was spelled out—written in the Bible. The beginning of the world would follow the preordained plan. Life, as Eva understood the teaching, began with Adam and Eve. Then after the sinning—children were born and the rest of the Bible was filled with begats and begats, and more begats as everyone had children and the world prospered. That, at least, was how I heard it the first time Eva read to me. There were a lot of wars in between the begatting but my mind accepted that this was a natural thing that balanced out the birthrate since there was so much sharing of Love. I was due for a rude awakening.

"Something is definitely wrong," Eva repeated. "We need to get some help. And do not start again with those dreams of yours." Her meaning was quite clear and made clearer with a look from her flashing green eyes. I had made a mistake one morning—the first time she said that there was something wrong with our relationship. I was feeling particularly open and trusting, after a night of sharing a deeper level than ever before. It was both spiritually and physically satisfying, for me at least. So, on that fateful morning, I told Eva about Dreams that I had been having that involved her and myself, in another place or time though I wasn't sure the location. "In one of my dreams, we had children," I told her. "In fact we had twins. This was some time ago and our children would be grown now and we had many beautiful grandchildren."

Well, that did not turn out the way I expected, the telling about the dreams I mean. Eva became very upset and accused me of either having an affair or it showed that I wanted to be with another woman. And I could not convince her that the other woman that had our children in my dream was herself. I would regret the sharing of this dream with her—many times over. And in Eva's way of seeing life, she might have been right. I learned a very valuable lesson about respecting another person's beliefs—no matter if I were to see things in a broader or different way. Eva wanted a life and children, in the here and now—with a husband that was grounded in this reality.

Following this last encounter, we agreed to seek out other spiritual answers with her immediate friends. She agreed that since there was "something wrong", it was time to at least read the books and listen to the viewpoints of the group of people who were responsible for rescuing her and bringing her to this valley. There were a number of different-coloured people that had been Eva's friend—mostly at arm's length for as long as she had lived here. She had been thankful for their help but not open to trusting them when it came to questions of her religion. This turned out to be the strangest part of it all, since most of Eva's religious beliefs were directly related to the man who pretended to be her father. She had the presence of the living spirit, that was undeniable, and he had provided the hard-lined Christian belief. And at the time when I began to see this, my relationship with Eva had already re-awakened me to my dreams. Otherwise, most of it would have been beyond the understanding of a boy who wandered naked into "Eden".

When we began to spend time with the group of people that had brought Eva to the valley, I learned that they had collectively followed the prophesies that foretold the end of the world, for years before the great "shaking" occurred. Then when the Earth began what appeared to be its death throes, these people were already seeking the one who would be part of restarting Life. They used many mystical and spiritual methods to locate this person. Much to their surprise, they found Eve—instead of Adam. But then, this group of individuals did not base their beliefs on one set of prophesies. The group was made up of many different coloured people and some found it almost offensive to think that a woman would be the source of a new beginning. I was not surprised to find that there were none of my people included as part of this group. It would have been a natural thing for the People of the Earth to find a woman at the centre of the Circle of Life. In sharing time more closely with this group of people, I chanced to meet one among them who was seemingly not as aged as the others. This woman, who called herself Sardana, was introduced to me as a

Buddhist monk. Her head was shorn—with a short cropping of white. Other than this symbol of age, she was remarkably agile and young for whatever age she might have been outside this valley. She seemed to know Eva quite well, to my surprise. I discovered that the reason I had not encountered this woman was that she spent most of her time in meditation—and of course, until this time, my focus had been on Eva. Eva had asked that I not become "involved" with the members of this group and their beliefs.

Astrology was one of the tools that the group had used. Their form of this sometimes logical art involved a mapping of the past, present and future based on the position of the stars. But the outcome was dependent and required a sign. "Who could know what this sign would be," I wondered. That was not something that they would reveal to me. But it became evident to me that Eva possessed this knowledge—even though she was not prepared to reveal it. At one meeting, the monk Sardana mentioned a certain artifact but Eva dismissed this remark with a look from her flashing green eyes. Eva evaded the question altogether, insisting that everything that anyone needed was to be found in the Bible. All the while, it became clear to me that she was extremely sensitive and spiritually intuitive. As we spent more time among these people on Eva's side of the water, I could see that she did fit in, all too well, with their mystical ways. But even as this truth grew, so did her resistance, until one day, she refused to continue.

"There is a problem," she stated as though it were so obvious. "But we will not find the answer in this black magic. And I am beginning to lose my trust in you for suggesting that we become involved in this sinful occult lifestyle."

By this time, I was aware that it would have been contrary to our relationship to point out that these "occult" people had been her friends—before I paddled my way into her life. But my new closed-lipped approach did not stop our once passionate relationship from going downhill. And rightly so—it could scarcely be called a relationship, if there is no relating—no real communication. After many moons passed over our valley and our relationship, or lack thereof, I began to realize that I had grown more in my time with Eva than all of the time with my tribe—from boy to man. If I didn't have my dreams to support me, I would easily have become an angry man who was ready to blame his wife and friends for the state of his life. In the beginning of our relationship, even though I had completed the Vision Quest, I was still a boy. And as a boy, I entered into this not knowing the true meaning of Love. In the course of loving this woman, I found passion, anger, resentment and a range of emotions that I failed to understand until I re-covered my dreams. I began to remember a man called Shiloh, who lives within me, as the "One who came before" lived within him. Forgiveness is not something we earn. It is our birthright. Sometimes it takes the challenge of loving someone who is not easy to Love, to bring out the best in a man.

"There is a problem," I agreed. I suggested that we take this to my Grandmother on the other side of the water. When I opened my heart to what Eva was telling me, I began to see things from a different perspective. And I began to feel that pull, the one that I experienced when I first paddled across the river. I began to believe that whatever we sense as an answer to the questions we face in our lives and our dreams—whether it is a person like Eva or a particular sacred object—it is most likely part of a Greater puzzle. This is about respecting the Mystery as the true Source of life. Life is a Mystery and when we are drawn to embrace it through Sharing, we are able to experience it but we can never truly "know" it. And the moment we attempt to define this Mystery—to name it—is the moment we began to lose touch with it. This is the moment we find ourselves outside "the garden". The best I could hope for in loving Eva was to show her that there was a choice and then it is up to us to take responsibility for the path we each choose. And even if she does not acknowledge that there is a choice, then that is her choice, too, and it is not for me get in the "way".

It would be some time before Eva would agree to take our problems to Grandmother. The fracturing of our relationship took its good time to go from a "shaky" beginning to the "big bang". And then one morning, Eva announced: "it is not part of my religion that a marriage of a man and a woman can be dissolved. It is 'til death do us part." Then she left our hut and sat gazing out across the water, in silence. Although I did not have a good feeling about what Eva said, I believed that this was her way of saying that she had reached her limit and did not have an answer in her book to solve our problem. At another time, I would admit my failings as a converted Christian. If I had been the Christian that Eva expected—if I had been her "Adam" then the Book might have provided the answer. Eva's Buddhist friend might have supplied that answer: "it is about suffering. This is the truth of our time on this Earth. And in that suffering we learn to endure, until we gain enlightenment." Or in Eva's religion, Jesus returns to save us from our sins. But Eva did not marry a Buddhist—or a Christian.

Eva was quiet as we paddled our way to the other side of the water. She seemed almost resigned but my experience told me that this was not necessarily true. And I respected this as her right. It was a necessary part of my experience of the Mystery. I am learning to follow the Path of Beauty. In walking or paddling on the Path of Beauty, we acknowledge that the Creator has a plan—and that free-will is also our Gift. To embrace both is to walk the Path of Beauty. Eva had agreed to come over to my side of the river but only as a last resort. In the Buddhist way this could be a good sign, but in the Christian way this might signify selling your soul to the devil. I was not sure of the complete significance to Eva. Perhaps it was a "wait and see"? The Christian beliefs are usually about the battle between Good and Evil. Perhaps Eva had decided that the best way to defeat Satan was to meet him in his own domain. Either way, I would need to be on my best behaviour. I had one major thing in my favour: Grandmother was not the devil by any stretch of the imagination.

Grandmother greeted us on the opposite shore with a broad smile that she appeared to be attempting to hide. "I am happy to see you again." Her greeting was similar to the "good-bye" as though she had foreseen this visit and the reason behind it. I opened my mouth to speak and Grandmother silenced me with a hug, and whispered in my ear: "Be patient. Wait for the time to be right. First let there be a sharing and the right words will come."

Later when everyone else had gone to sleep, Eva and I joined Grandmother by the fire. We talked for a while, bringing Grandmother up-to-date on the events of our lives. And then Eva became silent.

"In the ways of my people," Grandmother began, "a young man or woman goes on a Quest to find out how they will go about living the purpose that the Creator has for them. This is a two-fold quest since they have already been given a life of purpose by being born as a man or woman. This quest will be more about how they will fulfill that purpose. A boy, who is to become a man, will go to the top of a mountain for this quest and a young woman will go into a forest or valley. This is because a man is about to re-enact the Spirit of the Sky by joining with a woman who is at One with the Spirit of Mother Earth."

When Grandmother finished speaking, she waited for us to say something or ask a question. Eva and I were both silent.

"You should both think about how you came to be here," Grandmother continued. "Before you were ready to complete your quest, there were beginnings that would contribute to your beliefs. A child is shaped by the actions and teachings of their mother and father—that is if their parents were present during their early years. You came to me for answers to questions that both of you hold within you. Please think about being a child again. Hold this piece of bark that is the skin of a tree and think upon this—for as long as it takes." Grandmother gave us both a piece of the tree that had become my canoe. "When you are ready, feed the fire with your thoughts that are part of this tree and gaze into the fire. If it is right in your heart—you can share with me what you see."

My mind became a blur of the Dreams that I had lived while on my quest. It became difficult to hold a thought. I was once more within these dreams. I wondered, what more could I learn about myself that these dreams did not hold. And then when I was about to feed the fire with my piece of bark, I halted. Eva was talking—about what she saw within the fire.

"I see myself as a young girl. I am the middle one of three. My mother is telling us about how our father is the brother of a great man—a Shaman who is about to sacrifice his life so that our people can live. Our mother is not one of the Red-skinned people, but my father is a Shaman like his brother. This cannot be the truth," Eva exclaimed. "I want to look away but I can't."

"Peace child," Grandmother's voice was soothing. "There is nothing to fear. Think of this like a dream—the truth in dreams may be hidden from us by taking the shape of our fears. It may be a symbol or an animal that we see that will talk to us about something that we need to release from our hearts. If you do not wish to see this, you can look away. Give yourself the right to do this."

"Yes. I can look away," Eva acknowledged. "But I want to learn what this is about—even if I do not believe it. I am now a bit older. And my family is leaving our home. We are running away from some disaster that is about to happen—it is a terrible thing!" Eva began to cry. And then she got hold again. "I am OK, It is just a dream. As we are running—no, our family is together in a transporting device. As we are running away, my mother is explaining that the Shaman's sacrifice was in vain. I want to call him Jesus because it is the Story that I know in my Bible. It is the story all over again. But I am part of the story. This must be a dream."

"It is a dream," Grandmother repeated in a quiet voice. "You can move ahead in the dream—to a place where you are safe. Where are you now?"

"I am in a cave," Eva said. "We are all safe—except," she choked back the tears, "except my mother is not with us—she could have been safe but she chose to abandon us. She turned around and gave her life for the people that were not even her own. Why would she do this?" I wondered how Eva could make it through this. I was learning about a side of her that I had not previously been witness to. Eva was a brave and strong woman.

"Your mother was a brave and wise woman," Grandmother said in her soothing voice. "She knew that we are all part of the same Spirit. She gave of herself so that the knowledge to start again would not be lost. You are much like her—I can see that you have accepted this gift."

"Yes…I guess so," Eva sniffled. "She did give me a gift to share—but I am in fear of revealing it, because it might change all that I believe. I will be like a naked child again lost in the wilds."

"Is that where you are now in the dream?" Grandmother asked.

"Yes, it is a different time. I only remember that our father gave us a potion that would allow us to sleep for a long time until the world was safe again.

And when we woke, we became changed. But I did not want this change. I wanted my mother back. And soon I was myself again. I returned to the cave where one of my sisters was still asleep—like dead. I could not awaken her, although I shook her and called the name that we knew her by. I remember this from my father just before we went to sleep. How could I not remember the name of my little sister? I am alone. I gather my belongings including the gift that my mother gave, and leave the cave to try to find the rest of my family."

"And did you find your other sister and father?" Grandmother asked.

"No, but a man found me. I was alone. I was hungry. This man became my new father. He said that he saw a light around me—like I was an angel. But that did not stop him from becoming angry at times and beating me. He was always sorry after but he explained that it was necessary. He explained that we are all sinners—especially women. He explained that women will tempt a man to sin, so she must accept the punishment for her curse. He explained that I bore this curse much more than most young women because my temptation was so strong that even he, as my new father, was tempted. I was happy just the same because I was not alone any more and I knew that Jesus loved me and would save me from my sins. I know this because I read the Bible every day."

"But this did not last," Grandmother gently urged.

"No. My father visited the small groups of people that survived the end of the world. He preached to the people that he said were left behind. One day, I was with my father and while he preached, I saw a woman making a motion with her hand. I looked to see that my father was deep in his sermon and went to meet the woman at the side of the gathering. She said that her people had recognized me and were here to take me to a place of safety. She said that this was not over. I believed her because this was part of the sermon that my father preached. He said that God's chosen had been taken and we were left behind, until the reason for the shaking returned to complete Ezekiel's vision. I was tired of being beaten for a curse that belonged to the Original Eve—who was my namesake. So I left with this woman called Sardana and the others, while my father was screaming about sin, to come to the safety of this valley."

After a moment of silence, Grandmother thanked Eva for being brave and for sharing her story. And then Grandmother said in her most sincere voice: "Our people, of whom you do have a connection through your real father, do not believe in sin. If you feel a need to live your mother's truth, you should know that she chose to share her life with a man who would have believed that the Creator blessed all women. The God that you will come to know in your heart is about Love. The Creator gave Eve the blessing of being a mother."

"And what about you." Grandmother's voice brought me back to my thoughts. "You still hold the bark of your canoe. Are you ready to see more of your path? You should be aware that even when the quest is finished, it is not complete until you leave this Earth Walk for another Dreaming."

I took a deep breath and gave the fire my piece of the tree.

"Nothing," I shrugged in wonder, "...except another four-legged. I see this beast that I do not recognize. Does this mean that I have found another totem?"

"Tell me about this creature?" Grandmother requested.

"It is a large, white, hairy beast with horns. Do you know of this animal? What do you think this means?"

Grandmother drew in a breath. "Yes I know of this creature and her kind. They have been our providers as long as our people have roamed this Earth. These four-legged people are called the Buffalo and you have seen the Great White one of our legends."

"And what does this mean?" I asked. "Why should this Great White Buffalo appear in the fire before me?"

"It is about the reason that you are here this night," Grandmother explained. "This is your dream that is not finished. This is your dream that we are sharing. When the Great White appears in your dreams, it means that she is giving herself to you and the people who are your tribe."

"But my dream is not about one tribe," I explained. "And now my dream includes Eva and the beliefs of her people. It is all about starting this world again—in a good way. And it will be about the birth of children."

"Yes," Grandmother agreed. "It is about the Circle of Life. And the Buffalo is saying to you, it is ready to start this Circle again."

"But—how can this happen?" I was still confused.

"You will need to go into the world outside this valley and bring back the flesh of the Buffalo. This will begin the Circle once more."

"Do you mean that I must kill this creature?" I was shaken. I had not considered this at any time in my known life.

"Think about the lives that have come and gone in the quest that you call a dream. All of those lives are Sacred. And they all still have a purpose in preparing you for this moment. Yes—you will be required to hunt and kill the Great White so that this Circle can begin again."

Chapter 25
THE HUNTING

"If this is my dream, why can't I refuse to kill?" These thoughts filled my head as I began preparations as best as I could for the hunting. "But you are not alone in this dream." The words came back to me just as quickly as I put out the question. And this dream was about honouring the Circle of Life. I recalled how Shiloh waited on the hilltop as the other men killed the Buffalo that would provide the sinew for his bow. His reply was: "If I am part of the hunt, it is the same as if I were the one who killed the Buffalo." I realized that part of the truth about when I have a thought that is associated with a strong emotion, then the act is already begun or completed as though I had carried it out in this reality. To be completely responsible—to live the Spirit-life like the One who has gone before, meant I have to learn to "own" my every thought. This means that I'm acting as though Forgiveness is the gift of Fore-Giveness. Meanwhile I wondered if I would actually need to go through with this or if my acceptance would be enough?

The trees supplied the bow like they gave the wood for the canoe. Grandmother gave me the twine that was part of her knitting from a plant that she had once used to create clothes for me. "Mother Earth provides for those who are part of the Creator's plan," she explained. "The Earth and the creatures that are our relatives will always provide for those who are grateful for the sacrifice. You should be aware that everything is alive and all life is Sacred—the trees and plants are not less than the Buffalo or the two-legged for that matter. Some of the two-legged have just forgotten their part of the sharing and think that everything belongs to them. The Earth does not belong to us—we are the children of a marriage of the Great Spirit and of Mother Earth."

Grandmother gave me feathers that she had saved and helped me to gather stones that we shaped into arrowheads. There was an honouring ceremony for everything. "We do not have a religion," Grandmother explained, "a religion is for the two-legged to justify their actions. Our ceremonies are part of honouring the Gifts of the Creator and our relatives. It is about them—not just us."

And then I practiced with the bow, from daybreak to sundown, until I could draw the arrow and send it on its way almost as easily as I remember a young man called Shiloh. But there was a problem—I still lacked his unwavering confidence. Some of the arrows found the target and other arrows were lost in the tall grass and I wasted too much time hunting for them. Eva just watched and appeared to share in my frustration.

"This is the lesson of sin," she remarked one morning, finding it hard to hide a smile.

"I fail to see the point," I replied, searching in the grass until I found what I was looking for.

"Sin is really about missing the mark," Eva sighed. "At least that is how it should be without the heavy judgment added." She surprised me.

I sat beside her in the cool morning grass. "You surprise me," I acknowledged.

"I didn't think that anything I could do would surprise a husband who had shared all that I had given," she replied.

"We need to call a truce," I suggested. "I need your support in what I am going to do. It will not be easy for me to be a hunter. For you—it is your natural instinct to be a mother and perhaps a wife like our ancestors. But a man like me has lost the instinct to hunt and kill for my family."

"I believe that," she replied. "But you do not know me as well as you think you do. When this is over I pledge that we will reconsider our relationship. Perhaps I was too hasty. Maybe I…"

"You were not," I affirmed. "It was as much my choice as yours. I will agree to think about your description of sin since I have been experiencing it first hand, in more ways than one. In return I ask that you consider the belief of my tribe that a woman is not a tempter of a man and that it is part of the natural plan of the Creator that we be drawn together to share. How else would the Creator expect us to continue our species?"

"Perhaps we were meant to live forever—in this Valley I call Eden?" she replied. Why would there be the story of Adam and Eve in the Bible? It is becoming a Mystery to me."

"For me, too!" I rose to me feet to resume practice. "I hope that it will always be a Mystery for me." I refitted the arrow slowly this time, only to hear her quiet reply.

"I have kept something from you," she said.

"Of course you have," I mildly cursed the arrow that missed the target once more. "And I have sinned again. You have a right to keep your womanly secrets. Even a man like me who is inexperienced in this kind of relationship would know that."

"No. I mean a greater secret. Do you recall that time that Sardana mentioned an artifact? I have an artifact that will most likely mean, if it is what I think it is that you will be able to give up chasing arrows in the grass."

"You do?" I stopped in mid stride, quite ready to give up on the search—to let this one error—this lost arrow be forgotten.

"I have something in my personal belongings back in the teepee that is our temporary home on your side of the river."

"There is no my side any more than your side—except through respect for your beliefs," I said. "Even if we were not joined in marriage as is the custom of your people, all that I have belongs rightly to anyone of your tribe."

"I am slowly beginning to believe that," Eva replied. "Come back to our home away from home and I will show you the Gift I received from my birth mother."

Grandmother met us as we approached the camp. "You two are in good spirits," she noticed. "I think that the problem is on its way to being solved?"

"You may be right," Eva agreed. "I have something to share with all of you." Eva entered the teepee, and returned quickly with a bundle. It was a long carrying pouch made of animal hide. "I think this is deer skin," Eva remarked. "I have never checked and did not show it to anyone except my Buddhist friend on the other side of the river. And no—not even my once-adopted father, although he did try to find out what it was without results. He took it from me, and pulled it apart, and, after a while, he threw it to the ground saying, he didn't know how I could be so stupid and full of spirit at the same time. Then he slapped me. He did not find anything within my pouch. Perhaps one of you will know what it is? If you can see it, I mean."

Eva pulled a parcel out of the long pouch and began to unwrap something.

"An arrow!" Both Grandmother and I exclaimed at the same time.

"Yes!" Eva shouted gleefully. "And I can see it now, too! I could only feel it under the deer-hide wrapping before this. And my friend Sardana was the only one who could see it. She told me that sometimes having religion will stop us from seeing beyond our own beliefs. And that put me off to no end. I do not understand why I can see it now."

"I have heard about this arrow," Grandmother smiled. "Can you tell your wife why it is visible now," she asked me.

"I recognize this Arrow," I replied transfixed. "I wonder about Dreams—but this should allow me to give-away the doubts. I remember that only a person with an open-heart and mind can see this arrow."

"I hope that is true," Eva replied. "And now I can give it back to you and your People. It represents something that my people attempted to steal."

"This is a symbol of our acceptance of change," Grandmother hugged Eva. "Change is not the constant thing as some people believe. Love is the only constant thing—Love with the Gift of free-will. We did not give up—we will never give up. We will fight to the death to protect the Earth and its creatures. But we know that respectful change is part of the Creator's plan, if we are to share this Earth Walk with all of our relatives. And now, perhaps we begin again—together?"

Grandmother accepted the arrow from Eva and passed it to me. "Now you know that your vision about the Great White was true."

I could not disagree but I still had questions. "I will hunt this creature," I agreed. "As my ancestors hunted her tribe. But this is not something I am meant to do alone. We are all in this dream together, are we not?"

"I will go with you," Eva spoke up immediately. "Maybe it is not your custom for a woman to go hunting but I can see this arrow now—this must mean something. Right?"

"I would agree, as well," Grandmother replied. "But this is not for me to do. We will take this to the rest of our tribe to see if they will want to accompany you on this hunting party."

None of the other members of my tribe could see the arrow. I wondered at the meaning of this. Grandmother could only say that this was part of the mystery. "I believe it means that you are all happy with this life in this valley, or that you are trapped in the time not entirely of your own choosing. If you leave this valley, you might be stepping back into time that has left you behind. You might turn to dust. It might take the sharing of the flesh of the Great White to bring your bodies back into the Circle."

The young men of my tribe insisted that they would still take a chance. "We have a saying that today is a good day to die. This is not just words. This is something that our People have lived for."

"I cannot let this happen," I answered. "You may be right, but this is about following the plan of the Great Spirit. We have been given the gift to experience many Mysteries. This valley is part of this. Our gift of free-will does not mean that we will forget that the Creator has a plan as well. This is my dream vision. It is part of my quest. Please let me do what I can. I know through our sharing around the fire that we all live in different dreams, as well as this. If I do not return then it might be up to you to make a different choice at another time."

Eva and I took the canoe across the water to see if any of her friends would go with us to the outside world. None of them could see the arrow—except Sardana. And they were openly happy about remaining in the valley, until the end of time—whatever that might mean. Sardana however asked to be part of the hunting trip, as an observer. "I cannot kill—and I would not eat the flesh of an animal," she said. "But I have been in a world that life and death and the suffering in-between are a part of the Circle, as you call it. In my vows of Buddhism, like the original Buddha, I have vowed to remain on this earth to help all creatures gain enlightenment. If it is the wish of the Eternal Spirit however, that it is my time to pass into another Dream, I will gladly go. This is all a Dream after all."

The group on Eva's side of the river gave us warm clothing that they had worn on their journey to the Valley. "Outside it might be winter—if our beliefs are correct. It is only in this valley that the seasons remain sunny, like a Spring that does not end." Eva, Sardana and I took the canoe back to the side of my tribe where we were given a stock of fruits and berries to feed us during the hunting. I had a sense that the way to find the Great White would be back the way I came as a small boy.

When our hunting party of three arrived at the entrance to the valley, the beliefs of Eva's friends about the seasons and the weather were confirmed. Just beyond the entrance a different world awaited. This world was asleep, as Grandmother would have explained it, but in a different way than the valley. Life was continuing outside which is something Grandmother had known. The ground was covered by a blanket of white. Grandmother explained to me once before that in the season called Winter, the Earth will be healing herself. The three of us put on the warm clothing that had been given to us before venturing out into something I had only heard about. I was quickly acquainted with the reality of a storm of snow.

In the first day of our search for the Great White, I had to smile through the wind and cold. If it were not for a sense that the creature was calling to me, I do not believe that we had any hope of finding a white four-legged in the world of the same colour. And as the first day passed, I became re-acquainted with the part of Eva that had surfaced during what I had come to believe was the death of our relationship. The traveling in the snow was not an easy matter, especially for people who had become used to the mild and sunny valley. But it soon became apparent that Eva was affected the most of the three of us. She began to complain about the bitter cold and the difficulties of this whole hunting trip that might be ahead. But it was the way she complained that made it all the more difficult.

"I do not know why I let you talk me into this," Eva began. And when I replied that she volunteered to come along, her retort was: "If you were the husband that you should have been—you would have tried to talk me out of this ridiculous hunting party." Sardana did not complain. On the contrary, I saw her smiling and it lifted my spirits to know that in this world of suffering, she can find amusement at the bickering of her two companions. I reminded myself then that any argument requires two participants. I was aware of the value that our friend already brought to the hunting. I had wondered aloud before leaving, that it would not be possible for a man and two frail women to bring back the flesh of this great beast, even if we were successful in killing it. Grandmother's reply was of little help. "You will have the help you need." And now, I was able to see how much help one of these "frail" women could be.

Further on the trail, Eva began again, but I think she caught the look from Sardana this time. She stopped and began to laugh. "OK—I can be a 'B'...if I don't watch myself. I promise to try to look for a better way. And, well, here we are, just the three of us—freezing our buns off and no sign of civilization for miles. For all we know we may be only living humans this side of the valley. I guess I should look at the brighter side." At that she packed a handful of snow, and threw it at me and then at Sardana. After we all vented our frustrations with a snow fight, I suggested that we press on. "It will be dark soon so let us keep a look out for a good place to camp for the night. I can feel the creature getting closer, but it is hard to say how far away she is. She seems to be traveling in the direction of where the sun comes up, so that will put us on a direct path to meet her or at least cross her path. I can see the beast in my mind, but it is all snow so I have no way of telling where she is."

We stopped for the night in a natural shelter—a grove of trees. I searched about and easily found enough wood to see us through the night. The rest was easy, too—Grandmother had taught me how to create a fire—to call it from the wood. We huddled together around the fire wrapped in the blankets that Eva and Sardana's people had provided. That night I slept soundly, knowing that the Great White was on a tireless course to meet us.

Another day passed quickly in the numbing cold. We discovered that moving toward our destination, our appointment with destiny helped to keep us warm. And then we were gathered around another fire, eating our ration of fruit and nuts. This night was clear and the stars lit up the sky for us. Early in the evening, a large pale moon climbed higher in the sky. "A wolf's moon," Sardana remarked, as she watched her words and her breath rise like pipe smoke toward the Spirit in the Sky. And on cue a mournful, far-off howl seemed to agree with her observation.

"What would you know about that?" Eva asked. "I would not think that a woman who follows the Buddhist religion would know about wolves and Native beliefs."

"In the first place," Sardana smiled serenely, "Buddhism is not a religion. The true followers know it is a Spiritual Philosophy of life. Buddhism is a lot like the Aboriginal beliefs. I guess that is why it was easy for me to accept the teachings and make them my own. In my heart, I am still Anishinabe, you know?"

"Still?" Eva inquired. "What do you mean? You never told me that...?"

"I was waiting for you to recognize me," Sardana replied.

"Recognize you?" Eva squirmed uneasily. "I do recognize you."

"What are you saying?" I asked. There was something unspoken that I sensed in the calm way that Sardana spoke. Her voice held a slight quiver that was different somehow.

"I am saying that seeing the arrow comes natural to me. It was a gift to our family. My sister has suffered more than she tells. It was like the legacy of the Residential schools but as a-one-to one experience. She was taken as a young child and her soul stolen away. Sardana paused and breathed deeply so as to regain her composure. "Before I accepted my Buddhist name, I was called Mussohquamin by my father. This means 'a Ripened Ear of Corn'. This was because of the white tuft of hair that I have had since I came from our mother's womb." She slid down the hood that had been covering her head, to show that her hair was already growing back. "My mother, who was not born aboriginal, thought that my father had said my name should be..."

"Mouse!" Eva exclaimed, her eyes overflowing with tears. "Our mother thought that he had named you Mouse! I remember father telling that story about my older sister," she clasped her knees and rocked, until...."

"Great Friggin' Jesus!" a voice sounded from the underbrush and a man stepped into our fire light. "What the hell kind of hunting party are you people? A friggin' Injun and two sisters that don't recognize each other? What a motley friggin' crew we have here! And one sister is an Irish Catholic and the other living her life like an Asian. Where is your token black?"

Both women and I were stunned. This bearded, grizzly man appeared out of nowhere and the first words out of his mouth are remarks about us—as if he knew us personally.

"Who are you?" Eva jumped to her feet and grabbed one of the fire logs.

"Settle down. Don't get your knickers in a bunch," the bearded man waved what appeared to be a weapon in Eva's direction. "If I had a mind to kill all three of you, I could have done it while you were sleep. I have been following you since I saw your campfire last night."

"So why didn't you come forward until now?" I asked.

"I just wanted to find out what you were about?" The man answered, as he made himself comfortable on a nearby rock. "And I just about heard enough. You are just lucky that you do not have anything I need—like food. I am so hungry I could eat that Buffalo that you talk about rare—on the hoof."

"You heard about the Buffalo?" Eva asked.

"Well, why do you think I would bother to drop into your little campfire—to socialize? I would have just followed at a reasonable distance, until you found that Buffalo and then helped myself to a share. Except I was listening and I just couldn't hold back. What the frig are you people doing out here? In the old days, I might guess that you were city folk out for a stroll in the snow. But the cities are things of the past—gone are my grandpa's days with the big bang. My grandpa used to tell me stories about them though and the people who lived there. Never thought I would see the like. I would not have bothered but your Injun friend seems to have a thing left over from his people. And I have been on the trail of this Buffalo for too long. She just up and disappears every time I get close."

The shock of seeing this man walk into our camp had interrupted a conversation—an amazing discovery had taken place. Eva and Sardana were sisters—it seemed. How could this be so? I was almost ready to agree with this stranger's assessment of our hunting party. "Before this man appeared..." I began, and then Eva continued.

"I just found my sister that I believed to be dead."

"I might have been," Sardana replied. "When our mother stopped to look back, I did too. I discovered that she was not with us and ran back to find her no longer part of this world. In the distance, I saw the light that transformed her and it was like a moment in frozen time. I turned again to seek the safety of the cave but the next moment I was on the ground stunned. Our father grabbed me up and took me to safety as the light passed overhead. It was not until I awakened from the transformation that I discovered that the light had touched me. When I regained my form that you see now, I was helped by a man, a Buddhist that was seeking to join up with the group that eventually took Eva to the Valley."

"So you got caught in what must have been the aftershock from a nuclear bomb—the big bang that ended the world," the bearded stranger mused. "If the radiation touched you, then I am surprised to find you alive."

"I was ill," Sardana confirmed. "But the man who found me, unlike the person who adopted my sister, was kind and compassionate, He was in fact a healer. He showed me how to heal myself by living the Buddhist Way. I came away healed but without my hair. So I kept it short afterward—even when we found Eva. And the rest is what you would call history."

"But now your hair is growing since we left the valley," I noted. "And it is growing fast. Do you think you are catching up in time—like Grandmother said?"

"Perhaps. There is much water that has run under the ice. If the Eternal Spirit that is in me is ready to move on to another dream, I am ready."

"But what about this world?" Eva urged. "I have just found my sister again and we can start a new world together."

"Start a new world together?" the bearded stranger mimicked Eva's pleading voice. "Give me a break—for God's sake. How many times have I heard that? Get a grip on your shorts and pull them up and soldier on. The only religion I have found faith in is the Salvation Army! Just get it together and soldier on."

"You? Who are you to talk to us like that? You are a stranger in our camp and are enjoying our hospitality. And you dare to tell us how we should live our lives?" Eva was vehement in her reply. This stranger seemed to be able to say just the right things to set her off.

"Your hospitality? Your camp? Give me a friggin' break!" the man laughed loudly. "This forest belongs to no one—except maybe the wolves. And forgive me for intruding on your life. My name is Joe—Joseph Adams—and now that you know that, if your hospitality does not include offering a stranger a cup of coffee when he visits you in your part of the forest, then I guess that Sarah and I should be movin' on."

"Sarah?" I asked. "Do you have someone else with you? A wife perhaps?"

This brought about another round of abnormally loud laughter. "Sarah? Good God, no. I don't have a wife. And if I did—I would not be leaving her shivering in the cold, waiting until I say my how-de-doos." He rose and stepped back into the bush at the side of the camp. Eva and Sardana (or should I say Mouse, as we now know her real name) and I exchanged wondering looks. Joe came back in a few moments leading an animal that looked like a horse. Grandmother had told me about horses and I had dreamed about them. But then my mind returned to the moment that Joe—or Joseph Adams said his name. I had been looking directly at Eva as she continued to press this conversation about his reason for being "in her space". The minute he said "Adams," her eyes lit up. It was not hard to guess her thoughts. And then that seemed to ignite another fire—a further reason to dislike this uncivilized stranger, if not just for his name.

"Let me introduce you all to Sarah," Joseph's voice abruptly broke my train of thought. "Sarah is my mule. Got the name from an old vid that I saw once called *Two Mules for Sister Sarah*. Oh I can see from your faces that you don't know what a vid is? It is—or was—a form of entertainment. A play—you know what that is? Eva and I shook our heads in unison. But Mouse had seen a video before. "Our group had a video player and a collection of inspirational movies. This is a device that will show a re-enactment—like a vision that you can watch over and over again whenever you want. Our video player was powered by the sun."

"Yeah sure—that's the thing," Joseph interrupted her explanation. "Any way this movie was about a group of penguins that had a mule like mine."

Mouse chuckled. "Penguins—I think he means nuns."

"Yeah," Joseph agreed. "Must you people always be cutting in while I am interrupting? I do not need a running commentary, thank you—even from an attractive Buddhist woman like you. You seem pretty sharp. Maybe you would consider leaving this religious 'save the world by killing it' hunting party and join Sarah and I?" Joseph's mind and conversation jumped from one topic to another without a pause. I began to think that Eva would be more his match and I smiled a sly smile just to myself.

"I don't think so," Mouse replied evenly and unperturbed. "We may have been around that circle—you and I. You might call it a past life. I thank you for the offer, but I've been there, done that—and in the words that you might understand—got the tee-shirt. Compendre?"

"What did she say?" Eva asked. "I do not know what that was all about."

And neither did I.

But it seems that Joseph did—understand it quite well. And I got my first glimpse that this man might not be the blustering uncompassionate creature that he pretended to be. Something in his eye flashed just a moment. A recognition and then it was gone. "Penguins? Yes—I grew up next door to a whole flock. Trying to carry on as though nothing had happened. The world has ended and it didn't mean a thing."

"But that is just the point," Eva replied. "It does mean a thing. And that is why we are hunting this Buffalo—to start the world again—in a Good way."

And then it was my turn to be surprised—at Eva. Her words spoken for Joseph's ears did not go unnoticed, as being part of the Anishinabe traditional teaching!

"Those are some pretty sage native words for a Bible thumper," Joseph remarked.

"Yeah? Well I have lived with a Native man for longer than I would care to admit—and we did not disagree all of the time. So there!"

There were some times that I recall as well, that the sharing was particularly good—even beyond the physical. But as I listened to Eva at this point, her sister's words rang wise and clear. "Been there—done that—and have the tee-shirt, whatever that is? I imagined that coming from a Buddhist, this tee-shirt must be something symbolic of a "right of passage". Now it is time to get on with the starting of a new world—in a Good Way.

"I am still waiting on your hospitality," Joseph reminded. "Or, let me guess—you probably don't even have coffee, much less consider drinking it. You probably have—let me guess, green tea brewing in that pot?"

"Bingo!" Mouse answered him at his own level. She really did seem to have a connection. "Green tea. It is good tasting and it helps to keep you in good health. Let me pour you a cup?"

"Keep your good china for the more sophisticated guests that might drop in. The night is still young." Joseph waved his hand to indicate his disapproval of the offer. "I have a tin pot in my pack and good supply of java that I will be happy to share. Don't have any food left but I still have coffee. I have been going on coffee for a couple of weeks—almost. The beef jerky ran out awhile back and I was about thinking of making a meal of Sarah when I saw some tracks in the snow. Then the storm the other day took away my hope."

"How far away was that?" I asked. I had a sense that the Great White was close.

"Way over the ridge—that a-way," he pointed. "At least a day. She was heading the other way. Running from something, I gather. Maybe wolves? There ain't much else here abouts."

"Maybe." I considered his words and began to voice my thoughts on the subject. "She must be circling then because when the snow was heavy the other day, a couple of times I could sense that she was getting closer."

"See," Joseph spoke directly to Eva, "I had the idea that an Injun would be the best tracker for a Buffalo—even if he is a tea drinking Red-skin." He put some coffee in his pot, filled it with snow, and set it on the fire to boil. "No offense meant," he winked at me.

I really didn't know what to think of this man. But Eva obviously had preconceived notions. While I was telling him about the Buffalo, she was slowly shaking her head to indicate that it might not be a good idea. Too late—I shrugged in response.

"No offense taken," I replied. "What do you think about sharing the Buffalo flesh, in exchange for helping us take it back to the valley?"

"I don't think about that at all," he replied without a blink. "I am a loner. I think about me—and that has served me pretty well until now."

Before Eva could add her comments, Mouse spoke up. "Maybe so—but sometimes things can change when the situation is right. You were not always that way—in fact I do not believe that is how you really are—on the inside."

"Well let me tell you this," he settled back on his rock. "If a certain Buddhist woman would consider getting to know me a bit better, then I might be convinced to reciprocate."

"Not in this lifetime," she smiled, not unkindly. "My life is already spoken for. I have committed to helping heal the Earth and the people that are suffering."

"What about me?" he did not give up easily. "Sometimes on the trail I am suffering from loneliness and could use a bit of comforting?"

Mouse chuckled. "Maybe the next time around? This is a Circle don't you know, and for me it is about to begin again."

I was about to ask her to say more about her thoughts, but Joseph's coffee pot began to boil over and my questions went unanswered for the moment. He grabbed the pot and proceeded to pour it into a tin cup that he also got from his pack. "Any takers on the coffee?" he offered. And when no one replied. "OK—the offer stands. On both counts. Think I will turn in after this java. Tomorrow will be a long day tracking the Buffalo. If she is circling, as you say, then we should plan to cut her off. If it weren't for this damn snow, I would have no problem tracking the beast. But it looks like we will have to depend on the Injun-sense to get close enough to bring her down."

Chapter 26

Death—and new Beginnings

Joseph Adams and Sarah joined our hunting party and for the next few days traveled with us as we hunted the Great White. But by the end of the third day, I began to notice something strange. We did not seem to be getting any closer to finding the object of our hunt. In fact the Buffalo seemed to be mysteriously avoiding us, where a couple of days ago, it appeared to be destined to cross our paths. I didn't say anything about this until Joseph remarked: "I have a suspicion that the beast is leading us in circles. You see that ridge? That was on our North the day I joined you, and guess what—there it is again. We traveled East and then South and West—and here it is back again. We are going in a circle."

That night when we made camp, Eva announced that our food supply was getting low.

"Don't blame me," Joseph replied. "I don't eat your nuts and berries. I would sooner live on coffee."

"Don't want to blame anyone," Mouse spoke up calmly. "But the Buffalo was moving toward us before Joseph joined our group. I have nothing against you but I suggest we split up."

"Just what I think, too," Joseph replied. "Tomorrow I am heading out on my own. It seems like this Buffalo has Injun sense, too. I saw some squirrels back on the trail and squirrel meat seems like a good thing right now. I had my mouth all set for Buffalo and I didn't want to be shootin' to alarm it. But my stomach is almost eating itself."

The next morning, we went our separate ways with Joseph heading back the way we came. My thinking was that if the Buffalo really was leading us in a circle, then one of us—hopefully our hunting party—would meet her coming around in the opposite direction. In the early part of the day, I found that Mouse was right in her assessment of the problem. I began to feel the creature drawing close. "The Great White is coming toward us," I told the women. I began to think about a particular feeling that I experienced while Joseph was with us. It was part of some hidden memory—from a childhood that I had forgotten. That was in the back of my mind when I saw the Buffalo lumbering along in the banks of snow. Just like I predicted, she would be passing the grove of trees where we waited. I put one finger to my lips, then pointed and carefully fitted the arrow to my bow and waited.

As the beast passed close by where we were hidden, I drew a deep breath and the bow-string at the same time. I uttered a prayer of thanks for this Gift of life and let loose the arrow in the direction of the creature's heart. But at that very moment—while the arrow was still in the air, the silence of the winter afternoon was shattered by a deafening roar. I cannot say to this day which weapon must have struck the beast first but the sound—or something she sensed—caused the Buffalo to swerve, and she shuddered. The arrow was lodged in the Buffalo but she was not mortally wounded as was evident while I instinctively reached for another arrow and she moved on through the snow. The other arrow was in my bow in one smooth motion—a reflex similar to a Zen master. And in the space of a thought, the arrow was on its way—not in the direction of the fleeing Buffalo, but to find the source of the sound that had broken the moment of sacrifice. There followed a scream of pain and then a curse. Joseph Adams staggered into the clearing and fell to his knees, dropping his weapon to the earth.

Eva was the first to react. "You've killed him!" she screamed loudly, and rushed to where he lay in a pool of blood. Mouse was at his side one step behind Eva and when I rushed to join them, he was struggling to sit up.

"Just a flesh wound," he muttered weakly. He sat with Mouse's help and I saw the arrow lodged in his right forearm. It had passed through the fleshy part of his arm and stuck out the other side.

"Be still," Mouse instructed. "I am going to remove the arrow. Break the tip off will you?" She looked up at me with calm, collected, non—judging eyes. I did as she requested and she gently removed the arrow. Then she instructed me to apply pressure to stop the bleeding while she tore off a piece of her blouse to bind the wound. Meanwhile, Eva was hysterical, cursing and accusing me of trying to kill him.

"I am sorry," I said while Mouse completed the binding, "It was the sound (of a gun?) that must have triggered a memory. My mind was filled with the time I was a small boy and my mother was killed. I am so sorry."

"You should be. You really should be," Eva was calmed down but her eyes were flashing in anger. "I would never have thought you could do something like this!"

"He will be OK," Mouse assured Eva. "Just a flesh wound—right?" she enquired of Joseph.

"Yeah," he replied rather weakly. And to me: "You really are an honest to goodness Injun. But I am not the White man who murdered your mother. Just remember that in the future—OK?" And then he asked: "What happened to the Buffalo?"

"It ran in that direction," I pointed.

"Then you had better go after it. Do you hear that sound? The wolves will be on its trail. And if you don't find it before they do, then we will all die of hunger out here. And you can forget your plan to take the magic meat back to your valley."

"Joseph is right," Mouse agreed. "Go after the Buffalo. We will look after him and follow."

"When you find the Buffalo, start a fire for us to find you," Joseph instructed. "It is more than the loss of blood—I am already weak from hunger. I think I could try a bit of those berries and nuts—it you have any left?" he asked Eva.

I gave Mouse the pouch that I had carried. "This is all the food that I have left." I told her to share amongst the three of them. "I still have arrows. I will follow the Buffalo. That is what this is all about." Eva was still angry, and she looked like she wanted to say something more to me, but I was not about to go into that at the moment.

"Go, we will find you when Joseph is able to travel," Mouse urged me once more. And I followed the trail of blood and the tracks of the Great White in the snow.

At first I ran as best as I could in the deep snow. And then I slowed down from sheer exhaustion and plodded on through the drifts. "How could the Buffalo have made it this far, fast enough to stay ahead of me?" I began to wonder and I was still thinking these thoughts when the sun dipped low and a round pale moon filled the sky. "How can this be? It was only days ago that the moon was full. Something has happened to the passage of time." I began to realize that I was doing this all wrong. The way I found the Buffalo before was to seek out a connection in my mind and heart—to ask for the gift of life from one who has been a relative of our People since the beginning of our time on Mother Earth. I stopped and quieted my thoughts. Soon I felt the presence of the Great White. She was close. But other relatives of my People were close as well. I no longer needed to hear the wolves. I felt them, close, around me—drawing closer with every heartbeat. And the voices of the wolves began to change. My imagination ran wild as I began to hear them talking to me. "Come. Join us, Brother. Come join us in the hunt." And just as I was thinking that I was in the persuasive grip of an evil force, and I attempted to break contact, another voice called out, and it was sweet and strong. "Remember me. I am close now. Please remember me." And I did. I sank to my knees in the snow and found a soft, deep dream. And I dreamed a long dream that I didn't want to end—of running wild in the woods—with the wolves and she was there—beside me. And I was startled! "She looks so much like...Eva!"

And I woke to find Eva bending over me—shaking me.

"What happened to you?" she asked.

"I don't really know." My mind was in turmoil. I realized that I must be coming out of a dream and bits and pieces remained. And just for a moment, I imagined I was back in the dream and a soft voice called out "Remember me. Come find me again." And then I snapped awake to Eva's scolding voice.

"You are naked!" she said accusingly.

And she was right. I hastily drew the animal skin back over my body to hide my nudity but it was too late. I knew that there would not be any way of explaining this to someone whose beliefs were based on a logical world. That world would not have room for someone who might change into a four-legged creature. And my recent memories were not clear enough to say who might be correct.

"This is the end for us," Eva said sternly and with great conviction. "I know who you were with. This is the end for us. You can have your freedom—right here and now—I am officially granting you a divorce. Here in the presence of the Great Spirit. I am releasing you from any vows. My religion would never grant me this but for the part of me that is Aboriginal—somewhere back in my ancestry, I declare this to be done!"

"Wow! Eva! I didn't know that you had it in you? The Native ancestry, I mean." Mouse sat on a log beside a crackling fire. She was enjoying a good laugh at both of us. She appeared older and thinner than I remembered. The time was catching up with her, just like Grandmother warned might happen.

"Me, neither," Joseph chuckled. "And it still boggles my mind trying to understand how two sisters could be so different? Are you sure that you had the same father?"

"Mind your....mind!" Eva replied abruptly. "How many times have I told you to keep your sinful thoughts to yourself?"

"Many times—I have about lost count," he shot back. He appeared to have recovered from the wound quite well—although he had a bandage on his arm to show for it. What happened to you?" he looked at me with a smirk. "Other than getting caught with your pants down, I mean? And don't spare me the juicy details."

"Nothing that I remember exactly," I shrugged. But the moment I said that, it started to come back. "You look pretty healthy for someone who was wounded and weak from hunger the last time I saw you," I said to Joseph. "I am sorry about that." I wanted to change the subject, as well.

"No problem. I forgive you—just don't fire that bow in my direction again and we will be best of buddies—almost. It did give me the opportunity to spend some quality time being coddled by two of the cutest nurses this side of Eden." And for this he received a scolding look from Eva but not a blink of an eye from Mouse. He laughed. "I am getting use to this by now. And by the way, those squirrels were quite tasty. Weren't they ladies?"

"I wouldn't know about that—I just finished off the last of the food we brought," Mouse announced. I took a vow against eating meat and I am not about to give that up—in this lifetime." She sounded quite final and I wanted to ask more, but Eva interjected:

"I have to admit, I was ready to eat almost anything when Joseph bagged the Squirrels. I am surprised that you didn't hear the sound of his old rifle. But I guess you were busy doing other things." She paused to let that sink in. "But even after eating the squirrel meat, nothing happened—I mean to me. But when we got here—we saw the smoke from the fire and the Buffalo meat was all prepared—I was so hungry again that Joseph and I cooked a bit over the fire. We were going to see how long it would take you to wake up—and after I ate some of the Buffalo, it happened," her face reddened.

"She started to bleed," Joseph explained. "Eva was going to run into the woods—to hide. I don't know. But Mouse and I convinced her that it was a natural thing."

"A natural thing?" I reached out, and Eva drew back.

"Being on her Moon is a natural thing," Mouse replied.

"Do not touch me," Eva stated firmly.

"Yes, of course. Where have you babes in the woods been living all your lives? Don't you even know where babies come from?" Joseph shook his head in mock disbelief. "Oh yeah, that valley where time stands still. Shangri-la or Eden. Is that what you call it? I guess I will need to tag along to see it? You will need me and Sarah to bring back the 'magic meat' any ways."

"What about you?" I asked Mouse.

"I don't eat meat—remember," she smiled weakly.

"I felt better after eating the Buffalo," Joseph continued. "But I didn't bleed or anything. I just feel like I could father the world. Maybe I am the true Adam? What do you think?"

"In your dreams," Eva stated blankly.

"And not in this lifetime," Mouse chipped in. And for a moment the old spark was back in her eyes.

"Hey." Joseph did not give up. "I was good enough company for the two of you while we were in search for the wild Injun. Wasn't I?

You should have seen the three of us snuggled around the fire every night."

"Give me a break!" Eva spat out. "Mouse?"

"In his dreams—you said it right before."

Joseph shrugged. "So—getting back to what happened here?" He gladly switched the conversation. "And don't say that you don't remember. We saw the smoke from far off. And when we got here we found you out cold with a big smile on your face. There was a fire blazing like someone had left just before we arrived. But there was no one else here. The Buffalo had already been cleaned and the meat hung to dry. The strangest thing is the mixture of wolf tracks and human foot prints. How do you explain all of that?"

"I blacked out. And woke up when Eva started to shake me," I answered. I left out my dreams of running with the wolves. I really didn't want to get Eva started again.

"I think I know what happened," Mouse smiled her most serene smile. "There are legends about how our people once talked to the wolves. And if you combine those stories with the ones that the Elders tell about a tribe of shape shifters...well that about explains it for me."

"Oh sure," Joseph stifled an out and out laugh. "And there are stories about forest spirits—and little people who look after the trees. I think it is my turn to say the part about it being in your dreams?"

"And you might be right on both counts," Mouse answered with nary a smile.

"Well, I know one thing for sure," Eva replied. "There was a woman here. I know that look on his face."

"What?" If a Red-skinned person could blush, it would have been evident. "I have never knowingly cheated on you."

"There is an old saying," Joseph replied. "If you think it—you have done it. That originated in the Bible—I think?"

"Pretty close," Eva agreed. "And there are those dreams you told me about. Maiingun do you still expect me to believe that those dreams were about me?"

"I admit—there were other dreams about someone I spent time with when I was just a boy. But that was before I met you." I was not about to tell her that I might have mistaken her for the person in my dreams. But then again, I did dream of another life with Eva. "I was not lying when I told you about the dream where in which you and I had children and Grandchildren that was as real to me as anything that has happened here. To say what Joseph said, in another way, when we put emotion into believing a dream, it is given life—somewhere."

"But I wanted that here," she stated. "Here and now—not in some elusive dream world. But that is over. And we can start a new life now. When we take the Buffalo flesh back to the valley, the people there can decide if they want to start a new world. Then you and I can go our separate ways and you can go chase that wild woman—whoever she is. And I will be free to choose to live out the life that I was destined by my name or to start a new story about Eva who is a strong woman and the mother of creation. We will stay the night here and head out in the morning for the valley."

Joseph remained tight-lipped and went about packing up the dried strips of Buffalo meat.

"I am so happy to hear you talking like that!" Mouse exclaimed. And then her voice took a weary sound to it. She sat down. "I am not going on from here. My job is complete. I have lived to be reunited with my sisters and to know that both my sisters are safe and happy in their new lives."

"Both sisters?" This dawned for me.

"Yes," Mouse smiled. "There were three of us. The three sisters like in our People's story. Our father and mother liked to joke about that, saying we were what fulfilled them. "Oh? You didn't know? Eva had a twin. Even I began to believe that Sky had died, until now. But then she always had a greater magical connection than Eva or me. Mom named Eva and Dad named Sky—her Native name was Bright Sky. When Eva was born they thought Eva was the only baby but after a few minutes, our mother excitedly said—there is another!" And just as the morning sky became bright, another small baby was born.

"But I was first;" Eva interjected "That was why mother named me Eva."

"I guess. Strange—don't you think? Mom had taken to reading the Bible while she was waiting for her baby to be born. Everyone thought there was only one baby, but suddenly there were twins. Sky was so small that everyone thought she would not survive, but she did and there is the story of the three sisters. And after a while, the only way you could tell Sky and Eva apart, was the colouring of their skin and then Sky always seemed like the way she was born—like the Creator gave us a sister from some other family."

"Anyways," Mouse smiled and said to me: "I guess you met Sky?"

Eva let this pass and concentrated on what Mouse had begun this conversation about.

"What do you mean?" Eva asked, "of course you are going home with us."

"Oh yes. I am going on but not with the three of you. This is the end of my journey on this circle. My disease came back when I left the valley and slowly but surely it began to reclaim my body. But then I am aware that I am not my body. I have found a way of life that rings true for me. This body is a temple—a sacred temple—and at some time when we have completed the Circle that we came here for, we will leave this world and travel home—and perhaps begin another Circle. Who knows? There is enough of our People in me to believe that this may be the way to explain it, but it is still a mystery."

"How long do you think you have remaining?" Joseph asked with genuine concern in his voice.

"Perhaps a day or two—but not much more. I need to rest now. I have a long journey ahead of me."

Joseph borrowed the animal skin that I had been covered with and made a bed for her. "Get dressed will you?" he whispered out of the corner of his mouth. And I hurried to find my clothing that was heaped beside the fire. And so our trip back to the valley was to be delayed—for a sacred time, yet unknown, while the eldest of the three sisters who was named "Corn-Child" at her birth (and then re-named "Mouse"), gave her body back to the Earth.

Chapter 27

SOME OF US RETURN TO EDEN: IN OUR OWN WAY

"I almost feel cheated," Eva said to me when we finally stood at the entrance to the valley. Joseph and his burro Sarah were with us, loaded down with the flesh of the White Buffalo.

"Why is that?" I asked. "You did what you set out to do—we both did. It was my job to hunt the Buffalo and it seems that you will play a big part in starting the world again."

"But it will be different than I believed it would be at the beginning of our journey. And I found my sister only to lose her again. Mouse seemed so clear about her part in all of this."

"It may be just my thought, but maybe the future is not a plan that was written out in a book—and that there was only one way for it to begin and end."

"The best laid plans of Mice and Men?" she quoted.

"Yes. Except that Mouse who is your sister could see beyond her simple life—to the greater plan. One that includes the dreams of all creatures—and perhaps the living dream of the Creator which is still a Mystery."

"Listen to him," Joseph spoke up. "But also remember that it is your choice to start the world, your world, in a way that is right for you."

Joseph had mellowed during the last part of the trip back to the valley. Part of this began when we were preparing to say our prayers for Mouse. Joseph and I were digging the grave that would return her body to the earth. We took turns with the shovel that he had brought along strapped to Sarah's pack. "When my Grandfather died," Joseph told me, "I set out to prospect for gold. I soon learned how stupid that was since the metal really has no value in a world where the most important thing occupying your mind is where you will get your next meal. But in the last few days, I found that gold in the friendship of an unconditionally loving woman that I was only allowed to know for one moon—as your people would say."

And on that trip back, Joseph changed—or did he only show us his true heart? He revealed to us about how he did not really live next door to the "flock of penguins" as he said, when we first met him. He became orphaned at an early age and the nuns took him in and raised him until at the young age of 13, he ran away to find his grandfather. He joked to us about his memories of the many raps on the knuckles that he received for his outspoken ways while in the school that the nuns struggled to keep running.

We stopped for the night beside the stream that we would follow back to the valley and Joseph disappeared into the woods with his knife. He returned a while later, clean shaven and bathed—still shivering from the cold but proud as could be. "And I do know the Bible," he said to Eva.

"You will have to prove to me that this is not another one of your big stories," she shot back.

And then began banter—an exchange that would go on for the rest of our journey back to the valley. Every evening around the campfire, with coffee in hand, Eva and Joseph shared passages from the Bible—each trying to top the other. Eva would quote a verse and challenged him to tell her where it came from and the meaning. Then he would answer—proving that his knowledge was second to none. And then he would challenge her to explain another verse. As so it went—until I had heard the story of revelations and the end of the world so many times that I had to call out: "Please stop? It is all over and done with. We have seen the end of times. The prophesies have all come and gone. And it is time to start new."

"You are so right," Joseph agreed. "But as your people say: 'This is a Circle', so it is time to start again. We should think about how the Bible tells us how to start again in Eden." And that became the new topic for the rest of the journey.

And when we stood at last at the gate, the path into Eden, Eva expressed her concerns about what should happen next, and that maybe she and I failed to fulfil our duties.

"We have not failed," I repeated, almost what Joseph said. "We just did not do it by the book. If this is still a failure to you, I can't change it in your mind. You have to decide for yourself and live the life you choose—the best you can." Then I hugged her good-bye that is not a good-bye. In the ways of my people, it is: "until I see you again".

And the same for Joseph. I shook his hand in the manner of men of my tribe—no woman-hug for him. "I remember the words of an Elder. Our ancestors may have done terrible things to each other. But you and I can still part as friends. Please forgive me for the arrow?"

"No problem," he replied. And he retold the story that his grandfather told to him—about the times past that arrows were given away for free to the White man.

And that is how I will remember this man and this woman—until I see them again …meenawa! The telling and re-telling of his stories—many grand in their repetition—but isn't it similar to the stories of my People? And Eva? I wonder what she will choose to follow—her heart or the logical teaching in the book she holds so tight to her chest. I have to smile when I think about a world that might be started by this Eve and this Adam? The Creator must be part coyote—the trickster—as the old ones say.

And after waving them on their way to take the flesh of the Buffalo to the people, I stay behind for awhile to climb to the top of the nearest mountain overlooking the valley. I have much to think about.

I think about the Buffalo and I hold up the skull of the four-legged who represents all of the creatures that give of their life-spirit so that our People may live a strong and Spirit-filled Life. I will accept the sacrifice and be fully a part of this Circle of Life, which will be with Respect, to complete my part of the pact. I will do all that I can in helping Mother Earth to heal, so that my grandchildren and all of our brothers and sisters will be able to experience the Path of Beauty, in all ways.

"Great Spirit, please look into my Heart—see what I really need, and give me that."

Epilogue
EDEN?

I think about the other gift of the White Buffalo Maiden—the gift of companionship. This is all about the voice that calls out:" Return to me—come find me again." The first time I heard this voice there was just a name whispered in my ear. And that was the start of this dream for a small boy.

And I call out: "Great Spirit, please help me to be a Good and True expression of your Love."

This is my story and is not meant to be world-changing—except it is for me. We each need to learn to respect and to follow our own dreams and to learn to listen to the voice within our Hearts. And now, as a mist forms at the base of the mountain, I know that when I go down this path, all that I know might be changed. Like the mist that Shiloh witnessed when he urged the Emperor to seek his new life and to face his fears. I do not pretend that I am some present-day Shiloh, or Soma—but these are men whose lives and memories I have discovered within my Heart. They are alive within my dreams and are a part of me. This is my story…

It is about a Circle…

…Until you become aware that it is also a Dream…

CPSIA information can be obtained at www.ICGtesting.com
Printed in the USA
LVOW07s1926230913

353745LV00001B/14/P